THE
MERCURY
UNIVERSE

DAVID BERNER II

BOOKBERNER PUBLISHING
1999, 2000

Published in Port Townsend, Washington by David Alan Berner II dba BookBerner Publishing.

Printed in the United States by:
Morris Publishing
3212 East Highway 30
Kearney, NE 68847
1-800-650-7888

www.bookberner.homepage.com

The Mercury Universe: ISBN 0-9677633-1-2

Iustum enim est bellum quibus necessarium,
Et pia arma ubi nulla nisi in armis spes est.
"For a war that is necessary is a just
one, and when arms are the only
source of hope they are sacred."

-Niccolo Machiavelli, *The Prince*

CHAPTERS

To my mother and father:
For showing me a boundless universe
only a poet could create

The Explosion

It was a time that seemed to produce no wrong. A golden age for the masses who lived in a time of freedom. What could possibly shatter this beautiful, yet delicate state?

Deltrin was a traveler of worlds, a creature of adventure, standing on the brink of completing his extraordinary quest, which all began with a fortunate discovery of a treasure map.

The planet concluding his hunt possessed a past so deeply hidden not even the sharpest sense could exhume its secrets that Deltrin had intended to reveal. But what secrets could be so intriguing to make this man want to travel for five long years, visiting worlds filled with danger and beauty? Unlimited wealth, the fountain of youth, or the origin of life. Whatever it was that drove this questor to repeatedly chance his life, it was powerful, but it was hidden. Concealed somewhere within the walls of the temple.

How to describe such a celestial presence. The temple was a vision for the gods. Standing erect upon a remote island in the middle of the ocean, alone as if it were the home of a deity. It was made of crystal, gleaming proudly in the presence of the four suns in the sky, making it difficult to distinguish the diamonds in the ocean from the crystals in the temple.

Deltrin had spent five days inside, searching for clues, waiting for a revelation, but nothing had happened. The crystal statues decorating the rooms kept their silence, giving no hints to the treasure's whereabouts. He had been through every room ten times over, but nothing was to be found that remotely satisfied what the treasure map described. Deltrin repeated the final stanza of the riddle in his head, hoping that something would click. *Alone I sit in a temple of shards, coming out when my fathers embrace. The skeleton bands, with the jewels in their hands, will uncover my illustrious face.* Deltrin could not solve the riddle. What could it be referring to? The entire riddle gave the impression that this treasure was something more than wealth. It was tangible power, translated through some kind of instrument. But what does power look like?

The air in the temple was sweet, warm, almost inviting nostalgia, but the candlelight softness of the atmosphere could not subdue his impatience. He simply could not find what he was looking for.

Frustrated, he fell to the ground and sat for a while, running ideas in his head that he hoped could help him in his discovery. In time he laid down on the crystal floor and stared up through one of the spires of the temple into the blue sky, slowly falling asleep.

Minutes passed, feeling like days, until Deltrin felt a shift of temperature. It was getting mysteriously warmer within the temple. He opened his eyes and looked up into the sky and noticed something new. A tiny ray of light had broken through the cloak of space and had gently laid its warmth upon Deltrin's cheek. He brushed his face to see if he was still dreaming, and found to his pleasure that the heat was real.

Another tendril broke free and fell to the surface, followed by another, and then another. In seconds, thousands of rays of light found their freedom on the planet below, raining their glory upon Deltrin's willing body.

Finally, an explosion of light ignited in the sky, and a fifth star was unveiled with pure radiance, slamming its energy upon the surface with divine power and grace. The crystal temple swelled with light in response to this brilliant incantation. The statues in the rooms came alive to the will of this deity and invoked the spirits of the temple to send a beam of fire back into the sky that stretched to the farthest reaches of the galaxy.

Deltrin sat in silent awe of this display. There was no doubt in his mind that this mysterious awakening was the precursor to the treasure's discovery. His eyes were glued to the hypnotic ballet of lights, until something disturbed his attention.

A new light appeared, isolated from the main beam of energy. It was coming from one of the walls. Deltrin walked closer to the strange occurrence and noticed that part of the wall had become liquid. He peered into the mellifluous crystal and saw that something was inside the wall.

With trembling hands, he forced himself through the living structure and pulled out the treasure inside, his eyes aglow with wonder. As his hands emerged from the liquid, he realized he was holding a heavy casket in his hands, roughly a cubic foot in volume. The casket was cold, but the heavy beating of Deltrin's heart pulsed through his fingertips and rejuvenated the ancient tomb.

A pulse began to beat from within.

Was he dreaming or did his arrival give birth to the contents inside the box? It did not matter, for whatever it was, dream or no dream, it was magnificent.

Deltrin's hands no longer trembled. The two heartbeats formed a rhythm and harmonized. Energy surged through his veins, smoothing out his strains of fatigue, and flew outward in all directions. Baptized by this release of life, Deltrin was born again. He could see light and color in hues he had never seen before. The voices of ages past could be heard whispering in his ears, and on the tip of his tongue, life and youth left a sweet flavor.

He took a deep breath and felt the warm air rush into his lungs. He was one with life, one with nature, one with the treasure. What was this sublimity he had awakened? Rather, who was it?

The five stars rested in the sky as Deltrin left the celestial temple behind on the planet. Stumbling with anxiety to his map room, the Questor placed the tube on the table. He took a deep, rewarding breath and removed the hatch that protected the contents inside, where he found two books.

One was filled with mathematical equations, theories, notes, most everything Deltrin tried to avoid in his life. He placed the book back in the casket, hoping his frustration would be remedied with what the other book had to offer. The second manuscript's cover was decorated with a mysterious insignia. There were many different figures surrounding a single sphere, like something found in an ancient religion.

Flipping through the pages, Deltrin found to his delight no equations of any kind. Instead, the book seemed more like a journal of the past than a laboratory book. Intrigued by the historical document, Deltrin took the book and found solace in his sleeping quarters. He fell comfortably in his favorite chair and dropped the book in his lap.

"So, this is what power looks like." He thought to himself, staring at the book. "I figured it to be something else. Maybe it's a book of spells, or a revelation of life's secrets."

He thought back to the book of equations.

"Perhaps these books are blueprints to something. Something grand."

With the company of a refreshing drink by his side, Deltrin opened the engraved cover and read the title page.

"For Us." Was all it said.

He smiled, hoping for a brief moment that the 'us' the title referred to included him. Feeling part of something grand for the first time, Deltrin continued to read...

A thousand dreams have colored their worlds in my mind, but not even my imagination could paint the marvels I have seen throughout my journeys. If only I could describe beauty as well as nature can create it. Perhaps, if I begin my story, the words will create the pictures themselves as I proceed. For so many years, I have not been able to articulate my past. So many years have I had silent memories I could see only in my mind, in my dreams, and in the reflection of my tears.

I have lived a long and wonderful life, traveling to distant worlds with my comrades. I am alone now, but have not forgotten the extraordinary quest to which my friends and I devoted our lives, and the many wonders we encountered in its duration.

I have seen the birth of worlds, the death of stars, the creation of thousands of civilizations and their evolution. Now that I have nearly completed the mission, I have one final objective that will consummate this quest; a quest that has persisted for nearly four billion years, which will eventually be revealed.

You, who have found this monumental piece of work, will realize your importance once you have read the history of the great experiment that I divulge on this parchment. You may not however, understand the manuscript you found adjacent to this book. That is to be expected. You must take the manuscript to a group of scientists whom you trust. Once they read it, they will come to know what to do. But first, please read of our history. It is the only way that I, as well as my beloved friends, can stay immortal.

Deltrin took a sip of his drink, toasting his apparent importance. Growing up, he knew he would spend his life roaming around in space, participating in risky missions that he made important for himself. At twenty-five, he became a Questor, a title given to travelers who worked for a government. They would occasionally work surveillance missions, but usually, it was geared more towards reconnaissance. Only those who had the experience in trekking around the stars, as well as having a personal knowledge of the planets could earn their title. Deltrin was very young compared to the others, but was exceptionally talented and bright. When he reached thirty-eight, he had completed several missions, but nothing could have prepared him for the mission at hand.

Now that his mission was reaching its termination, he would soon add to his repertoire a journey that would be told to endless generations, but not as soon as he had hoped. He had spent half a decade of his life seeking the conclusion of his mission, but as he would soon find out, his mission was only half over.

He did not know many people, and certainly he did not know any scientists personally. He was, however, familiar with a group working on a project known as "Hyperlight".

The project had a simple objective: To build a machine that could decelerate the rate of consumption of hydrogen in stars. Some scientists of the universe knew that the universe would eventually become a valley of lifeless planets and rocks as soon as all the stars' energy was depleted. They decided that if they elongated the life of stars, the eventual termination of the universe would be pushed further into the future. There were obvious complications involved in the experiment, however, the main problem was finding out how to get into the star itself. No one knew what the internal blueprints of a star looked like. Even worse, there are no two identical stars, so the lifeline was not a constant.

It was obvious that the scientists had several things on their minds, and were busy enough with their experiment, but Deltrin knew no one else who fit the requirements. He had no choice. He read on...

The mission was an experiment of significant proportions. Everything seemed to be in place, but for one final link, gravity. It was the final piece of our puzzle. We had toiled over the equation for years, and all the while, the solution was right in front of us. I cannot remember how we found it. Perhaps it was just an ambiguous attempt at trying something different on the blackboard. I do not know. What I do know is that the discovery opened a door that would forever change the meaning of our existence.

Our project was two billion years in the making, which, even for us, seemed like a very long time, but we knew the effects of our creation would unite life in a way that has never been achieved.

Most of the time was spent experimenting with models, which were greatly reduced in size. We placed our models in different atmospheric situations, which gave us ideas as to where we would ignite our creation. We discovered many things in our experiments; things that we had never even seen occur in nature. The discoveries in the lab made the wait for us almost unbearable, which may have sped things up. Do not get the wrong impression. We knew exactly what we were doing, and made sure that all our calculations worked. Two billion years gave us plenty of time to make certain. However, as I have found, even two billion years of experience can leave room for error. Unfortunately, I could not see this during the experiment.

When we were ready to complete the most important step in our project, we decided that we could not simply witness the success alone. It was expected that we share our glory with others and not bask in the greatness alone.

We initially invited a small group of beings from different planets, mostly other scientists and royalty. In the end, we decided to fill our entire ship with guests. The only reason we invited a few guests was because we feared we had no room in our ship. Our oversight was quickly remedied. We enjoyed the thought of having more beings on our ship, considering the project was to benefit all creatures and not just a select few.

It was fortunate for all of us to have such a gathering. Not only was the congregation a pleasant way of seeing old friends, but it was also a wonderful opportunity to meet new ones.

I knew I would remember the day we journeyed into a new era for the rest of my life, however long it would last. The excitement glittered in everyone's eyes. All were staring into a void that we assured them would soon become a vast array of light and colors. No one knew how the experiment would turnout, except us, to a certain degree.

Our ship was billions of light years away from where the initial stage of the experiment was to take place. We told our guests that the distance was necessary and the effects would still be seen.

We were all ready to start with the countdown when we were interrupted by an incoming message. All it said was "greetings" in a language that I had to have translated for me. We all stared out of the window in the back, to see where the message originated. To our surprise, there was another ship behind us. The crews had heard about the secret gathering and had no desire to miss witnessing such a momentous occasion. They were not alone.

We could see distant lights coming closer and closer. More ships had decided to join us. In minutes we were surrounded by hundreds of vessels, all having the desire to see the blast that would be heard ringing in our ears for eons to come. Within thirty minutes, we were leading a pack of over fifteen thousand interstellar cruisers, joining us to see what our guests called "the display of magic."

I was pleased to see so many beings had come to witness the outcome of our experiment. I cannot begin to describe the emotions I felt when I saw all those ships adjacent to ours. For a brief moment of time, the many disagreements and oppositions between all the different races and civilizations were put aside. Everyone came together to unite as one, all because of a single event; our single event. The scene must have looked incredible from a distance.

Ships of all different sizes gathered around us, meeting for the first time and creating relations that would last for as long as the stars. Our altruistic attempt to unite worlds had worked, and as soon as we had finished the introductions, it was time to show why members of twenty-two thousand different species had come to join us.

We sent a universally translated message to all ships, telling them to turn off all their primary and non-emergency lights, in order to view the first stage of the experiment without any unnecessary interference. Obviously, some systems could not be shut down, so there were ships with some light interference, but the pollution from the lights would not be enough to take away from the view.

Lights began to flicker off in the distance, one by one, until the once brilliant Zirconian sector that we were in turned black. Our hearts pumped our blood so fast, we could feel the heat generating, seeping through our veins, and spreading into the air around us. The experiment was ready, and so were we.

We received thousands of blessings from all the ships in the fleet. In response, we sent to every ship a universal countdown. The seconds were like years and I could feel myself aging as they crawled across the clock. I couldn't wait any longer. The anxiety was burning my skin. I never knew that I would feel this way. After all, I spent two billion years in the laboratory, fixing and constructing everything with my fellow scientists. So why all the commotion now? I knew what was going to happen, but that didn't matter anymore. It seemed like I had forgotten everything that happened in the lab, and every single second told a secret. The anticipation was genuine.

Ten seconds.

My hands were fidgeting and my fingers were dancing so fast I could no longer control them. I looked around to see if I was the only one who was feeling the same fire. Everyone was consumed by the imminence of the ignition. I could see it in their eyes, growing larger and larger as the time crept closer and closer to its entirety.

Five seconds.

The past was flashing before me, like some slide show. I saw the first stages of the experiment, frustrating and painful. It was as if someone had been watching our every move, and now I was observing what this phantom spy had seen. Then the time sped up, showing me the highlights of the experiment, the day when everything culminated into one glorious device. The smiles and congratulations pervaded the entire laboratory.

I snapped out of my little trance and noticed there were only three seconds left on the timer. We were close.

Two seconds.

One second.

I held my breath.

Nothing dramatic happened suddenly, but rather a subtle birth of something grand, very quiet, almost mysterious. A ripple in the void emerged from where the experiment was to originate, and traveled close to what we figured to be twenty billion light years in all directions. After the ripple, a blue cloud emerged from the void, spherical in shape. This phantom orb glowed brightly, but as it continued to grow, it lost its illuminant luster, losing the appearance as a source of light and taking on the shape of a crystalline prison.

The outer ring of the orb was filled with billions of specks of lights. A blanket of stars encircled the void, finally ceasing to grow as soon as it reached as far as the ripple. For a while, nothing else happened. There was the blue orb, hollow with nothing inside its belly, at least not yet.

Our guests looked around at each other confused, not knowing if there was something else to expect. They saw we were still keeping our attention on the spectacle in the void. Following our lead, they turned back to see what was next to come.

Inside the center of the orb, a new light began to glow. It was faint at first, almost mistaken for another star, yet its intensity began to grow. The light became incredibly brilliant, separating it from the rest of the stars in the outer ring of the orb. My eyes grew wider with anticipation, waiting impatiently.

The light in the center flashed and sent another ripple so powerful that the orb itself expanded in attempts to keep the blast from escaping. The white light blew apart in all directions, throwing multi-colored trails of light further out within its container.

"Augment, one-hundred thousand percent." I told the helm.

"Aye sir."

With a close-up view, we were able to see clearly what was happening inside. Thousands of explosions ripped open the black insides of the orb, revealing an endless spectrum of colors within the dark hollow void. The detonations increased exponentially, filling up the entire screen with iridescent light; an area close to one million light years in diameter. All this happened in about fifteen seconds.

"Helm, pull back view by ten thousand percent."

"Ten thousand percent sir."

At this range, we were able to see that the separate explosions consolidated to form another sphere of activity inside the blue cloud barrier. A few stray tendrils of light separated from the globe of explosions, erupting into what looked like fingers reaching out for something unattainable. In time, the commotion began to cease and the spherical light within the blue orb slowed its expansion almost to a halt.

"Bring her back to normal view, helmsmen." I said relieved.

At that view, the inner light was no larger than the size of a small egg. I held out my hand and placed this apparently small container of shimmering iridescence within my fingers and thought for a second if I would ever hold this realm of a trillion stars in my control again. Our tiny universe was newly born and looked magnificent beyond words.

Deltrin paused at the last sentence. He had to read it again, not believing his eyes the first time they scanned the sentence. *"Universe? A baby universe?"* Intimidation took over his emotions, suddenly making him feel that he was way over his head. However, that had never stopped him before, so he swallowed his fear with his next drink and continued on with sheer excitement...

From the other side of the room, someone breathed, awakening us all. I blinked a tear and smiled. I looked at my friend beside me and laughed. It was either that or crying, and considering the jubilance we were all feeling, crying would have dampened the mood.

People came out of their dream state eventually and reacted in whatever way their emotions thought appropriate. A new sensation overtook me as I brought my focus and attention on the baby universe once again. Something greater than anything I could comprehend had embraced me, putting its warm hands over my eyes, allowing me to see existence in a new light. It was a very humbling experience, making me feel somewhat smaller, knowing that there will always be new doors to open with every new discovery.

What I saw next I must tell you about, for it may explain a few things that will come later in the story.

When I had finally sat down, taking the opportunity to look at the universe, I fell into another dream-state. This time, it was more than just a dream.

The picture was ambiguous at first, but eventually, it focused into incredible detail. I saw before me a single branch, which at first, was cryptic with its symbolic presence. That single branch was then placed on another branch that had hundreds of little twigs attached to it. It was as if some force was displaying some fantastic glimpse of an oracular future to me. Thousands of branches appeared in sequence, all connecting in some way to a single, sturdy tree.

Then it stopped for a brief moment. I thought the vision was over, but I was wrong. New branches with multitudes of their own extremities become visible, as the imaginary canvass flourished with life. They continued to multiply, until I could no longer see the initial branch. I was left in a daze, watching the tree spread out, growing in all directions, making the branches look like a web. The sturdy trunk of the tree finally appeared and my apparition shifted its shape, and then suddenly disappeared.

I blinked and wondered why I was shown such a strange display. I then looked out beyond the blue halo, where the tree reappeared in the center of the infant universe.

To this day, I do not know if I was the only one who received that vision. The fluorescent tree, which I have dreamed of these many long years, changed me forever. It was a premonition, whose significance will be revealed as you read on.

Deltrin quickly got up from his seat, and rushed over to see the map he placed on his desk. Something had clicked in his mind and he had to quench his pondering. The figure displayed on the map was finally explained from what the last statement had just mentioned. Satiated, he returned to his seat and read on...

Several ships began to depart, leaving us with their warmest congratulations. Our passengers also decided to board other ships that accommodated beings of their own race. Within time, our ship was alone once again, allowing us to proceed with the third stage of our experiment.

The closer we approached the blue halo, the more it seemed to glow. It was much more resplendent close up than from an extreme distance. Our shadows danced upon the floor of the bridge, until our ship was completely immersed in the blue mist. We were surrounded by a myriad of stars, born instantly from the explosion. The blue mist changed into a more violet color the further we traveled into the fog.

We sailed through this sidereal ocean for several hours, observing all the different shapes and sizes of the stars we could bear to watch. They were celestial with their pure eminence pouring into our ship, splashing against every wall. We were swimming in a pond, blanketed in pure light. Every color we could name spread itself throughout the room. We were ghosts in our ship, feeling the light pass through our bodies, each ray more purifying than the last.

We were in no danger in this realm. Our ship was at a safe distance from any star's gravitational pull or intense heat, so our journey was a pleasant one. The shield was several light years thick, accommodating billions of stars. The orb stretched for what seemed an indeterminable distance, which was exactly what we needed it to do. The main purpose of this entity was to keep the inner universe safe from any other outside universe, and vice versa. All the other universes in our system had protective barriers to basically hold in the activity, so nothing interfered with, or partially destroyed part of another universal realm. It was unnatural, but it was necessary to preserve the harmony that already existed.

The bridge had increased in temperature from the amazing light of the outside sources, but we didn't mind. The warmth was life and we could feel its power surround us, strengthening us. We could have melted to a liquid, and would not have noticed.

The temperature of the bridge began to decrease as we found ourselves leaving the shield behind. The windows began to get darker and darker, until our only light source was the tiny universe in front of us, growing steadily in the center. Everything in between was nothing but black.

We gave our silent good-byes to the mist behind us, perhaps thinking we would never see it again. The bridge was cold inside, lacking the warmth the stars provided. I still felt the youth souring through my veins, but it was not the same without the stars. I did not, however, worry about it too much. I knew our upcoming adventures would be satisfying enough.

We would not breach the inner universe for many thousands of years, so it was time to get some rest. We had gone through a terribly long day and our sleep was greatly deserved and needed. Our course was set, and soon enough we all retired to the de-animation chambers, where we would sleep for millennia to come. I did not think my dreams could compensate for what I saw earlier, but it was worth a try.

The Blue Planet

Deltrin set the book on his lap and relaxed for a brief moment. He had never considered the idea of actually building a universe. What scared him more was being the messenger who bore the news of this imminent creation. He was becoming terrified with his burden, yet strangely excited. Now, like a ferryman rowing down a placid river in the twilight with no land in site to dock upon, Deltrin took his oar and plowed his way into an unknown ocean...

I awoke fully rested, excited to see where we were. I imagined something incredible, just waiting to be seen out in the deep black. I felt giddy and almost ran down the hallway to the bridge, like a child expecting a gift at the end of the stretch.

I ran down the hall; a trek that seemed to last for days. I couldn't hear anything around me, nor could I pay attention to anything. Finally, I reached the bridge. From the moment I crossed that threshold from reality to fantasy, I knew my life would never be the same. I was in a new universe, a new existence. Whatever it was that my comrades and I left behind was now a vague memory that none of us could recall. We were newborns.

Octan and Terinsa were the only officers on the bridge. Both were silent, probably unaware of each other's presence. I think that my attention didn't stay in the room for more than two seconds before it journeyed beyond into the outer space, colliding with the planet we were orbiting.

I was left with not a thought in my mind, except for a passage that kept repeating itself in my head as I gazed at the planet. I whispered it to myself, not knowing if the others could hear me. It didn't matter. It wasn't really for them to hear anyway.

And he opened his heart as wide as his eyes. His blood pulsed, echoing through the silence around him. In his son's eyes could nothing be seen but the reflection of himself, looking out from within.

"There are two orbitals around the planet." Octan said, never looking away from the captivating planet.

The heavenly body was already stable, passed the violent stages of its growth. The white and blue clouds hovering over the brown land moved swiftly through the atmosphere, caressing the tips of the mountains. There were bodies of water of variant size laid about the surface deliberately, separating each continent from one another, naturally.

The moons Octan mentioned had little growth on them, but possessed the potential to accommodate several different forms of life. Clutched within the powerful grip of the planet, they gracefully danced around their guardian.

I broke out of my trance and focused on Octan. "They're just as beautiful as their mother."

He smiled and turned to show me his complacent face; his glassy eyes telling me enough. Terinsa didn't say a word. Still in reverie, she slowly got up from her chair, walked over and embraced me like a sister.

"Good morning." she said, whispering through her tears.

How passionate we all were; poets lost in a new world. Can you blame us? Two-billion years of diligence and the release thereafter will wreck havoc on your emotions. But I was through with shedding tears of joy. I was ready to see just how much we created.

Terinsa released herself from the embrace and lifted her head to see me smiling back at her. I loved to gaze into those pristine eyes of hers, always wondering what she was thinking.

She was a soldier during the project, ranking as captain, recognized for her talents in espionage. Her furtive characteristics were valuable assets during the wars.

For many years, she and I fought together, side-by-side, and not even I could always tell what was going through her head. Octan was also with us during our missions. I don't think he could tell what she was thinking, either.

He was the weapons specialist, I was the pilot and commander of operations, and Terinsa was our infiltrator. The many missions we embarked on and the countless deaths we witnessed had made our hearts cold and us uncompassionate. But those times seemed to be over now, thankfully. Seeing those tears in her eyes made me certain that our days of reticence and death were finally over and forgotten.

We named the planet Eve. It was to be our headquarters. We knew we would rarely ever visit home base, but it was nice to have an establishment in those dark woods.

We all met on the bridge after we landed on the rocky surface of the planet. Stage three was now ready to commence.

Our next mission was to travel around the cosmos and document as much as we could. We planned to meet every billion years on Eve and share what we found. Only the Admiral would stay back, being the overseer of operations.

The main objective, however, was not to go gallivanting around the stars just to have fun. Each of us

19

had in our possession a certain amount of information pertaining to the universe equation, which we had to distribute to a worthy culture that we encountered. That was our mission: To pass on our knowledge, very slowly, one piece at a time. We all figured that by the time every intelligent being was in contact with each other, they would most certainly be advanced enough to complete the equation, and do exactly what we did.

Deltrin knew most all of the civilizations had established contact with each other, in one form or another. There were a few cultures who either refused to make treaties with other planets, or did not yet evolve into intelligent beings who knew how to travel. Be that as it were, he did not feel that any of the scientists had the maturity of holding such information. They did not have the potential to become gods. Yet, according to what he just read, and as ironic as it seemed, they already were, if a mortal could create life.

A billion years was not that long of a period. I had been alive for two billion by the time we said good-bye to each other. Time has its importance, but not nearly as much as existence itself. We knew the time would pass exponentially fast, at least we'd hoped so.

I was not sad when I said my good-byes. I felt rather excited, looking at the control panel in my transport vehicle, just waiting to have my fingers dance along its buttons. I knew my comrades and I would meet again soon. I was even more certain the stories we would have to tell each other would be breathtaking.

I can remember sitting down in my pilot seat for the first time. It was daytime, and the neighboring star that the planet circled nearly blinded me. I never really had taken the time to do so before, but for some unknown reason, I had this overwhelming sensation run through me. Everything was crystal clear. When I passed the gravitational barrier of Eve, I noticed things on the planet that I never saw before. The reflection of the star on the water below, how it was much stronger in some areas than others. The way the plant-life could be seen miles above the surface. I noticed how the moons around Eve were rotating at different intervals. I especially loved the purple and green nebula behind the planet, blanketing the system. I must admit, I was reluctant to leave this masterpiece of art, but I reminded myself this painting was just a preview of the vast beauty I would soon encounter in my travels. I also noticed from this epiphany that I was beginning to lose my senses as a scientist, and acquiring the senses of a poet. I no longer saw any equations before me, or spatial quantities that dictated how things would grow and turn out. The mathematical matrix disappeared and all that was left was the simplicity of nature.

I fired the ship's rockets and blasted into the black unknown, having no concept of which direction to go in. We were given orders to distribute the manuscript, but we were never given any mission parameters concerning the path we took. I picked a star in my panoramic horizon and set a course directly for it.

Before I continue, there is something that I must explain to you, considering that there are probably a few things that seem inconsistent to nature. First of all, the amount of time that it took for things to form. A planet that comes into being in less than two million years after the birth of a universe is physically impossible, however, we were able to modify the growth pattern in the calculations. Without help from an outside force, the appearance of a combined molecule does not occur until after the first fifty thousand years have passed. You see, as the atoms disperse and move around a more vast area after the initial explosion, they begin to combine with other atoms. Another thing to consider is that the ratio of existent hydrogen atoms to any other atom is significantly greater in any universe. By making a greater abundance of other elements, we increased the attraction, which made more complex atomic structures, inadvertently making more complex elements.

This increased the speed of the growth process exponentially, allowing us to not have to wait for the universe to grow at normal intervals. Because of this tampering, we realized that evolutionary changes would occur, which would be unpredictable, but I assure you, the manipulation of the calculations was worth the change. We were able to see things never before documented in any of the other universes, nor in the lab. Believe me, unpredictability was sometimes therapeutic when one keeps in mind the possibilities that unexpected events reveal.

I was a little nervous when I set out on my own. Like I mentioned, I was wandering aimlessly into an unknown world where anything could happen. However, It was for the same reason that I was excited to venture off.

The star that I had set my sights on did not have any nearby planets orbiting it. Instead, there were four other younger stars circling around the older and larger star. However, I did not leave the system without even searching the neighborhood, and to my delight I found a suitable planet to set my anchor upon.

The violent birth of the chosen planet seemed to have passed, making the surface sedate and cool. There was still volcanic activity, but most of the land was verdant with plant-life. It was too early for the emergence of any other life to have occurred, so my trek upon the land was undisturbed.

I took several tests to calculate the growth pattern of

the life on the planet, and to my surprise, the rate of growth, though accelerated from the aforementioned tampering, was still extremely slow. It would be a few hundred million years before any other intelligent life would spring into existence. Too many other civilizations would have emerged by then in other systems, so I had to consider moving on to a different planet.

To make a long story short, I hopped from one system to the next, and before I knew it, Two-hundred million years had passed and I had not found the right place for my manuscript. I was not, however, impatient. I was rather enjoying the search for a perfect planet, if one existed. I had seen planets that had the makings for promising evolution but not what I was looking for. I wanted to find a civilization that was already on the way to becoming a complex and advanced society: A civilization with intelligence and experience, not an amoebae colony with the intelligence equivalent to a handful of sand. You can say that I was picky, friend, but I knew what I wanted and what I wanted was right.

Egotistical little bugger, isn't he? Deltrin thought, almost admiring him.

My search continued for several more million years, and I had seen wonders that only poets could describe. However, the pursuit for the civilization I desired was still unfinished.

The worn controls had my fingerprints imbedded into them and my hands had completely shaped themselves around the steering mechanism. The ship and I had entwined ourselves together and had become one. I knew its strengths and weaknesses, and it knew mine. When I felt the fatigue of travel take over my senses, I knew my ship was also tired, but time has a way of presenting solutions.

23

After soaring through the cosmos and penetrating a galaxy-size nebula, I had found my vision. There was my planet, floating silently on a dance-floor made just for it. I could almost hear the music it glided to. Granted, I had no idea what I was going to find, but deep down inside, I knew that I had found my euphoria within the black walls of this labyrinth.

The atmosphere around me was terribly warm, created by the four stars that were in the neighborhood. There were two other planets around this system, one was incredibly larger, and the other a little larger. The two smaller planets must have been in orbit of the larger one. I decided I would journey first to the smallest of the three, and charter its big brothers later.

It glowed blue, with the exception of a few black dots strewn about the surface of the planet. It didn't have a very strong gravitational pull on my ship, but the atmospheric wall was difficult to penetrate. My ship bounced around the different densities of the atmosphere, but it was eventually able to get us through in one piece.

The undulating world was certainly a sight to behold, with the stars turning the placid water into glass. The docking process was not difficult at all, at least, not until I reached the surface, considering there really was no surface at all, apart from the water itself. A quiescent crystal blanket flowed beneath me. Apart from the strange black objects I saw from space, there were no continents to implement any waves.

I could see the bottom of the sea floor from my cockpit. The depth was probably no more than two-hundred meters. I could see all sorts of marine animals of various size swimming back and forth through the bio-matter that scattered itself along the reef floor. My curiosity flared, coaxing me to journey beneath the surface to see what I could find.

I submerged through the surface layer, finding

myself immersed in a kaleidoscopic world of creatures, some that I had never seen before. The iridescent cloud of finned animals swarmed around me, repeatedly brushing itself on the protective glass of my transport.

The tremendous amount of solar energy from the four stars was probably the reason for the brilliantly colored community of pelagic life forms. Unfortunately, I had not come across anything that resembled what I was looking for. I had hoped the vision I previously had of this planet was not going to shatter, but it looked as though my search was going to continue on to the neighboring planets. However, my luck changed as soon as I confronted one of the "black dots".

It was an enormous tower, covered with lifeforms, making it look more colorful than it did from outer space. I traveled up the cylindrical formation, until I reached the surface. It protruded from the surface only a few meters, but it was still hard to see from a distance, due to the incredible reflection from the stars on the ocean surface.

Considering the intense mirror effect of the water with the stars' rays, I was lucky to be able to see the seafloor in the first place. I floated above the surface to take a peak inside the spire, only to find a hollow inside.

My ship was too large length-wise to slowly and gently descend into the abyssal pit. I had to rotate my vehicle about ninety degrees in order to fit through the hole, which proved to be not the brightest idea I've ever had. My rockets were pointing my ship downward, which was, incidentally, not the right direction. The gravity of the planet took hold of my transport and pulled me down into the tunnel.

The next few minutes were nothing more than a blur to me, but the whole way down, I was still able to constantly remind myself of my incredibly foolish notion, and vowed never to trust my curiosity. Lucky for me, there was no hard landing; instead, there was a rollaway ending that brought my ship to a nice halt. At least that was pleasant.

I took a few minutes to un-suction my body from my seat and dig my eyes out of the back of my brain before I decided to get out of my transport to have a look around.

There were two waterfalls, one on each side of me, both pouring into a connecting stream that flowed off the side of the cliff, making a third waterfall. I was curious to see how far the water fell until it hit the bottom of the canyon, if there was a bottom for it to hit. Again, my curiosity took over, so I went to have a look. As soon as I looked over the edge of the cliff, I suddenly forgot about the waterfall. There was an enormous glow coming from below.

I did not have much time to scrutinize the surroundings of where I was, being preoccupied with the brilliant light that soared to the ceiling of this subterranean world. I slowly walked forward to view the base of the cavern, feeling the light crawl up my legs to my chest. I then stopped at the edge of the cliff and stared at the presence before me. A source of light so grand, it could have stretched to the edge of the universe if it weren't being held in by the cavern's roof.

My eyes must have grown to incredible size when I looked down upon what had to be the light of creation. I found what I was looking for and even though I had just told myself never to trust my curiosity, it was a matter of seconds before I found myself in my cockpit, flying down to the jewel below.

What was this force that compelled me to journey down to the city? Perhaps it was the simple majesty of an underground city that sparked my curiosity. However, I would like to believe this city was the mystical force that invited me to come to this planet in the first place. The light was so thick, I could have left my transport and climbed down the light as if it were a stairway to the civilization below. Further and further I descended down to the unknown source, having to watch my speed, for I could see spires and towers piercing the dense fog of light. Buildings; just what I had hoped to find.

Deeper and deeper I sank to the bottom, immersed in an ocean of radiance. I could only dream of the great finds that remained imminent to my discovery, wondering if they, whoever 'they' were, were as excited to see me as I of them. Questions rapidly flew through my head almost blurring my vision.

The descent continued and I could now see the buildings at a close-up view. Engraved into the sides of the enormous structures were incredible designs, which I could not translate. Some were pictures of flying creatures, others were of land creatures, engraved in magnificent detail that made the walls come to life. These murals seemed out of place, because there were no apparent objects to inspire such artistic creations. I was led to believe the world only consisted of water creatures. *They must be travelers*, I thought. *How else could their depictions of such creatures be so vivid? They must be an advanced civilization, capable of space travel.*

I was getting more thrilled and anxious to meet these creatures. What secrets of the past and what wild adventures they must have to tell.

The Trocties

I landed on the rocky surface, with hardly a drop of patience left to meet these aesthetic creatures. My arrival was by no means surreptitious, considering the large gathering that accumulated around my landing area. I had hoped the species of this civilization did not think me a threat.

Just for safety precautions, I tucked a small firearm under my belt.

The warm welcoming smiles on their faces cleared up my suspicions. As soon as I jumped out of the cockpit, I figured they knew I meant no harm, as well. I still kept my weapon.

They were not tall at all, probably reaching a maximum of one meter in height. There was no outer hair on their bodies, nor on their heads, which, might I add, only had one ocular cavity. They did have ears, a nose and a mouth, much like I had. They had two legs, but no upper extremities that I could locate. Strange, I thought, but I was sure that the mystery would soon be solved.

Most of the creatures came forward and gathered around me, no doubt as curious of me as I was of them. Their eyes were beautiful, each one a different color. A swarm of rainbow eyes blinked and stared at me with extreme vivacity. I could not help but to laugh with pure joy to see such an ineffable scene.

I wondered for a moment if this is how a diplomat

feels when encountering a new species for the first time. The attention, the glamour, the admiration, I was loving every minute of it.

The crowd was soon parted, and a brightly decorated creature emerged from the back. This one was regaled with several shining medals indicative of a high member of this society.

Out of his torso grew a single arm, displaying a form of greeting I had never seen before. The extremity gelled into a solid arm, solving my little mystery of their lack of natural tools. His newly formed arm extended towards me with his hand nearly touching my eyes. A flash of light emanating from his palm exploded in front of me, and suddenly, all turned black.

I awoke in a well-lit area, lying on a soft surface in a dimly lit room. A light above my head was shining into my eyes. I was expecting a sense of pain in my head or at least a bit of drowsiness, but fortunately, there were no side effects to my induced sleep. The only thing that brought me pain was the annoying light above me. I brought my arm to my face to block the light as I lifted myself off the bed, feeling surprisingly alive.

There was a wall size kaleidoscopic mirror on my left. To my right, there was a mantle in the center of the other wall, surrounded by more engravings, much like the ones I saw in the murals on the sides of the buildings. There were also several paintings hanging in display. I walked over, curious to see what wonders these creatures thought to be art-worthy.

There were paintings of the stars that I saw on the way here, as well as paintings of the two other planets found in the system. There was, however, one painting I did not recognize.

It was not a painting at all, but rather a map, with five stars gathered in a circle all pointing to the center.

There was a symbol in the middle that I could not recognize. It looked like a jewel or stone with five sets of hands holding on to it. A treasure map of the past most likely, but it was unclear. I do love solving puzzles, but now did not seem like the right time to do so.

All the paintings were of outer space, but not one of the paintings included any of the little creatures who greeted me in the city. So what was the mirror for? They were obviously not self-conscious, considering they had no artwork of themselves. It must serve another purpose other than vanity.

"Which one do you like best, my friend?"

I spun around to see whom it was that emerged from the shadows. It was the same one who brought me into this situation in the first place.

He walked over to the painting of the four stars circling the water planet, right next to where I was standing.

"I find this one to be the best of my collection."

He was very calm, speaking in a low and relaxed tone. He noticed my frustration to the situation.

"You must forgive me for putting you in the sleep. I know that it has made you upset, but you must realize that it was necessary. We had no form of communication. You see, while you were in a trance, I was able to read your subconscious, which allowed me to learn your form of communication. I am now able to talk to you and we now have the chance to get to know each other."

I understood his motives and forgave him.

"I should have known you meant no harm." I told him, feeling a little foolish for overlooking the obvious.

"That is quite all right," he said.

He walked over to the desk on the other side of the room. He stopped in his tracks and turned around to face me.

"I trust there were no side effects to your sleep?"

I shook my head. "None. I thank you for that."

He smiled. "I must admit, I have not encountered a more effective way of breaking down language barriers."

He sat down in the chair behind the desk and motioned for me join him in the other chair. I acknowledged and walked over to sit down. Two arms grew from his torso and placed themselves on the desk. He leaned towards me.

"You are not the first to visit us. On the contrary, we have had many guests from far away. Some of what you see has been inspired by outsiders, but mostly from our neighboring planet that you most likely saw on your journey here. Have you been on the largest of the three bodies in this system?"

Again, I shook my head.

"No, this is the first planet I have visited in this system, however, I do plan on going to the other two as soon as I have finished what I came here to do."

"Which is what?" He asked calmly, yet intrigued.

"I'll tell you later." I said, knowing it would be wise to skip the revelation until a later time.

He smiled.

"Well, you must accompany me to the outside city. I'm sure you want to know all about our civilization. I figure that the way we live has something to do with your presence here."

I smiled and told him I couldn't wait.

Secrets revealed in the manuscript were becoming familiar and making sense to Deltrin. The system of the three planets, which the narrator was describing, was the same system where he found the temple. Before he got there, he had no clue that there were intelligent life forms on the other planets on or below the surface.

There were many things that did not make sense

31

to Deltrin, and as soon as an old secret was revealed, a new one was hidden. He could do nothing more but read on, hoping to find all the answers he was looking for. Completely hypnotized by the fascinating tale, he glued his eyes to the book and picked up from where he left.

The city was not clustered with buildings. On the contrary, the space was well organized, with plenty of room to move from place to place. The city was so beautiful, it almost seemed a shame for it to hide within the walls of the cavern. That reminded me of something. I turned to face my tour guide.

"When I first came into the cavern, I noticed there were two waterfalls joining together and falling off the edge of the cliff. Where does the water go?"

"That water is our source for drinking." He answered. "We have an inexhaustible supply of water, considering the planet is one giant ocean. The water you saw falling off the cliff drops into a system that captures it and circulates it throughout the society. We do not need to take anything out of the seawater in order to drink it. We have evolved to the point where our bodies can use the salt in the water as a nutrient, and drinking the water straight does not hurt our systems."

He took me to the main funnel that captures the falling liquid. There were several tubes that split the water flow, transferring the supply to different areas.

"Is there enough to supply the entire civilization?"

He smiled at my question.

"Actually, there are several hundred civilizations scattered all over the planet. We all live underground for obvious reasons, the main one being the fact that there is no land piercing the surface of the water outside."

He pointed up to the ceiling of the cavern.

"That waterfall is one of hundreds underground. In answer

to your question, yes. The waterfall is sufficient enough for us to live on. The other societies have their own waterfalls to live off of."

"But, why not just go up to the surface and collect the water from up there?"

"There is no need to. We have enough."

I didn't get the answer I was looking for.

"What I mean to ask is; if the supply was cut off, would you be able to reach the surface and gather enough water to live on. Can you survive on the surface?"

He paused for a moment, finally realizing what it was I was searching for.

"So, it is our history you wish to learn." He stated. I nodded, urging him to continue. "Very well. For about two-thousand years, our race has lived underground. We were not here when the planet was born. We just found it. But, since we never have had much exposure to the neighboring stars we orbit, our bodies adapted to the amount of light underground. Because of this, too much heat would kill us if we were exposed to the stars' rays. We are able to travel to the surface, but not for too long. When we do need to have prolonged amounts of time in the presence of the stars, we have machines that allow our bodies to adapt to the solar rays. I believe you had the chance to see one of them."

I responded with a confused look.

"The mirror that looked back at you in my room was actually a panel that captures a certain amount of solar energy from outside. By capturing the rays that emanate from stars, we can store the energy in a containment unit. The energy can be released any where and still have the same effects as if it were coming from the stars themselves."

He paused to see if I was confused. My countenance assured him I understood exactly what he was talking about, so he continued.

33

"When we need to travel to the surface for some reason or another, we gather enough of the star's rays into the panels of the mirrors, and then subject ourselves to the heat by exposing the rays to our bodies at a controlled amount. The inoculation of the rays allows our bodies to adapt to the outer atmosphere, but only for a little while. After a certain amount of time has passed, our bodies lose their abilities to stay in the direct path of the star's rays and we are forced to return underground. The only real reason we go onto the surface is to conduct space travel, which we do quite a bit of."

I was pleased to hear how highly evolved this civilization was.

"Impressive." I said, "Your civilization is quite advanced."

He proceeded to give me the tour, showing me several different areas of the city, as well as explaining certain cultural activities. Eventually, we began to walk back to the building I awoke in.

"I just realized, I've not even asked for the name of your species, nor for that matter, *your* name!"

He stopped in his tracks and turned to face me. His scrunched countenance showed me he also realized the error.

"My name is Retnar." He quickly said. "I am the leader of this particular city. We are known as The Trocties. There are several other civilizations accommodating this planet of the same species, which I told you about earlier, but I am not their leader. As a matter of fact, I barely keep in contact with any of them, but we are on friendly terms with each other, nevertheless."

He paused, waiting for my response.

"I am pleased to meet you, Retnar. My name is Tyran."

I was reluctant to disgorge the rest of my story, but nevertheless, I continued.

"You may find this hard to accept," I said with slight hesitation, "but I assure you, what I am about to tell you is the truth."

He waited in silence, confused at the sudden change of mood.

"I am over two billion years old and am one of the nine scientists who took part in an experiment that resulted in the creation of this universe."

Did I mention subtlety is not one of my virtues?

The silence between us after this revelation lasted long enough to give me time to build another universe. In all fairness, he took it rather well.

"It's not everyday you meet your maker." He said, with a bit of reluctance.

"Please don't think of me any higher than you, my friend. I did not come here to press my rights as your leader, or anything remotely similar. I am here to observe the growth of the many different forms of life in this universe, not to declare any authority."

He paused, feeling a little safer. I could see his curiosity was beginning to overpower his confusion and fear. His interrogation picked up again

"How many worlds have you seen?" He asked.

"Millions. Each one different than the one before."

"How is ours different?"

I paused, thinking about the vast explanation I could give him, but that was not my intention. I wanted to tell him a force beyond my power of description and definition pointed out the way to this planet. How could I tell him this planet was my choice to be the receptacle for my manuscript, for reasons being I was silently told to choose it by an invisible voice? I am a scientist, not a priest, but for some reason, everything that made me who I am told me this was the planet that deserved a piece of the formula.

"All I can say is that your children's children will follow my footsteps and be the catalysts to a new order of life."

He staggered from the unexpected comment and

admiration, but was still able to smile in response.

"I did not tell you the entire reason for my mission, so here it is, as brief as I can make it. Eight of us are traveling throughout this universe, searching for a worthy civilization that will receive a piece of the formula that explains how to build a universe. It has all the notes we took, all the mathematics, all the errors we found, and all the solutions. It is our life's work and I have decided to give my piece of the manuscript to you and your civilization. It will not make much sense to you now, considering it is incomplete, but in time, your future generations will come to do exactly as we have done, and continue the long chain of scientists before us."

He gathered the information as well as expected, but still looked with obvious confusion.

"So, you're a scientist who's searching for a colony that will follow your footsteps and continue the universe recipe?"

I nodded. "That's the plan."

"Well, I'd hate to take away your excitement of finding a fresh civilization," he said, with sincere sympathy, "but you are too late."

I was not expecting this. "Too late? What do you mean?"

"Ten years ago, we were greeted by a traveler, much like yourself, who gave us a manuscript filled with equations we could not decode. He told us that in time, the mathematics would make sense."

I hadn't expected this, either. The surprise widened my eyes. I couldn't tell if I was pleased to hear that one of my comrades had the extreme luck of finding such a wonderful species, or if I was angry about my extremely bad luck of being too late.

My future was starting to look long, filled with many more years of endless searching for another planet. Retnar did not understand my frustration, probably thinking I should be pleased to hear that a fellow scientist was having a successful journey.

"I'm sorry your adventure has not come to a happy conclusion here. At least let me show you the manuscript so you can determine which of your friends it was who made it here first."

I must admit I was wondering who it was that found this secluded paradise. I did not hold a grudge. It was not the fact that I was beaten. That did not bother me at all. The only thing I had a deep foreboding about was the fact that I was going to have to spend several more millennia trapped in my capsule of a ship, trying desperately to find a civilization such as this. I could almost feel the seat in the cockpit sticking to me.

We traveled back to the building from which we came. The whole time, I moved extra slow, trying to avoid what was inevitable.

The inside of the first floor was new to me, considering my pleasant little sleep kept me from seeing it. However, the room up on the top floor was recognizable. It was nice to be in a room that was relatively familiar.

Retnar came into the room holding a thick manuscript of which I was all too familiar. He handed it to me and sat down in his chair, watching, waiting for a reaction.

Volume Seven. That was Octan's volume. That sneaky little...He was always good at finding things before me, always on top. Despite the fact that he had beaten me, I was rather happy to see it was he who got there first. I would not have wanted anyone else, except maybe Terinsa.

I began to flip through the pages, feeling nostalgic. I missed my friend. Perhaps looking through his manuscript would be the closest thing to hearing his voice. The equations were all there, as well as the gravity mathematics.

You see, each volume contained one of the eight major pieces of the experiment. Octan's was the gravity portion, which, in my opinion, was the most important of all the pieces.

I found myself reading through the book, remembering the experiences of the project. Though the times were both good and bad, my ambivalence found a harmony and I looked back on my past with elation, accompanied with a small yearning to be able to live it once more. It was odd that I could feel such emotion by simply glancing at a multitude of mathematical equations. I often felt a sense of pride in discovering new things, but never like this. I was beginning to look at science in the same light a poet sees an ocean, watching its waves dance on the shore, in a unique ballet that needed no explanation for its actions.

My fingers continued to caress the pages of the book, probably entertaining Retnar. I got to the last portion of the manuscript and noticed something I had never seen before.

According to what I could remember from the experiment, the primary explosion should have had a gravity constant that acts as a barrier. That is what we saw when the blue halo expanded to the outermost reaches of the new universe.

The only way we can keep enough space for other universes to be created is by putting a limit to the size of the explosion. Once the barrier reaches a certain point, it stops and makes an orb, where the universe grows inside. What I saw in the manuscript was an equation that left out the barrier's dimensions as well as the gravity constant, which made the force of gravity incredibly weaker than the explosion's intense force. The explosion rate was too great for the gravity to have any reactionary force to hold back the blast. If this equation were put to use, there would be no barrier, making a blast wave that would never end. All the universes that had been created in the past would be destroyed in the wake, as well as all life existing. My passion towards the experiment turned instantly to extreme fear, and Retnar could see the horror flushing into my eyes.

"Something is wrong." He stated.

"Yes. This equation is not what we printed."

I sat down in the seat next to Retnar. I looked at him with consternation, trying to think of what to do next. The operation was now at a critical moment, and I was the only one who knew about it, aside from Octan. I feared the worst, already knowing that my friend was dead, killed by the hand of an unknown opposition.

I looked up at the frightened Retnar, who had no presumption of what was happening.

"Can you remember what the person looked like who gave you this manuscript?"

He began to describe the mysterious being, recalling details from his memory as best he could.

"The creature that came to us looked much like you, however, he did not wear similar clothing. If I remember right, there was a small insignia on his left shoulder that you do not possess."

My fear grew even worse, for I already knew what he was about to tell me. The situation was more critical than I thought.

"The insignia that you speak of," I interrupted, "was it an oval shaped medallion with a hollow center?"

He nodded.

"Was there a sword stabbing through the center?"

His nod was somewhat more reluctant than the first he gave me. He knew, as well as I, that my journey had just come to a screeching halt. What he didn't know was that the project had just turned into a full-scale war.

The Start of War

"Eve-one, this is Eve-four, do you copy?"

I spoke into the Tele-communicator inside my cockpit, hoping that the Admiral was listening. After a long moment of silence on the other end, his clear voice finally came through.

"I read you Eve-four. What news have you got?"

I figured that there was no reason to cushion the blow, so I simply stated the facts, pushing my emotions aside.

"Seven has been eliminated. I'm with the being he gave his portion of the manuscript to, but it was not Seven who delivered it."

"How do you know this?" He asked, confusedly.

"The leader of the city who received his portion of the manuscript described the being and it was not Octan. To make matters worse, the gravity equation in the manuscript has been tainted. It's missing the outer-barrier mathematics."

The first bit of news was enough to stop the breathing on the other end of my communicator, but it was the latter half of the news that returned it promptly. He stabbed his next words through his communicator.

"Who was it?"

"As I said, the leader of this civilization gave me a description of the traveler, which included the description of a familiar medallion of a sword stabbing an oval."

There was another moment of silence.

"So, the Rashouwe have decided to rekindle the flames that we thought were extinguished?"

His hypothetical question needed no reply. He and I already knew that. War was about to begin and our project was only half done.

The name was finally familiar to Deltrin. He recalled hearing stories about these forces, always hopping from planet to planet and destroying whatever life they could find on each of them.

"Notify all other team members and tell them to rendezvous on planet Eve. We have to make a few changes. I will be waiting here for all of you."

He paused for a brief moment.

"Tyran?"

"Yes sir?"

"Tell the others to watch their back. You do the same. Eve-one out."

"I may be of assistance to you and your friends." Retnar began. "From what I gathered from your conversation, it's obvious that a battle is imminent. I cannot supply your friends with much fire-power, but at-least let me try to protect you on your journey back to your base."

I must admit, I had no idea what he was talking about. His civilization did not strike me as a warrior race at all.

"You have weapons?"

"I should have mentioned that we've not battled with any species for a very long time. However, we do have a storage facility containing several battleships that have remained dormant for many years. Most of us know how to operate them, in preparation for an attack, but we've not had to use them in real battle for a very long time"

His posture and tone changed a little, indicating that a wise notion was about to emerge from his mouth.

"I'm an intelligent being and can be a valuable asset to your mission. Please, let me help you in your cause. You have already included me in your project simply by your presence here, so why not go the distance?"

A smile appeared with his last comment. I assured him that his help would greatly be appreciated. Protection from any outside threat would be nothing but helpful.

With no argument to his proposal, I followed him. He escorted me to the basement level of the city, where the armada of sleeping vessels awaited us to wake them from their slumber.

I followed him for what seemed to be miles down the heart of the canyon. Several stalactites trickled off the ceiling, decorating the stairway down to the underworld. The path in front of us could barely be seen. Only a small collection of lights that Retnar activated kept us from going blind on our way down. My life was in his hands. If I lost sight of him, I might as well have lived the rest of my life down here. One thing's for sure; whatever it was they were storing down in the pit was more than your average squad of battleships. The farther we went down, the more I anticipated.

We finally approached a large door that was regaled with several different security systems. I thought that the identification process would take hours, but all Retnar had to do was place a newly formed hand on a dimly-lit board for a few seconds, and all the locks protecting the jewels behind the door were undone. I guess it helps to be in company with a high member of society.

The door opened slowly, exhaling a breath that fogged the view of the room inside. The mist slowly dissipated as Retnar activated the lights in the room. I stood in awe as they flickered on one by one in sequence.

The dimensions of the room seemed infinite, as well

as the number of ships, which kept increasing as the lights continued to activate. I couldn't breathe. It was like what I saw at the countdown before the universe's birth. Thousands of ships were docked all adjacent to each other, stretching for several miles. Retnar proudly walked down the aisle, paternally fixing his eyes on the plethora of flying beasts.

"You must have really had some kind of war." I finally said.

He ceased to stare at his metallic trophies and turned around to answer my question.

"Wars to be exact, Tyran. There were several invasions."

I tried to coax him to tell me more, but he did not budge. Perhaps another time, I thought. To be sure, it was better not to waste our time with story telling. We had more important things to accomplish.

"So, which one will it be?"

He began to walk around, deliberately towards a particular spacecraft.

"I have been trained to operate about eighty percent of the vehicles you see. Of all of them, I prefer this one above all."

His attention was glued to the incredible machine in front of us.

"I have never tested any of these machines in actual combat, but from what I've learned from this craft, I have found that it can perform many tasks that allow for instant evasion. It is also capable of fending off multiple attacks with its extensive armory."

He really didn't have to tell me all that. I was ready to jump in the moment I set my eyes on it. Being cooped up in a single passenger transport would cause me to jump into anything. Just looking at the beautiful craft was enough to get me excited. My expression was answer enough to Retnar's invitation.

The smooth contours of the ship softened the glow

43

from the lights above. It had three wings of equal length and distance from each other, all of them armed with triple 90 mm. Plasma rifles. On each of the two avian wings used to guide the hull, there was a circular insignia with a bolt of lightning inside. On the dorsal wing, there were two large hyper-light speed conductors on each side, about three meters in diameter. The wingspan of this incredible beast was about fifty meters, making it look like a monstrous raptor of ancient lore silently resting in its nest, waiting patiently, studying its prey. The mouth of this winged omen slowly opened, inviting the two of us inside.

We both hopped into the cockpit, which was about the size of my transport itself. The controls did not look familiar, but were not intimidating either. The panel contained controls for flight and attack: it just had an incredible abundance of them.

"When was the last time you piloted this machine?" I asked, not taking my eyes away from the countless controls.

He looked over pensively, trying to remember when his last ride amongst the stars was.

"It hasn't been that long, actually." He replied. "Relax, my friend. This ship and I are connected, literally."

As soon as he said that, a dome shaped apparatus descended from the ceiling and attached itself around Retnar's head. Then, a single plate of glass attached to the helmet lowered and set itself in front of his single eye. It listed several figures and symbols on its translucent screen.

Two more connections emerged from the bottom of his pilot seat, both molding around the sides of his torso.

"You and I can still converse with these connections." He said. "These controls create a neural connection between myself and the ship. My instincts control the movement of the ship with much more speed and accuracy than simply steering the ship with primitive sticks and wheels. What's even better," He continued "is that the ship's atmosphere creates a type of solar shield around me."

This was new.

"How does that work?" I asked.

"To tell you the truth, I really don't know. It's one of those things I don't understand. All I know is that the head-gear I'm wearing sends a harmless electrical circuit through my body, which attracts certain elements in the atmosphere. Ultimately, the elements mix together and create a biological shield around me, allowing me to traverse upon star-lit land for an innumerous amount of time."

"Um... do I need to worry about these elements attaching to me? I asked nervously.

"No, not at all. They are only attracted to the current. The ship's atmosphere is perfectly harmless."

The ballet of lights continued to flash on the panel.

"Are you ready to leave, Tyran?"

I nodded, still trying to absorb the wild atmosphere phenomena, and proceeded to give him the coordinates to Eve. From what he told me about the speed of the ship, it would only be a few days before we reached Eve's orbit.

The lift-off of the ship was very smooth, as it should have been. We sailed over the vast fleet and exited the deep canyon through a massive tunnel. After we penetrated the underground, we flew past the ocean surface-level and were nearly blinded from the light of the three stars in the sky.

In seconds, we cleared the gravitational pull of the water planet and were ready to set a direct course to Eve. I looked over at the eager Retnar, waiting to feel the speed of this immaculate contraption.

"Hold on" was all he said and in the blink of an eye, we were rocketed into deep space.

Deltrin was tempted to go down to the water planet and see this swarm of ships for himself. Unfortunately, he knew he had a long journey ahead of him and could not take the time for little vacations. Still, he made sure that he would come here again to visit this lost colony.

He finished the drink he had and placed the glass on the table. He marked his place in the book and set it down next to his empty glass. He got up from his chair, stretched his stiff body, and proceeded down the hall to the cock-pit. He plotted a direct course for his home planet, hoping that his family would still be there. Perhaps they would even recognize him. Strangely enough, Of all the places he had been, home was the most relaxing for him. Right now, relaxation was exactly what he was looking for. He sat back in his pilot seat and within seconds, he fell sleep.

He awoke after a long rest, a little disoriented. He lifted himself off the chair clumsily and stumbled down the hall, holding his hand to his forehead. The slight headache went away after he showered. As soon as he had completed his morning ablutions, he sat back down in his favorite chair, and continued with his reading...

The Presence of a Threat

As far back as I can remember, I've always loved space travel. I can still remember the first time I had the opportunity to travel outside my home planet other than using a simulation unit.

The planet that I grew up on orbited only one star. It was mostly land, with some small bodies of water, some stretching for several miles. The plant-life was beautiful there, blanketing the land with breathtaking vivacity.

I was born and raised in one of the major cities, but never became accustomed to the life in the metropolis. There were too many people, too much commotion.

My parents did not enjoy the big city either, so they decided to move when I was about fifteen. The city we moved to was much smaller and the beings there were much more friendly and familiar with one another. I received a marvelous education, learning science, technology, mathematics, and language skills. I felt I had no need for anything else.

My last year's entirety was spent in a simulator, preparing me for my final flight, which incidentally, would not be in a stationary machine. Like all young beings, I was impetuous and wanted to pilot a real transport. Finally the day came when I would pilot my own craft. Rest assured, my excitement could barely be contained.

On that particular day, our sun was high in elevation, making the land glow with intensity and luster. There were a few clouds in the sky that blocked some of the star's light, but not enough to muffle any of the star's radiance. I think that since it was the most exciting day of my life, everything was intensified with majesty. It was the final day of my flight school.

I had practiced many times on a simulation machine and passed successfully through every mission, but, like anyone will tell you, a simulation will not prepare you for the intense rush that you feel when you are controlling a space craft without the training wheels.

I was manning a craft that was designed to accommodate only one crewmember. It was a science vessel, not a battle-craft, so it had no need for a second member. It was just a simple vessel designed to surface on a planet and gather material for scientific purposes. But no matter what it was, on that day, it was the greatest ship ever built, and I was its next pilot.

It was docked in a hanger where several other ships rested, waiting to be launched by other students in my class. I walked around searching for my ship. Docking bay forty-two was my destination. I walked past several ships, wishing my comrades a safe and successful flight, receiving the same best wishes from them. I finally came upon docking bay forty-two There it was, glowing where it stood, perhaps only for me. I stood in front of the beautiful creature feeling its aura surround me. My shadow crept closer and closer to the doorway. Soon we were joined, flesh to metal, soul to soul.

I climbed up the ladder to the seat and walked in, feeling every inch of my body mold into the wrinkles of the pilot seat. I never had this kind of a connection to any simulator, but then again, if something went wrong in the simulation unit, I could simply restart and try again. This was not the case now. I depended on this machine and placed my life into its power and protection. Likewise was the trust the machine placed in my hands.

I glanced down to the control panel, acquainting

48

myself with the many gadgets that decorated it. All pre-launch systems were in tact and I was ready to launch myself to the stars. I notified my superior that I was ready for departure. He acknowledged my eagerness and prepared to open the dome shield.

Slowly, the doors spread, and the light from the star peered through the opening. Its radiance spread throughout the cockpit, almost blinding me. I saw for a split second our neighboring planet, which incidentally, was my destination for this flight.

My mission was to successfully navigate my ship through space and dock on the other planet. Then, I was to gather specific materials on the planet's surface, contain them properly and head back home to complete the mission.

The materials that we gathered really had no significance to any experiment or other laboratory work. The whole idea behind the project was to show our superiors we could gather items in a particular environment and categorize them.

The other planet was heavily populated, much like ours, and contained many scientists with whom we often communicated. There were many people on the planet who were told in advance about this mission and were asked to help out if anything went wrong. Personally, I didn't worry about any potential dangers. Rather I was looking forward to meeting my friends on their home-planet.

My superior commander wished me success on my flight and launched me into orbit. The takeoff was, for lack of a better word, extreme. The immense rush from the power behind the blast sent all my nerves into shock, but I was still fully conscious. The reverse-pressure modulator protected me from the immensity of the G-forces at work. I took my concentration away from the incredible physical forces at hand and averted my attention towards more natural forces.

I turned around to look back at the blue sky that suddenly turned black, and for the first time in my life, I was beyond my planet, floating in the greatest frontier any species has ever traveled. I looked around, amazed at the clarity of the stars. Never before have they been so bright, free from all light pollution. Even the clearest night on my planet couldn't compare to this.

I submitted the coordinates of my landing place into the machine and let the computer do the rest. As my spacecraft floated towards the planet, I relaxed in my seat and glared into the dreamlike world before me. After about three hours of space flight, I reached the orbit of the planet and took control of the craft. Gently, I descended into the blue atmosphere of my sister planet and softly landed right on the mark.

I shut down the vessel, hopped out of the cockpit and landed on the rocky surface. I pulled out the list of materials that I needed to gather. Before long, I was greeted by my partner in the mission, a native of the planet. He and I had worked together many times before, but we had never met each other face to face. We conversed mainly through Tele-communications or radio devices during our final year of education. It was gratifying to finally meet him in person.

Together, He and I found several materials and placed them in their appropriate containment units. We searched for hours, finally finding all the materials. When we were finished, I thanked him for his help and told him we would meet again. Soon enough, I was in the cockpit of my ship, on a direct course back to my planet.

I landed successfully in the same docking bay, almost at the same time as my fellow scientists. I hopped out of the cockpit, and grabbed a cart on which I placed all the materials I gathered. My Commander was pleased with my success and told me that my performance throughout the entire period of the class was very impressive. Then, he gave me a name to contact for a special mission, and congratulated me on my achievements.

For a long time, I stared at the name, wondering if I should make contact. I was not paranoid by any means. I was simply unaware of what my Commander wanted me to get into. The manner of which he presented the information was clandestine, almost military-like. But I was starving for more adventure, so after a couple of days of deliberation with myself, I decided to take a chance.

I contacted the person whose name was given to me, curious to see what this special mission was all about. This man was very large and adorned with medals, most likely a decorated veteran of war, so my assumption of this mission being operated by the military was confirmed. His voice was below the normal tone, almost grating. With serious execution, he told me that I was one of eight scientists selected to conduct an experiment, which would result in the birth of a universe.

He made the plan of the mission sound plain and simple, which was the exact opposite of what I expected. I admired the Admiral's talent for stating just the facts and the brevity of which he did so, but I was also very intimidated. However, being adventurous and willing as always, I accepted the great honor.

Building a universe was an idea that had been thought over for several millennia. The concept was nothing new, but it had never been tried before, at least not by anyone in this universe. The Admiral of the mission had explained to me that we were going to follow in the footsteps of scientists before us. The allegory was a little strange, but I continued to listen.

According to him, the scientists of the oldest universe found a way to create another universe and did so after a few billion years of research. They did not want this information to go to waste, but they knew that it would be several more billion years before the inhabitants of the second universe would be ready to handle the power of the universe experiment. So, they hid several pieces of their notes around the baby universe, hoping that when they were found, the scientists would be ready to make another lap around time's circle.

This chain of events led to the building of four more universes, and it was our turn to build the sixth universe in existence. It was the opportunity itself handed to me that was completely unexpected. It was a great honor and privilege to be one of the selected scientists and I had no idea how to take it. All I could do was ignore the immense pressure that was placed upon me and try to complete the tasks that were presented to the best of my ability.

A few days after my conversation with the Admiral of the operation, the elite eight were invited to attend a mandatory meeting. There I met six new scientists, all of whom I knew I would immediately enjoy working with. The seventh, however, I had met before. The last time I saw him was on the planet I had just studied. Fulfilling the last promise I gave him, I walked over after introducing myself to the other scientists. I extended my arm to shake his hand.

"It's good to see you again, Tyran."

"The pleasure is all mine, Octan."

I awoke from my nostalgic journey to the past, feeling the streak left behind by a stray tear on my cheek. I wiped it away and sat up in my chair. Retnar was silent, paying some attention to the flight and some to me. He spoke up, realizing I had finally awoken from my sleep.

"I know this may be a bad time to ask such a question, but I am curious to hear more about these creatures that have infiltrated this universe."

I had no idea how to describe the Rashouwe, except to say they were quintessential evil. One of their clan members murdered my best friend, so how could I give any description that was unbiased? Then again, all personal descriptions are biased.

"I will make a long story short, my friend, for I don't think the flight is long enough for me to give a full description."

Understanding my actions, Retnar nodded his head and then turned to face me, fully attentive to the story I was about to give.

"Before the experiment, my race had lived through five hundred years of peace. About five years after we began with the project, our universe became acquainted with a race of warriors. At first, we did not think their presence too much of a threat, but as soon as we got the news of their part in the annihilation of an entire solar system, it was obvious that we had a major problem. Most everyone in our system enlisted themselves in the battle-forces, including three of us; Octan, Terinsa, and myself. We were told to help out in the technological field, such as making new weapons and learning how to protect our soldiers with better armor. It did not turn out that way. Instead, the three of us were made into a team of special operatives. We completed several missions during our tenure as warriors, receiving first hand information concerning the movement and method of fighting that the Rashouwe exercised. They did not have a planet of their own or a base to which they could dock for supplies. Rather, they attacked large vessels and gathered the supplies they could find in the derelict and simply moved on. At first, the Rashouwe were just small clans of warriors, attacking small areas on planets. But as they grew, they formed a band of ruthless warriors with extreme solidarity. With the supplies and weapons they stole, they were able to take on the larger star cruisers that patrolled the allied space in which our planets orbited and eventually began to attack planets themselves. We ignored the potential danger of the Rashouwe for too long and paid dearly for it. After they destroyed the solar system, most every being in the galaxy united to destroy

53

the Rashouwe completely. The Rashouwe won the first battles, but since they had no planet to retreat to, they were forced to constantly fight, no matter what their losses were. It was like they were fighting just for the sake of war. They had no diplomacy to expand, nor did they have any need for the natural resources on our planets. They simply enjoyed killing everything. Many planets were destroyed in their wake, but were never commandeered by the Rashouwe. The planets were left to silently orbit in space, completely devoid of all life. Finally, we were able to manufacture a fleet of destroyers in a system that was unknown to the Rashouwe. My home planet was one of them. Our squadron, which totaled over twenty thousand heavy battle-ships, was then launched. We ambushed a huge Rashouwe fleet, taking them by surprise with our incredible fleet, giving our side a tactical advantage. On one particular occasion, we met up with an incredible fleet. Four groups of five thousand ships gathered on all sides of the advancing enemy and closed them in a box formation. The Rashouwe fleet was in chaos, for they had no where to run. In panic, one of the ships fired on us, causing every one of our ships to retaliate. The fireworks were incredible. Hardly any of our ships were damaged. Some were destroyed by the Rashouwe, but it was nothing close to what the Rashouwe fleet suffered. A few ships were able to escape, which we thought were nothing to worry about. We scouted all the allied systems and devastated the Rashouwe clan with incredible force. Our side was victorious. This incredible event ushered a new era of peace, where every race involved in the war became united, with the exception of the Rashouwe. The losses suffered in the war were soon resurrected and eventually, everything was brought back to normal. Terinsa, Octan, and I returned to the other scientists with valuable information that could help us with the project. We also figured out a way to enhance our life-expectancy at exponential rates."

I looked over at Retnar. "Naturally, our bodies could survive for maybe two-hundred years at tops."

"I'm relieved to hear that." He chuckled. "I've never heard of anything living that can last as long as you."

"Well, we found something in our studies that gave us the ability to elongate our lives." I do not want to go into the details, but to give you an idea, we injected into our bloodstream a type of liquid that gave youth to our internal organs, instead of tiring them out. So, in essence, our aging is moving in the opposite direction. However, the injected potion will eventually wear out and our bodies will flush out the potion, making us age as we should."

I paused to take a breath and continued on.

"Anyway, since then, we have not heard anything about the Rashouwe, until now. What I am most worried about is the fact that they are trying to start war when they know we are well equipped for one. They would not try something unless they were well prepared to withstand a devastating counterattack. In all probability, there may be a huge Rashouwe force out there and now they have control of a planet, or perhaps many planets, somewhere in this universe."

"But why you? " Retnar asked, "Why are they attacking you and your fellow scientists."

"That's what I'm hoping to find out."

I looked over at Retnar.

"I told you, they only like to kill and destroy and nothing else. Our only chance now is to kill every last one of them to make sure they don't have a chance to return and I don't know if there is a way to do that. By now, they are too scattered."

The Plan

Planet Eve lacked the beauty I remembered it once had, now that my mind was clouded with despair. I knew that the reunion with my comrades would not be a pleasant one.

Retnar docked the craft near the headquarters, close to the other ships that were already there. We were greeted by the Admiral at the entrance to the building, who had a justifiable countenance of anger and sorrow smeared on his face.

"Welcome home, Tyran. The rest of the clan is waiting inside." He turned over to my companion. "You must be Retnar. I'm pleased to meet you. I am grateful for your willingness to help us in our mission, as Tyran has informed me. I am sure the rest of the team shares my opinion. So please, follow me into the meeting room, where they are waiting to meet you."

The Admiral led Retnar and me through the halls of the palace. After two billion years of being absent, I barely noticed any change. I had hoped to be greeted with something new. Unfortunately, the walls sang a monotonic dirge that echoed down the halls. Why was I so partial to what the walls were lamenting? I had just lost my closest friend and the mere triviality of the stagnant walls was what was bothering me the most. My whole life had changed once I was informed of Octan's demise and in respect to his death, I wanted everything around me to change as well. Why didn't the universe grieve with me? Was Octan's death not enough to make a single star stop in its orbit, just for a moment, to honor his departure?

I began to question my own immortality, asking the same questions concerning my own demise. Would anyone notice? Would I be the last of my kind? What emotions or thoughts pound the mind of the sole survivor of a species, who feels their end approaching?

The thought of a war being conceived in this universe disgusted me, for I knew that the imminent battle would lead to the end of thousands of civilizations. I also knew that for every species who would perish in the whirlwind, there would be one creature who would have to suffer the realization that he or she is the only one left of their kind.

I wallowed in this disheartening premonition as I continued to follow the Admiral. I pictured in my mind the soldier who succeeds everyone in battle. The glow of his aura roaring like a lion as he realized his victory, glaring at the panoramic view of death and its smell that fowled the air surrounding him. The way he would triumph over all his enemies, but in payment to this victory all those he could tell of his glory would also be littering the battlefield.

Along with this thought, I was reminded of the Rashouwe, constantly fighting just for the sake of killing. They had no purpose in their ways except to prove some presupposed conception of greatness to themselves. I wondered what would happen if they eventually destroyed every known civilization in their campaign. What would it prove? They would have no one to rule except a barren universe where once a million species thrived. They would perish themselves, considering that the drive in their life was no longer present, due to their short-sightedness and lack of respect for life. I knew in my heart that something had to be done to stop this advancing army of death. The purpose of our great experiment rested on this very goal.

We made this universe to spread life and watch it flourish so that every creature may grow in knowledge and strength and follow in our footsteps. It was essential that we preserved this right to every species in our universe, and we would die to save this privilege.

I rolled these thoughts around in my mind the whole way there and finally, like an epiphany, I came to the conclusion of what to do.

Enraptured by the suspense of the story being told, Deltrin barely noticed that a noise was coming from the cockpit of his ship. Annoyed that he could not read on, he marked his place and walked to his pilot seat, rather hastily.

A small light was flashing on his control panel, indicating that the ship was caught in the orbit of a planet. He looked out through the window of his ship and saw a large brown planet looming ahead. He took control of the ship and prepared to dock on the planet, somewhat curious to see if there was anything worthwhile to look at, as if he hadn't seen enough already. Perhaps old habits are hard to break

He landed on the rocky terrain and climbed out of his transport, instantly realizing he had made a big mistake. The planet was covered with thousands of bodies and smoldering machines, obviously the aftermath of war.

He quickly climbed back in and restarted his machine, but before he could lift off, his ship was being dragged down to the surface by some unknown force.

Fearing the worst, he armed himself and climbed out of the vehicle. There were seven warriors dressed in some sort of body armor, all pointing their weapons at him.

"Throw down your weapon." One of them commanded, showing with extreme assertiveness that he would not ask again.

Being the wise person that he was, Deltrin did as the assailant asked.

"What faction are you with?" the creature asked.

Confused by the question, Deltrin had no choice but to feign ignorance.

"I am with no faction."

The Commander looked at his men and asked another simple question that would either save Deltrin's life or kill him, but before the Commander asked it, Deltrin noticed a familiar insignia on the left arm of the Commander and the rest of his men.

"Are you a follower of the Rashouwe?" He asked.

Deltrin considered the possibilities of answers, but decided that not even in death would he join such a race of monsters. He shook his head slowly, but not reluctantly.

The Commander looked at the man beside him and then glanced back at Deltrin with a reassuring countenance. The Commander walked toward Deltrin, lowered his gun and extended his arm in friendship. Deltrin could not believe his eyes.

"I don't understand." He said. "I thought the insignia on your left arm represented the Rashouwe."

The Commander took a look at his left shoulder and snickered.

"We are Rashouwe warriors, but we do not fight for the their faction. We fight for a better cause. What's your name?" He asked.

A better cause? Deltrin thought. This was something to ponder.

"My name is Deltrin. I'm a traveler of these worlds."

"Really." The Commander responded, interested to hear more. "What is your latest find?"

"You wouldn't believe me if I told you." Deltrin said.

"Try me."

"Okay." He said, as if he were warning them of an incredible tale. "The quest that I just finished actually lasted for five years, until I got to this temple, where I found this casket."

The Commander seemed even more interested now. "What did you find?" He asked with a more stern voice.

"I found two manuscripts. One had numerous calculations and notes. The other turned out to be the chronological history of several scientists who claim they created this universe."

He waited for them to laugh at the notion. Instead, their faces displayed astonishment.

"You have the manuscript of calculations?" the Commander asked, stupefied.

Deltrin, a little scared that this secret manuscript was really not a fantasy, nodded his head. The Commander was relieved to hear that the great work had finally been recovered. He placed his hand on the shoulder of Deltrin and spoke in a voice that almost praised him.

"You're the great traveler that we have been waiting for! This is wonderful. But what are you doing here? You must get that treasure to a group of scientists. Do you know any you can trust?"

The extreme change in moods left Deltrin in a daze, and all he could do was shake his head.

"Alright, well, have you heard of a project called "Hyperlight"?"

Of course he had. But didn't confirm it out loud.

He just nodded.

"Great!" the Commander outburst. "Let me give you the coordinates to where they are located."

The Commander jumped into Deltrin's ship and plotted a course directly for the destination. When he was done, he shook Deltrin's hand once more, this time with more of an enthusiastic jerk. He then told him how much of a pleasure it was to meet "the savior".

Deltrin had no idea how to take all this adulation, but played the part very well. He shook the Commander's hand and told him not to worry, everything would be under control. His stern voice made the Commander believe his confidence. Good thing too, because Deltrin sure as hell didn't believe it.

The Commander left the ship and waved good-bye on the surface. He seemed refreshed, knowing that fate was tipping the scales in their favor. Deltrin waved back and soon enough, he was back in space with a new destination.

It wasn't enough that the manuscript was confusing, but now, Deltrin had to live up to the title of "the savior".

The Savior? He thought *Hell, I can't even save my own self. I must have done something real good. Or something real bad.*

With that thought, he ran back to his favorite chair and read on, hoping to find out what it was he did, or was about to do that made those fighters believe he would save them, along with everyone else...

The three of us finally reached the entrance to the meeting room. Inside, all six of my comrades silently awaited our arrival. Like a mist, we entered the room, not making our presence noticeable. Perhaps it was not our silence that cloaked our entrance, but rather the gloomy atmosphere that clouded the room. The first to see me was Terinsa. She stood up and managed to produce a smile, happy to see me.

I walked closer to her and embraced her as if she were my sister. She did not cry. Instead, she placed her warm head on my right shoulder and relaxed her entire weight on me.

"Seeing you now Tyran fills me with joy, but it is the vengeance in my heart that quenches my tears." She whispered.

She brought her lips close to my ears.

"You and I both know what needs to be done, and I am quite certain you have already thought of a plan."

She released herself from the embrace and looked deep into my eyes. I glared back at her, silently answering in agreement to her thoughts. She lowered her head and walked back to her seat.

The Admiral took his cue and introduced Retnar to the other six scientists. He then glanced toward me and walked my way.

"I know you too well for you to hide anything from me." He began. "Terinsa, Octan, you, and I all had a relationship where we could all predict each other's movements before they could be executed. I am sure that's exactly what Terinsa reminded you of when she spoke to you just now."

He was right. The four of us were inseparable. Like in a game of chess, each of us were able to anticipate any move we made. This connection allowed us to move at incredible speeds during the experiment simply because we did not need to waste any time explaining our actions.

I realized that Terinsa and the Admiral knew exactly what had to be done, on the simple premise that I knew as well.

"I need to address the others, Admiral. None of us here

should be left in the dark of what needs to be done." I paused to take a breath. "You and I are both aware that we have only one option. Otherwise, there will be no stopping the Rashouwe."

He nodded in agreement, and quickly began to assemble the counsel. They had all been able to acquaint themselves with Retnar, so I now had the chance to deliver my proposal. I positioned myself in the front of the room so that everyone could see me. Once everyone was seated, I was ready to speak.

"My dear friends, there is no need to be elusive to cushion the horrific force that has entered our lives uninvited, so I will be blunt. There is no escaping the Rashouwe forces. You will remember that many years ago the Rashouwe forces destroyed many civilizations in our universe. Fortunately, we were able to survive and fight back and eventually beat their forces down to a minimum. They were thought to have been finished, but we have been proven wrong. I have thought this over and have found that in order to make our universe safe, as well as every other one in existence, we have to completely eliminate every creature that is identifiable as a Rashouwe."

I inhaled the air around me and continued.

"We must enlist the aid of our allies to help us in this battle, for I am sure the Rashouwe force is beyond powerful. They would not have attacked us if they did not possess the army to back their actions and withstand our counter-attack. While our allies are covering us in the battle, we will be completing a mission of our own. Ironically, the Rashouwe assassin that killed our beloved comrade gave me an idea. It will seem that this idea was conceived from insanity, but I assure you it is our best option."

I took the manuscript I received from Retnar from out of my jacket.

"There are crucial components missing from this

63

manuscript. The formulas are lacking any type of constant for gravity, which would lead to the malfunction of the experiment. Without a gravity constant, the experiment is unstable, and unpredictable."

I closed the book and looked up to my audience.

"Do you remember me telling you that our only escape is to eliminate all Rashouwe? That is exactly what we are going to do."

I began to perspire, finally realizing the immensity of my plan.

"We must keep the manuscript as corrected and give gravity no barrier."

They all broke into a unified feeling of disbelief to my suicidal proposal. Frolton, our mathematics engineer spoke up from the back of the room.

"Surely you realize what will happen if there is no barrier. There will be no stopping the blast wave of the universe's birth. Everything in its path will be destroyed. Everything."

He delivered his last word with conviction and extreme emphasis, hoping I would reconsider my thought, but I didn't. My mind was made. I was content in my decision and nothing could stop me from carrying out my plan.

"I realize your concern, my friend, and I have tried to think of an alternative plan, but I cannot. I am sure the Rashouwe have an incredible force and it's going to take every last creature to fight them off. By eliminating everything and starting anew, we will ultimately annihilate any threat to the new universe. By sacrificing our lives, and the lives of all existence, we will pave the way for a new order of life, a life that will have the chance to thrive and grow without anything helping it or detracting from it. We have all given an oath to serve life and see to it that life comes first, in all situations. A no-win scenario has been presented before us, armageddon being its conclusion and a new order of life at the crest of its wake. In the name of science and of existence we must do this final action."

The counsel remained silent. The very thought of destroying existence was nothing to take lightly. Neither was the Rashouwe threat. Slowly, all my comrades began to realize that what I spoke was the truth. Then Terinsa and the Admiral stood up.

"I'll stand by you." Terinsa spoke with pride.

"As will I, comrade." The Admiral emphatically followed.

One by one, each of the scientists, as well as Retnar, stood to show their allegiance with me.

I stood amongst my comrades with pride I have never felt before. Their bravery and devotion made me proud and I knew my death would not be in vain if I were to perish in the company of such creatures of valor. I was not scared anymore. In a grave time such as this I would have thought it inappropriate to smile, but I could not help myself. Through thick and thin, we were all bound to each other, and not even our death would separate us.

"If fighting solves nothing, we are in defiance of truth, my friends. Not until we fight and win the day will we find our peace. The Day of Judgment is upon us. We all knew that some day our fears would return to haunt us. Now that they are here, let us face them, and defeat them."

The eyes of my comrades were fixed upon me as I finished my speech. The Admiral nodded his head, impressed and proud.

"Life after death." He said with a smile. "To your stations."

War had been declared.

The Memory Awakens

Deltrin stared at the words written on the parchment, not believing what he read. If he did not know how important it was to finish the mission, he would have kept the manuscript and prevented the Pyhrric victory from occurring. However, he knew the gravity of the situation and knew that the sacrifice was for a noble cause. Being cognizant of an imminent death was not what Deltrin hoped to achieve. But who was he to question fate? With all the risks he had taken, it was a miracle he was still alive. Besides, by the time the experiment would be complete, he would be long dead anyway. It was the fact that billions of creatures were going to be killed that was hurting him inside.

It had been a long time since he felt anything for anyone, and vice versa. Now, he was the key player in the game of existence and the chance for life to go on depended on him. He did not feel the need to hand the job to someone else to relieve himself of his burdensome duty. Instead, the primal instinct of protecting life arose from within his spirit and he accepted the responsibility, only fearing a death of shame, which would not find him if he continued to follow the path he was taking. He felt good about what he was doing, and continued to read...

The Admiral set up a com-station during the time the rest of us were out exploring. We all picked a station to seat ourselves and began to notify all our known allies.

We had been informed by several other species that the Rashouwe had in fact been deploying several fleets all across our old universe and had already annihilated thousands of worlds. Terinsa was lucky enough to contact a star cruiser that had been able to capture an assassin of the Rashouwe clan.

"Is he saying anything at all?" Terinsa inquired.

A faint transmission was heard from the other end. "He has kept silent ever since we captured him, Captain. What do you want us to do?"

Terinsa looked over to the Admiral, who was listening to the conversation.

"Shall we give it a shot?" She asked.

The Admiral thought for a moment and then looked over to me.

"Captain Tyran, you and Retnar rendezvous with their ship and see what you can get out of the Rashouwe. We'll stay here and continue with the mission. By the time you get back we will have your portion of the map ready to be delivered and you and Retnar can find your planet."

I hadn't been called 'Captain' in a long time. Every time I heard it, it reminded me of the days of war. For many years, I had tried to forget the horrors that the war had brought with it. I guess it had not occurred to me that we were in a time of war now. The funny thing was, I didn't think we ever left it. Not a day had passed without me thinking about it. It had haunted my thoughts and dreams and without me realizing it, my nightmarish fantasies were materializing before my eyes.

A nodded in compliance and was halfway out the door with Retnar when Terinsa grabbed my shoulder.

"Come back alive." She whispered in my ear. "I don't

67

want to lose my other brother." She leaned forward, gently placed her hand around my neck and kissed me. When we parted, I gave her a reassuring smile. "We'll return," I said, and in the blink of an eye, we were off to face the enemy.

I had to keep calm. If I lost my temper and felt the rage of vengeance for the death of my friend, I would be tempted to kill the prisoner, eliminating a valuable weapon against our oppressors.

We arrived at the rendezvous point in a few hours and docked with our ally ship. As soon as we docked and hopped out of Retnar's transport, we were greeted by one of the officers.

"Welcome aboard the Phantom Hunter, Captain." He extended his arm. "I am Captain Phantos. It is an honor to have you here." He swung his arm around my shoulder and began to guide me down the hallway.

"My crew and I have heard many stories about the great experiment. Of-course, none of us were alive to see it, but several generations have passed the stories to their children. I wish you could tell me what it was like. Information from a key witness would be wonderful. Unfortunately, we have to take care of the business at hand and not reminisce of the past."

He led us to the ship's prison.

"As you know, Captain, he won't speak or do anything. I hope you have a way of making him talk."

I thought for a moment and then came up with an idea.

"Retnar, put him to sleep like you did me when we first met. That way, you can read his thoughts and find out what the Rashouwe are doing."

Retnar emphatically smiled at the cunning plan and proceed to go into the room. There sat the assassin. Retnar walked toward the creature, without saying anything to him. He extended his hand towards the forehead of the

Rashouwe. Sparks of lightning appeared out of his palm, frightening the life out of the Rashouwe, but before he could die of fright, he was put to sleep.

Several hours passed, leaving Phantos and me in suspense. I paced back and forth in the hallway, anxious to hear what Retnar found out. Finally, the door opened and from the gloomy cell emerged the fatigued Retnar.

His single eye was red with tendrils of blood, spreading throughout his iris like bolts of lightning. His countenance was melancholy, most likely brought on from the exposure to the horrible world of the Rashouwe. I sympathized with my friend, knowing exactly what he went through. He slowly approached me, stunned, wishing he had never gone through the emotional torture he just experienced.

"I had no idea." He spoke through his trembling. "Such misery. Death was not just a state of being in there. It was tangible. I could feel the coldness all around me, creeping up and down my spine, penetrating my soul, touching my life with its malignant fingertips."

He slowly walked past me, straining for a breath of fresh air. He stopped in his tracks and turned around.

"You were right, Tyran. We have to completely destroy them. I have seen many evil things in my life, but nothing like this. There is no equal binary to compete with this force. Peace and goodness have no chance against these foes. They will win as long as one of them survives."

"So what do we do?" I asked, impatiently. "Tell me what you saw."

"I can't," he said, shaking his head incredulously. "It would take me a thousand years to give you a description of what I witnessed in there."

"An impasse is not what I wanted." I replied. "There must be something you can do."

He thought for a moment and then came up with a

plan.

"There is something that I could do to make you see what I saw." He said. "I'll reverse the process of the mind sleep and have you read my thoughts."

Now I was confused.

"You can do that?"

"Of course I can. I'm surprised I did not think of it before. You see, the mind sleep works by means of electricity. Most all life forms exist by means of electrical currents. Their brain waves, like yours and mine, are all currents, sending millions of thought patterns. During the mind sleep, I simply steal your messages. Since electricity can flow in different directions, I can reverse the flow of the current. Instead of me taking your messages, you will take mine. You will still be put to sleep, but you will be awake in your subconscious, able to study what I have learned."

I must admit, I was skeptic on the 'stealing' part. Nevertheless, I was persuaded to try out his idea. There was, however, one question that I had.

"How do I steer my way through your subconscious?" I asked.

"You won't." He replied. "Consider my subconscious as a ride, where you are the passenger and I am the pilot. You do not need to worry about steering at all. Since this is unknown territory for you, I feel it would be wise for me to guide you through everything, instead of you walking through my subconscious alone. Also, this may be a good time to allow you to read all my thoughts. That way, you will get a showing of the history of my species and the history of the beings before us.

I could not help but to chuckle at the growing difficulty of my task.

"So, what you're saying is that you're going to show me all your memories, everything you've ever learned?"

He nodded, smiling. "In chronological order, to make it less confusing. I must warn you ahead of time," he continued, "You may not understand everything you see. I won't be able to interpret things for you while you're asleep. Chances are, you might only understand the memory I have of the Rashouwe assassin. Some things may seem familiar, because you have visited my home planet, but the story behind the familiar scenes will be nebulous."

Among the many questions I had running through my head, one managed to escape and made it past my lips. "Then, how were you able to interpret my memories?" I asked.

"I didn't. I only took the time to find and read the memories that allowed me to learn your form of communication. In your case, you had more than enough to choose from."

"*My* case?"

"You told me yourself that you are over two billion-years old." He chuckled. Why do you think I was so surprised at you telling me about the experiment, or your age, or the Rashouwe themselves? I only had enough time to learn your ways of communication. Everything else was a blur. I saw a huge room filled with models, blueprints, and experimental tools, but you told me you were a scientist, so I took it for granted that you spent most of your time in a lab. I had no idea you were creating a universe. All I saw was a laboratory, then a huge explosion, then several different planets. To tell you the truth, It made no sense. But now, I know what they mean. My time-line will not be as condensed as yours, so the memories will be easier to read. However, the scenes will still be confusing, so you may need me to interpret them for you."

"That probably will be necessary" I responded.

As strange as it may sound, I was looking forward to the journey I was about to take. I love puzzles and it looked like I was about ready to travel through an enigmatic world that would prove to be quite challenging.

The only reason I was reluctant to go through with this was because I would not be in control of my body. Granted, Retnar assured me the ride would be safe, but I still didn't like the idea of some electrical force taking over my every move, as well as my subconscious. In all honesty though, I really did not have much choice, so I picked the lesser of two evils and prepared myself to take a trip on memory lane. His memory lane to be exact.

The Captain escorted the two of us into another room, much more cheerful than the previous cell. There were two chairs in the room, and nothing else. Retnar and I sat down, facing each other, while the Captain left the room for us to conduct our experiment without any distractions.

"The sensation you will feel shall be slightly different from what you felt when I put you to sleep. Instead, you will feel your body become relaxed, almost paralyzed, but your mind will still be awake. Also, the background of the room will change into something else."

"Like what?" I asked.

"It all depends on what your subconscious chooses to be a suitable atmosphere. Don't worry Tyran. No pain will come to you. I promise."

He formed a single arm from his amorphous torso and placed the hand near my forehead. Threads of electricity appeared and cycloned around the edges of his hand. The swirling tendrils of lightning culminated into the center of his palm and sent a concentrated beam of energy into my right eye. The fulguration placed my whole body into this immobile shock. I was stranded in my chair. Anxiety took over and I began to tremble, but my body would not move, not even shake in fear. In my mind, I could feel the temperature of my body rise radically and then drop just as fast. I was going into shock in my dreams, but I was still awake. And then for no explainable reason, my fears left me, and I was at peace with my mind. The temperature found a suitable level, and I felt relaxed.

Retnar was no longer in front of me, even though the atmosphere of the cell still remained. It was somewhat dark, even blurry. It was like my mind was trying to choose what type of scene would be best. Then, all turned black. From out of the darkness, a tiny glow appeared in the distance. I was no longer seated in the chair, but rather standing up. I walked toward the beacon and realized it was a torch. *That's odd.* I thought.

Behind me, about a hundred meters away, another torch lit.

One by one, torches lit all around me. Finally, the spontaneous combustion had ceased and all the torches were lit. I found myself standing in the center of a spacious cavern with hundreds of tunnels presented before me. Each torch lit the threshold of the tunnel below it. I stood in the middle, motionless from disbelief.

I'm supposed to visit all of these tunnels? I thought.

Suddenly, an even stranger sensation overtook my soul.

Some strange type of vacuum-like force was pulling at me and I felt my body begin to separate. In seconds, my body went from solid to being lighter than air. I was turned into millions of particles and being sucked into one of the tunnels. I felt no pain. Come to think of it, my body had never felt so relaxed. *"This must be what Retnar was talking about."* I thought, *"I'm being turned into electricity myself and being led through every tunnel in order."*

Like a bolt of lightning, I was transmitted through the tunnel and found myself lying down on a sandy surface. I felt like I was awakening from a thousand-year slumber, slowly lifting myself up off the ground. I was whole again and still free of pain, thankfully. Whatever type of crash landing I made on this surface did not leave me wounded.

I looked around to study my surroundings. I was on

a beach, looking away from the water towards a hill. The sky was dark, but the surface was not. The land was almost glowing. There was an abundance of stars that must have lit the surface of the planet, but kept the atmosphere dark. I turned around to face the body of water and walked toward it, feeling the sand harden under my feet with every step I took.

The water was very warm, soothing. I dipped my hands into the tepid water and caressed the liquid, feeling it flow through my fingers. It was as if I was really there, even though I was in a dream.

I breathed in the air around me, feeling the warmth enter into my lungs. Everything around me was warm with life. I looked up to the sky, hoping I could sketch the heavens into memory. There was a huge blue nebula that stretched over the ocean like a blanket. Magnificent. It almost covered one half of the sky. Everywhere else, the sky was black with thousands of white pinholes, revealing pieces of light behind the shaded cloak of night.

I could hear sounds in the distance, but could not identify their origin. They grew louder and echoed off the ocean surface, intensifying the strange noise. They sounded like explosions, most likely being detonated beyond the hill at the other edge of the beach. *Was there a war?* I asked myself. Curiosity overpowered my reluctance and I found myself leaving the warm ocean and confronting whatever battle lied beyond the beach.

I crept up the hill and peaked over to view what was going on. I was right; the sounds were explosions, hundreds of them. I remembered I was just an invisible observer who could not be seen or harmed by anything, so I picked myself up and dauntlessly walked down the hill.

The air kept its warmth, but that heat was created by the mixture of explosions and the lifeless odor of death that hovered over the field. I walked down the hill and found myself treading in a river of blood. The battlefield was littered with thousands of bodies.

Pieces of bodies were strewn about the ocean of death. I looked around the area to see if there were any other creatures standing, but I could find none. There were no more foot soldiers in this particular area, but the action was far from over.

Where once a thousand creatures walked, hundreds of metallic soldiers waged war with each other. These machines of mass destruction towered over the lifeless bodies in the pool of blood and marched over them, splashing in the red streams and stepping on the corpses. There was no life here. There was no emotion or passion behind this war. The machines had no feelings and were simply fighting because their now dead creators had programmed them to do so. Death was fighting itself in a cyclical battle that would have no absolution.

Beams of crude plasma erratically flew all over the field, sometimes hitting a target, crippling a machine. The number of machines reduced rapidly, until a lone craft came into view and hovered over the field of death. It floated above for several seconds until it dropped a bomb of some sort, concluding the battle with one incredible explosion that completely eliminated all the activity on the field. I was not hurt at all by the explosion, nor was I blown back from the blast wave. As soon as the smoke cleared, I could see that the bomb had left a huge crater in its wake, taking out everything, including the suicide bomber itself. Slowly, the blood on the field flowed down into the pit, forming several estuaries that culminated into a lake in the center of the hole.

I was the only thing left standing, immersed in a sea of fog with the stench of death and melted metal. I could still see the effects of the bomb. Thousands of pieces of metal and flesh were entwined and tangled together, embracing for the final time.

All of a sudden, I began to feel my body begin to deatomize. I felt like millions of air particles again and was being transported back to the cave, but before I left, I caught a glimpse of what the other adjacent fields looked like. Hundreds of battles were being fought all over the land. The battle I witnessed was simply a little skirmish, but it did foreshadow how every other battle would end. I left this world, hoping that I would never see this landscape again; a landscape that was red with blood and black with death.

I returned to the cave, wondering where I would be conjured next. I looked around the cave at all the tunnel entrances and noticed that one of them was blocked by some sort of force field. I obviously could not enter a memory room more than once, so I had to pay close attention to everything I saw, no matter how horrifying it was. A familiar feeling came over me and I found myself being rocketed through another tunnel.

This time I could actually see where I was going. It looked as though I was going to crash land into the ground once more, but to my surprise, I did not stop. I broke through the surface at lightning speed and tunneled through the planet's core until I fell through the ceiling of a subterranean area, splashing into a river below.

Face down in the water, I felt like I was dead. I lifted my arms to see if they were still attached, forgetting I couldn't get hurt in this realm. I shook my head and stood up. I walked out of the river and took a look around.

The entire cavern was coated with a brilliant blue rock that illuminated the underground world. It seemed so peaceful, like a heaven untouched by any creature and I was the first to feel the grace and majesty of the flawless mountain. I placed my hands on the silk stone and caressed the smooth contours of the giant bijou.

Where were the lifeless machines now? This river flowed peacefully, colored crystal blue in this world and not the glowing red, like the rivers that stained the fields of the world I left behind. Let nature paint a new picture for me to see in this blue paradise. Here, there was no death. There were no machines to crush this world or any corpses to taint the atmosphere with its stench. The sounds of explosions were absent, for all I could hear were the gentle sounds of the river, echoing clearly from one stone to the next. What was this place that Retnar stored in his dreams? Incidentally, where was Retnar? If these were his memories, should he not be in them somewhere? This nebula of memories was already confusing and I was only in the second one. What surprise was in store for me in this realm of beauty?

I stopped with the questions and took a moment just to absorb the magnificence. All too soon I felt my body begin to change once again and I found myself leaving what might be the last paradise I would ever see. Just then, a single shard of the blue stone fell from the ceiling and dropped into the river. From the splash, a single drop managed to reach a piece of the blue mountain. Instantly I was the lone audience member of the most angelic musical performance I had ever heard. A single drop was all it took to trigger the melody of the stones. The music traveled along the walls, chiming every single shard until it circumnavigated the entire core of the planet. How dissimilar the two worlds were, and yet how alike. I had heard two symphonies, one being death and the other being life. These polar worlds were just the beginning, however. I had thought that I had seen the worst and the best of what Retnar had stored in his mind. How wrong I was.

A second tunnel was blocked by a shield now. Soon enough, I was jettisoned beyond the third threshold. This time I materialized inside some sort of bunker. At long last, I was in the company of living creatures, instead of dead ones. They looked very similar to Retnar, only their skin was not as pale and they had two eyes instead of one. Their upper bodies were amorphous, just like Retnar's, so I deduced that they were somehow related to the Trocties. The room was dark, with the exception of two lights overhead.

There were five creatures in all, all crouching over a map of some sort that was placed on a table in the center of the room. They were speaking a dialect that I could not understand, but I could tell that they were planning either an attack, or an escape. I walked over to the map to see what exactly they were planning. It was obvious; they were planning an escape.

The map was actually a star map of the neighboring galaxies with a single one circled in the upper right-hand corner. I couldn't help but to notice that the stars on the map collected together in a formation that like a tree. On each end of the eight great branches, there was a galaxy. It was almost like someone painted this galactic system, piecing everything perfectly together.

I studied the map to see if anything looked familiar and strangely enough, there were recognizable features. Before I reached Retnar's home planet I noticed that the entire galaxy was being blanketed by a very unique nebula, the same blue nebula that I saw covering half the sky of the war planet I just left. It looked like a winged guardian of some ancient religion. The wings of the creature spanned beyond the width of the galaxy, making it seem like the guardian was protecting the galaxy. This nebula was also in the vicinity of Retnar's home planet. Finally a connection was made.

Suddenly, a bright flash of light took all of them by surprise, including myself. I hurried to the only opening in the room to see what all the commotion was. There was a cloud of smoke blocking my view, but as soon as it dissipated, I could see what was outside the bunker. It was another battle, and to my horror, the same machines that will forever haunt the battlefield I once saw were marching over an all too familiar land that was covered with the dead.

The puzzling history was beginning to solidify into clarity, but there were many questions still unanswered. For example, why were the stones in the underground river system so important to include in the memories? The only things I had seen were two battlefields and a subterranean kingdom of jewels. What did the stones have to do with the war? Hopefully, the answer would be found in the next memory, for before I could make another thought, I was back in the familiar room of tunnels.

So, the war that Retnar had briefly told me about was what I just saw. I was still left in the dark. Where was Retnar? Were these his memories, or someone else's that he stole many years ago? Too many questions and I had only visited three out of the two hundred and seventy four tunnels.

The fourth tunnel transported me into a spacecraft of some sort. The crew that was visible totaled five; the same five that were plotting the escape plan in the bunker. I must have been placed in their escape ship and was on my way to visiting the circled galaxy, Retnar's home.

I walked to the window and watched the many planets and stars go by as we passed them on our trip. I recalled from my own memory a time when my comrades and I first ventured into this universe, so many years ago. I looked behind us and saw a collection of ships following us. It must have been a huge evacuation.

The familiar galaxy finally came into view. The blue nebula was not much different in the past as from when I saw it, possessing the same beautiful qualities. I remembered how nice it was to find such a wonderful place during a time where there was no war. I chuckled to myself at the contradiction. A time without war? There's no such thing. I have seen a million worlds, a million births, and a million deaths. As routine as the cycle of life and death, so is the cycle of peace and war. With the vast amount of space, it would be impossible for there to be absolute peace throughout the entire realm of existence.

I dreamt of the possibility of having a time without war and didn't even notice the ship I was in had reached Retnar's planetary system.

I looked around to see if anything was different and found that everything was virtually the same. Two moons circling around a water planet with five stars in the sky. *Wait,* I thought, *there were only four stars when I visited this place.* I could feel myself slipping away and returning back to the cave, without having any time to actually study this mysterious star. The transmission could not have had worse timing, but I was not too frustrated because I knew that Retnar could explain it to me as soon as I woke up.

Four tunnels were now completed, but my journey was far from over. What treasures or horrors awaited me? Time would only tell.

A trip through the fifth tunnel left me on the beach of an unknown planet. I looked around hoping not to recognize anything, in fear of the possibility of a recurring scene. With trepidation I walked over the hill at the edge of the beach, curious to see what mysteries could be found.

I stood at the crest of the hill motionless, frozen in time, staring in awe at the landscape of immaculate beauty.

There, in the center of the plateau, stood a magnificent castle that seemed to me an impossible incantation, even in a dream. But after all these years, my memory of the temple is as clear now as it was the moment my astounded eyes first gazed upon its beauty. My search was over. I knew that this immaculate presence was to be the resting-place for the manuscript.

I approached the temple to get a better look at it, but

eventually, my journey was cut short, for the threshold of the temple was not accessible. A huge labyrinth guarded the temple's doorway, and I knew that I would not have enough time to make my way through the giant enigma. It did not matter. Just being on the same planet with this pristine palace was reward enough. With the time I had, I decided to just sit down on the hill to behold this masterpiece.

Oh, the memories hurt. It's been so many years since I have mentioned this breathtaking memory, and even though it was not truly mine, I still cherish it like it was. So long had I been travelling, never establishing any roots, or settling down on any planet. But here, I was home, and I was not even walking on solid ground. I gazed into paradise, remembering what once I had read in training, that reality is what you see, and fantasy is what you feel. I was in a dream that I did not want to end. Perhaps it was the dream state that enhanced my emotions and made this view so humbling. But throughout the many years I have been alive, I have never seen anything so incredible, where it was fantasy that I saw, and reality that I felt.

The temple had an aura that lit up the entire valley. All the stars that spread their light like a blanket covering the land with their warmth struck the temple with their radiance. Like a mirror, their light bounced back in glorious blue and violet. The structure was made of some sort of crystal, but not clear enough for me to see what the temple held within its walls. On the sides of the temple were five spires, with a sixth standing erect in the center. All of them pointed towards the sky, for a purpose I could not determine; a question that would soon be answered as soon as Retnar would enlighten me. I did, however notice that there were four stars in the sky, resembling the same type of sky on Retnar's moon. Perhaps the temple was a tool built to understand and calculate the stars' movement.

The labyrinth below reflected on the walls of the castle, making its base look like a glass garden. I continued to scrutinize the castle and glanced down to get a last look at the gigantic labyrinth. At the threshold, there was a tiny figure I could not make out. Feeling inspired, I ran down the hill, hoping to make it down there before I was transported again to the tunnel of memories. Soon enough, I could see the creature that welcomed any traveler into its maze; a skeleton figure, holding a map of what seemed to be a guide through the maze.

I studied the map and found that the directions were not at all simplistic. Riddles were strewn about the map in a language I could not understand. There were also drawings and measurements even more confusing. I tried desperately to translate just one word, but could not. However, the map itself gave me an idea I would have to remember when I woke up.

I could feel my body being overcome with a familiar feeling, and soon enough, I was back in the cavern. I held the temple in my eyes as I left, vowing I would visit it again in the near future. I could not wait to feel the grass on the hill with my own hands, or see the labyrinth with my own eyes, or breath the life of the temple with my own lungs.

I shall spare you the details of the next few transmissions, considering they were quick and were scenes of familiar war. What you should know is the fact that the soldiers fighting each other were Retnar's ancestors and once again, their bodies littered the valley that was once verdant and full of life. I must admit, I was very happy to have only a minimal amount of time to be in the presence of these warring factions. Nonetheless, I still had to witness them.

Finally, I was sent back to my paradise, where the crystal castle stood in the distance, but now, the world of which it decorated was covered in ice. I could not see any trace of life as I wandered around this barren world. I

82

wondered what catastrophic event could have caused this planet to freeze, causing all life to simply vanish. Walking around this cold planet, I stumbled on the slippery surface, hoping to find any hints that would solve the mystery haunting this realm. My search on land did not uncover anything. So like the astrologers of my own universe, I looked to the sky for the answers, and found it.

Only one heavenly body could be found in the sky, where once were six. The other moon and five stars had left the sky mysteriously, but the closer I looked at the moon that could be seen, I noticed its outline had several different shades and colors. The other celestial bodies were cloaked behind the blue moon, whose familiar glow made me realize where I was. Only Retnar's water moon could produce such a familiar glow. Only now, it could be seen in the sky with its brother moon and five stars lined up in an eclipse, blocking out all the rays that kept this planet warm. I began to shiver, feeling the lack of heat. Luckily, I was conjured back to the cavern in the blink of an eye, leaving the dormant world behind. Where was Retnar?

I could see I had barely begun, considering dozens of tunnels were still left to explore. The question of whether or not I was going to see Retnar was soon answered. Before I knew it, I was sent through the next tunnel and found myself being a witness to Retnar's birth.

Everything went so fast, I could barely tell what was going on around me, but I knew it was Retnar's birth for two reasons. First of all, the eye color of every Troctie has a different hint to it, as well as a different retina. Their shapes were all different, as well. I recognized Retnar's instantly. Secondly, The room we were in was the same room in Retnar's building, where I awoke from *my* mind reading.

There were two other Trocties hovering over the newborn Retnar, most likely his parents. They smiled at the magnificent child, without any knowledge of how important Retnar would turn out to be. Unfortunately, I could not stay long enough to enjoy the moment. It was nice, though, to finally see Retnar. I must confess, I was feeling a little lonely in this unfamiliar world, but as soon as I recognized someone, it made me feel more accustomed to my surroundings.

Memories rapidly flashed before my eyes, as I was thrown from one tunnel to the next, watching a highly accelerated version of Retnar's growth into the being he had become. The scenes were very short and somewhat jumbled, but that was to be expected. Ancient memories are hard to see clearly, for the mind is not fully developed at the time of birth or infancy. What I saw was all that Retnar could remember and see with his mind's eye. During his infant years, his mind's eye could barely see. I can only conclude the memories I saw before were clear only because Retnar assimilated them at a later age.

Eventually, the memories became more organized and comprehensible. I was now watching Retnar's evolution in memories, watching his training in leadership, his teachings, as well as his development in mind reading. His mind-reading class I must tell you about.

There were only seven in his class, which made me think that mind reading was not a widely practiced art. They all gathered in a circle, facing the center, and simply closed their eyes. What happened next, I can only describe as an artist's conception, Retnar being the artist. In the center of the circle appeared a mist, and all the students eventually de-materialized in the room and suddenly appeared in the mist, as did I. Being in the body of Retnar, I could not choose otherwise.

There were several thousand doorways, tunnels, arches, and other thresholds that led to different realms, much like the cavern I was in, only this was not just one cavern. Since there were seven students, there were several worlds.

One was a cloud-like world with several golden arches that led to different memories. Another was a mountainous region that had several caves to enter. It was like standing in the center of a map, having the choice of seven worlds to explore. All the students chose different areas to explore, expanding their 'reading' capabilities. Retnar chose one of the cloud arches to travel through. As soon as he crossed the threshold into a new memory, I followed.

From then on out, most all of the memories were of other types of species, which told me that I was soon to encounter the Rashouwe assassin. I had almost forgotten him during the journey, but after I had seen the best and the worst of Retnar's life, I remembered the reason why I had begun this journey in the first place and the information I wanted most of all was soon to be revealed.

Finally, I found myself in the cavern with only one tunnel left. I knew that the world beyond the tunnel was going to be nightmarish, but I had to find out what secrets the Rashouwe held. I began to walk towards the tunnel and was instantly gunned through the last doorway and into the prison room, where the Rashouwe assassin was sitting.

I looked into his frozen eyes that made the ice-planet seem like a paradise. Within those crystals of ice, I could see all the horrible things that he and his clan had done. Scenes of war reflected in his eyes, as thousands were being cut down by warriors, crashing to the unforgiving earth, their spirits trapped where they lay. Cities fell in the wake of the Rashouwe as the unsuspecting civilians were being torn to pieces. Even crying infants were quickly silenced with the heavy weaponry the Rashouwe extermination units carried. Endless generations were eliminated by the Rashouwe juggernaut, as the army of darkness wrecked havoc on every planet they encountered. I could not recognize any of the faces of the countless beings who were murdered for the first few scenes, but to my horror, I was soon able to identify some of the beings.

To my horror, I saw the death of Octan. He was stationary, fixed to the ground, almost waiting for the Rashouwe assassin to kill him. A single bullet was all it took to send my brother crashing to the ground. A friendship that endured for millions of years, a life that was more precious to me than my own, was ended with a single action. I could not hold back my tears, watching the endless death spread as the memories progressed.

After several more scenes progressed, I thought I had seen the worst of it all, but I was greatly mistaken, for more was yet to come. What I saw next, I still have trouble believing.

For billions of years, I had thought that the Rashouwe clan was nothing more than a reckless team of mobile death machines that never fixed themselves on a planet. Yet, right before my eyes, I saw four planets that were overrun and stationed by the Rashouwe. How odd it was to see that, because I had never heard of such a thing. A distressing feeling came over me, as I realized the Rashouwe force was much more organized than I had thought. This threat was more severe than anything I could have conceived.

I recognized all four of the planets, each one residing in a different universe. My sorrow grew even more when I recognized my own home planet being one of them. More scenes of war emerged from the Rashouwe's heartless stare, and I was forced to witness the death of my family. Try to imagine the rage within my blood, for such a scene is ineffable. Forever will I be cursed with that memory, and yet, I knew then that the Rashouwe would eventually pay for their reign of darkness, but that didn't stop the anger within. Therapeutic though it was to know that the Rashouwe were doomed, I still wanted to tear the life away from each one personally. Finally, I could feel myself awakening from my dream state, but before I did, I was left with another disturbing piece of information. In the reflection of the Rashouwe's eyes, I could see a single battle cruiser, its destination being planet Eve.

My awakening was violent. I was completely disoriented and did not recognize anyone or anything. Retnar immediately jumped from his chair and held me down until I began to recognize my surroundings. He took a moment to let me control my breathing, and stood me up.

"How do you feel, my friend?" He asked.

At that moment I knew he was feeling excited to hear what I had to say about my journey, remembering what it was like his first time. I really didn't know what to say. I knew that he was expecting a grand description, much like a magician would after his apprentice performed his first spell, but I knew I could not give him one. How do you tell someone about their own memories?

"Give me a few hours, and I'll get back to you on that." I replied, still somewhat woozy from the trip.

He chuckled. "That's exactly what I said my first time!"

He let me sit down for a few minutes and then finally asked me the question I was hoping he wouldn't ask.

"So now what do we do?"

I looked at him, trying to figure out how to answer his broad question, but before I could, there was a knock at the steel door. The Captain entered the room, looking as if war were declared, which had been anyway.

"There's a distress call from planet Eve that I think you should hear, Captain."

Remembering what I saw as my dream concluded, I acknowledged.

"I know."

The Demon's Plan

"We were able to defeat the first ship, but we're sure there will be more. I hope the information you drilled out of the Rashouwe was worth the trip, Captain."

"Admiral, the things I have seen will prove to be very helpful. Rest assured, the information I possess is valuable."

"That's good to hear Captain. So, tell-"

"There is one thing you will find disheartening, though, Admiral." I interrupted.

The silence indicated he was listening.

"The Rashouwe have evolved into a more sophisticated civilization."

There was a pause.

"What do you mean sophisticated?"

"Well sir, they have based themselves on four planets and I am pretty sure Eve was their next target. The planets they have are Tycran in the Mon Universe, Frychne in the Deo Universe, Necroy in the Trec Universe, and my home planet Euphon in our universe."

"I suppose you are suggesting we evacuate Eve and proceed with the second phase of our mission somewhere else?"

"That would be best, Admiral." I replied.

"It's a wise idea. But, where do we go?"

"Why are you asking me, sir?"

"Well, you have the secret information concerning the

movement of the Rashouwe, so you're the only one who could guide us to a planet that's safe and isolated."

I looked over to Retnar for help because I had no clue where to go. I took it for granted that the Rashouwe were probably spreading everywhere as we spoke. He walked over to where I was sitting and mentioned something to me.

"There is one place safe enough to base ourselves."

I was pleased to hear that.

"Hold on one moment, Admiral. We may have something."

Once again I turned to Retnar, waiting for him to reveal this secret place.

"It is the Temple of the Jewel of Souls."

That did not help out much, but his reassuring nod jogged my memory.

"*You* have seen it, Captain."

Of course. I thought. *The beautiful temple I saw in my dreams. How could any other castle deserve such a title?"* I smiled at the entitlement.

"How aptly named." I told him.

I brought the communicator to my mouth and spoke to the Admiral.

"I have a rendezvous ready, Admiral. It should be just what we're looking for. I'll have Retnar transmit the coordinates to you."

Retnar did as I asked and the coordinates were given to the Admiral.

"Is this place safe, Retnar?" He asked.

"Yes, sir." Retnar replied. "I know this place very well. It has been bereft of all life for centuries now and I am pretty sure that its present condition will not change for a long time. I assure you. You have my word."

There was a slight exhalation heard on the other end of the communicator. I couldn't tell if it was out of relief or out of terrified realization.

"All right," he finally spoke, "I trust your judgment. Captain Tyran?"

I took the communicator from Retnar.

"Yes Admiral?"

"When will we expect to see you two?"

"As soon as possible sir. There's still one last thing I need to do."

"Do it quick, Captain. We have no time to waste. I don't want to lose you like I did Octan."

"You can count on me, sir. We'll see you soon. Out."

I got up from my seat and turned toward Retnar.

"Come with me. We have one last piece of business to take care of."

The cell with the Rashouwe was darker than last I saw it. How strange the evil of his presence so quickly tainted the room with its epidemic gloom.

I walked into the room, remembering what I had seen in Retnar's memories, wanting to tear the creature apart. The callous monster glanced up to sneer at my presence and turned the other way, insulting me even more.

"Look at me." I sneered. "You're already dead. It's just a matter of how long it will take."

I can remember a time when I could not possibly torture any creature, but things were different now. Besides, this creature had no soul. I wanted to take out all my anger and rage on this monster. This thing had no good qualities to make me reconsider my desired actions.

He slowly turned to face me, his cold eyes pierced my heart. A sadistic smile appeared on his tormented face.

"I'm afraid you are mistaken. Not only will I die, but you, and everyone on this ship. All of you aboard have about five minutes before you join me."

"What do you mean?"

90

"You are a mindless creature. You and your pathetic friend, whom I've finally recognized. Yes; you're the one who accepted the manuscript."

He looked at Retnar and sneered joyfully. He then turned his attention to me.

"And you must be one of the scientists who created this little universe."

He smiled wickedly. "So sorry about your friend."

I slammed my fist into the side of his face. His head whipped back and returned to face me with the same smile. He wiped the blood near his eye and licked it off his hand.

"Four minutes." He said.

"How is it possible for us to die with you?" I asked. "We're alone in space."

"I would have thought that you, being a scientist, would have guessed this."

I listened patiently; almost.

"Do you really think that we would let any information fall into enemy hands and let them get away with it?"

He turned his head around, revealing a small mechanical device in the base of his neck.

"We are all equipped with one. It is a homing device that is connected to my nerve column. Our locators are monitored at all times. Once the mother ship got word that I was on a foreign ship, they knew I had been captured. I'm sure they did not waste any time in making plans to find this ship and blow it to pieces. They won't mind killing me in the process. That's a risk all our soldiers have to take."

He slithered back into his chair like the snake he was.

"We are a much more sophisticated race than you would like to believe."

"You're nothing!" I snapped. "I look into your eyes and see a lifeless abyss. I see no reason to believe that anything as evil as you and your pungent race could evolve into anything worth more than a speck of dirt."

"Evolved?" He quickly asked. "What do you mean evolved?"

"I know about your bases. You and your clan have never based themselves anywhere before."

Again, a wicked smile smeared itself on his face.

"I see." He whispered. "You thought we never based ourselves? You thought your tiny victory was the last of us?"

He chuckled to himself, while Retnar and I waited for the reasoning of his indecent laughter.

"Incredible. I thought you were much more intelligent. I can't believe that you were so oblivious to the fact that we were so dug deep into your universe, it would have taken you more than the length of your life to find us all, and even longer to eliminate us."

I couldn't believe what he was telling me, but I didn't stop him. He was giving away information that could be considered useful. His voice became more iniquitous the more he spoke, making it hard for me to stand his lecture.

"Your myopic vision of peace in the universe will get you no where in the future. You think that we're the only ones who start wars? You are gravely mistaken. Even more pathetic is the fact that you think that by eliminating all traces of war, you will have a realm of peace."

He got up and walked toward me. I could feel his virulent stare sinking its teeth into the back of my neck.

"Creatures will get bored with this pink vision of existence and will want a little excitement in their life. You need to have just as much war as you do peace in the recipe of life. Without us, you have nothing. Without us, you are nothing."

My heart was pounding with hatred. I could feel my arms surging with the desire to end his sadistic reasoning with one quick attack to his heart, if he had one, which I doubt. I managed to speak again.

"There is no way that you could help our survival. Your presence has done nothing but hindered our progress."

"On the contrary." He retorted. 'We were the impetus to your discovery in the lab. If it weren't for the war, it would have been several more lifetimes before you could have come up with the right formula. We knew about your little spy missions. You thought you were so crafty stealing the information that led you to the creation of this universe."

He walked back to his chair and sat down.

"We *allowed* you to take the information. We had planned on you stealing it in the first place. You fell right into our trap, and the sad thing is, you won't have the pleasure of seeing why we wanted you to. Too bad."

His smile became more unbearable and sickening.

"Admit it." he pressed on. "You need us. You needed the war to continue your project. How ironic that your instrument of peace was given birth from an instrument of war."

I had had enough. I turned to Retnar and silently asked for his weapon that he brought into the cell. He gave it to me without question. I turned and fired a bullet into the chest of the Rashouwe finally silencing him, for a moment. The blow swiveled his chair, spinning him around. He gasped for air, surprised from the unsuspected attack. He placed his hand on his wound and looked down to see the blood that stained his hand. Then, a familiar smile appeared on his face as he lifted his head to face me.

"Thank you for proving my point." He whispered through the pain. "Even you, a creature who honors peace is capable of inflicting harm."

I didn't listen to his comment. I holstered the weapon at my side and walked toward the wounded beast.

"Your friends are late." I whispered in his ear. "By the time they get here, Retnar and I will be long gone, safe from the attack and carrying valuable information that will tear down your race."

"Referring to war again?" He chuckled. "How contradictory you are. At least my race can make up its mind."

He managed to grab the collar of my jacket and pulled me closer.

"Besides. You're wrong. Look out through your window."

I rushed to the window outside the cell to confirm. He was right. We were too late. A Rashouwe battleship could be seen in the distance, approaching our ship at great acceleration. There was little time left before the Rashouwe would open fire.

I hurried back into the room, content on ending the prisoner's life before he could see anymore death. I fired another bullet through one of the cold eyes. Perhaps it was convenient that the last thing he saw was a piece of war machinery flying through his twisted mind.

His blood flew against the back wall of the cell, adding to the dark atmosphere. His death was the last thing I saw before Retnar and I rushed to our ship, hoping to escape in time before the Rashouwe would attack.

"Alert everyone aboard to abandon this ship." I told the Captain. "We are about to be fired on, and I'm pretty sure that this ship will not survive any bombardment from the Rashouwe."

The Captain did not argue. Without any hesitation, he grabbed the intercom and ordered everyone to abandon ship. Before he could end his orders, the enemy began to fire.

Retnar and I wished the Captain good luck and rushed to our battle cruiser, barely evading the many explosions blowing apart giant holes in the ship's hull.

We finally reached the docking bay and threw ourselves into the cockpit of Retnar's ship. Before I could blink, Retnar donned his headgear and blasted out of the bay into outer space. I looked over to Retnar, still worried.

"How do you expect to get past that ship?"

He remained focused on the task at hand, but still answered my question.

"This ship is equipped with a type of cloaking device."

"I hate to be the one to tell you, Retnar," I interrupted, "but the Rashouwe are very advanced and have the technology to see past cloaking devices."

"You didn't let me finish." He replied. "By absorbing all the light from the stars or any other source, the hull of the ship turns into a shadow. The design of the ship's frame allows it to be untraceable by any space radar, but the fact that it can camouflage into the night makes it impossible to trace."

He turned to face me with a reassuring glance.

"Don't worry, my friend. We'll get out of here all right."

I felt better, but was still worried about the other people aboard the ship. I looked out the window to see if any other ship escaped the attack. Only three managed after the main ship exploded, but their escape was very quick and unsuccessful. Three ships detached from the main Rashouwe battle cruiser and tracked them down.

Within seconds, the escapees were turned to dust and the Rashouwe departed from the area, thinking they had eliminated every trace of life. Even though I felt terrible about the lives that were lost, I was still able to smile, for the first time in a long time. I knew that with the information we had, our cause would have an advantage over the Rashouwe that would prove to be their final downfall. Retnar and I had escaped and were on our way to completing our mission, finally with a bit of optimism.

I was troubled by the words of the Rashouwe. I knew fully well that binaries need one another to exist, but it was the fact that a creature such as a Rashouwe was capable of speaking such logic. How could I have been so blind? I spent billions of years of my life completely devoted to creating euphoria, a vision of peace, which I

95

finally realized, did nothing more than cloud my mind. I concentrated too much on the notion of tranquility and forgot that acquiring such a thing is difficult and requires many battles to be won. I wanted to have a universe that would be free from any harm and I wanted to complete this task the easy way, hoping that everything would fall into place naturally. My own selfishness and shortsightedness left me oblivious to the truth. Now, in the ultimate act of irony, I bestowed a mission upon my comrades and myself to fight for peace.

It's strange the respect you can get for someone you despise. I was beginning to realize that this fight was much deeper than a good vs. evil dispute. True, the Rashouwe were evil, but they were also intelligent. If only we could have settled our differences so long ago, the things we could have accomplished together would have been phenomenal. What troubled me the most was what the assassin had mentioned about existence becoming boring. He was right, as painful as it is for me to confess it. A peaceful life without any type of aggression, as wonderful as it may sound, would seem empty. We would forget the purity of peace and happiness and take for granted the gift we had. With the constant threat of war making our dreams of peace so hard to achieve, we create a more beautiful concept of peace, simply because the pursuit of the dream enhances our perception of it. But when the dream is achieved, the fantasy becomes reality and almost instantly loses a bit of its majesty. The glory of life is the fact that every living creature embarks on a personal quest to achieve the impossible, only because they know they will never accomplish it. That way the life force never ends, it simply concedes.

"Troubled?" Retnar asked.

I shook my head, amused by the pedantic question.

"Before I heard the Rashouwe speak, I was sure we were doing the right thing. Now I'm not so sure."

"How can you possibly say that, Tyran?" Retnar burst out, seemingly confused.

"We have constantly fought against an opposing force, may it be the Rashouwe or some other faction. I never realized that the battles made us stronger and more experienced. I always felt that fate was on our side at all times and we had nothing to fear, nor did we need any more experience. I felt that our side was immaculate and could never be defeated. It never occurred to me that we were simply playing a role in the chain of life and the risk was just the same for us, as it was for our enemies."

Retnar turned to look at me.

"Is it so wrong you are part of life's circle?"

"For years, I felt I was above life, considering I was one of the constructors who created it. I had forgotten that even the creator of life still has to play by the rules and be humble to nature."

"So what have you deduced form your epiphany?" he asked.

I thought for a moment, wondering what I had learned. "There is no beginning and no end to anything." I replied.

He nodded, glad to hear I was beginning to succumb to my own arrogance.

"I never thought I would hear myself saying this, but the assassin was right. We do need each other. He realized this, and I didn't. That's what hurts me the most. I am feeling inferior to a creature who was part of the race that is responsible for the desecration of millions of planets."

"Life can be horrible just as often as it can be wonderful, Tyran, and we all need checks to make sure we don't forget that. But I don't agree you are *inferior* to that race. What you should remember is they need you even more than you need them."

"How do you mean?" I inquired.

"Well, you honor life and have dedicated all your time and

energy to see that it continues to strive. You and your team have created and populated an entire universe."

He paused for a moment.

"True, but what has that got to do with the Rashouwe?" I nudged.

He turned toward me again.

"Without you, they have no food. You are supplying them with the things they need to survive. If the Rashouwe lived in a realm with no other forms of life, they would eventually die out, because they would be deprived of the one thing they need to survive. Do you really think they would want to rule over a graveyard?"

"The thought had occurred to me they probably wouldn't mind, but you do have a point. Their life would become boring, just like the assassin mentioned about our life."

There was a little bit of silence before I asked him another question.

"Retnar?"

He turned towards me and listened.

"Are you afraid of dying?"

I couldn't tell if he was thinking about an answer, but the amount of time it took him to respond seemed like an eternity.

"No. I can't say that I am. I know I am helping out a cause that has to be the most honorable in the history of existence. I have to admit I am sad that so may life-forms have to perish because of it, but I feel that a rebirth is probably best."

"I agree." I continued. "But you do have to look at the flip side of the coin. It really isn't fair that the new-born universe is surrounded by other universes that accommodate so many other advanced creatures, before the new universe has a chance to grow and not be infiltrated by an outside force."

I sat back in my chair, realizing I had never considered this.

"Your universe never really had the chance to grow on its own, having so much interference from outside forces. Besides, the universe was an easy target for beings like the Rashouwe, who took advantage of the situations."

I turned to face him again.

"Perhaps the universe we are planning on building is the real reason why we created this one. It never really occurred to me that maybe all the universes created were failures."

"I hardly think the great experiment was a failure, Captain." Retnar began. "I happen to believe that you and the scientists before you have accomplished something greater than anything else conceivable."

I agreed with what he said, but something still bothered me. "I know that what we did was great, but I think we all forgot something."

"Well," Retnar chuckled, "considering the size of the experiment and the infinite amount of variables, I don't doubt it."

I couldn't help but to laugh. I guess I needed the break, but I was still pondering the problem.

"Seriously, Retnar, I think we overlooked something. The main objective of the project was to allow life to continue to grow and to allow it to expand, but we never allowed that life to grow on its own. There was always something that spoiled the purity of the universe. What's more, the Rashouwe assassin's manuscript allowed for this to be possible. I wonder if they realized this before they gave us the other manuscript."

Retnar seemed puzzled.

"Are you saying that there could be a possibility that the Rashouwe are trying to help?"

"Such an unbelievable plot is somewhat perturbing. However, an idea such as this could almost be credible." I said. "But why would the Rashouwe be trying to help us? There's the possibility that a resistance of Rashouwe rebels exists, but if that were true, they would not have needed to kill Octan, unless it wasn't a defector who killed him. Maybe it was an actual Rashouwe who killed Octan, which would mean that...Oh no!" I blurted out.

"What?" Retnar asked, frightened by my outburst.

"If the Rashouwe were trying to help out, and Octan was still killed, that would mean he stumbled onto information he was not supposed to get. Besides that, no one knew about the second stage of our mission in the first place, not even the Rashouwe. Only we scientists knew about it, and only we scientists had the capabilities of finding out where each of us were in this universe. That could mean only one thing. Some of the scientists are turncoats."

I was terrified. I knew that Octan was not a traitor. He was my best friend for several years. I knew him almost better than I knew myself. There were only two others I knew would not betray the project; the Admiral and Terinsa, and right now their lives were in danger.

"Where is your communicator, Retnar?"

He hurriedly grabbed the COM and handed it to me.

"Eve one, this is Eve four, please come in."

Several times I tried to get him, but I could not. I threw the communicator down on the floor, fearing the worst. Then, miraculously, a faint transmission came in.

"Tyran, are you there?"

It was the Admiral. I grabbed the communicator and spoke gibberish the first few seconds, but was able to control my excitement.

Success. I thought. "Admiral. Where are you?"

"Safe and away from those traitors. Don't worry, I have Terinsa with me and I have the manuscript."

I was ecstatic to hear this.

"Who were the turncoats?" I asked, curious to find out.

"Everyone but You, Octan, Terinsa, Keltoy, and myself. Keltoy, however, didn't make it alive. Frolton, who was the ring leader, tried to kill me, but Keltoy jumped in the way of the bullet, giving his life so Terinsa and I could escape."

Frolton. It was he who opposed my decision to change the plan of the project in the first place. Why would he want to do this? The Rashouwe don't give rewards for help or good deeds, so what was going on?

"Have you any ideas as to why they were doing this?" He asked.

"I think Retnar and I came up with a plausible idea. But I'll tell you it as soon as we meet at the temple."

I paused for a moment, fearing the worst.

"You didn't give the coordinates to anyone else, did you?"

"No, Captain. You, Retnar and I are the only ones who know where we're heading. And don't worry, no one followed us."

"How do you know?"

"We're still alive. That's why."

Good point, I thought.

"Understood, Admiral. Stay on course and we'll meet you at the temple. And Admiral...I didn't doubt you for a second."

There was a silence. I knew he was not a traitor and he knew that I knew, but I wanted to reassure him I was still behind him one hundred percent.

"Thank you, Captain." He responded. "Good to know we're still a team. Terinsa gives her regards and can't wait to see you. Out."

I placed the communicator in its appropriate place and sat back in my chair. Retnar looked over at me, probably amused at my facial expression. I was overwhelmed and could not think straight. Just half an hour ago, I was sure I knew what was going on. Now I was lost. I never would have thought our project was this important to everyone. I knew the birth of the universe was a momentous occasion, but I had no clue that it would be the pivotal point in history that would later reveal the outcome of existence. The idea of building a universe just to expand life was simplistic.

"It was a test." I thought out loud.

"What was?" Retnar asked, still looking out into space.

"The universe. It was just a test. I was completely unaware that there were other intentions. Frolton and his crew were helping with the project for the sole reason to build another shooting range. They were creating a lair, or a holding tank that would eventually produce a tremendous amount of species, whom they could eventually attack."

It was the equivalent of spawning thousands of tiny fish inside a containment unit, waiting for them to mature, and then dropping a dozen sharks in the tank. I continued.

"The Rashouwe resistance must have allowed the project to continue simply because they were seeing if the experiment was a success. That is why they didn't attack when we completed the first stage. Once they saw that we accomplished our task, they began their own mission; to seek us out. The real Rashouwe didn't attack either, because they got what they wanted; a new playground. So now, we have two problems, and one of them is solved. We know who the traitors are in the team, but we still don't know which Rashouwe to trust, if any"

"Do you think the prisoner we just killed was on our side?" Retnar asked.

I thought about the possibility for a moment and then dismissed the notion.

"No. Because if he was part of the resistance, he wouldn't have killed Octan."

"How do you know Octan wasn't a traitor."

The sudden turn my emotions took squeezed at my heart. I was disgusted by that idea, but had to let go of my anger at Retnar for even suggesting it. He had a right not to trust anyone, so his suggestion had to be made.

"I just know." I finally admitted. "For one thing, if he was a traitor, he would have asked me to join him. If I had refused, he would have killed me."

"Something still confuses me, Tyran. If the Rashouwe was not a rebel, why would he have changed the manuscript?"

"I don't think he did. I think Octan did. Octan must have come across one of the rebel Rashouwe during his journey. The rebel must have informed him of the resistance and their plan to stop the real Rashouwe. He must have also known about the leak in our team and told Octan. Octan must have agreed with the rebel that the best thing to do was to exterminate the Rashouwe completely. *He* changed the manuscript so that the next team of scientists would create a universe that would end old life, so that a new order could emerge, untouchable by any outside force."

My confusion was dissipating and things began to fall into place.

"Why would the Rashouwe have contacted Octan?" Retnar asked, still confused. "Couldn't the rebels have changed the manuscript by themselves, without the help of Octan?"

"The resistance had no conception of what the calculations were like. They had to find someone on the inside, whom they could trust, to change it for them. Octan knew the experiment inside and out and was able to change the equations without tampering with the constants. He knew exactly what to do. The manuscript was not changed by the Rashouwe after all."

Retnar began to understand as well and threw in his two cents to the conversation.

"That would explain why the Rashouwe gave me the manuscript, even though it was changed. He couldn't tell the difference."

"That's right." I replied. "The Rashouwe assassin must have tracked the rebel down, killed him after he conversed with Octan and then followed Octan until he got to your planet and then killed him. He must have thought that

103

Octan didn't trust the Rashouwe and failed to change the manuscript. The Rashouwe assassin was just being systematic and followed his mission, taking the risk that the manuscript was not changed. All he had to do was kill the rebel and Octan, and deliver the manuscript to your planet. You had no idea that he was not who he claimed to be."

"Well, at least the problem is remedied. So who else knows about our little plan?"

"As far as I know, we four. The other scientists think you and I were killed in the attack on the Phantom Hunter and must think that the Admiral and Terinsa are incapable of becoming a threat now that they are alone. Besides, they have no idea where we are, or where we're going. I think we are safe, for now. But make no mistake, the war has begun. We're going to need all the help we can get."

We continued to discuss what we thought was going on. Before we knew it, the guardian nebula was finally in view, and I knew we would be at our rendezvous soon. I saw the familiar system up ahead; the two moons, the ice planet, and the four stars, which reminded me.

"Hey Retnar. I had to ask you something. Well, actually, I have many questions, but I will ask them all in due time."

To this day, I still do not know how Retnar was able to predict what I was going to ask. He and I must have had some sort of psychic connection, perhaps a side effect of the memory-reading. Either that or my thought pattern was becoming predictable.

"You want to know about the fifth star, don't you?" He asked, confidant in his presumption.

He began to explain. "I have only seen it once and that was many years ago. At first, I did not know why my parents took me to the surface. There were many other Trocties on the surface of the water, all waiting for something spectacular to happen. I, for one, had no idea what was going on, and just waited, thinking my parents knew what's best. It was nighttime, with only one of the main stars in the sky. I kept my eyes glued to the sky, unaware of the glorious event about to take place. Finally, a brilliant flash of light sparked in the western sky and like magic, a new star appeared."

"Just like that?" I asked.

"Just like that. The fifth star is a very unique phenomenon. The first time I saw it, I thought it was a sign from the gods and was so enthralled by it, that I spent the entire year studying its movement and cycles. It stayed visible for only one year, each day fading away ever so slightly, until it finally disappeared."

The star sounded intriguing, so I made sure he would continue with his lesson. "So, did you ever find out why it disappeared?"

"Strangely enough, the star acts much the same way that the cloaking device on this ship works. It absorbs a type of element inside its belly that increases in mass, until it finally reaches a certain point and bursts into light. You see, the star is a black star that blends into the color of the atmosphere around it. The star is made of some sort of chemical that causes the light to curve around its body, therefore, making it invisible. It is not until the light-producing element reaches a critical mass, does it becomes visible. At that point the star stays visible, burning off the element until it depletes its supply. That's when it becomes veiled by the atmosphere once again."

"Fascinating." I have never heard of such a thing before. That's what I love about nature. It's simply unpredictable.

"The element absorption process obviously takes much longer than the burning process." He continued. "From what I know, the star becomes visible every one-hundred and fifty years. I have been alive for one-hundred forty-eight, so I am sure we will be seeing it soon."

I was pleased to hear that. This star was truly a treasure and a sight to see. I couldn't wait.

We reached the ice-planet and saw the Admiral's

ship orbiting around it, waiting for us. We hovered along side his ship and extended a bridge between our two cruisers. Retnar and I hopped out of our seats and went to the air lock to welcome aboard the two survivors. The door opened and there were my two friends. I never felt so happy in my life to see them. Terinsa ran up to me and embraced me.

"When Frolton informed us that the Phantom Hunter was under attack, I feared the worst. You don't know how relieved I was to hear your voice when the Admiral and I escaped."

She kissed me repeatedly, holding me tight.

"We're not going to leave each other ever again. The four of us have to stick together and finish out the mission."

She let go of her embrace and smiled, allowing the Admiral to approach me, who was amused at the extremely warm welcome I just received. He extended his arm to shake my hand.

"It's good to see you again, Captain. I was worried when I got the news about the Hunter. But here you are, with Retnar, the two escape artists who may have saved this entire operation from its demise."

The Admiral turned around to face Retnar. He extended his arm to shake Retnar's hand. Retnar, glad to see this, formed an arm of his own and shook the Admiral's hand.

"It is a great honor to have you on our team, Retnar. We couldn't have asked for a better ally then yourself."

Retnar was obviously pleased to hear this. His smile stretched from ear to ear.

"Thank you, sir. I can't think of a more honorable cause to fight for, and to die for."

"Well spoken, friend." The Admiral responded, patting Retnar on the back, speaking the last sentence with more sincerity and favor. "Well, spoken."

We all convened in the cockpit and detached the

Admiral's ship, leaving it in orbit till we got back.
"Okay, Retnar, take us to the temple." I said
"With pleasure."

The Search For Paradise

Thankfully, the planet was no longer under a blanket of ice. Instead, the surface was glowing blue, as if there was a light underneath the waves. We seemed to cruise over the water for an eternity until we finally came upon an isolated structure, seemingly floating in the middle of the ocean. This structure was actually a cylindrically shaped island emerged from the depths of the ocean, reaching about a mile into the sky with its highest peak.

"Now what?" I asked, hoping that Retnar knew the way.

"The temple cannot be accessed by just flying to it. We have to clear the mountain in front of us and submerge into the water by flying through the hollow belly of the island."

He proceeded just as such, hovering over the mountain, and then traveling down through its belly, crashing through the surface of the water and diving to incredible depths of the sea.

The sea was dark, cold, and lifeless. I felt somewhat claustrophobic.

"Is there any way to light our path?" Terinsa inquired, feeling the same way.

With the flick of a switch, Retnar turned on the outer lights of the ship. Instantly, the dark world lit up, displaying its thousands of meters of clarity and visibility. Retnar detached his headpiece and got up from his seat.

"From here on out, the planet does the steering."

We all three looked at each other, baffled at Retnar's last comment.

"What do you mean, 'the planet does the steering'?" the Admiral asked.

"Have you been here before, Retnar?" I asked.

"I have not been here before myself, but this planet is a legend in our civilization. I've heard so many stories about this place and have been told extensive amounts of information concerning the features of this planet."

"Why didn't you travel here, anyway. Say, for curiosity's sake?" Terinsa asked.

"There was no point in making the effort. This planet does not offer much in the field of sightseeing. The only thing worth coming here for is the temple. And as you will soon see, the temple is not exactly easy to get to."

I looked over at Terinsa, who was obviously content with the answers she received, apart from the last comment. I could tell that the Admiral and Terinsa were not looking forward to the journey we were about to take from the tiny hint of fear that showed itself in their eyes, but who could blame them? They had not yet seen the temple and did not know how glorious the prize was at the end. I for one could not wait. I didn't care what obstacles would be thrown at us. All I wanted was to see the temple, and fulfill the desire of being able to behold it with my own eyes.

The ship sank further and further down, its lights uncovering several bizarre creatures that lurked in the extreme depths of the ocean. The bottom of the sea came into view and I almost told Retnar to get back in the pilot seat to steer us clear from hitting the bottom, but I had forgotten that he told us the planet would do the steering.

The ship began to slow down until it was sucked into a vacuum of some sort on the bottom of the sea. The vacuum placed us into a small hole, which, I did not realize then, was actually a launching pad. The ship stayed in the hole for a few minutes. All the while we could hear a slight whisper echoing throughout the ship's hull.

"You'd better hold on." Retnar warned.

We all heeded his warning and found available seats for each of us to harness ourselves in. The whisper stopped, and like a bolt of lightning, the ship was sucked into the hole and rocketed through a vast tunnel system in the planet's core.

We could feel our innards splashing from side to side in our bodies, as the ship was thrown from one tunnel to another. The ship barely fit through the tunnels, for we could hear the piercing noise of the rocks scratching against the hull. We could see through the windows sparks flying everywhere around the ship, heating the cock-pit to an intense temperature, but before it became unbearable, we could see an opening in the distance. The vacuous tunnel seemed to speed us up the closer we got to the opening, until finally, it spit us out about a mile into the air. The ship then came hurling down at lightning speed, crashing into the blue ocean, which concluded our fantastic ride.

"Is anyone injured?" Retnar immediately asked.

"Did anyone see where my lungs went?" Terinsa asked. "I think they fell out of one of my ears on that last turn."

"Give me a minute." I said. "Let me pull my eyes out of my brain so I can take a look."

Eventually we were able to peel our bodies from our seat to exit the ship and survey the land.

"What was that?" The words rolled out of the Admiral's mouth as best they could.

"It was a tunnel system." Retnar said, claiming the obvious. "The only way to the temple is through that transit. You see, the planet's core has an intense gravitational pull and the vacuum that forced us through the tunnel system was created by the gravity. Neat, huh?"

"But, why couldn't we have just flown to the temple, instead of traveling through the tunnels." The Admiral asked, a little confused and disoriented.

"The temple is guarded by an invisible dome. The beings who built it protected their paradise with all their capabilities so that no force, natural or other could harm it."

He jumped out of the ship and began to wade around in the gentle ocean tide, but we stayed put, still uncertain about what he was talking about. He turned around and saw the blank stares we returned.

"This area is sacred. The constructors made sure it could not be accessed without using the secret tunnels. They wanted to keep it safe from everyone. Even if there was a natural disaster that destroyed all life on this planet, the builders made sure that this area would be untouched even if they themselves had to be sacrificed. Look around. This is the only area of the planet that was unharmed by the great eclipse, which *was* the natural disaster that once destroyed all life on this planet."

"The great what?" Terinsa inquired.

Retnar remembered that there were some things that were still unknown, and he would have to do some serious explaining.

"Several hundred years ago, this planet was plagued by an eclipse of the five stars that this planet orbits, which resulted in the deaths of every living creature on the planet. The planet was frozen for many years, until the rays of the stars could penetrate the surface once again. This planet used to be home to many creatures, including ancestors of mine, but their civilization came to a crashing halt when this blast of ice occurred. Only a few creatures managed to escape the planet's freezing temperatures and were able to travel to my water moon you saw on our way here. Our civilization helped them out as best we could, but the sudden change in temperature from warm to cold to warm again was too much for their bodies to handle. Within days, they all died. They were, however, able to give us several books and written material, which gave us vital information about their planet and their culture. That is the only way I knew about this temple and the way to get here."

"Well," I began, "Let's go check out this temple. I know I can't wait."

The rest of us dropped out of the boat, carrying with us the manuscript, along with all the notes Terinsa and I took from our travels. We also took some equipment to set up a small base of operations.

Into the water we went and waded our way to the beach. It was like I was still in the dream. The hill was much the same, as it was in the memory. I ran from the group and climbed the hill in seconds to see the temple. It hadn't changed a bit. It was still perfect, after all these years.

As giddy and impetuous as a young boy, I called out to the others to hurry up My excitement couldn't be held in, so I impatiently flew down the hill, not braking for a second, until I reached the entrance to the labyrinth. I looked back to see if the others had followed me down the hill, but to my amusement, they had barely cleared the crest.

They stood there for a few minutes, beholding the majesty, like I had the first time I saw it. They slowly walked down the hill, taking every step with emphasis. It was as if they were trying not to disturb the beauty's slumber, thinking that if they made too much noise it would disappear forever.

After several years of walking, they finally reached me.

"You boys certainly know a good place when you see it."
Terinsa said to both Retnar and me.

"I can't believe how incredible this place is."
She turned around to Retnar.

"Are you sure it wasn't a god who built this?"

"Pretty sure." Retnar answered her. "Although, I am having trouble believing it right now."

"Now the real fun begins." I interrupted, pointing to the skeleton at the entrance. "We have to somehow interpret the writing on this map."

Almost simultaneously, the three of us stared at Retnar. He turned around to see if there was anything behind him, hoping there would be. As soon as he realized we were staring at him, he turned around and displayed an uncongenial face. He sighed, and stepped up to read the writing on the strange map.

"Well, I should be able to translate the language, but as far as the riddles go, your guess is as good as mine."

That was a start, and we were all grateful that we at least had a chance with Retnar translating the writing.

The map was not securely fit in the hands of the skeleton, so we were able to free it. It's a good thing we didn't need to memorize anything, otherwise we would have been in a real heap of trouble.

"All right, Retnar." The Admiral implied. "You're in charge now."

The Labyrinth

Deltrin placed the book on the table and rubbed his tired eyes. He took a deep breath and then a long drink, eventually deciding it was time to eat something.

He traveled down to his little kitchen area, which was actually a hole in the wall with a cabinet he stored his food in. He picked out a few pieces of meat and nearly inhaled them. He then pulled out the bottle he had been drinking from and closed the door to his pantry.

He walked down the hall to the cockpit, with a few pieces of meat in one hand and his drink in the other. He glanced down at the computer terminal and saw that there were still twenty-three hours left before he would reach his destination. Content that he had enough time to take a short nap, he went back to his room and collapsed in his bed. He curled up, getting warm and comfortable and fell asleep.

After a forty minute nap, he woke up fully rested. He stayed in bed, looking into space, thinking about everything and nothing. Now that he had completed the most challenging quest ever conceived, what was there left for him to do? There was no way for him to top what he had just accomplished. Thoughts of his future danced in his head and when it became too much for him to consider, he cleared his mind and sat up.

He stretched, got up, and walked to his favorite chair and sat down upon its comfortable cushion. The bottle and pieces of meat were still lying on the table where he left them last. He grabbed for the bottle and poured a little into his glass. He then picked up the book and continued to read where he left off...

"So what is the first riddle?" I asked, following close to Retnar.

"Well, the directions basically say to travel along the green path until we come upon a party."

"A party of what?"

He looked at me with an annoyed countenance, wishing I would understand he knew as little as I.

"Sorry."

We traveled along the green road until we came upon an area with two steel doors, each having their own knocker. The knockers were actually faces of an unknown creature. They were made of some metal, most likely brass or copper. They had two eyes, one nose, one mouth, and two ears, much the same as myself.

Terinsa approached them both and studied them. After she scrutinized them enough to become even more confused, she turned to Retnar.

"Does the map say which one to choose?"

"It says to choose the one who cannot see."

I walked over to them and got a look for myself. There was a problem. Terinsa and I looked at each other and relayed a confused look to the other two.

"They both have their eyes open." She said

Retnar and the Admiral now joined in on the fun and took a look at the two silent figures protruding from the doors.

"Ah ha!" Terinsa exclaimed. "Look at this one."

We all took a close look at the face she was pointing

at.

"These eyes have no iris. It's just a plain surface. The others have an iris in their eyes. The first one is blind."

With Terinsa's discovery, we unanimously agreed to choose that door and proceeded to open it. The door swiveled against the ancient rock on the floor, shrieking a horrible noise and cursing us for disturbing its slumber. We swung the door open as best we could and saw our next puzzle, which might I add, looked a little more difficult to solve than the door-knockers riddle.

"I think I know what the party is now, Retnar." I sarcastically uttered.

The whole room was circular, like a small coliseum, if you mind the contradiction. All around the outer ring there stood twelve skeletons upon the grassy floor, each frozen in a unique pose. They were all standing at the threshold of a path to take.

We walked around the timeless room and gazed at the peculiar statues. None of them had eyes, but we all knew they were watching us. My nerves were dancing up and down my spine as the eerie feeling of death pervading this room sank into my soul. Whispers of the past could be heard from each of the dormant skeletons. I could feel spirits brush up against me as I studied the bizarre menage.

"Please tell me the map says something about this." I uttered, still shivering from the uncomfortable feeling.

Retnar turned his attention away from one of the figurines and glanced down at the map. He read what it said and chuckled sardonically.

"You're going to love what it says." Retnar replied.

I'll bet. I thought, remembering all the things he said I was going to enjoy in the past.

"To pass the test, I'll tell you how, but let me have some fun. Some look up and some look down. I'm staring at the sun."

"WHAT?!" I exclaimed. "That doesn't make any sense.

The sun is up, so if he isn't looking up, how could he be staring at the sun?"

"Calm down, Tyran." Terinsa said. "This is a riddle. It doesn't need to be scientifically correct."

I guess I did get a little out of hand, but I wanted to get to the temple. Could I help it if I was impatient?

"Sorry." I said. "I'll try to be a little more tolerant."

The four of us studied the different figures, examining the direction they were looking at, seeing if the shape they took would give something away.

"So, what type of skeletal structure is this?" Terinsa asked, studying the bone construction of all the statues.

"These are skeletons of the creatures who lived here and built the temple. I know that they are different from what I look like, the major difference between us is the fact that they have two eyes and my species only have one."

"No," She continued. "That's not the only difference. These guys have arms."

"Well, so do I."

She looked at him with a funny glare.

"I'd hate to be the one to tell you this Retnar, but if your species are supposed to have arms, you're in serious trouble."

Retnar chuckled.

"You don't understand." He explained. "We have the ability to make our own extremities. It's just that the bones in our arms are gel-like, and are able to fold into our torso cage. It is a form of protection. We only use our arms if we need to, otherwise, we keep our bones concealed within our bodies. The rest of our bone structure is exactly like the ones in this room, with the exception of the upper extremities."

He turned his head to Terinsa.

"Do you understand?" He asked playfully.

"Vaguely. So your arms are made of a substance that can solidify into a stable extremity, but can also turn into an

117

amorphous gel at will?"

"Exactly that."

"That's fascinating, Retnar"

After he explained his unique talent, we continued our search for the quiescent mystery host.

There was a figure covering its eyes, so we figured that wasn't it. There was a figure holding some sort of telescopic device, looking up at the sky. We figured this was not the one to choose since the map told us that those who looked up were not what we were looking for. The next two figures we studied were actually a parent holding the hand of a little boy, but their eyes were closed, so they weren't it. Four down, eight to go.

Another figure was holding a jewel in the palm of his hand, looking at his prize. It was a black pearl.

At first, I thought this was the one, so I asked the others what they thought. My explanation included the fifth mystery star Retnar told me about. Considering the star itself was very close to this planet and holds importance, I thought it was the one to choose.

"You are forgetting the star is not black, it's invisible. I think the black pearl is a trap, because only an inhabitant of one of the two moons or this planet would have known that fact. Remember, this labyrinth is designed to keep foreigners out. You might say the builders of this temple were a little xenophobic."

"Is there any way we can find out if it is the right path?" I asked, still holding on to my theory.

Retnar handed me the map and took the black pearl from the hands of the skeleton. He then threw the pearl through the threshold of which the skeleton was guarding. The second the pearl hit the ground, the surface collapsed, exposing a huge cavern below with no way out. My question was answered, emphatically, and the search continued.

"Maybe it's a play on words." The Admiral suggested.

118

"Perhaps the word 'sun' is not referring to the astronomical sun, but something else. Maybe it's talking about a son, like a boy."

With this thought, we all rushed over to the skeleton of the little boy.

"I think you're right, Admiral." Terinsa said. "Apart from the black pearl, this is the only other skeleton that even fits."

Convinced that the Admiral was not mistaken, Terinsa began to walk through the threshold that the son was near, not realizing her mistake. Just in time, I grabbed her arm as the floor beneath her collapsed. She nearly fell down into the oubliette, but luckily, I had a hold of her. As quickly as I could, I pulled her up to safety.

"The parent is not looking at his son, Terinsa." I explained, trying to get my breath. "Don't do that again."

She took a few deep breaths and looked up at me. A faint smile appeared on her face.

"I think my impatience is getting to me."

She placed her hand on my shoulder.

"But thank you. I owe you one."

Considering the situation that we were in, I didn't like the implication that a bad move on my part was in the near future. But then again, I was glad to know that when I did do something foolish, I would have someone there to help me out.

"We need to find the skeleton that is looking at the son." The Admiral said, finishing his theory.

We all looked around to locate this mystery skeleton. There was one that was sitting down, with its legs crossed, but it was looking up. The figure right next to the sitting skeleton was looking straight across the room and had its arms stretched out, as if it were about to embrace something. We went around the back of the skeleton to see what it was looking at. To our good fortune, it was looking straight at the little boy. We cautiously treaded over the path the skeleton was guarding. Fortunately, the Admiral's idea was correct. On to stage three.

"So, how are we doing?" I asked Retnar, still impatient.

"According to the map, we only have three more stages to go."

"That' s good. Any hint on what to expect next?"

"Hey guys." Terinsa spoke out, answering my question for Retnar. "Look at that."

Up ahead, there was another skeleton figure. I was getting a little sick to my stomach over this death motif that seemed to be everywhere we went.

The skeleton had two outstretched arms, each holding a key. However, there were no doors in sight.

"What are the keys for?" I asked Retnar.

He looked down at the map and began to read aloud.

"To open the soul will take plenty of might, so look in your heart and choose only right."

He glanced up at me, about to answer my question.

"I think it's the key to open the front door to the castle."

We all looked at the two keys trying to decide which one to choose.

"What happens if we take both keys?" Terinsa pondered, coming up with a valid loophole to solve our little problem.

"There's more to the riddle." Retnar continued. "It says 'Be wise in your choice, be sharp as a knife, for if you are wrong, it will cost you your life.'"

"Cute" She said with a little acerbity.

Choose the right key, I thought. *I wonder if it's another play on words.*

I glanced down at the two choices and tried to look for the hints I needed to confirm my suspicions. It was obvious to me that the teeth of the keys would be different, but to my surprise, there were no apparent differences.

"Do you guys see any difference between the keys?" I asked.

They all shook their heads, not finding one tiny contrariety.

"Well, if that is the case and we can't distinguish one from the other, than we have to pick the *right* key."

I extended my arm and picked up the key that was in the skeleton's right hand, while the others held their breath at my impetuousness. Luckily, my hunch was correct and we now had in our possession the key to the front door.

"How the hell can I owe you one if you don't give me a chance to do so?" Terinsa asked, still trying to breathe. She hit me on the shoulder, rather hard I might add.

"Well it seemed most logical, so I tried out my hypothesis. It was a fifty-fifty chance, so I took my fifty and came out with one hundred."

She shook her head, frustrated with my stubbornness.

"Tyran." The Admiral began. "I know that risks are all part of the game, but next time, consult with us before you do something like that again."

Retnar looked at me as well, but said nothing. He just shook his head with a smile. I guess it is safe to say he enjoyed the challenge and was glad to see that all of us were not afraid of taking risks. Off we went to stage four.

Most of the directions on the map were simple 'take a right, take a left' instructions. However, It was a good thing that Retnar was with us, considering only he could read the writing. Finally, after an hour of what seemed to be us going around in circles, we came up to five doors, each having a different inscription on it.

"I think this one is mine." Retnar said, still reading the map. "The map says 'to find the way, do not be scared, for you are not that far. The symbols speak of ancient lore, so find the shadow star."

He looked up from the map and stared into my eyes.

"I must do this one alone. The riddle is obviously talking about the fifth star that you mentioned at stage two. But only I know what its symbol looks like. It is a circle with five rays pointing outward. The rays create a perfect pentangle if you were to connect their ends. Also, inscribed in the circle, you will find the two ancient symbols that mean 'cloaked light'."

Retnar began to study the symbols, which were very similar in design. There were two symbols that had a circle with five rays, but only one had two little symbols in the center. Retnar chose that one and we were on our way to the last stage.

The map continued to give us simple directions and to our surprise, it led us straight to the threshold of the temple. The blue glow emanating from the crystal was celestial. I wanted to stare at its magnificent aura, but couldn't, for it would have blinded me. I moved closer to the entryway, shielding my eyes. I wanted to use the key, but unfortunately, I couldn't. There were five doors, again.

"What does the map say to do?"

"It doesn't say anything." Retnar answered.

He placed the map on the ground and looked at me with a confused look. We all looked around hoping to find a clue, and found one. A little skull balanced on a pedestal was found near the far right threshold. It had a tiny piece of paper wedged between its jaws. I took the note from the host and handed it to Retnar. He looked at it, and read what it said.

"To have come this far, you must be wise, so here's your final test. Place the key in the right hole and it will do the rest."

I knew I could not pull the same 'right' thing again, so I was stumped, as were the others. We all looked at the doors, trying to find something.

Each one had a different color stone in the place of a knocker. There was a red stone, a blue stone, a green stone, a white stone, and a clear stone.

"Okay, here's my idea." I began. "I think that the note is taking for granted that we already have all the hints we need. That would mean that the past riddles are all part of this test. Let's consider all the main points of the other riddles."

"Well," the Admiral began, "The first riddle spoke of a creature not being able to see."

I nodded in agreement.

"The second one," Terinsa continued, "Talked of a baby boy. The third was showing us the 'right' way."

"And the fourth," Retnar concluded, "was the fifth star."

They sat in silence, hoping I had a point to this. I stalled for as long as I could.

I pulled out the key from my jacket, desperately searching for something. There was a small diagram on the handle of the key, which I hadn't noticed before. There were three circles on the outside of the handle with a single arrow in the middle pointing to the smallest of the three. I thought for a moment, hoping that this latest clue would fit with the other four. Finally it made sense. I called Retnar over to have a look at the key.

"Is the other moon smaller than your moon, Retnar?"

He shook his head. "No, we are much smaller compared to it."

That was just the answer I was looking for.

"Okay." I said. "Now I know the answer. All the clues point to a single person with us. And that person of course, is Retnar."

They were confused at what I was trying to get at.

"Me? How do they all point to me?"

"Well not at you personally, but to your entire race. Let's start with the first clue. Can't see. Now obviously, you can see. For one thing, you have an eye in the middle of your face that's bigger than my head. What it's talking about is the fact that you live underground. You can't see natural light. The only time you go to the outerworld is to 'stare at the sun'. Let me ask; did any of you notice anything strange about the skeleton who held the key?"

Retnar, still confused, shook his head, as did everyone else.

"He only had one eye. Now, from what I remember, the people who lived on this planet had two eyes, unlike their younger neighbors, the Trocties. That was a hint. A Troctie was showing us the 'right way'."

"So how does the shadow star come into the equation?" Terinsa asked.

"The fourth stage," I concluded, "Was testing whether or not a Troctie was the one solving the riddle. Retnar himself said that only he knew the right symbol, and no one else. The fact that it was the shadow star is irrelevant. The fact that a Troctie solved the riddle *is*. Therefore, the color of which we want to choose is the color of the moon where the Trocties live."

A glow emanated from Retnar's face as the pieces of the puzzle fell into place for him. Retnar smiled at my ingenuity, while the others looked up to see the brilliant blue moon sparkle in the sky. I placed the key in the blue-stoned door and magically, it opened, exhaling a thousand years of breath stored within its lungs.

The Temple's Keepers

So long did I dream of the moment I took my first step into the temple. I did not cry, nor laugh, nor do anything. All I could do was simply stare, motionless in time, feeling a connection with the temple. It had been asleep for a thousand years, but I could not tell this from the fresh atmosphere surrounding me like a warm blanket.

There were no marks of age on its reflecting walls. No cracks on the floor or ceiling. Everything was silent and frozen. Every step we took echoed with purity, the notes ricocheting against the crystal shards that held the temple up. There were no crude stones or rocks that made the foundation of the castle. Only crystal was the floor, the walls, and the ceiling above our head.

We walked around the first level, pacing from one side to the other, studying the objects that inhabited the temple. There were only three objects that could be found on the first level. In the center of the room, there stood a crystal pedestal about one-meter in height. The top of the pedestal was a circular cauldron, about four meters in diameter. Resting in the cauldron, roughly the same size, was a brilliant turquoise stone. I still have trouble believing the size of that jewel and yet, it was perfect to have a stone of those proportions found in a temple of such magnificent euphoric beauty. The other two objects were just as extraordinary.

On opposite ends of the room, there were two

skeleton figures, each of them placed at the bases of two of the five spires of the temple. The quiescent figures were both sculpted out of crystal and were both frozen in an intriguing pose.

The farthest one from the pedestal was engulfed in flames, but showed no signs of agony. Instead the flames were like clothing, covering everything except for his two arms and his head.

In his right hand, he was holding a red stone, placed directly under the spire's opening.

The figure on the other side of the room was resting on an ocean wave. He was relaxed on its crest, and in his right hand, he too was holding a stone, this one was of a blue aura.

"What do these figures represent?" I asked our expert.

Retnar was still over at the pedestal, gazing at the mountainous turquoise stone. Caught in a trace but still able to hear me, he eventually lifted his attention and walked up to me.

"These jewels are pieces of rocks that were broken off from the five stars in the sky. The fire figure over there is holding a shard from a huge rock that broke off the large red star, known as the Star of Ages. The rock crashed into one of the volcanic mountains located on the other side of the planet. The stone eventually splashed into a pool of plasma and lava, violently exploding from the heated impact. A piece cracked off due to the immense temperature and floated to the side of the cavern. No other portion could get out of the lava quick enough, so all of it melted, save one piece. This surviving portion rested safely on land, until a group of scientist studying the effects of the volcano found the stone. They deduced that the chemical build-up of the star mixed with the lava. Somehow, the inside of the stone turned pellucid and created a compound, which you see resting in the crystal hands of that skeleton."

I shook my head, incredulous at the tale. "I never

heard of that happening in the laboratory." I said.

"There are some things," Retnar continued, "that nature will not allow you to see in the lab, my friend, no matter how well you calculate things. Sometimes things just happen without any possible explanation because we are not equipped to define the phenomena. It is no insult to your intelligence or your expertise in the laboratory, Tyran. You have proven to me on several occasions that you are a highly intelligent being. I'm just saying that nature has a way of telling its smartest beings that there is always something new to be seen, a phenomena that cannot be clarified with reasoning or words."

I always loved how Retnar could demean and elevate in the same sentence. I remained silent so that he could continue explaining the origin of the stones.

"The other stone that the water figure is holding has a similar story. It too came from one of the stars. The star it broke from is the only blue star of the five in our orbit. It crashed into the ocean close to the beach that we just came from. After the stone had settled down on the bottom, it mixed with the chemicals in the ocean eventually shattering the rock into several hundred pieces from intense erosion. One of the pieces emerged to the surface and eventually washed up on shore. When it was found, it was completely crystallized by the contents of the ocean. Only the outer layer of the stone is reflective. The middle is still the same material that the star is made out of."

Retnar walked toward the blue stone. He looked at it for a second, like it was his own.

"I have wanted to see this stone all my life." He said caressing the stone as if it were a child.

He looked at the stone a little while longer and then turned to me.

"You know how a child falls in love with something; may it be a toy, a pet, a ball, or something even more simplistic?"

He turned to gaze at the stone once again.

"I fell in love with this one stone the instant I saw it for the first time, in a photograph, of course. I don't know if it was the blue color that I cherished, or the sparkle it possessed. Whatever it was that captured my heart, it made me believe that this was the most beautiful thing that was ever created. I would sometimes concentrate and could feel the stone in my hand and for some reason, a reason only a child could know, I would feel safe holding that stone. It was as if something was inside that stone; a living spirit or protector, that watched over me. The pureness of the vision kept me alive. And now, being close to the stone for the first time, I can feel the life surrounding me, like a cloud of energy, as if it was emanating its warmth for me alone. Touching this stone is like a dream come true."

"Strange." He quietly spoke, "It's even more beautiful now than in my dreams."

He took a moment from his memory and relished in it. He closed his eyes for a moment and then released the stone.

"But come," he finished, awakening from his mystic abstraction. "There's still more to find."

"I thought this was it." The Admiral said, speaking for all of us.

"Oh no!" Retnar exclaimed jubilantly. "We have another level to find somewhere in the castle. There are five spires, not two."

"You mean there's three more stones?" Terinsa asked.

"Three more stones." Retnar confirmed. Like a bunch of children looking for a new playground untouched by anyone, we all began our search for the stairway to the next level.

Finally, the Admiral found the staircase, camouflaged within the walls of the temple. None of us could tell where it was, not even the Admiral. The only reason he found it was because he stumbled over the first

128

step of the stairs while he was searching. That is how clear and beautiful the temple was.

All four of us walked up to the next level and found three more skeletons at the base of each of the three other spires. The closest crystal statue was a skeleton sitting down at the base of a tree, holding in its right hand, a green stone. The tree itself was beautiful, its branches raining down to the ground, almost touching the head of the skeleton. The skeleton seemed young, like a child playing with the stone in its hand, using the tree as a shade from the stars. Retnar walked up behind me with the other three close behind.

"This stone came from the star that never sets, the third largest star that we orbit around. According to what I have been told before, this stone is a small shard from a rock that crashed to the surface about two hundred thousand years ago. The rock was about an eighth of the size of this island, which incidentally, is exactly where it crash-landed. After the stone impacted with the surface, the island basically grew and evolved around the star-rock. The outer layer was not fertile, but amazingly, one tree was able to grow on this patch of land."

He pointed at the statue. "That tree."

He walked toward the statue and kneeled down to look at the jewel.

"Years of weather broke off several pieces of the rock, this stone being one of many. It one was chosen simply because of what was found inside it."

We kneeled down to look at the jewel to see what other jewel could be found. In its center, there rested a single flower, violet in color.

"The mixing of the land with the star made a very fertile material, however the only growth that emerged was locked inside the rock. It had only one root system, but that life form was able to grow throughout the inner-stone, branching everywhere. The roots of the plant were long

129

enough to reach to the ocean, so it had an inexhaustible supply of water. Also, the stars were able to penetrate the layers of the rock, so there was enough energy to survive for several million years."

"Could the plant survive for that long if it had to?" the Admiral asked, curiously.

"It has survived for this long and I am pretty sure, considering the rock protects it from all harm, it will survive for many years to come."

He turned to face the crystal tree with a pondering look.

"The tree that grew on the outside did not last for very long, unfortunately. You cannot see it anymore, but it did serve its purpose. Since it was very conspicuous, and because it stood out from everything else, the scientists were obliged to find out why nothing else grew near it. When they reached the tree, they looked down to see the plant growing beneath them, instantly cognizant of the lands uniqueness. They did not, however, carve any pieces away from the stone, fearing they might interfere with the plant's natural growth, causing it to die. In time, pieces eventually broke off from weather and age, but none could be found that had a flower from the great plant inside it."

"This stone," he said, now placing a hand on the jewel, "was the only piece of the rock that did."

"It's very beautiful." Terinsa added.

Retnar turned to her, smiling with agreement.

"You should see it when it lights up."

I must admit, I enjoyed this enlightenment. The stories he told made this place even more magical then before. He too, was obviously enjoying himself. The way he gazed at the stones with his hypnotized eyes told me enough.

The fourth statue seemed like an idol made for worshiping a certain deity of ancient religion. The rampant figure was dressed in a cloak and was raising his left arm into the air, catching a single bolt of lightning. His other arm was balanced, pointing away from his body. In its hand, was a white stone.

"This stone was emitted from the second largest star that we orbit, called the Star of Purity. We do not know why the piece broke off, but its origin is not why it was chosen. What's important is how it fell to this planet's surface. According to those who actually had the chance to see it approaching the land, the piece was several meters in size. They watched it fall from the atmosphere until it reached about two hundred meters from the ground, which is where the jewel got its story. You see, there was a violent electrical storm occurring when this happened. When the stone reached its height of destiny, a bolt of lightning struck it during its descent. The explosion blew the rock into several million pieces, resulting in a rainfall of small white jewels. This piece was found resting near the observatory, where the astronomers watched it fall to the ground. The real oddity of this stone is the fact that it is the only piece that retained the electrical current of the lightning that hit it."

He walked over to the statue and placed his hand over the stone, being careful not to touch it.

"If you place your hand over it, you can still feel its power."

I was curious to see what it felt like, but Terinsa beat me to it. She placed a hand over the stone and shivered a little, smiling at the tickling sensation. Her hair began to rise and stand on end. After she left it alone, the Admiral and I got a chance to feel it, each of us enjoying the tingling sensation it made.

The final statue was caught in a pose of grace, but there was no jewel to be found on or around it. The skeleton itself was being encompassed by a twisting flame or a gush of air, I couldn't tell what. Whatever it was, it covered nearly the entire figure except for the skull and

131

arms. The arms were outstretched, as if the skeleton was welcoming an embrace from above.

Terinsa, the Admiral, and I all walked around the statue, trying to locate the hidden jewel. Retnar was amused at our attempt, obviously hiding something from us.

"This jewel came from the shadow star that you have heard so much about." Retnar spoke while we still searched. "It was found, or rather *it* found a traveler who was trekking from one island to the next, trying to map out the planet for himself. One day, a piece of the star fell from the sky and landed right into one of his nets. He looked to see what fell, but he could not see anything because the star had not yet reached critical mass and remained invisible. He grabbed his net and pulled it in to search for the mystery object."

"The stone eventually fell to the ground, making a small dent in the deck of his ship. You can imagine his surprise when he saw a dent appear out of nowhere. Somewhat reluctantly, the traveler stuck out his hand to examine the dent and felt the stone resting where it landed. Even more confused now, the traveler picked up the invisible stone and had no idea what to do with it next. His hand must have felt forty kilograms heavier, but all he could see was his palm and nothing else. Little did he know the star was within seconds from critical mass, so while he stared at his hand, the invisible rock burst into a brilliant light and the traveler was blinded instantly. He dropped the stone onto the deck and screamed for help, but no one was around to hear his cries. Luckily, the piece of the star attracted attention with its brilliant light and eventually, another ship found the traveler drifting helplessly on the currents of the ocean. When the rescue boarded his vessel, they found the blind traveler on the deck, eating what little food he could locate throughout his ship. The brilliant rock was lying by his side. The rescue team could not even look in the general direction of the traveler for more than a second before the light became unbearable. They were finally able to get close to the blind man and carried him off his boat along with the jewel, which they placed in a steel case, so not to blind anyone else. When the traveler was finally calm and well fed, the crewmen tried to reopen his eyes, which had been burnt shut from the intensity of the stone. With much tribulation, they were finally able to open his eyes and to their extreme astonishment, the eyes of the traveler were white as pearl and glowing from the brilliant light and puncturing heat of the stone. The crewmen were able to protect the stone until they got to the shore, where they gave it to a couple of scientists who were able to study its composition. By the time they got to the scientists, the stone had burnt all of the element within, so it had returned to its original invisible state."

"So, where's the stone?"

"The jewel cannot be seen for two reasons." He finally admitted. "First of all, as you know, the star from which it came is the shadow star. It cannot be seen until it absorbs enough of the element that makes it glow. Furthermore, the jewel cannot be seen because it is in the skull of the skeleton."

He walked around to the back of the crystal figurine.

"You can't really see it, but there is a small hole in the back of its head. The star's rays travel through the spire up there," He explained as he pointed, "and hits the jewel through this hole. The jewel itself also shines on its own, but the addition of the outside light basically aims the reflection to its destination."

It was befitting that the jewels of this immaculate building had fascinating origins. It seemed that it was beyond coincidence that all the pieces of the stars had such incredible journeys and lives before they were found. It was almost like something chose this planet to be the facilitator of the greatest temple ever built. But I was still confused as to why the temple was built or why there were five skeletons, each holding a flawless jewel in their hands.

"So what is this place, Retnar?" I asked, most likely speaking for the rest of us.

"Haven't you figured it out yet?" He asked in return.

We all shook our heads, hoping that Retnar would enlighten us.

"It is the greatest timekeeper ever built. It designates the cycle of our sidereal system. Judging from how long it's been since the last cycle, I'm sure you will see how it works very soon. But first, we need to discuss what to do with the manuscript."

The Malacts and the Pactals

A couple of items from Retnar's story gave me some ideas. I knew that we needed to find seven planets to place the pieces of the map on, but I had no idea which planets to choose, let alone the systems they resided in.

I then recalled the map I saw in the bunker during the memory sleep. I remembered there were seven other galaxies on the map besides the one the rebels chose. I recalled the map from memory and drew it as best I could for the others to study. I also drew the huge nebula in the background. As soon as I did that, Terinsa recognized the strange nebula and informed me she had been there in her travels. Retnar also knew a little bit about the neighboring galaxies, but it was Terinsa that provided the most help. It turned out she had visited five out of the seven galaxies, and found many planets to choose from.

She gave us an abundance of information about many different planets, including the types of life forms that inhabited the planet, its geographical structures, along with specific locations of certain landmarks. Without having to leave the area and search the galaxies, we were able to decide which planets to choose from right inside the temple.

"The first planet," Terinsa began, "I think we should choose should be..." She shuffled through the many notes lying on the table, searching for her planet, finally finding the schematic she was looking for. "This one."

We waited for her to give us a description.

"This planet was found in a dual sidereal system with no other planets or stars in the neighborhood. If we are trying to find a safe shelter for one of the pieces of the map, then this planet is perfect. The planet is young, but is past the violent and chaotic stages of its birth, so it is safe to travel on the surface. There are traces of potential life, but there will not be any intelligent life on it for billions of years. Nothing will harm the map."

"What is the geographical formation of the planet?" the Admiral asked.

"There are several bodies of water, but three-fourths of the planet is land." She replied. "It is very mountainous with a few valleys; Mostly rocky terrain with a few forest areas, but nothing grand. The climactic situation can be violent at times, but that is to be expected with all the mountains and the oceans. I assure you, this planet is what we are looking for."

We all respected Terinsa's judgment and agreed that what she told us was more than enough to clinch our decision. The first planet was chosen.

I scrambled around the table to find other planets to choose from. I came across a planet that seemed familiar to me, so I picked up the diagram and the notes that went with it to confirm my suspicions. After studying the planet's description, I came to the conclusion that I had been there before, but it was long ago.

"What about this planet?" I asked Terinsa, giving her the details. I gave her a moment to look over her notes and then continued.

"I think I've been there before."

She did not look up, still reading what she had written before.

"Oh yes." She finally said. "I remember this world. The plant world." She finished.

"Right." I answered back. "Wasn't this planet completely covered by trees and flowers and all sorts of other types of foliage?"

She nodded her head. Then for a moment, she began to think something over and gave me a flustered look.

"You know, I never found out how the plants survived without a water source."

"There was a subterranean water system." I answered back. "You must have never traveled underground."

"I never considered doing that." She said.

"Well, below the planet's surface, there was a vast river system where all the roots of the trees dug to in order to get the water they needed. It was really neat, actually."

"How did you get underneath the surface?" She asked.

"I was curious as to how far the roots went down, so I drilled a huge hole in the ground. Before I knew it, I had broken through the ceiling of a cavern. I went down inside the hole and found the water." I became more excited with my description, which made my gesticulations a little exaggerated. "Thousands of roots were dangling from the ceiling, submersing themselves in the water."

I couldn't help smiling at the scene that I recalled from memory. I pictured in my mind, thousands of trees, sticking their straws into a community glass of water. Now that I think about it, I was lucky that I didn't get tangled in the vast amount of roots.

"If I remember right," I continued, "there were four stars in the system, keeping the planet lit at all times. However, there was nothing else near the system. Like the other planet we have chosen, this planet is secluded from everything else, and would most likely keep the piece of the map safe from any harm. I think we should choose this planet to be the second candidate."

They agreed with me, feeling that a green planet would be a nice home for a piece of the map. Terinsa still had a question.

"Where did you get the drill?"

"I actually built the drill bit out of some spare metal I found in my transport. It didn't take me long to construct a large and sturdy drill. The real problem was getting it to work. Being as resourceful as I could be, I unhooked one of the retro-rockets from my transport and attached the drill bit to it. I pointed the drill downward and fired the rocket, making a well."

"Impressive." She said.

We continued to look for the third planet, throwing papers all over the place. Finally, Terinsa broke the silence.

"I know it's around here somewhere." She blurted out.

"What?"

"There was a water planet in that system." She answered me, pointing to one of the galaxies on the map I drew.

"Were there two moons around the planet, all three orbiting one star?" The Admiral asked, finally breaking his silence. We were pleased to see he had the chance to learn about the universe.

"What? You think I spent the entire time stuck on planet Eve? No way would I do that. I traveled some of the time. I knew I was supposed to stay there at all times, but I got bored."

He looked at the both of us. "Could you blame me?" He emphatically asked.

We chuckled at the comment. Terinsa inquired him on what he knew about the planet. He responded vividly.

"The planet is not what we should focus on. It's the larger of the two moons that we should. The planet is nothing but water and there is no way we can leave a piece of the map on it, or rather in it. Also the smaller moon has nothing special about it. It's basically a large dead rock that got caught in the pull of the planet. The larger moon, however is a tiny planet, filled with all sorts of different forms of life. The landscape is also very diverse; having mountains, plains, islands, forests. You name it, it has it."

"How did you find it, Admiral" I asked, curious to hear

more.

"I have a thing for water. I was attracted to the planet, but when I found out that there was nothing *but* water, I left and landed on the moon. Besides, I didn't have to do much searching. The equipment on Eve allowed me to survey all the galaxies within a ten billion light year radius. All I had to do was pick and choose. Believe me, when you get as bored as I did, watching mold evolve into a small community was getting annoying."

"How many planets did you actually visit and study?"

"Thousands. That's not much compared to you guys, but it did give me a feeling for the types of planets you were surveying."

"So, do you think that this planet will suffice for number three?" I asked the Admiral.

"It should do the trick." He responded.

All this time, Retnar had been studying a particular planet. Now that it was his turn to choose a planet, it seemed he had already made his decision.

"I know this planet." He spoke out. "I've been there before. If I remember right, It only has one star in the neighborhood and even that star is no where near being close enough to heat the planet up. The planet's covered in ice."

He began to pace the room, recalling the details of the planet and its history.

"From what I have been taught, the only life that survived on the planet was this type of insect race that burrowed through the subterranean levels of the world. The only way they survived was by burrowing holes directly to the core of the planet, which caused the heat to rise to their hive. However, the queens could not survive and breed quickly enough to have the broods expand, due to the extremely cold temperature that sank through the surface. They also couldn't survive because there was not enough energy to distribute to all the eggs. The survival ratio of the eggs at best was twenty to one. Pretty soon, all the queens died and the workers could not think on their own. Eventually, the entire insect colony died out. Since then, the planet has floated aimlessly in space, orbiting around a distant star. If you want an isolated planet, this is it. The closest planet with life on it is about four light years away and I am pretty sure the inhabitants have ignored this one."

"Good choice, Retnar." Terinsa responded. "Funny. When I came into contact with that planet, I thought it would never amount to anything. How ironic." She smiled at him and received a matching smile back. Only three left to find.

We must have gone through two thousand planets. Because of the stars in Retnar's solar system, there was never any night, so we ignored our need of sleep by using the excuse of never having the right time to do so.

You know." Terinsa said, finally breaking the silence. "This planet wouldn't be so bad." She handed the paper over to the Admiral. "Have you been there before, sir?" She asked.

He sat silent for a moment, trying to recall if he had been or not.

"No. I can't say that I have."

He handed the planet's biography over to me to see if I had been there before, but unfortunately, our responses were the same. I had never even heard of the planet before.

I did not, however, hand the papers back to Terinsa. Something about the planet caught my attention and I was intrigued to hear more about it.

"It says here," I began, "that there are no stars, planets, or moons anywhere near the system."

I looked up to see if Terinsa was listening. She nodded her head.

"It's all alone. And the interesting part about the planet is that it does not need an outside energy source, like a star."

"So, how does the life on the planet survive?"

"Well, if you read further down in my report, you'll find

that the planet is its own energy source."

She scrambled and shuffled all the papers, looking for a clear sheet to write on. She found one and grabbed a writing instrument.

She drew a circular object, which represented the planet and then drew another circle inside the first one and then drew a final circle that surrounded the planet.

"The core of the planet is not really rock or stone at all, but rather a condensed mixture of gases. It is a very active core, which causes quite a bit of surface activity, like natural geysers or volcanic eruptions. The atmosphere, which is represented by the outer circle, does not allow any of the gases to escape into space. Since they stay within the boundaries of the planet, the life-forms had to adapt to the virulent gases and turn them into forms of energy."

"So how did the life-forms survive without any solar energy?" Retnar asked.

"Well, I never was able to fully understand that, but I think that since the core's buildup was similar to that of a star's, but not as intense, the solar energy came from within."

"Hmm." Retnar muttered. He turned his head and looked at me. "I don't know about you and the Admiral, but I have to see this to believe it."

The planet had my vote. We both pivoted towards the Admiral.

"Sounds like fun." He said with a smirk. He shifted his eyes to Terinsa. "Obviously, we won't be able to breathe the air, right?"

"Right. When I was touring the planet, I had to breathe through an Air-regulation Mask. Otherwise I would have been poisoned."

"Do you think the map will be safe if we put it on the planet's surface?" The Admiral asked, concerned.

"We can lock it up in a protective tubing of some kind, but I'm not worried about the map. It should be just fine. What I am worried about is the traveler who has to go there."

"Do you think the traveler will be able to handle the planet's atmosphere?"

I nodded my head. "I think that if the traveler is as advanced as we hope he or she is, they will have studied the planets we have chosen and will prepare themselves for their journey."

She agreed with my logic and we all decided to make the fire-planet our fifth.

Since there were only two more choices to be made, we all decided to pick one planet each and then pick two out of the four. I have never had to make a more difficult decision in my life, but I must admit, it was fun deciding the fate of the universe, and of existence. About twelve hours had passed and we all had picked our choice. Retnar went first.

"I have been to this planet before and feel it is worthy of holding a piece of the map. It has three moons around it, all lifeless, and orbits around four stars. There is no form of life on it because the elements were insufficient to create life. It is a mountainous world, filled with caves, which will prove to be a challenge for our traveler. It is completely isolated from any planet with intelligent life, so the map will be untouched until the traveler gets to it. The only reason I know about this planet is the fact that it was one of the other worlds that the Malpact rebels had considered to travel to. It is a very safe planet."

He finished and placed the planet's biography on the table as choice one. It was my turn next.

"Like Retnar, I have been to the planet of my choice. It is a night planet, for reason being that all the stars are too distant from the planet to produce any daylight. However, the amount of stars in the neighborhood is tremendous. Because of this, there is an abundance of energy released, giving the plant-life on the planet enough to survive on. It is mostly covered in water with several islands on it. When I got there, the planet had no life except for the plants and from the experiments I performed and the data I recorded, I concluded that no other forms of life would emerge for a few more billion years. It is the only planet in the system and there are no moons caught in its orbit. I had considered it for the resting place of my piece of the manuscript, but since such a vast amount of time would have passed before any civilization evolved, I chose to move on. Also, the fact that there were no neighboring planets didn't help either. Now, because the situation is completely different, I choose this planet for the exact reasons I refused it before."

Terinsa was next.

"The planet I have chosen does not have any incredible eccentricities, like the star-planet, but I do believe it's unique. The abundance of tree-life is breathtaking. Everywhere you go, you're in a forest. When the single star breaches the horizon, its rays reflect off the dew on the leaves of the plants and turns the surface into a plate of glass. However, that's not the most incredible aspect of the planet. It's the mountains. There's a single mountain range that completely circumnavigates the planet. The largest mountain in the range has a height of thirty thousand meters. That should tell you something about the size of the planet itself."

She paused a moment, most likely recalling the majesty of the planet. She blinked her eyes and smiled in slight humiliation. She regained her focus and carried on.

"Now, if we put the piece of the map on one of the mountains, it will most certainly prove to be a challenging journey for our traveler. Believe me, this planet is perfect. No one, except for a brave and risky traveler, would have the courage to traverse on this planet."

"But you did." I butted in, smiling.

She turned her head to look at me, not showing any sign of humor.

"Like I said. Only a brave and risky traveler has the guts."

"Well, that's a compliment to me." I said. "For I have been

there, myself."

"Really?" She said. "Well, then I take back what I said. Anyone could do it."

"Ha ha."

She smiled and nudged me with her shoulder. With that, she left the floor open to the Admiral.

"Now that I have listened to your choices, I feel that mine fails in comparison."

You must realize the Admiral never gave up a chance to speak his mind, so this choice took both Terinsa and me off guard.

"Therefore," He continued. "I have decided to pick one of your choices for my own, and I choose Terinsa's."

Terinsa smiled at the agreement.

"Since two of us have agreed on a certain planet, it is only right to have that planet be one of the choices."

Now his personality was coming back.

"For the final choice, I believe that it would be fair for you two to discuss it and make a decision, without us interfering."

I must admit, it was a good idea, and Retnar agreed. He and I deliberated for a while, until we came to the agreement that my planet was the better of the two.

Our seven choices had been made. Luckily, each one came from one of the seven galaxies on the map. Coincidence was becoming something that I enjoyed. Now that we had had our fun of deciding fate, we had to focus our attention on how to distribute the pieces of the map.

The Riddle

We did not want to give the planet's coordinates away without a challenge attached. We wanted to make sure the being that found the manuscript would be very intelligent and exceptionally powerful. That is why we chose such unique areas to be the shelters of the map. You had to prove your worth before you had the right to wield the power of the manuscript. Since you are reading this now, you have most certainly proven your might.

With the planets chosen, our first step was completed. The second step required us to come up with a way of making the map's presence known.

With the threat of the Rashouwe and other opposing forces, we could not simply tell everyone about it. Granted, the Rashouwe knew nothing about what we were doing in the first place. Keeping in mind the many surprises we endured in the past, we knew not to underestimate them.

We figured that since you would have to be a great explorer to complete the mission, you would be able to find something in space without knowing about it beforehand, like stumbling over fate. For that reason, we planned to place the information about our mission, along with a huge star-map of the eight galaxies, inside a small orbital. After we were finished with writing down the information, we would lock the map and the declaration into a tube, which would eventually be placed into orbit around a particular planet or moon. It seemed like a good plan, but we never considered the time it would take us to complete everything.

Choosing the planets was simply the icing on the cake. Our skeleton of a plan desperately needed meat placed on its bones. We all studied the dozens of notes and drawings about the planets we chose, investigating everything about them, and marking the obvious and unique characteristics, which could be used in our nebulous directions. We had decided earlier that a riddle would be the best medium to use in conveying the message.

Our inspiration came from the maze we had just ventured through to reach the temple. We wanted to protect our creation just as much as the beings who created this temple wanted to protect theirs, so we followed their footsteps and guarded our masterpiece with a similar puzzlement.

We worked with the planets in the same chronological order that we picked them in the first place. We had to make the first test relatively easy so we wouldn't scare the traveler away. We chose not to do this until you were too far to turn back.

The riddles were actually not that difficult to make, because the planets were so unique. As long as we pinpointed the major characteristics that made the planets recognizable and discussed them in the riddle, we didn't have to write down too many stanzas for each planet, trying to explain the terrain word for word.

The first planet, as you recall, was a very young planet that was mostly mountainous, with a few small bodies of water in between. There was also very little plant-life that was growing on the surface.

"Okay, how 'bout this?" Terinsa began, who was put in charge of writing down the riddle.

"The cloak upon me is brown and red, and I have some blue,

But you will see some little trees, but I'm still very new."

We all thought it was rather catchy, but needed something more.

"It's missing something, isn't it?" she asked, open to suggestions.

"Well", Retnar began, "I like the cloak part, but 'cloak' isn't the word that fits. How about 'blanket'"

She raised her eyebrows, impressed with the proposal. She crossed out cloak and replaced it with blanket. We all looked at the change and silently sang the line in our heads, seeing what else needed to be changed.

"The blanket I wear is brown and red, and has a little blue. I have some green, as well, you know, 'cause I'm fairly new."

They all looked at me, liking some of the changes, and disliking others.

"Oh wait!" Terinsa said with a burst of energy. "You just gave me and idea, Tyran. How's this?"

She wrote down the words as she said them aloud.

"The blanket I wear is brown and red, with little spots of blue.
There's green in me, but hard to see, for that's because I'm new."

We all liked the improvement immensely and almost clapped when she finished.

The other information about the two stars the planet orbited around and the mountain that held the piece of the map eventually came into the riddle, as you well know.

After about an hour of writing down four stanzas, we felt we had made a great accomplishment, but we were far from over. Six more riddles were still needed just for the map alone.

The next planet had an obvious detail that we jumped on immediately.

"The place is one giant garden." The Admiral said. "The second you mention that characteristic, our traveler will know exactly where to go. Let's try to make it a little harder to get the piece than last time."

We would have agreed with him anyway, considering he was the Admiral, but the suggestion was a good one to begin with.

"So the question is," Retnar added, "which area do we pick to hide the map?"

Terinsa got up and walked over to find her notes.

"Actually, this planet holds the illusion that it is one giant garden, when in fact, the land is separated into several different gardens."

She walked back to the table with the planet's compendium.

"In every garden on the planet, there was always a particular type of flower that would rule over all the other flowers in the vicinity. You could find the flowers elsewhere as well, but only once would they overpower their own garden. There was, however, a type of rose that only grew in one garden and nowhere else. It was a very light blue rose."

She passed the page of notes over to me. She pointed out the illustrious flower.

"It was very beautiful and very rare." She continued. "I think the garden it's in would be the perfect area for the map to be placed."

I looked over the notes and eventually agreed with her. I passed the paper over to Retnar, who in turn passed it to the Admiral. Both of them nodded in agreement.

"Good." She said. "So, what do we write for the riddle?"

"I think we should include something about the underground river system." I said. "Something like 'within the belly', or 'inside my heart.'"

"'Inside my heart'. I like that." The Admiral said.

"So do I." Terinsa included. Retnar nodded his head, smiling in agreement.

"From inside my heart, a garden springs. Do you like it?"

148

Terinsa didn't even answer. She just wrote the stanza down.

"Okay, so we have a start. What else do we want to say?" Terinsa asked.

"We need to include the four stars in the system and say that there's nothing else around." Retnar spoke up. "We also need to include the turquoise rose and the fact that it's a garden they are looking for, and not a tree."

The second riddle was only two stanzas long, but it took us two hours to build. We were obviously becoming very tired. It was necessary for us to step away from what we were doing and go outside to get a breath of fresh air. We put everything down, got up, and walked out the door, letting the air pervade within our inviting lungs and the four stars in the sky beat upon our pale skin.

After a brief vacation, we went back into our paradise turned dungeon. Don't get me wrong, the temple itself still held all its majesty. It was the papers and notes and machines that tainted this perfection.

The water planet was next, so we let the Admiral take care of this one, considering it was his to begin with. He felt the riddles could be more mysterious in its hints. The last two were very good, but they were not true riddles since they didn't really use much symbolism, such as giving anthropomorphic qualities to objects, or using animism as a way to relay a message.

"I think a conversation would be a good riddle." The Admiral said, getting our attention. "Like something simple between two people."

"That's a start." Terinsa said. "What would they talk about?"

"Well, let's consider what we have to work with. The planet we're going to put the map on is really not that different from other planets, so we can't use its characteristics in the map. It would get too confusing."

He rested his hand upon his chin and pondered for a

moment.

"I think we should use the water planet for the riddle. It's perfect. There are not that many planets made entirely of water. In this galaxy," he said, pointing at the third one on the map, "there's no other planet like it."

He looked at Terinsa and me to confirm what he just said. We did not oppose anything mentioned about the planet's uniqueness in form.

"So, if we are going to use the water planet as our subject, let's have the conversation be between a father and a son. That way we can both talk about the water planet, and give away the hint that there is one star in the system."

I thought the idea was very clever, as did the others, considering their enthusiastic nodding.

"What could they talk about?" The Admiral asked, hoping for a suggestion.

We all mulled over what the conversation could include. The planet was nothing but water. Water is blue. What else is blue?

"I got it!" I blurted out. "Since the dominant feature of the planet is its blue color, we could have the planet be sad."

"Why would the planet be sad?" Retnar asked.

"Because it didn't get to hold the map."

"Oh." Retnar said, thinking about the idea. "That's really good."

"We can have the star trying to console the planet, but later get sick of his son always crying."

I must admit, it was a great idea, but I had no idea what to write. We continued to think about a good dialogue for the father and the son, but you must understand it was rather difficult. Finally, the Admiral came up with the perfect piece.

"How about this one?" He began. "I'm very sad, the planet says, but I haven't got a clue why I shed a tear most every year, and why I am so blue. It's because, his father says, you silly little sap. Your eldest son, instead of you, was picked to hold the map."

Perfect. Absolutely perfect. We all loved the speech, especially the 'little sap' part. That was great. We didn't even bother to change one bit of it. Terinsa wrote it down in an instant. Since the Admiral was on a role, we didn't step in his way. Instead, we sat silently, waiting to hear what else he wanted to do.

He looked at the notes about the planet to see where an appropriate place would be to hide the map. Something jogged his memory.

"Oh, this would be great." He spoke up, obviously excited about something. "I had forgotten about this."

He placed one of the surface diagrams on the table in front of us.

"Around this area," he said, circling his finger around a point on the map "there's a well with an opening about ten meters in diameter. The inside of the well, however, is about fifteen hundred meters in depth, with a floor about two hundred meters in diameter." He poked his finger a couple times on the target area. "This is the best place on the planet to put the map. There's no other area even half as good as this."

"Do you want to continue the conversation between the father and the son?" Terinsa asked.

"No." he answered. "I think that we should break the dialogue and continue with the other form of speech we've used for the other two riddles."

We agreed and finished up the third riddle with little difficulty. The fourth planet was next, which we handed over to Retnar, since he seemed to know the most about it.

He took all the notes about the planet and began to pick out as much as he could. He didn't come up with much, but we expected that. The planet did not give him much to work with in the first place.

"There are three things we can mention, which should be enough for the fourth riddle." He commenced, with us being as attentive as possible. "The characteristic we should begin with is the obvious one; the ice. We should mention the one star it orbits around and its extreme distance. Next, we should talk about the insect-like colony that lived there, since they were the only creatures that could survive on, or rather, within the planet. The last thing we should mention is a geographical structure on the planet's surface. The reason this is important is because it only has one structure on the surface. There is a large protuberance that extends to about two hundred meters in height. It actually resembles an arm. If we tell the traveler to land on the hand of the extension, we can place the map somewhere on the platform."

He stopped for a second to contemplate something. "I think the appropriate theme for a desolate planet would be loneliness. The riddle could be like a plea from the planet for someone to come and visit it."

We all looked at the Admiral who responded with a refusing gesture.

"I'm all out." He said. "I can't think of anything."

Out of the silence, Terinsa began to think out loud. I don't know if she was caught in creative inspiration and was talking to herself, or if she was actually giving us her idea. Whatever it was, it certainly did the trick.

"I beg of you, come visit me and show me that you care. I'll give you what you're looking for, now doesn't that seem fair? Trust in me to hand to you, the gift that you have earned. You're a friend I'd like to keep, for that is what I've learned."

She didn't move for a second, caught in a moment. We were stunned as well. Her poem captured the soul of the planet. We could feel the bitterness in the voice of the planet, lamenting its sad and lonely state. It needed to feel life caress its frozen skin to remind it that it really isn't alone in the vast blackness, much like ourselves.

Terinsa looked up to see our stunned faces. We all

were feeling the same emotions. Even the Admiral shared the moment, reflecting a similar expression. We knew that there was no need to change or improve Terinsa's aesthetic recitation.

The other two additions to the fourth riddle seemed to flow out of Terinsa's spirit just as clear and serene as the first. We did not interfere with her stream of consciousness. We simply watched her magic work, and what a pleasure it was to see her invoke this wonder.

I wish I could explain the transformation that passed through our soul when the day concluded. Before we began the work on the project, we all dreaded the amount of time and work it required. Now that we had finished four of the poems, we began to see our project in a different and much more brilliant light. We had poured all our life into our work and were finally feeling its effects upon our tired bodies. We felt a deep connection with each other, much more than what the two billion years of working together could have produced. Our emotions possessed the words we wrote on the parchment. The garden that sprang forth into the second riddle seemed to spring forth from our voices, the passion from within clothed the empty parchment. We could feel the breeze on the planet surround and embrace us with its ambivalent touch. The sadness of the water planet was a tear shed from all of us. But nothing pulled the tears out of our eyes like the loneliness of the cold, forgotten planet. We began to feel all the emotions pry into our hearts and we began to forget who we were really speaking for, or to.

We needed to rest. That was obvious. We all had the same idea and decided to go outside and sleep under the beautiful sun. Strangely enough, there were a few stars that could be seen beyond the intense light of the sun. We all slept close to each other and dreamt of the same thing; angels.

I awoke from a dream I will never be able to

describe, so I won't even try. I knew the others had the same experience. They never confirmed it. I just knew.

We entered the temple, fully refreshed and filled with energy. The Admiral picked up the notes for the fifth planet and began to study its contents with the excitement of a schoolboy. I think it was the rest that allowed him to be more perceptive, because there were things he found that made the making of this riddle much easier than the others.

There were the obvious attributes that could be used in the riddle, such as the different gas pervading the atmosphere, or the fact that the planet was its own energy source, but there was one thing he found in the map that I would never have caught.

"It says here that there's a cave right at the base of this huge canyon." He began. "At the threshold of the cave, there's a tiny geyser that has a constant flame coming out of it. I think we should make this geyser act like a guardian. We can put the map inside the cave. Nothing too complicated. We'll save our efforts for the next one."

"Besides." I emphasized. "He or she is going to have enough trouble with the atmosphere. They don't need to have another obstacle to hurdle."

The riddle took only half an hour to complete, and believe me, we were thankful for its brevity. The sixth puzzle took most all of the day to complete.

We had decided that since we were getting close to finishing the riddle, we felt that we needed to impose much more difficult tasks on the two final planets. We knew you'd thank us later.

If there was one thing conspicuous on the sixth planet, it was the many mountains that spread throughout the landscape. That was a start. Incidentally, it was the final choice for the map's destination. After a long bout of thinking, I decided to dismiss myself from the table to walk around and get some blood to my brain.

I looked at the statues for inspiration. I stared at the large blue jewel in the middle of the room, but nothing seemed to give me the inspiration I was looking for. I sat down in my chair, staring now at one of the statues. I watched the shadow from the sun slowly crawl across the floor. The statue's silhouette glided like a marionette as the star led the way, which was exactly the inspiration I was looking for.

I grabbed a sharpened pencil from the table and walked over to the statue. The others curiously watched me, trying to see what I was experimenting with. I stood the pencil upside-down, with the sharp end sticking up. I then steadied the pencil on the ground and watched the shadow of the pencil move across the floor with the statue's shadow moving close by. The culminating point of the pencil looked like an arrow, pointing the way to something unknown. That's what I needed to see. I got up from the floor, taking the pencil with me and sat back in my chair. I took the notes from the table and found that my plan would work perfectly.

"All right." I said to my curious friends. "According to this, the star always rises in the same place everyday. There is a mountain that sits right in its way. It doesn't clear the peak of the mountain until a good two hours have passed."

I grabbed another sheet of paper in front of me, showing a different angle of the mountain.

"In the distance, you can see another much smaller mountain that sits right in the shadow of the rising sun. We can use this placement to our advantage."

I took the pencil and found a blank piece of paper to write on. I began to draw my plan.

"We can build three statues somewhere on the smaller mountain, who will act as the guardians to three possible caves for our traveler to take. Behind two of the caves entrances, we can build a fire-pit that won't be seen until it's too late. Behind the third will be the piece of the map."

I drew the three statues on the layer of the mountain with the caves they stood in front of.

"Now, the only way the traveler will know which one to take is from the shadow of the taller mountain. You saw how the tip of my pencil acted like a directional arrow. That's exactly what the peak of the mountain will do. We will build the correct statue in the path of the rising sun's shadow. When the peak is stabbing the sun, its shadow will point the way to the map. If they wait too long, the shadow will be pointing in the direction of an incorrect choice."

I drew the peak's shadow, pointing at the correct statue and then placed my pencil down.

"What do you think?" I asked.

"Now that's what a riddle should be like." The Admiral said.

Terinsa agreed, as did Retnar and the sixth riddle was complete.

It should be no surprise that there was quite a bit of anticipation riding on the seventh and final installation of the riddle. Like all great adventures, there should be a rewarding conclusion when the trekker reaches the end. There was a problem to this truth, because I felt that if the finale were too great, there would be the possibility of the traveler forgetting there was another task to complete. You might have been clouded with a terrific ending to the seven riddles and would overlook the fact that it wasn't the end at all. The acquisition of the manuscript was to be the treasure at the end of your conquest, not the map with which you were to find it. For that reason, we decided not to place any puzzles or mazes on the seventh planet. Instead, we kept the planet just as it was, so as not to deprive it of any of its majesty. The true specialty of the planet was its symbolic representation of the manuscript itself. The planet was a single pearl, floating silently in a black sea that was circumnavigated by a ring of stars. Just like the treasure, it was a glowing angel in a dark universe.

The Admiral took the notes and diagrams of the planet and placed them on the table for all of us to see. He sat down next to me and made himself comfortable.

"You know." He said, thinking out loud. "This planet really is beautiful. It only seems right that we aren't doing anything to it. Incidentally, the traveler will probably be saturated of puzzles and riddles by the time he gets there."

"I sincerely hope not." Terinsa blurted out with joking exasperation "He still has one more after this!"

He laughed at the remark and continued to scrutinize the papers.

"Well," I began after clearing my throat. "Since we have decided not to install any type of brain-teaser on the planet, or in the riddle, we should focus mainly on the eccentricities of the planet."

I looked over at Terinsa, who was cradling her tired wrist in her other hand. Retnar noticed this and offered to take over for her. She gladly passed the privilege of writing the last riddle over to him and relaxed in her chair, continuing to massage her fatigued muscles. Retnar took the pen and paper and looked up at me with an encouraging glance.

"How should we begin the seventh riddle?" He asked.

"Let's start with the position and placement of the planet, but let's color it a bit." Perhaps my suggestion was unnecessary, considering the planet really didn't need any help from me to make it beautiful. "Begin with something like...'a single pearl in a sea of black'"

"That's a good start. Retnar said. But he didn't write anything down. Instead, he took a blank sheet of paper and began to jot down several little lines to work with.

After brainstorming for a few minutes, it seemed that he had created his desired prose and read it aloud to his anxious audience.

"Encircled in a ring of stars, I have no where to run." He paused to look up and see what we thought. We gave him reassuring looks and he continued on. "A pearl afloat a sea of black, and family I have none. The stars are far away from me. I've never seen the day. Yet, my surface glows in the night. It seems we've found our way."

He set the paper down on the table and picked up his pencil, awaiting any suggested changes. He received none. We all felt that the first sentence was a good hook for our adventurer. He was glad to know that he did a job well done, and finished up the three-stanza poem.

Our map was ready to be placed in its resting area. Now all we had to do was figure out where to put the manuscript in the temple. Coincidentally, a few minutes after we had completed the map, our solution presented itself in the form of the fifth star.

Deltrin chuckled, remembering how excited he was when he found the beacon orbiting a small moon in the middle of nowhere. He left the story for just a moment thinking to himself, almost sad the journey was coming to an end.

He relaxed in his chair, put the book down, and took a drink of his relaxing beverage. His eyes traveled around the room, looking for something to grab his attention. Finally, his eyes passed the window in his bedchamber.

He looked out amongst the stars and slowly began to reminisce on the last five years of his life. He could hear a voice in the back of his head, telling the story of when he came upon the grand tomb of the map...

The Discovery

After searching for something to do for the past week, Deltrin became very bored and would have taken any mission, no matter what it required. He sank in his pilot seat, staring into the void he called home, hoping that something would fall into his lap.

Drifting endlessly in space, waiting for something to come into view, he began to get discouraged, almost sorry he hadn't chosen a better occupation than being a drifter. Feeling sorry for himself wasn't going to release the monotony from his life.

He had been traveling for most all of his life, and hadn't seen another soul in the past four years. That's the price you pay when you travel your whole life. He never knew anyone who wanted to jump from planet to planet with him, so he was forced to make the choice of either staying put or being adventurous and never establish any roots. The choice was not that hard for him to make, considering he had always wanted to travel all his life. As soon as he could afford his own spacecraft, he said his good-byes to the very few friends he had and sped off into the night, looking for any quest he could find. On occasion, he traveled back home to see his parents, who were always pleased to see him. But no one else remembered him, so his visits were always brief and quite rare.

He had just finished a mission that bought him some new parts for his ship, with a little extra for the future. The mission took four years from his life, but he did not want to go back home. Instead, he wanted to find a new mission, being disappointed with the last one.

The cloak of space finally lifted itself to reveal a small planet in the distance. Deltrin was relieved to see that there might be something down there, waiting to be discovered. He closed in on the planet, only to find that it was actually a dead moon drifting in space. Jaded with disappointment, Deltrin turned his ship around, not even noticing his ship's control panel was flashing a message that read "Object detected".

He glanced down at the annoying light to see what it wanted. Not realizing his stroke of luck the first time, he made a double take and finally saw that a miracle had happened. He was ecstatic to see that the equipment he had just purchased was worth the money it cost him.

He immediately turned the ship back around to face the planet and headed straight for the unidentified object. It was a small tube, about a meter in length. Deltrin fished the treasure out of the black sea with his retractable arm and brought it into his ship.

Time had worn down the outside of the casket, but to his fortune, he found that the contents were unharmed. He pulled a large parchment from the belly of the tube and unraveled it.

On one side, there was a huge star map that he recognized, slightly. There was a large blue nebula, resembling the wings of some flying beast, like a gargoyle, which covered the entire system. Inside its wings, there was a constellation that looked like a tree of some sort, with eight spiral galaxies on its eight large branches. Each of the galaxies were accompanied by a designated number, except for the one in the upper right-hand corner, which was left blank.

Deltrin recognized the nebula, as well as the tree constellation and was obliged to find out the point to all of this. He turned the parchment over and found a series of riddles, each of them corresponding to a number similar to the numbers of the galaxies. He began to read the riddle, having no idea what he was getting himself into...

1) Are you brave, do you take risks? I'm waiting here for you.
Hold your breath, you're in for a ride, here is what to do.
Connect the dots from one to seven and you will have your prize.
But watch your step and keep your wits, and always trust your eyes.

The first is simple, trust me friend, compared to all the rest.
Just walk the path that's beat for you and you will pass the test.
Cross the bridge to a darkened world and you will find me there,
A star to my left, another on my right. Welcome to my

161

lair.

The blanket I wear is brown and red, with little spots of
blue,
There's green in me, but hard to see, for that's because
I'm new.
I'm all alone, no one's around, an only child am I,
Besides the parents I circle around, I have an empty
sky.

Come through my door, undaunted knight, and claim the
prize you seek
The largest isle, I'm waiting here, atop the highest
peak.
The first test done, six more to go, and now you have a
piece.
complete the map and you will have a rare and golden
fleece.

2) Within my heart, A garden springs a vivid world to
see.
The son of four, no brothers have I, who look exactly
like me.
Come down on my throne, for I am alone, apart from

the billions of trees
Who keep me at peace, as I watch them glide and
happily dance in the breeze

Feeling lost, my green-thumbed friend, Amongst the
green so vast?
Not in trees, I'm below your knees, in a garden that
you've passed
My carpet is soft and smells divine, tickling the hairs in
your nose.
You'll know me best, when I confess, I'm near the
turquoise rose.

3) Two are down, five more to go. We've barely just
begun.
But do not fear my little dear. Aren't you having fun?
Miss the sea? It gentle waves that pierce the sandy
beach?
Well not for long, I must concede, for it's within your
reach.

I'm very sad, the planet says, but I haven't got a clue
Why I shed a tear most every year, and why I am so
blue.

It's because, his father says, you silly little sap.
Your eldest son, instead of you was picked to hold the
map.

So seek the well that's large in size and look inside the
cave
Find the tomb inside the womb and open up the grave.
Inside you'll find another piece, just what you've had in
store.
Hold on tight and buckle in, it's off to planet four.

4) Not even the flame I see all day can save me from
the ice.
I've been frozen all my years, this is no paradise.
A species lived for many years, inside my heart of
stone.
But they could not survive the ice and left me all alone.

I beg of you, come visit me and show me that you care.
I'll give you what you're looking for, now doesn't that
seem fair?
Trust in me to hand to you the gift that you have
earned.
You're a friend I'd like to keep, for that is what I've

learned.

My extended arm will welcome you, come rest upon my
hand:
The only thing that I can lift above this barren land.
Open up the only ring, you won't believe your eyes.
Within the stone, the fourth piece sits. Go on and claim
your prize.

5) Unique am I amongst the rest of other planets
you've seen
I live alone and have no friends, it's not because I'm
mean.
I have no need for outside stars to help and play a
part.
For deep inside my reddened veins, I hold a star-lit
heart.

You must be warned, my brilliant friend. Don't come
unprepared.
Fools have tried to walk my land and they could not be
spared.
I breathe a different gas than you, so bring a separate
lung.

I wouldn't want to see you hurt, or die so very young.

There is a cave that you will see, that's guarded by a flame.
But do not fear, he'll know you're here, he even knows your name.
Within the cave, the next piece lies. Don't worry, there are no tricks.
Five are yours, two are mine. Are you ready for planet six?

6) A ring of mountains rules this realm, where a single star rolls on.
The trees bow down to this range of gods, until the sun is gone.
No turning back, you've come too far, remember what you have done.
I warned you what we had in store, it's time now for our fun.

A tower stands on the planet below, it isn't hard to find.
Walk up the stairs and trust your wits, for you will need your mind.

Three statues wait for you up there, be sure to use your head.
Trust not their smiles, except for one. The others want you dead.

My father holds the only key to help you make your choice,
When he comes, heed his advice and listen to his voice.
Only in morning will he speak the truth, his wit as sharp as a knife.
Wait too long and your choice will be wrong; that's the end of your life.

If you succeed and chose the right, you've passed our little test.
Proceed through the door and find the tube that's resting in its nest.
One piece left, you're still alive. One more step to heaven.
You're going to love what you will find awaiting on planet seven.

7) Encircled in a ring of stars, I have nowhere to run.
A pearl afloat a sea of black and family I have none.

The stars are far away from me. I've never seen the day
Yet my surface glows in night; it seems we've found our
way.

And so have you, I have to say, my bravest of the brave
It's good to see that you have not been put inside a
grave.
The seventh piece is in my grasp and soon to be in
yours.
It's been here resting peacefully along my crystal
shores.

Only one island has risen above the crest of my ocean
blue.
Find it, friend, the map is there, waiting just for you.
Your quest's half done, the map's complete, there's one
last thing undone.
Find the treasure by solving the maze and then our side
has won.

Deltrin stared at the incredible riddle, thinking
that maybe it wasn't such a good idea to read ahead. He
still had a chance to reconsider taking the job, but how
could he pass up an opportunity like this? If he were to
pull this off without getting killed in the process, he

would be well rewarded not only with the gift that awaited him, but also with the praise he would get from everyone else. No other assignment or quest could match this. Plus, what did he have to lose? Apart from the ship that he put so much time into, as well as the nice pantry he just installed, not much. His family would probably encourage him to take this mission.

He left the map on the table and walked down the hall to the cockpit. He immediately set a course for the blue nebula. That was his best start.

He walked back down to where he left the map and read the first riddle to himself many times, getting the clues into his head. A better idea sprang into his head, so he took the map and walked back into the cockpit. He sat down and swiveled his chair to face a new machine that he had just purchased with his earnings and installed only two days ago. It was now time to put the machine to test.

Before he typed any information, he took the riddle and decoded the clues. The riddle mentioned two stars in the vicinity, as well as the planet being an 'only child'. Considering the other riddles talked about parents and siblings and children, it was obviously referring to the stars, planets, and moons near the particular planet in question.

The only child meant that there were no other planets in the sidereal system and since the riddle mentioned that the planet was all alone, Deltrin could only assume that there were no moons either. Deltrin set the map aside on the desktop near him and began to work on the terminal.

The machine he had purchased was a locating device that could give all possible planets that would fit the description the user typed in. It was a little ancient compared to its newer and more efficient models, but those were used for military purposes. All Deltrin needed was for it to help him out in doing his job.

Deltrin typed in the information he could decipher from the riddle; two stars, no moons, no other planets. Just before he began the search, he realized he was forgetting something; the galaxy itself. If he were to have neglected to mention which galaxy to look in, he may have ended up searching every known system in every known galaxy in every known sector. The list would have been enormous. He quickly left his pilot seat and ran back to the map room, where he located a map of the universe. He took it and ran back to the computer. He quickly located the nebula on the map and found the appropriate galaxy. He typed in the coordinates, adding it to the rest of the information and then began his search. He waited for a response.

After about five minutes of hunting through several thousand systems, the computer concluded its search and found six planets that fit the description. Deltrin was happy to see the first planet would not be so hard to find. He picked up the riddle and read the third stanza. Red and brown with little spots of blue. *Mountainous* he thought to himself.

He continued to condense the search by looking over the descriptions of the different planets. The first planet the search revealed did have mountains, but it was about ¾ water. The riddle spoke of little spots of blue, not gigantic smudges. That was the wrong one. The second planet was very green and had been around for several hundreds of millions of years. The riddle said the planet was new. The second choice was incorrect. The third planet that was chosen was a very young planet and fit the description nicely, having very few bodies of water. Deltrin highlighted that one, but kept on with his search. None of the other three were close to the description. Since the third planet in the selection seemed to be the one, he confidently chose to travel to it.

He brought up a screen that gave the necessary information about the planet, as well as its coordinates, and turned around to see how far his ship had traveled. There was still about an hour left of travel, so he put his feet up and began to sleep until he got there...

The Quintessence

The memory began to fade and Deltrin awoke from his slumber taking a deep breath into his lungs. He looked at his watch to see how much time had passed. To his surprise, only five minutes were spent in his daydream. He grabbed the glass from the table and took a drink, still looking out through the little window in his room. He averted his eyes from the window and focused on the book that was still in his lap. He picked up the book and continued to read where he had left off...

The timing of the fifth star's appearance could not have been more impeccable. It was like we told the star ourselves that we had finished the map and were ready for it to make its arrival.

Before the star appeared, we had just put all the notes away and were just about ready to locate where to hide the manuscript.

Then, like a flash from the heavens, the jewel in the skeleton's skull produced a light that flew straight down into the turquoise gem on the bottom floor. All the other jewels did the same, and the culmination of rays fed the turquoise jewel with energy, until it finally spread its luster in all directions.

We had trouble finding our way out of the temple with such a blinding atmosphere to walk through, but when we did, we could see the sixth spire in the middle firing out such a tremendous light making everything glow on the planet's surface, especially the temple. The light was pale blue, with a hint of gray. I wish I could have been out in space to see how far it reached, but I was just fine right where I was standing. I suspected that everyone else had the same expression as I, but I couldn't take my eyes off the light for one second to see.

We left the temple through the labyrinth to get a full look at the spectacle. On the hill, the entire island could be seen. The trees were violently swaying back and forth, as if they were dancing ritualistically to this incantation. Their leaves broke free, gliding through the air, decorating the island where they fell. The labyrinth had become much more resplendent due to the clarity of light. Details I could not even see close up were suddenly springing from their invisibility.

I turned around to see what was happening in the ocean. The waves were crashing upon the shores with intensity, throwing our transport back and forth on its unstable surface. Luckily for us, our ship stayed afloat and did not sink.

The effect the star produced on the ocean was astonishing. Besides the dancing of the waves, the surface had a new appearance within it. Above our heads, the sky gently turned from blue to silver, making the clouds seem like a collection of feathers hovering over us. The new hint of color spread throughout the planet and dashed the water with streaks of glowing silver along the surface. It looked like mercury flowing independently through the blanket of water, like strands of yarn stitching a quilt.

I turned my head with great effort to the temple once more, and could see the jewels inside, blazing with incandescence. Any other light would have been muffled by the intensity of the temple, yet these souls of stone made their presence seen for miles.

The temple's radiance began to dissipate after a long while had passed, but the main stone was still glowing from within.

"It's now safe to go back into the temple." Retnar said, still smiling with excitement.

We were all sitting on the ground, enjoying the warm grass. We lifted ourselves up and walked down the hill back to the temple, a little dazed by the brilliance. The turquoise jewel on the main floor was still affected by the stars, but, as Retnar informed us, one of the stars would eventually move out of the spires' opening and the jewel would stop glowing. There was, however, one phenomenon that not even Retnar knew about.

I must tell you first that we had spent some time looking at the jewels and their magnificent glow. We first stared at the two jewels on the bottom floor and basked in the light they produced. The blue stone created a light so dark, it almost looked violet. The crystal statue holding it absorbed most of the dark light, but it was still able to maintain a blue tint.

The red stone turned darker, filling its statue with blood red color. Excited to see what the other stones were doing, we all ran up the stairs to the next level, which is where we made the discovery I referred to before.

In the skull of the fifth statue, there were two stones, not just one. Each eye had a different stone. The one on the right was pointed down to the jewel below, but the left eye was pointing to a spot in the wall, creating a translucent material that made the wall look like a liquid surface. We approached the apparition in the wall to see what the statue was looking at. To our amazement, there was a book revealed behind the crystal door.

"Is it safe to touch?" Terinsa asked Retnar.

He shook his head and shrugged his shoulders. "I have no idea. This book's a mystery to me, as well."

The Admiral stepped up to the wall. "I guess there's only

174

one way to find out."

He placed his willing hand on the undulating crystal. His hand penetrated the surface and sank into the tiny pool, until he had a grip on the book. He pulled his hand out of the gel and retrieved the book. His hand was dry. He looked at the distant statue that looked straight at him and obscured its line of sight. The light that punctured the wall could no longer reach the resting-place of the book and the wall turned solid crystal instantly. Terinsa placed her hand on the wall, trying to push into the hollow cavity, but could not. The Admiral cleared the path of the light again, making the surface mellifluous once again. Terinsa fell through the wall and jammed her hand into the other side of the wall. The Admiral turned to see what happened and quickly jumped back into the path of the light in hopes to remedy the situation. Unfortunately, as soon as he blocked the light's path, the area turned solid again.

"Ah!! It's crushing my arm! Jump out of the damn light!"

The Admiral moved hastily out of the way and freed Terinsa's arm.

"Sorry about that." He said as he rushed over to see how she was.

"That's okay." She said, cradling her arm. "Just stay out of the light." She gave him a look of acceptance for his apology, with a tiny hint of warning. The Admiral received this subtle threat clearly and kept a distance away from the beam.

The Admiral opened the manuscript to see what it contained. Within seconds, he looked up with a confused look and quickly handed it to our interpreter. Retnar took the book and began to read it silently.

"Oh my." He whispered. He looked up from the book with astonishment glazed in his eye. "This is the history of the temple. It talks about all the trials and tribulations that the builders went through, the stories about the crystals and their origins. It talks about everything." He looked back

175

down to the book and then looked up again. Do we have time to read some of it?"

We all nodded our heads and soon enough, we were back down on the bottom floor, sitting down in the chairs we were all too familiar with.

Retnar read aloud the contents of the book. Retnar skipped over the stories of the jewels and only read to us the different accounts the builders made during the construction of the temple.

Most of them talked about why the temple was built, which was really simple to explain. According to their testimonies, they were new to the planet and had no idea how to predict the natural phenomena of the planet. The appearance of the fifth star was especially difficult to cope with because it heated up the surface at least ten more degrees Celsius during its season. They needed a way to predict the coming of the fifth star, so they built a structure that could be used to alert the inhabitants of its approach. The technical aspects of the device were not that sophisticated.

Each of the four stars fall on their stones periodically, but never at the same time, until about two years before the fifth star makes its appearance. When the four stars are seen through their spires at the same time, that's the warning that the fifth star is close to bursting with light. Once the fifth star appeared, the inhabitants were already prepared for its arrival.

What Retnar said was right; this was a gigantic clock, but it didn't tell time the way the Trocties thought it did. They thought it was the beginning of their sidereal cycle, which it was for them. According to the beings who created the temple, they built the structure as a warning system. It may have been used for similar reasons, but the ones who made the accounts didn't mention anything about a new beginning or a recycling of time.

The book continued on, giving records of the star's

movements, its build-up; the usual things that one writes down in a record book. Retnar finished the book and placed it in a bag with the rest of the notes. He told us he was going to take it back to his civilization so they could study the star with first-hand information.

"How much time do we have before the jewel in the skull loses its ability to glow." Terinsa asked, forming an idea.

"I think we have about an hour before it turns lucid again." Retnar answered.

That was more than enough time to get the manuscript ready and placed in the wall. That was the best place to put it, since it would be hidden and only a traveler who had decrypted the riddle would know where to look.

We gathered all the pieces of the manuscript and placed them all in a sheath. We took the case upstairs and placed it in the hands of the liquid stone. We only had one thing left to do before we left this place. We had a final riddle to create that would reveal the resting-place of the manuscript.

Deltrin was getting tired. He could feel the sweat of fatigue building on his brow. He took a final drink and placed his empty flask on the table next to him.

"Guess I'll have to read you later, friend." He spoke out-loud. He had only been awake for about four hours, but the release of a long journey had finally caught up with him. He would have to expect this narcoleptic state to be with him for a few days. He languidly set the book down next to the glass and slowly got up to walk to his bed. He laid himself gently on the mattress and began to dream, continuing where he left off from his earlier daydream…

The Blue Rose

The first piece was found with hardly any trouble for Deltrin. He didn't let the effortless task go to his head, though, for he had been warned that the first planet was a cakewalk compared to the other six.

After he settled down from his first step of the quest, he set his ship on course for the second planet. He found the plant-world with ease, considering there were no other planets that fit the description. With the first step taken care of, Deltrin knew better than to take the next step for granted, for finding the piece was going to be the hard part.

He got up from his worn pilot seat and walked back to the map room, where he left the first tube he found. He didn't bother to open it on the surface. He wanted to get out of there as soon as possible, to continue his quest.

He opened the tube, which exhaled a small breath of air inside, and found a small parchment lying peacefully in the cradle of the container. Deltrin pulled it out gently and placed it on the counter.

It was obviously torn off from a larger piece, on account of the serrated edges, as well as the fact that the picture on the piece was incomplete.

There was a type of garden drawn on the segment

of the map, seemingly to be a great distance from the eyes of the observer. The map seemed to be drawn from a hill, but Deltrin couldn't tell what the observer was looking at yet. There were still six more pieces to find.

At the bottom of the drawing, there was a single stanza.

Great Deltrin thought. *Another riddle. As if I didn't have enough puzzles to decode, they give me another one.*

He read to himself the tiny writing, which was just as nebulous as the original riddle...

Alone in the dark, a mighty tree stands,
That's colored as white as the dove.
Seven great worlds entwined in its leaves,
With an eighth that's floating above.

Hmm. This riddle motif is getting monotonous.

A red light attached to the ceiling of the map room began to flicker and make an ululating noise. Deltrin glanced up at the annoying light and realized the second planet was in range. He hurried to his pilot seat and began to steer the ship to the planet's surface.

The world glowed green in the black space around it. The atmosphere was a little difficult to puncture, but Deltrin managed to break through. He found a suitable place to land, on top of a small patch of grass that was surrounded by a forest.

Before he left his ship, he took one last glance at the riddle to make sure he knew where he was going. The riddle counseled him not to look in any tree, but to look within the many gardens that were in abundance on the surface. He needed to find the garden with the turquoise rose.

He took a final breath before he opened the hatch. He climbed out of his ship and was nearly blinded by the brilliance of the four stars in the sky. He climbed back into the ship's hull to find his protective visors. He placed the shaded goggles over his eyes and made his second exit from the ship. He dropped himself on the soft ground and straightened himself out.

With every breath he took, he could feel the fresh air flowing through his yearning veins, filling his lungs with the sweet aroma around him. The fragrance from the flowers was tantalizing, yet gentle, much like the breeze caressing the rough skin on Deltrin's face, embracing his body with the coolness of its whisper. He could have stayed in that position forever and would not have complained, but he was too curious to see what fate held for him at the end of his mystical journey.

The expedition through the meadows of the ornate world made it hard for Deltrin to concentrate on the task at hand. The two suns in the evening sky danced upon the petals, their shadows entwined with one another in a forever embrace. It was a shame that Deltrin had to walk all over the foliage below, crushing some of the magnificent flowers. He tiptoed as gently as he could, but he could not dodge some of the iridescent blossoms. His search for the turquoise rose seemed endless.

There were gardens everywhere and every one of them had their own particular types of blossoming colors and flowers. But none of them contained the elusive blue rose. He decided to make his search a little easier for himself, so he left a type of marker on every garden or patch of land he encountered. This way he wouldn't backtrack.

Luckily, the planet's surface area was not that

large and Deltrin was able to traverse most of the entire planet within a couple days. However, his initial search wore him out and he decided to rest.

He made a small bed in the shade of a group of willow trees. The branches rained downed to the ground, making an umbrella to shelter Deltrin. A patch of moss was growing on a stump close by on the ground, so Deltrin seized the growth by the roots and pulled them off to make himself a pillow to cushion his head.

The stars in the sky were cut into tiny shards through the millions of leaves on the branches of the willows. An amiable wind smoothed out the tree's arms as they placed their cool hands on Deltrin's face. The atmosphere was more than relaxing and it did not take much coaxing to put Deltrin to sleep.

A ray of light cut through the fingers of the willows and awoke the dormant traveler. He rubbed off the sleep in his eyes and slowly sat up. The mattress of grass rose with the same celerity. He sat for a moment in the cool shadow and deliberated on what to do next. All he could do was search some more, until his luck had changed. He took a deep breath of the fresh air and propped himself up.

A little disoriented, he looked around, realizing the branches of the willows had shifted slightly and he could not find the opening from where he came. The green circle he was in was almost symmetrical, which didn't help him out. As soon as he realized the obvious fact that he had to begin his search over, he made his own doorway and walked out.

Perhaps it was a stroke of luck, or a stroke of fate that made him choose his path, but whatever the impetus was that forced his decision made Deltrin the great adventurer he was. Hidden underneath another range of willows was the intangible garden of the turquoise rose and beneath their verdant wings, the second piece of the map rested safely. Deltrin let out a sigh of relief and walked over to receive the guerdon. A smile stretched on his face from ear to ear, but only for a moment. He had just realized he had forgotten where he left his ship.

Another few hours passed until his search had really ended. He climbed into his ship, frowning at his stupidity. With the second treasure in his hand, he placed the other piece adjacent to it. Thankfully, the edges fit together, completing more of the mysterious garden. The garden became more detailed, and began to look more like a structure made out of trees and bushes. He glanced down at the bottom of the second piece to read the next part of the riddle...

A splash in the sea and you're on your way
To a place you see in your dreams
A blink washes tears and my family appears,
Which isn't as small as it seems.

He scratched his head, wondering if the riddle was going to get any easier. Deep down inside, he was enjoying its difficulty, but this was a new type of adventure. He was not used to riddles and was using a part of his brain that had been dormant for many years. He kept the pieces where they were and calmly walked into the cockpit to charter his third destination, tired both physically and mentally.

The Violet Haze

According to the riddle, the third planet was obviously a water-dominated world, so the search was not that hard to conduct. Deltrin eventually rooted out the correct planet from four other possibilities and made his way into the third galaxy.

He picked up the map riddle that was setting on the counter next to the computer and read the third brainteaser. He chuckled at the nonsensical conversation between the father and the son and quickly deduced what the riddle was hinting at. The largest moon that orbits the planet was where the map was to be found. That was not too difficult. What would be difficult is finding the supposed 'well' in the earth. At the moment, Deltrin didn't worry about it and just sat back in his chair, watching the stars fly by through his window.

The brevity of the trip to the water planet was astounding. Deltrin was taken slightly off-guard when he caught a glimpse of the blue glow from almost a light year away. The one star must have really bombarded the surface with heavy rays to have produced such an illumination.

He quickly ran down to his supply room and made himself ready for whatever type of terrain the moon would present to him. Proper equipment would be needed for this hike, so Deltrin made the necessary precautions and heavily dressed himself with mounting tools for climbing in all directions.

He grabbed two different types of cables that were hanging on the wall. One cable was used for quick descents and was made out of a very elastic material. The other had no elasticity, which could be used for a pulley system, or for delicate climbing. He also grabbed four pneumatic guns that were used to fire anchors and cable attachments into hard surfaces to ensure stability and safety.

He took these tools, along with other things of necessity and laid them all out on the table in the map room. He strolled down to the cockpit to manually anchor his ship to the largest moon of the water system.

The atmosphere of the moon was very thick and the descent to the rocky surface was very violent. After Deltrin managed to shove himself through the thick clouds, he was able to maneuver with ease and landed his precious ship safely to the surface.

He got out of his pilot seat and went to the map room to hook all his gear onto his belt and vest. Before he walked out, he remembered to take another piece of equipment, which might be necessary to have if the well was as large as it was said to be.

He walked into the equipment room, lugging the tools attached to his body. He searched inside the room and finally found the oxygen helmet hanging on the wall. He took it and strolled out of the room with contentment. He was ready to scout the third world.

The air was fresh, with a little sting attached to the tail's end of every breath. The sun was nearly setting on the horizon, bleeding pale light upon the land. There were mountains in the distance that could have scraped the clouds away from the sky. Deltrin had landed on a small patch of land that was about ten meters away from the coast.

He splashed into the tide-pool and felt the warm water ride up his legs and chest. He instinctively looked down to see where he was walking, and to his surprise, he could see tiny organisms resting on the bottom floor. The water could not have been more than four feet deep and yet there was a huge colony of benthic life forms spread everywhere on the underwater carpet. Luckily, the oxygen helmet he brought along allowed him to breathe underwater.

Instead of requiring an oxygen tank, this helmet acted like a pair of gills, which isolated the oxygen from the liquid, filling the helmet with the necessary pressure and gas for Deltrin to breathe. Unfortunately, it did not work in gaseous atmospheres. Only in liquid ones.

He fitted the mask over his head and submerged to get a closer look at the microcosm. There were several little plants growing off the bottom, but there were also tiny circular creatures that were not completely attached to the floor. He picked up one of the little organisms and held it in his hand. it did not have much of a defense. There was no virulent sting applied when the traveler picked it up. All it had were simple little thorns adorned all around its circular body. If these creatures needed a form of protection that would mean there had to be a threat. Who? Or rather, what was threatening them?

Deltrin decided to prolong his stay here to determine why a species needed protection in this pristine world. He gently placed his new friend on the underwater sand along with the other tiny creatures. He walked back to his ship, making sure he was not stepping on anything.

The ship was able to travel to incredible depths,

along with its ability to travel through space. Deltrin wasn't planning on going too deep anyway, so he really didn't have to worry about the potential danger of the immense pressure at great depths.

He lifted off and traveled further into the blue, until he was hovering over what seemed to be deep waters. He plunged into the ocean and began his search for pelagic life forms. His search was quickly ended, for the clandestine world of predators was revealed at about twenty meters in depth. They were dispersed over a square kilometer in all directions.

The creatures were of all shapes and sizes ranging from two inches to twenty feet. The heads of the larger fish seemed almost armor-plated, with prominent scales on their bodies. Most of the fish had beaked mouths, while a minute few had a flattened jaw line made out of some sort of bone or cartilage.

Some of them were curious and bumped their steel heads into the hull of Deltrin's ship. They did not, however, make any damage. They were probably even more curious and threatened by the strange object that had just invaded *their* environment.

The evolution of life on this planet seemed very strange, considering that some life forms had managed to reach the tidal areas. It wasn't right to have pre-cartilage fish swimming around, when there were more advanced creatures almost on land, or already on land, for that matter. Deltrin thought to himself, wondering just how far the life had evolved, hoping that he would encounter other animals on the surface.

He ascended from the ocean slowly, depressurizing at safe intervals. He followed his trail back to where he landed before and set anchor in the same area. He climbed out and carefully walked to the beach, minding his footing to avoid the underwater city.

Deltrin traversed along the coastal area to have a look around before he began his search for the grand well. There was quite an abundance of tree life on the beach, but nothing out of the ordinary. The most prominent color was green, but there were also some reds, blues, violets, and yellows. The iridescent display of light almost kept him from noticing the little footprints indented on the sand.

Deltrin kneeled down to look at the tiny signatures, noticing they looked like clawed feet, with five digits on each one. They were very tiny, but physical characteristics did not matter at the moment. Deltrin was not alone on the surface. Something had evolved.

He hurried back to his ship and grabbed a couple weapons to protect himself. He armed himself and walked back to the beach, only this time he did not stop on the sand. He proceeded straight through the forest.

As he trekked through the woodland, he could hear keening noises coming from above. The trees blocked his view from the sky, however, so he couldn't locate any flying creatures. He continued to look, hoping to see the origin of the sound, but he did not find it. It found him.

A tiny winged-creature was perched on a limb from a tree in front of Deltrin. He was about a foot in height and couldn't have weighed more than five pounds. It was colored dark green and looked like a dragon. It hopped off the branch and floated down to greet the visitor, who was completely frozen from the surprise. He hovered in front of Deltrin and simply smiled, or so it seemed. Deltrin finally regained mobility and since he found no danger in showing amicability to the tiny being, he lifted his arm and offered a resting place. The tiny dragon fluttered his wings and stayed put for a second or two and then blissfully plopped himself on Deltrin's arm.

"Well, you're a lovely little thing, aren't you?" He asked the extroverted creature. The dark violet eyes gazed into Deltrin's stare, as the creature cocked his head to the side, trying to figure out what the stranger had just asked him. Deltrin lifted his other arm slowly, as not to frighten the little being and began to caress the tiny head with a gentle stroke. The creature welcomed the massage and after Deltrin had pet the head of the dragon for a minute, the dragon hopped closer to his face and began to pet the traveler's cheek with his petite hands. The questor couldn't help but to laugh at the adorable gesture.

"So, where are your friends?" He asked. The smiling creature stopped what he was doing and hopped onto Deltrin's shoulder. As soon as he reached his destination, he made a high pitched warble. Deltrin cringed at the note.

Within seconds, a swarm of tiny dragons all came into view, flying in from all different directions. This tiny fleet of mystical creatures hovered around the bewildered Deltrin. A couple perched on his head, some on his shoulder and arm, some hopped on the branches of trees, others on the ground and some just stayed in flight. There must have been a hundred of them in the small grove. They were colored in green, red, and black, and all had different colored eyes, every one of them fixed on the stranger.

The dragon who first made contact with Deltrin poked the stranger on the side of his head, trying to get his attention. He turned to look at the eager dragon, who was pointing into the distance. The dragons on the ground and the trees made themselves airborne again and began to fly with the others to where the little one was pointing. The others that were attached to Deltrin did not give up their comfy nests and stayed put. He did not mind, at the moment, but come time when he needed his arms, he was going to have to let them go.

The squadron gave him a tour of the land, which was to say the least, breathtaking. Life was different here. It was like a force had changed the formula of evolution, making the results incredible and unpredictable. Deltrin had never seen such a difference in evolution between species. There were fish in the ocean that were much more primitive than the benthic organisms that he saw in the tide-pool, and they were no where near as advanced as the flight of his little friends. He didn't want to question the uniqueness of this planet. He loved it, so he refused to ruin it with explanations.

Through mountains and valleys, the armada led the way to their mysterious destination. Some of the dragons were at great distances ahead of Deltrin, and eventually, he could see that they had stopped and rested on the ground. The immense luck Deltrin had experienced on his previous adventures was nothing compared to what he received when he found that the creatures were waiting at the mouth of the enormous well.

"Are you guys going to carry me down there?"

The creatures looked at him and then each other and then all flew down into the hole

"I thought not." He said to himself. Obviously, they could understand some things.

Deltrin took off some of his equipment from his vest and laid it on the ground. He realized that there was no need for his oxygen helmet, since the dragons didn't

189

look aquatic, so he placed that on the ground as well.

He left the four guns on his belt and took the non-elastic cable with him. He attached the cable to his vest. He shot a metal clip into the ground and hooked the other end of the cable through the eye of the clip. He then walked to the edge of the well, wrapped a light around his head, and slowly began his descent into the black. Inside the cavern, the tiny dragons were watching him make his journey to the floor of the cave.

When he got about five meters below the surface, he could feel the rope begin to give. Incidentally, this was not a good thing. The clip slowly dug itself out of the ground, so Deltrin did not have much time to act. He quickly attached the open end of the cable to one of the metal hooks on a pneumatic gun. As soon as he tied the knot in the bottom of the hook, the clip on the surface gave and Deltrin was sent plummeting down at tremendous acceleration. He aimed the gun at the ceiling and immediately fired the hook into the air. The miracle hook found a hold and broke Deltrin's fall. Lucky thing too, for he was about ten meters from the floor.

He slowly lowered himself to the ground with his bloody hands. When he stopped falling, he had to grip on to the rope, for his body was no longer attached to it. He slid down the rope about a foot until he stopped, but it left barely any layer of skin on his palms.

He jumped down to the grassy carpet and picked himself up. His violet-eyed friend came out of the darkness and perched himself on Deltrin's weak shoulder. *Where the heck were you when I was up there?* he thought to himself. It was no use asking the little being. He couldn't have helped and couldn't understand a word he said. Nevertheless, Deltrin was beginning to like him.

Deltrin could barely see anything with his faint helmet light. He took a flare from his vest and ignited it. It did not hurt the eyes of the dragon, nor did it bother the two thousand other dragons that inhabited the caves. Deltrin could not believe his own eyes.

They all swarmed down to him, all non-threatening. They scrutinized the stranger and eventually went back to their nests. Deltrin watched where they flew to and noticed there must have been a few hundred eggs strewn about their lair. This was the perfect hiding place. Nothing could enter, except for them and they could come and go as they pleased.

Deltrin looked down on the ground and noticed tiny skeletons and bones strewn about the floor. They were not skeletons of the dragons, but of little rodents that must be roaming around this planet. This place was beyond fantasy, as was its evolution.

Deltrin walked around the lair, greeting several dragons as he walked by, until he finally reached the third tube. Nothing was near the tube, no eggs, no nest, nothing. It was just waiting for him to retrieve it. He picked it up, seeing if the dragons approved of him taking something from their lair, which they did.

He stuffed the tiny tube into his vest pocket. He said his good-byes to the dragons and quickly made his ascent to the surface. Once he reached the surface, he was about ready to leave, when he felt a tiny tug at his right ankle. He looked down to see who it was. The violet-eyed dragon looked up at him with a sad look. Deltrin was sad, as well, to say good-bye to his little friend, considering he was his first companion for many years. Deltrin needed a partner, and felt this little being would be perfect. He lowered his hand to the little dragon, who gleefully hopped upon his palm. Deltrin lifted him up and placed him on his shoulder. He climbed out of the cave, and with his new friend, he trekked back to his ship and blasted away from dragon's isle.

Deltrin introduced the tiny creature to his new home. The dragon quickly found a place to rest and perched himself on the rim of Deltrin's bed stand.

"You're going to love it here, little one." He said, smiling more than ever before, now that he had a friend.

The little dragon squeaked at Deltrin.

"I can't go to sleep right now, friend. I have to see what's in that tube."

The dragon actually seemed to understand him and flew over to rest on Deltrin's shoulder, urging him to go to the map room.

"Well, I hope you can solve riddles better than I can."

The little dragon squeaked again.

"They don't make much sense to you, either, huh?"

The response he got from the question was shorter than the other ones, but Deltrin got the point.

They traveled down to the map room, where Deltrin left the unopened tube lying on the table. The little dragon hopped off of his shoulder and landed softly on the table, excited to see what was to be revealed. Deltrin opened the tube, releasing the captured breath of age. Inside was the third piece of the map.

Deltrin took the piece out and added it to the other two. The picture was becoming clearer and he could finally make out the entire bottom left hand side of the map. It was a labyrinth of some sort. The third piece of the riddle was smudged just a bit, but was still legible...

Eight is the count, including myself.
Five fathers and two sons of my own.

This one was shorter than the other two and Deltrin was not pleased to see there was still not much to work with. He stroked his hand through his sweaty hair and thought for a minute. The little dragon was still engulfed in the message. He looked up at Deltrin with a confused look. Deltrin looked back with a congenial countenance. He lowered his head at eye level with his little friend.

"I'm hungry. How 'bout you?"

The little creature did not move, confused at what he was just asked. Deltrin raised his hand and held out a finger.

"Wait here. I'll go get us something." The dragon stayed put and waited for him to return.

Momentarily, Deltrin was in the pantry, gathering a meaty meal for himself and his partner. He returned with several different types of meat and was amused at the happy expression that appeared on the dragon's face. He handed him several different meats, which all pleased the dragon.

"Well" he began. "I guess it won't be difficult to find food for the two of us."

Deltrin and his dragon finished the meal in minutes and were satisfied. He tapped on his shoulder, inviting the dragon to perch. The tiny dragon perched on his shoulder willingly and they both proceeded to the bedroom.

"Now we can go to sleep." As soon as Deltrin had lied down, the dragon left his shoulder and settled down on the bedpost.

"How do you like the name Violaze?" He asked.

The dragon smiled, but did not acknowledge the entitlement. Deltrin pointed to himself. "Deltrin." He said. He then pointed to the dragon. "Violaze." The dragon cocked his head, finally understanding and after considering the name for a few seconds, smiled and squeaked.

"It's a good name." He said. "My little haze of violet." He closed his eyes and began to sleep. Violaze watched Deltrin fall into his slumber. As soon as he was asleep, the tiny dragon hopped off of his resting place, nuzzled up against Deltrin's warm face, and slowly fell asleep...

Deltrin could feel his nostalgic dream begin to fade, but it wasn't its conclusion that woke him up. A familiar squeak emanated from a small weight on his chest. Deltrin opened his rested eyes and peered into Violaze's beautiful gaze. He was perched on his chest and smiling to see that his partner was finally awake.

"Where the heck have you been hiding?" Deltrin asked. "You missed the best part!"

Violaze pointed to a little cubbyhole in the corner of the ceiling that Deltrin had never seen before. There was a little blanket stuffed inside. Deltrin looked at the little creature.

"You were sleeping?! How could you have slept through that?"

Violaze blurted out a series of squeaks, answering him.

"Well I was tired, too. Oh wait." Deltrin paused for a second. "I forgot what happened to you on planet seven. Never mind."

Violaze gave him an indifferent look.

"Well, a lot has happened in the past couple of days. I found this casket with two books and got so involved in the reading, I haven't been thinking about anything else. Sorry. I would have looked for you, but I didn't know where you were. Well, that doesn't matter. What does matter is that we have one more task to fulfill. We need to deliver one of the manuscripts to a group of scientists. We should reach the destination in about twelve hours, so we have plenty of time to finish reading the other manuscript. Plus there seems to be some strange things happening. Before you woke up, I made a detour to a planet and found this huge battle going on. I met a few of the soldiers and from what I've deduced, this war is much larger than I thought."

Violaze was eagerly listening to the interesting story. After five years of traveling with his partner, he acquired an ability to understand what Deltrin was talking about. Deltrin acquired a similar talent, but he had a tougher time learning how to understand the dragon's form of communication, considering he couldn't speak legible words, just a few octaves of squeaks. It took time to learn, but it was eventually accomplished.

"We're going to have to watch out for the time being. We'll just take it easy for a few days, until we get rid of the manuscript. Then we'll figure out what to do. Is that alright?"

Violaze squeaked in compliance and in a flash, he swooped to the pantry and found something to eat. A five-day nap would leave anyone hungry. Deltrin laughed and walked over to his chair to continue his reading. He had to read back a few paragraphs to remember where he left off, but he was soon back on track...

The Beginning of the End

I suppose I proved to be a good artist with the first map I drew. That would explain why the others gave me the privilege of drawing the last map. I told them that I would do it, if they took care of the riddle itself. They agreed to the fair compromise and started with their task.

I thought another map would have been repetitive. An artist's conception of paradise seemed much more appropriate and since I felt we were in the greatest structure ever built, I decided to draw the temple itself.

It took time to consider how to draw the garden labyrinth around the temple. I couldn't tell if I wanted the labyrinth to overpower the temple or if I wanted the labyrinth to look as big as it really was. I eventually decided to use actual scale and drew an exact portrait of the temple and the labyrinth from the point of view that we had when we cleared the peak of the hill.

I put the finishing touches on my painting just about the same time the others finished the riddle. We traded creations to see how they turned out. I was very impressed with the riddle they made and from the reactions I received, it seemed I had done a good job as well.

Terinsa had the best handwriting out of all of us, so she took care of writing the riddle directly upon the parchment. The calligraphy enhanced the spirit of the riddle, as well as the map. It was beautiful. But, in an act of barbarity, we had to tear the painting into seven pieces. We knew it had to be done, but that didn't matter. Terinsa and I refused to have any part in the desecration and let Retnar and the Admiral do the job, who weren't enjoying it either by any means.

The map was ripped into seven pieces and the job was nearly done. Now all we had to do was distribute the pieces to the planets. Our tenure within the temple was up and it was time to say good-bye to paradise.

We had spent so much time together in this temple and had learned so much about one another. For a short time in my life, I felt safe, as if nothing could penetrate the protective aura of this palace. There was a universe inside these walls, where there were no threats, no type of killers that could take away our peace. Walking out the doors would mean I was no longer protected. For a moment, I was reluctant to exit the crystal cradle, thinking that if I were to stay here with my family, I would never have to worry about anything. But then, I remembered what the Rashouwe assassin had said about existence becoming boring and I realized I still had a war to fight and could not think about peace. Not even isolation could protect me anymore. My death, along with the death of every living creature had been anticipated and fated with the conclusion of our mission. I could not change the great plan. None of us could. We all knew this.

We packed up all our equipment and left the illuminated palace to enter the dark universe we created. Ironic, isn't it, how something that was once beautiful can turn black? I suppose beauty is in the eye of the beholder, but I could never see the glamour in death.

We climbed into Retnar's ship and took off to find the other ship that had been orbiting for quite some time. I looked back at the last sanctuary and held its beauty in my eyes.

How peaceful was the song the stars' rays played upon the crystal shards, yet how saddening. I closed my eyes and locked this ambivalent melody within the tomb of my memories, hoping it would never haunt me again. Yet, even now, I find myself listening to the enchanting music, losing myself in a past I wish I could feel once again.

Terinsa shared the moment with me, also staring at the crystal garden. I put my arm around her and squeezed her tight. She looked at me and asked me what I was thinking.

"I can't think of anything. I'm just lost in the view." At that moment, I realized I wasn't looking at the palace anymore, but I was still lost. I was looking in her eyes, finally knowing what she was thinking. I was thinking the same thing. I refused to tell her, though, for words would have ruined it. Instead, I kissed her for what seemed like an eternity, but lasted only for a second. She smiled and hugged me and then whispered into my ear, "me too." She unlocked her embrace and walked out of the room.

It was agreed that the Admiral and Terinsa would stay with us to finish the mission together. It was safer that way and we didn't want to be out of each other's sight. We took all the necessary equipment out of the Admiral's ship and placed it onboard Retnar's. We then sent the derelict on a slow, direct coarse for Eve, hoping that its return would confuse the traitors still there. When we were done with that, we began our journey to the first planet. That night, we got plenty of rest.

The two stars of the first planet came into view after a couple days of traveling. The two stars were on each side of the un-angled planet, which meant it was daytime all around the world. That was good; we had light to work with.

We took the first piece of the map and placed it into a metallic tube that would keep it safe from the wear and tear age would provide. We found a nice area to land on the island, right next to the highest mountain that our riddle spoke of.

We climbed out of the ship and felt the warm air surround us. The sea was crystal blue and was shining from the rays of the sun. All four of us climbed the mountain, rather quickly I might add, and laid the tube to rest. Terinsa looked at me and began to speak.

"You know, I'm not scared anymore."

"How do you mean?"

"Well, here we are planting the first root of a weapon that will both doom and save us. And yet, I'm not afraid of the outcome. To be honest, I'm rather happy to know that I'm not immortal. Being alive for almost two billion years has made me believe that it would never end, but now..." She chuckled. "I think I'm going to like the rest."

I never knew that she was scared in the first place. But who am I kidding? We were all scared. We just didn't want to admit it.

The other two began their hike down, but I wanted to stay and Terinsa decided to give me company. Together, we watched a sunrise and sunset in the same sky. It was quite beautiful. The center of the ceiling was an evening shade, surrounded by a circle of light. The entire horizon glowed with a purple and rose haze. Terinsa held my hand and shifted her weight to the leg closest to me. She placed her head on my shoulder and relaxed.

"I'm not scared because, no matter what, you'll always be with me."

I smiled but did not look down at her. I felt better just looking at the sky and feeling her warm body next to mine. I didn't need to see if she was still there.

"That was really mushy, Captain." I said jokingly. She turned around and whacked me on the side of my head. She laughed and told me it was the last time she'll ever try to be sentimental.

"But you're right. I'll never leave you."

Her smile lit up her entire face and before I could move, she pulled me in and kissed me passionately. It must have been a sight. A united being, atop the greatest mountain of the planet, in the midst of a sunrise and sunset. I wish that someone could have captured the moment. But I realize that some pictures, though beautiful they are, cannot convey the precise emotions through any means of expression.

It was time to get back to the transport, so we captured the radiance of the view for one last moment and started climbing down. The other two were on the foot of the mountain. When we came down, all they could do was smile at us and snicker a bit, but no words were spoken. We all climbed into the ship and made way for the second planet.

As soon as the course was set, we all found a place to sleep, for the climb wiped out all our energy. I didn't have the intention of falling asleep, though.

When I thought everyone was asleep, I quietly got up and crept down the hall into the cockpit to relax in the presence of the stars. I sank into the comfortable seat and placed my head back on the small cushion. I could have sworn the stars were playing music for me, but it did not matter. Their silence was just as peaceful as their singing.

I was thinking about everything and nothing and was lost in a trance from the hypnotic powers of the tiny bulbs in the distance. I had experienced so many adventures and had attached myself to so many beings, I couldn't tell if the pictures and memories I watched fly by in my mind were my own, or someone else's. My thoughts began to clear up and I could finally tell my own memories from the others. A small voice could be heard in the back of my head.

I didn't know who's it was at first, but as I listened more carefully, I could tell it was the voice of my mother. I saw her last when I was inducted to the universe project. I never knew when she died until I saw the Rashouwe destroy my family in the memory sleep. The project took my life and perhaps I was dead in her mind, since she knew she would never see me again, but I doubted that then and still do. Mother's don't forget their children. It's impossible.

I thought it was rather odd I was having flashbacks of my childhood. I heard it is a normal reaction for people to have when they are scared, or if they are about to die. I was not scared; I can admit that. However, the thought never occurred to me that I was dying. It wasn't the fact that my death was imminent due to the explosion, but rather, I could feel the deathless liquid begin to disappear from my bloodstream.

Time was finally catching up to me. I did not know how to accept this mortal sting that kept biting at my heart. Death never came knocking at my door. Instead, I simply ignored it, thinking that the magic within me would never stop. But now, I could hear the rapping it made and I knew my end was closer than anticipated. The thought of my demise gave my emotions a good twist and I didn't even realize that I had been crying in my nostalgic trance. But staring at those stars would forever quench my tears. I was at peace and if I could just look at the stars, I knew the end would never come, even though I would not live to see that truth fulfilled. Forever was the promise I gave to Terinsa and I would stay dear to my word, but what would happen to *me* when *her* forever came to its conclusion? I did not let the thought stay long in my head. I let it slip from my conscious and buried it into a small hole, hoping it would never emerge again. I was still in a trance, gazing into the realm of night, when I felt a gentle hand caress the back of my neck. I did not look back to see who it was. I didn't need to.

"They're beautiful, aren't they?" I asked her.

"Yes they are."

She came around to see my face and wondered why my eyes were clear as glass and why my face was glazed with shining streaks of emotion. She didn't bother to ask me why I was crying. She just sat in the chair next to me and stared at me. She did not speak for quite some time, but just looked into my soul. I remained focused on the stars.

"When I was a boy, I would climb up to the roof of my home and watch the stars rotate around the night sky. I didn't bother to keep track of their movement. I just watched them dance. It was a childhood fantasy of mine to dream of reaching the stars and I thought that if I could reach their ballroom floor, I could touch Heaven. I stuck with that dream throughout my entire childhood and it was not long until I made my first flight to the stars. At the time, I was thrilled to be in space, but the child in me was disappointed. There was no ballroom. No matter how far I went, I couldn't dance with the stars. Perhaps it was fate that I was chosen to take part in the project, because there, I could fulfill my dream. I held the stars in my hand and my own hand was their ballroom. Now, the stars have left my grasp and I am left here to dream of the time when I cradled the universe in my palm. My life is going backwards. Pretty soon, I'll do nothing more than climb on a roof, or a stone, or a mountain, and dream of reaching the dance-floor once again."

Terinsa was looking into the stars, just like myself, when I finished speaking. There was a moment of silent obligation, which concluded with her stepping into the pond of nostalgia

"When I was a little girl, my father used to take me out to a secluded area where I grew up. There was no light to pollute the night sky in our little grove. He would set up a telescope for us to look through, but I was never partial to it. I liked the distance. I never really wanted to get close to the stars. They were too magical. The closer I got, the lesser they became. My father died when I was very young, but I never stopped going to the grove to gaze at the stars. My innocence led me to believe that I could find my father if I looked closely enough, so I gave up my prejudice to the telescope and began my search. Little did I know I was developing a talent for astrophysics. Soon enough, I found myself graduating with honors in astronomy, and before I knew it, I was invited to take part in this project. I still don't know why I accepted. Perhaps it was because I had the chance to produce my own sky for other little girls to look at. Maybe I wanted to prove to myself that I could make my own distant stars. Maybe I just wanted to make my father proud. Now that the project is coming to an end, I cannot help but to look at the stars in the distance, instead of the stars up close. It's the presence of the unknown that makes me feel content."

I held out my hand and she placed hers around it, pulling it closer to her chest. Her time was running out as well, I could tell. That night, we stayed in the chairs, holding each other close with our memories, until we eventually fell asleep. We didn't need to dream. We were already in one.

I awoke after a few hours of peaceful slumber. Terinsa was still asleep and was still holding on to my hand. I released my hand from her grip and slowly got up to get closer to her. The serenity in her face was angelic. I tenderly caressed the soft skin on her cheek and brushed the golden strands of hair that tickled her eyelids. It hurts to still be able to see the radiant gleam of her features. I lie awake at night and dream of that haunting majesty. I knew that I would never forget how she looked at that moment, wondering what she was dreaming about that gave her such peace. Her eyes slowly opened and instantly she smiled at me. And then, she said something to me that, even now, brings a tear to my eye.

"I dreamt of you as a little boy."

After every one had woken up, we all had a tiny meal together and spent most of the time talking about our pasts. I was curious to hear about the Admiral's childhood, since I never really had the chance to get to know him. Now that I had the time, I took advantage of the opportunity.

"My childhood was rather brief." He began. "I grew up without a mother. She died at my birth. My father was a very good role model, teaching me self-reliance and how to survive. We lived in a secluded area, quite a ways away from any city. We lived off of the land and I can't think of any better way of growing up. I never received any formal instruction. What my father taught me was more than I needed. Soon enough, I was grown up. I looked for a job in one of the big cities, but I couldn't find a decent occupation available. I decided to join the military and put my survival skills to good use. In the many campaigns I fought, I proved to my superiors I was too valuable to be killed in the front line. They took me out of the battle and placed me in the presence of other intelligence officers. Eventually, I worked my way to becoming an Admiral. From studying all the planets in our system, I acquired a talent and love for the movement of the heavenly bodies, as well as their physics. As a result, I was chosen to lead this project because of my status and my knowledge. I must admit, I was pleased to get away from all the killing. It was nice to take part in the business of creating life, instead of destroying it. Now, I'm doing both at the same time and I can't tell which one is giving me more pleasure. As a boy, my father used to tell me there was no shame in killing anything as long as it was for a good cause. But what is a good cause? When I was fighting in the fleet, it never occurred to me that I might be fighting for the wrong side. The colonies we fought were no different from ours. It was just the fact they had a different way of living that seemed to threaten ours. There could have been an Admiral just like me, with the same morals, on the other side, and I would still have planned to take him down. Now, I'm doing the same thing, only I'm planning on wiping everything out."

"Well, sir..." Terinsa began.

"I know what we are doing is best." He interrupted before she could finish. "But that still doesn't help. I dream every night of the millions of potential life forms that won't have a chance to prove their worth. The only thing keeping me going is the knowledge that they wouldn't have a chance anyway with the Rashouwe parading around." He paused for a moment. "Don't get me wrong, I feel all right knowing that life will have a chance to thrive when our mission comes to an end, and if it's any consolation, for once, I know I am fighting for the right side with the right team. I can't think of a better cause to fight for, and I can't think of anyone better with whom I would choose to fight by my side. But I still don't feel good about us making straight what nature intended to make crooked."

The last line stuck into my heart. I knew exactly what he was talking about, but I had no way of making him think otherwise, because I felt the same way. We all did.

"I think it helps to know the creatures will come to understand our sacrifice." Terinsa began. "I have seen the torture that entire colonies have suffered from the Rashouwe. I don't want every being, every living organism to endure the same torture. I know in my heart that allowing a new era to come into existence is the best thing, and if it means making the grandest sacrifice, I will do it. I am sure every living creature who ever valued life will take part in it as well. We all have an instinctual desire to protect life in any way possible. We will risk our lives to see that life will continue, and what we are doing is a sure-fire way of making sure it will. I agree with you Admiral. I too have nightmares of the endless screams that will come from the wave of death, but I can't think of that. I look beyond the death and see the emergence of life. Ours is the most honorable cause no party has ever come close to taking part in. We are the chosen saviors, and we must make sure that life will continue, in any way we can. I know you are trying to look beyond the great toll of death, but it is difficult, I know. I still have trouble seeing that distant star, but I never stop looking for it."

The Green Orb

The second planet came into view after a couple days of traveling. Our spirits were as refreshed as the day we were born. I had forgotten about the diffusion of my youth within my bloodstream. Actually, that's not entirely true; I didn't forget. I just ignored it.

Retnar piloted his ship very nicely into the plant world and soon enough, our second trek was underway. The second tube was tucked underneath the Admiral's arm, as we all walked along the soft surface. The air was cool, which was strange because there were three stars in the sky. I would have thought the atmosphere would have been very warm.

I could feel the aroma of the flowers color my lungs with their sweet flavor. The gentle breeze was also something I missed from this place. It had been several million years since last I was here, but nothing changed. It was still breathtaking. Terinsa turned around to talk to me.

"Before we continue the journey, I would sure like to see this underground water system you told me about."

"Well, we're going to have to jump back into the ship and search for the hole I made." I looked to the others. "You guys mind if we go look for it?"

They both shook their heads, curious to see the cavern as well.

"Okay, let's get back into the boat."

We hopped in and began the search. Terinsa sat in

the chair next to Retnar. I stood next to him and navigated the hunt.

"I can't believe I left this place without looking harder." Terinsa said to herself out loud. "I really must have been eager to go somewhere else. At least someone else searched harder than I had."

I chuckled at her last statement and continued to show Retnar where to go. We finally came upon a large well in the ground and landed near it.

"Unless someone else dug a really big hole in the ground, I think we're there."

We all climbed out and walked towards the hole.

"If I remember right," I began, "We should be able to grab onto a large root and climb down."

It was not a difficult task and everyone agreed it was the best path to take. We all climbed down one by one and reached the floor of the cavern smoothly.

The river was still running as strong as when I left it. Terinsa took off her shoes and socks, and rolled up her pants. She then proceeded into the cool waters of the river and let its current massage her legs.

"If only I had known." She said, shaking her head. "I'm so glad you found this place, Tyran. It's absolutely beautiful." She waded through the thick foliage of roots that rained down from the ceiling and walked further down the river. After she had her fun in the river, she came out and dried herself off.

"How far do you think it travels?" She asked me.

"I'm pretty sure it circumnavigates the entire planet. I'm also pretty sure this is not the only river. To nurture all the life on this planet, there must be hundreds of river systems underground. I just don't think we should search for them, though. There is the possibility that other currents may be much more violent than this one."

She agreed and put her socks and shoes back on. We all climbed out of the cavern and reached the surface.

"Since we're on the surface now and have a long search ahead of us," Retnar began, "Why don't we just start the expedition from here, so we don't have to move the ship. The hole is a pretty good marker for us to find the ship when we're done."

"Great idea." The Admiral spoke up. On that note, we began the journey.

I walked along side Terinsa, while the Admiral and Retnar were close behind.

"Do you have any idea where the garden is?" I asked.

Terinsa shook her head. "Not exactly." She said, "But I do remember you can't see it from a distance. It's guarded by a ring of trees. I drew a pretty crude map of the area, but the exact coordinates are somewhat of a mystery."

"A ring of trees, huh? How convenient." I concluded. I turned around to speak to the others.

"We need to look for a ring of trees. The rose garden is hiding inside it."

They nodded in compliance and walked faster to catch up with us.

Even though we had a good idea on where the garden was located, our search still seemed endless. We finally found the garden covered by a few umbrella-like trees and made a nest for us to rest upon beneath their verdant wings.

"Do you think the trees will still be here when the traveler comes?" Retnar asked.

I paused a moment, considering the good point. Terinsa and the Admiral did the same.

"I'm sure that these particular trees will be long dead, but I'm sure that similar trees will grow here in the cycle. We have to put our trust into the risk we are taking."

"Oh, I know." Retnar said. "I was just wondering if we needed to hide the manuscript, just in case the trees spread their seeds elsewhere. The land will inevitably change, so why don't we just lay this in the grove and let the plants do the rest?"

Retnar made a valid point and none of us challenged his logic. I set the tube in the middle of the grove, partially covered it with leaves and left it there. We left the grove and walked back to the ship, with the joy of knowing that two were down and five were left. We were making incredible progress.

We found the trip to the third planet would take about a week to reach, so we made sure we got plenty of rest in the duration. We talked most of the time we were awake.

"My childhood was very brief, to say the least." Retnar began. "I did not have much time to enjoy the innocence early age brings. Being the heir to the leadership of a particular civilization leaves little room for playing around. When I was five, my training began. I was expected to attend all the diplomatic meetings my father went to so I could have the opportunity to see how things worked in politics. I hated it." He chuckled for a second. "But, I became partial to it after awhile. My father was a fair and just leader and I wanted to follow in his footsteps. During my formal education, I was taught mathematics, science, language skill, astrophysics, and the art of mind reading. Tyran has had the pleasure of witnessing the art, as well as doing it himself. Mind reading was my favorite class, because it was so unconventional compared to the other subjects. I was nine when I started learning how to do it. I should also add that only a select few had the opportunity to learn. We were chosen because of our high-ranking status, and our high intelligence. Talk about predicting how children will turn out. Anyway, since Terinsa and the Admiral do not know about the technical aspects of mind-reading, I will tell you a little about what I was taught." He paused, hunting for the right words to begin his explanation.

"Every action is made by the push of an electrical current. Movement, thought, words that are spoken; they are all performed by several billions of messages being passed along by means of electricity. And, like any form of electricity, the line of current can be diverted to another point. That is what mind reading is all about. By attracting the currents of other creature's brain waves to flow into our minds, we are essentially stealing thoughts. Once the flow is complete, we can read thoughts, memories, ideas, anything, just as if they were our own. It's really a useful trick to use if you want to know if someone is hiding something from you. I have never been in a war before, so I've never had the chance to try it out on an enemy, but considering how well it worked on the Rashouwe, I don't think any war against us would have lasted very long. We would have found out their orders before they had a chance to carry them out. To tell you the truth, I'm actually glad that I never wasted the energy on war. Mind reading was taught to us for diplomatic reasons, learning about other cultures, breaking language barriers and forming relationships between different planets. It was never used to take advantage of anything, but I must say, it sure was fun taking advantage of the Rashouwe." He smiled at his last comment, epidemically making us all smile.

"What I liked most about being able to read minds was the feeling of ease that I received every time I learned something new. I wasn't doing it to expand political relations. I was doing it so that *I* could expand. Meeting new intelligent beings made life seem less complicated. I felt closer to everything, as if the universe was not so big after all. I did, however, fear one thing."

"What was that?" I asked eagerly.

"That there were barriers. That I would eventually see everything there is to see. I thank the stars you came along to prove me wrong. Now, I know there aren't any barriers, and space really is infinite. I did not want to curse myself by getting what I wanted. I wanted to find all traces of life and to understand how they live, but then what? I would have had to find a new hobby, and being as old as I am, that would have been difficult." He hesitated for a second, and then looked up to face us all.

"I must thank you." He said. "I am very fortunate to be in the company of the greatest beings that could ever be found, or rather, who could have found me."

His speech was heart-felt, and we all didn't know how to accept the compliment. Random 'thank-yous' were all we could give in return for the gracious flattery.

The week went by very quickly and we reached the planet faster than we had expected. The deep blue glow of the water planet was enough to make anyone humble. I wished there was one island on that planet for us to place the map, but unfortunately, the entire world was covered with ocean. The moon, though, was nothing to sneer at. It was just as beautiful.

The planet's surface was not what I expected. It was almost dead, with barely any trace of growth of any sort. The air was smug and stuck to the insides of our lungs. I was confused, because the view I got of the planet's surface from outer space seemed very colorful. We must have landed in an area where there was no growth. Something was wrong, because the barren land stretched for a few miles in the distance.

"I thought you said the planet was beautiful." I asked the Admiral.

"It was." He responded. "This is highly irregular. There should be color all over the place. I don't remember seeing any desert area when I was here."

"How long ago was that, Admiral?" Terinsa asked.

"Not long enough for deserts to appear. This is not a natural phenomenon. Some outside force must have done this. I think it would be a good idea for us to find another planet."

The plan was a very wise, but we were unable to execute it, for right when we turned around, we found there was a small force of soldiers holding us up. To our extreme disappointment, they each had the emblem of the stabbed oval placed on their shoulder.

The Foe Turned Friend

One of the members came closer to the Admiral, who was holding the piece of the map.

"What's in the tube?" The Rashouwe venomously asked.

The Admiral thought that all was lost, and was reluctant to give up the game. However, there was no reason not to give away the secret, because they were going to kill us anyway and no one would be able to take over, so he finally opened the tiny casket, hoping for a miracle.

"Slowly!" Our captor loudly ordered. "This better not be a trick."

"No trick." The Admiral said. He revealed the small parchment resting in the cradle, and looked at the Rashouwe to see what he thought.

"What is it? Battleplans?"

"No." The Admiral mocked with sincere hatred. "It's a science project."

The Rashouwe peered into the Admiral's eyes, and then panned around to look at the rest of us, stopping at Retnar. I could see that Retnar's presence produced a change in the Rashouwe's temperament.

"You're a Troctie, aren't you?" He asked with less aggression.

Retnar turned around to look if he was asking anyone else. There wasn't a Troctie to be seen within a few billion miles, so I guess he must have been a little panicky about the situation. He pointed to himself and said, "Me?"

214

The Rashouwe shook his head, and produced a tiny smile. "Do you see anyone else who looks remotely like you?"

"No sir." Retnar responded. "How do you know that I'm a Troctie?"

I could see the wheels turning in the Rashouwe's head, working something out.

"Did you get the book? Did you get the *changed* book?" He asked with unexpected enthusiasm.

I couldn't believe our luck. I spoke up to confirm this apparent miracle.

"You're the resistance, aren't you?"

His impressed smile secured my theory. I can't remember any time I was happy to see a Rashouwe smile at me.

"You must be the other escapee." He said to me. "I'm glad to see the attack on the Phantom Hunter failed. Did you get any useful information?"

"We got some." I told him. "We found out where they are based and where they're headed. May I ask why you thought we were Rashouwe?"

"We didn't. We had to make sure. Your Troctie friend was what led me to believe you were not part of the Rashouwe faction."

"But still," I continued. "We're not wearing any regalia that even remotely resembles the oval and the saber."

"They have spies, my friend." He said, trying hard not to sound condescending. "A minute few of them will not wear their emblem while they are on mission."

"But some do, right?" I asked.

He nodded his head. That made me feel a little better. I had seen Rashouwe spies before, and all of them had worn their regalia. During the war, we used to tear them off their shoulders after we killed them and hung them up as trophies on the dashboard of our ship.

"So, what are you four doing on this planet?"

"We're completing the final stage of our mission." The

215

Admiral spoke up. "It will take a while to explain all the changes we made. Rest assured, you will hear about them, but I'll make a long story short, for now. We have made a map that points out the location of the blueprints for the universe equation. The map has been split into seven different pieces and we are distributing the pieces to different planets. We've done two. This planet is number three."

The leader of the group placed his hand over his brow in disbelief.

"You've got to be kidding." He spoke incredulously. "This planet has been under siege for quite sometime and each side has not made much progress. We know the Rashouwe has contacted other fleets to assist them, which should be here pretty soon. We have done the same, but our response is no where near as grand as the other side's."

"Sounds like we have no way of getting out of here and finding another planet to take this one's place." The Admiral pedantically stated.

"'Fraid not." He answered. "The only way out is by eliminating the Rashouwe force here."

"Pardon me for interrupting," Terinsa began, "But if I remember right, the Rashouwe don't quit on any planet until it is completely bereft of life."

"We've changed." He choked for a second. "I'm sorry, *they* have changed. If a planet is not worth taking and does not give them any tactical advantage, then they will leave it after awhile."

"Why are they fighting here in the first place then?" She persisted.

"Because we're here. A traitor is a much greater threat than any other enemy."

"How do they know you're here?"

"They have a tiny locator device at the base of their neck." Retnar explained, pointing to the back of his neck to illustrate.

216

"So the assassin told you that, did he?" The leader asked, curious and surprised. "He must have really counted on you getting killed. I guess they feel as content on killing you, as we are of saving you. Well, now we have something they really want. We're going to need to protect you guys with everything we can. Believe me, the fleet is going to land a million more angry killers on this planet in a few hours. When they find out that you are here along with us, they're going to march all over us with everything they've got. We'll have to keep you a secret."

"Can't you just turn the silly thing off?" Terinsa kept on.

"They only turn off when we're dead, and only then."

"Is there any way we can scare them off?" the Admiral asked, changing the subject.

"You mean like a huge victory or some doomsday tool? It would take a devastating weapon to deal such intimidation. In answer, yes, they would leave us alone if they found the death toll would be too great to risk. Do you know of such a weapon?"

The Admiral turned to face Retnar, who understood completely where the Admiral was going with his plan.

"We all do." The Admiral confessed. "All we need is a radio to contact one of our allies. Can you take us to your outpost?"

"Yeah. It's a couple miles towards the mountain over there."

He pointed towards the only mountain in view.

"We have a satellite up-link at the foothill. We'll take you there."

I walked along side the leader of the group, who surprisingly knew quite a bit about the universe experiment.

"So tell me." He began. "What happened to the original project plan? I was led to believe that it was the manuscript that was going to be split into seven pieces."

"It started out that way." I responded. "But as soon as Octan, was murdered, the whole plan changed."

"Now Octan. He was the one who changed the manuscript, right."

I nodded, finding it rather amusing the mystery we solved was hardly a mystery at all.

"That's right. I must say, it took us a while to figure out what was going on."

The leader glanced over at me, smiling as if he were happy to see that someone had figured them out.

"What gave us away?" He asked.

"Well, Octan wouldn't have changed the manuscript if someone hadn't warned him about the Rashouwe plan. I have fought against the Rashouwe before, and if there is one thing I have learned from my experiences, it's almost impossible to capture forbidden knowledge and live to tell about it. I figured the only ones who could live to tell about the Rashouwe plan would be the Rashouwe themselves. And since they didn't want the manuscript to be changed in the first place, the only explanation would be that there was a resistance, who lived to tell the secret."

"But the Rashouwe could have changed it, as well. How do you know they didn't change it for their own purpose?" He continued.

"Two reasons. First, they would not blow themselves up. The untainted manuscript allowed them to have another playground for them to do their killing. The changed manuscript would not give them this, so they had no reason to change it. Secondly, they wouldn't know what to change. It would be like trying to translate gibberish."

"I must say, you've really done your homework."

"I know my enemy. It's as simple as that. Long ago, I fought with your race and learned much about your actions. I didn't think we would make it, but we achieved victory in the end. I wish you could have been there to see it."

He chuckled and produced a privy smile. I asked him why he was laughing. I didn't find anything funny about it.

"I *was* there." He said.

"You were there?" I repeated, shocked at the revelation. "How is that possible?"

"You weren't the only ones who were injected with the youth potion."

This was very bad news.

"Oh god. How many of you took it?"

"All of us."

"Including the Rashouwe faction?"

He nodded ominously.

This is not what I was hoping to hear. If what he said was true, we were facing an entire army of immortals. Things were turning ugly.

"I'm beginning to feel the potion wearing off. Can you feel yours?" I asked.

"I can tell it is going away, but compared to what was being passed around, I received a very tiny share of the medicine."

He stared into my eyes with empathy. "It would seem you have all the more reason to eliminate them, wouldn't you say?"

I nodded, not believing how bad the situation had just become.

"To change the subject, which I'm sure you would like me to do." He began. "What is this weapon you speak of?"

"Retnar is our expert."

I turned around to get Retnar's attention. He came up and asked me what I needed.

"Why don't you tell our friend about our weapon."

He smiled and faced the Commander.

"Tell me, Commander. Have you ever heard of a stone called Amphiltrite?"

"Not that I can recall." He said nonchalantly.

219

"It's a rare blue stone that forms in subterranean levels, next to an underground water source. Its chemical build-up is somewhat unstable, but the outer shell of the stone is too strong for anything to disturb the electron ring of the rock's atoms. Except one thing. Have you heard of Tekteron?"

"Now that I've heard of. That's a special liquid only found on a few planets in this universe. I've never seen it myself, but I have heard that it was used as a weapon, but I never found out how."

"Well, the Tekteron is the catalyst to the Amphiltrite's explosion."

Retnar continued to explain how the bomb works. The Commander seemed anxious to try out this awesome method of destruction, once Retnar gave him the explanation.

"Sounds like my kind of weapon." He enthusiastically stated. "Problem is, do you know anyone who can find the ingredients in time?"

Retnar gave him a grin that matched the Commander's enthusiasm.

"I know just the people."

The base was dug deep into the forest area near the base of the mountain. There were a few hundred soldiers being handled by medics, while the others were getting ready to go to battle somewhere else. A stout General strolled out of the main tent and peered at us with curiosity. He turned to the Commander and asked who we were, with extreme contentment.

He too, was wearing a Rashouwe emblem. He obviously knew which side to fight for, but he sure didn't give up the Rashouwe personality.

"These are the scientists of the universe project. They are our friends." The Commander stated.

The General slowly twisted his head to get a good look at us. He pointed his fat finger in our direction and

220

sneered.

"These are scientists? They don't look anything like scientists."

I still wonder what a scientist is supposed to look like. I never got the impression that we inherited a look along with the occupation.

"I assure you, general." The Commander said. "They are who they claim to be. They know about the tainted manuscript."

"Lots of beings know about the manuscript!" The General shouted. "I want real proof. I don't trust these characters." He began to walk back, when something held him back.

"General Telkord." Terinsa exclaimed, taking the general off guard. "Trust your Commander's judgment. He knows us, we know him, and I know who you are. Don't be foolish, again."

The smarmy general slithered towards Terinsa and looked into her cryptic eyes.

"I will not be insulted by a scientist, let alone a female." He turned to walk back to his quarters, but didn't get very far. Terinsa grabbed his long hair and pulled him back. She swung her arm around to knock the general to his knees and sank her eyes into his fearful countenance. Her voice was quiet, but her intentions were something of a completely different nature.

"I don't care whose side you're fighting on, I'll take you down and end your life right here. Normally, I wouldn't think about killing anyone, but considering what I've been through, killing you might be therapeutic. We don't have time to question each other's loyalty. We are fighting for the same cause. When the Commander told you to believe us, you should have done as he suggested. I am giving you another chance to redeem your unspeakable rudeness."

The General was released from her grip and stood up rather clumsily, coughing sporadically. I don't think anyone alive would consider incurring Terinsa's wrath for a second time. The General was no exception.

"Alright." He said with a scratchy voice. "I shouldn't have lost my temper. Losing is not one of my pleasures, which is what I foresee happening to us. I have fought with the Rashouwe and know how powerful they are. I apologize for taking my anger and frustration out on you."

"Thank you." Terinsa said. "You should put more trust into your men."

He turned his glare towards his Commander and nodded, losing some of his ugly personality.

"And don't worry." Terinsa concluded. "The Rashouwe aren't going to win. I assure you of that. We'll discuss it in your quarters, while my friends contact our allies."

He didn't question her orders. Without hesitation, he led us into the control room.

She explained everything to him, right down to the details of the map. I could tell they were becoming better acquainted. Terinsa was good at doing that; beating the hell out of someone and becoming their friend all within an hour.

Retnar was the one working the communicator. After a couple of failed attempts, he was able to make contact with the desired party. He spoke a language that neither the Admiral nor I could understand, but I soon recognized the familiar dialogue and realized he was talking to his own civilization. After conversing with his old friends, he put the communicator down and produced a great smile on his face.

"They know exactly where to look and they will have the bomb ready within the hour."

"That quick?" I asked incredulously.

"Yep. I forgot to tell you that we have our own supply of the ingredients, just in case."

"In case of what? The entire universe declaring war against your planet?"

"Well," He snickered. "We do like to keep ourselves protected."

I couldn't believe it. I couldn't help but to laugh at the stupidity of it all.

"Forgot to tell me. How the hell long were you going to wait before you *were* going to tell us."

"You never asked. I didn't see any reason to mention it. We never needed it until now."

It wasn't worth the effort to comment on that last statement. I just let it go, as did the Admiral. I twisted in my chair to face the General, who was finished listening to Terinsa.

"How long before the Rashouwe reinforcements get here?" He thought for a moment and answered, "About three hours, if our calculations are correct."

"That gives us plenty of time for the bomb to get here. My friends should be here in about two."

"All right." The Admiral asserted. "We need to plan an attack that will wipe out all Rashouwe forces on this planet. This planet needs to be evacuated as soon as possible for us to complete our mission."

I never thought I would see the day I would be working with the Rashouwe. It was awkward at first, but working with the Commander was a privilege and I came to enjoy my time spent with him. He was a great tactician, and a good soldier.

The estimated manpower fighting on our side was less than a million foot soldiers, three thousand heavy mobile vehicles and five bomber/strafing squadrons with twelve ships in each. Our enemy had about three million foot soldiers, ten thousand mobile artillery, but no squadrons. As soon as their reinforcements surfaced and joined their friends, their count would double. Our only hope was to decimate their count with the Amphiltrite explosion, distracting the ground forces already here, which would give us the window of opportunity we needed. We couldn't detonate any Amphiltrite on the surface, because we would take out our own soldiers, as well as theirs. We would have to plan a quick and effective campaign to take advantage of the Rashouwe already on the planet. I had never planned a battle before, and I must say it was rather exciting, even though the Commander did most of it.

"I must admit." I said. "The plan should work." I took my eyes off of the map and looked at my new friend. "It has been a pleasure working by your side." I extended my hand, which he shook almost immediately.

"The pleasure's all mine."

"Tyran is my name, since we never formally introduced ourselves."

He smiled at our mistake.

"My name is Rinar. Again, it's a pleasure."

"Well, Rinar. Why don't we get ready and give our enemy reason to tremble."

His grin made the excitement even grander. He took the map and walked over to where the Admiral and the General were working.

"What have you got for us, Commander?"

"Well, General, I think Captain Tyran and I have come up with a plan that should work."

Rinar laid the battle plan out and explained every detail to the two superior officers.

"We have not been attacked yet, because we have the same battle tactics that the Rashouwe themselves have. We think alike and act alike. That is why they have alerted another fleet to make sure they have another million soldiers, setting the odds even more in their favor. Their plan is to eliminate our forces with as much power as they can get. If they had tried to execute a major campaign now, they would have lost just as many soldiers as we would. Now, they are going to launch a major attack, but it's not going

224

to happen until they get confirmation of the fleet's arrival. That is when our plan takes action. Tyran has informed me the Amphiltrite bomb will be here within the hour. That is about half an hour before the Rashouwe fleet gets here."

The Admiral quickly interrupted. "One hour?!"

He looked over at me, remembering Retnar had told him that the mixture was very rare and hard to find.

"I'll tell you later." I told him, allowing Rinar to finish.

"When the Rashouwe army on the surface begins to move, that means their fleet has informed them of their presence."

Rinar flattened the map out on the table and pointed to a specific area on the map.

"This is where the Rashouwe are based at the moment."

He moved his finger west of their base.

"This valley here is guarded by a wall of trees and is the best and most feasible place for their reinforcements to arrive."

"Are you sure?" The Admiral asked. "

"We would've picked it."

The Admiral turned to look at the General who was nodding in agreement. Rinar continued with the mission.

"The Rashouwe forces will meet the reinforcements in this area. From there, they will stage the first wave of their attack. Before they get there, we will place a ground force of one-hundred thousand soldiers with one-thousand attack mobiles here." He pointed on the map. "We will place two other regiments of equal force here and here. The remaining force with our squadrons will be their back-up in case of an over-sight, but that is highly unlikely. We should suffer minimal losses, if all goes well."

"Why will the soldiers be posted there, Commander?" The General asked.

"Have you ever seen how a creature will build a lair and then set a trap for its prey? Kind of like how some spiders will tunnel a lair into the sand and then make the walls of the funnel they created very slippery so that when a tiny

225

insect tries to pass over the lair, they get stuck and can't get out. Eventually, they fall into the mouth of the funnel, which is actually the mouth of the spider."

"Yes Commander, I have seen that before."

"Well, we're doing something similar, only it's upside-down. We're going to trap our prey into an inescapable terrain and surround them from above the funnel. They won't have a chance to get out. It'll be like shooting fish in a barrel."

"Excellent plan you two." The Admiral said, speaking for the General as well. "But I still have one question. What happens to the Rashouwe reinforcements?"

"Once the fleet has broken though the planet's atmosphere," I began, taking over for Rinar. "Retnar's friends will launch the Amphiltrite bomb towards the fleet. The fleet will not expect this and neither will the ground forces, who will be waiting for their allies in the landing zone. The bomb will take out all the ships in the fleet, causing the ground forces to panic. They will try to retreat back to their base, but our forces will trap them in the valley and wipe them out. Once this is complete, all of us can leave this place without any threats. The map will be safe and our mission, as well as theirs can continue on course. Now, we know that the explosion does not work in a vacuum." I emphasized, reminding the Admiral. "However, the blast will take place right below the outermost layer of the atmosphere. It will be too high to affect any of the ground troops."

"Well." The General said, excited to wipe something out. "Let's saddle up. Commander: wire to all the regiments and tell them the plan. Captain; I want you to inform the squadrons about their part in this battle. I want everyone ready to fight within thirty minutes. Commander? How long do we have before the Rashouwe get here?"

"In an hour and a half, sir."

"We haven't much time. Execute your orders as soon as

possible, Commander."

"Yes sir."

We got on the communicator to inform everyone about the plan, telling them to be ready to move immediately. The response we received was more than enthusiastic. Every Sergeant and Major sounded like they wanted to sack the Rashouwe all by themselves. They told us they would be ready to roll in fifteen minutes. Rinar and I were surprised at the predicted brevity of the preparation, but we didn't argue. We knew how excited they were and there's no greater driving force than a desire to win.

"Regiments will be ready in a quarter hour, General." Rinar stated loud and clear.

"Good. The Admiral and I will prepare for battle. You better go tell your friends to do the same, Captain."

I chuckled at his comment. "I'm sure they're all ready fighting the Rashouwe themselves."

The General smiled with charge. The Admiral did the same.

"Dismissed." He said, and we were out of the room in a flash to get ourselves ready.

We found Retnar and Terinsa together talking. They were both armed with two small infantry rifles attached to each hip. Terinsa had a large plasma gun wrapped around her shoulder. Retnar had a similar, but smaller weapon strapped to him.

"Good God, we do have others to help us out, you know." I said to Terinsa.

She turned around, not amused by my comment.

"You know that I have never fought in the infantry before, Tyran. I have no idea what I may need during battle. When I was a spy, all I needed was a small firearm, which I only used once. This is completely different."

She got off from the bench and walked towards me. She grabbed the cleft of my chin and looked into my eyes.

"You'd better do the same. I don't want to have to save

227

you when you've run out of ammo."

She winked. Rinar pulled me away from her and led me to the weapons shed.

"Come on. You'll have plenty of time for flirting when the day is ours."

By the time we were all armed and ready to go, I came to the decision that Retnar's friends didn't need to launch any bomb, at all. With our combined weaponry we had in our possession, they could have strapped the four of us to a trajectory and fired us at the fleet, doing more damage to their hauls than the Amphiltrite.

"Terinsa and I will ride in one mobile artillery. You two will ride in another right by our side." I ordered. "The Admiral and the General will be close by in their own armored vehicle. All of us will be coordinating the attack behind the lines for the primary stages of the battle, but when the Rashouwe are being mowed down, we join in and finish them off."

I turned to Retnar. "How long before the delivery?"

"We have fifteen minutes before they get here. The Rashouwe are an hour away."

"Good. Commander; Lets have the three regiments start out and secure themselves in their positions. The Rashouwe forces will detect them, but they won't attack until they know they have the upper hand. They'll think we'll be walking right into their trap."

The Commander informed the regiments to move out. Like an earthquake, the rumble of their engines shook the earth below us. The dust kicked up from the ground, nearly blinding our view, but we wanted to make their entrance be noticed. It would help create the false confidence of the Rashouwe. Terinsa and I hopped into our vehicle, as did Rinar and Retnar. The Admiral and the General strolled out of the control center and secured themselves into the belly of their transport.

"Everything ready?" The General asked over the COM.

"Already underway, General." Rinar responded.

"Well, let's not keep them waiting. Over and out."

Rinar looked over to Terinsa and me and gave us a nod.

"Ready Captain?" A clear and exuberant voice asked me.

"I've been ready for about as long as you've been alive, my young friend."

"Whatever Gramps." He replied. "I'll see you on the field. Out."

I looked over at Terinsa, who was chuckling at the comment.

"Well, darling? Have you missed this enough to do it again?"

She looked at me with a cynical look, but I could tell she found the irony as amusing as I did. "More than ever, old timer." She mocked.

I didn't give her the satisfaction of a witty comeback.

"Just get us out of here." I replied, over her snickering.

The Mistake

Violaze was perched on Deltrin's right shoulder, reading along. Unfortunately, reading a blank piece of paper would have been as good a read for him as the manuscript.

"You probably want to get out and stretch your wings, don't you?" Deltrin asked his little friend.

Violaze averted his eyes from the book and concentrated on what his partner asked. He chirped emphatically in agreement.

"Well, let's go see what's in the vicinity. We are in a rush, but I suppose we could make a pit stop for an hour or so."

Violaze chirped happily and flew down to the pilot room. Deltrin followed and sat in his chair. He searched in his computer for the closest planet they could take a break on.

"This place might be just what we're looking for. It's on the way, and we should be there in less than an hour. There are life-forms on the planet, so we may be able to stock up on food."

Violaze was pleased to hear he was going to finally get out of the stuffy ship and get some fresh air into his lungs. He was so excited, he almost flew out of the ship before it even landed on the luscious planet. As soon as Deltrin opened the hatch, Violaze soared out of the ship like a bolt of lightning. He spun around, did flips in the air, enjoying the purity of the atmosphere. While Violaze was wildly expressing his happiness, Deltrin looked over the surroundings, hoping that he would not run into any soldiers on this planet. The fresh air and undamaged ground made him feel secure.

Deltrin went on a little expedition to check the planet out, with Violaze gliding right above him. There were many different animals frolicking about the land, unaware of the two strangers present. Deltrin took advantage of the situation and hunted a couple of the larger creatures. He got enough meat to last them the rest of the journey, with a few days left over.

Violaze strayed off a little ways beyond Deltrin, curious to see what else could be found. Deltrin didn't worry about him, considering that there didn't seem to be any threat.

After a few minutes of being alone, Deltrin was suddenly met by his dragon, who was flying so fast, he didn't even notice Deltrin in his way. Violaze turned his head to see where he was flying, but did not have enough time to slow down, and collided into his partner's face.

The blow knocked Deltrin on his back, as well as gave him a fat lip. "What are you doing, buddy?" He asked with haste.

The squeaks were so sporadic, Deltrin barely understood what he was trying to communicate. Something was wrong, that was obvious. But what? "Take me to what you saw."

Violaze hid himself behind Deltrin's neck, and simply extended a trembling arm pointing directly ahead. A couple miles in the distance, Deltrin found what scared the life out of his partner. It was a war, but not a war of equal power. One of the sides was being beaten to a pulp.

Deltrin pulled out his binoculars to get a closer look. The army that was being torn to shreds was unidentifiable, but the other army was easily recognized by their familiar emblem.

"We need to get out of here." Deltrin told Violaze, who had managed to stuff himself into Deltrin's vest.

Deltrin cradled his friend and began to run as fast as he could, but as soon as he got to his ship, he could hear voices inside. Thoughts ran as fast as they could in his mind, but he couldn't do anything, because in seconds he was seen by a Rashouwe, and was instantly taken hostage.

"So good of you to join us." The Rashouwe spoke. "We were hoping you would show up to translate the manuscript for us."

His evil stare peered through Deltrin, almost focusing on a point behind him.

He pushed Deltrin into the ship harshly. Another shove and Deltrin fell to the floor, smashing his face against the metal grill. He whispered to Violaze to find a hiding place when the Rashouwe wasn't looking. While he was on the floor, Violaze managed to crawl out undetected and found a suitable place to hide. Deltrin knew that if the Rashouwe knew about Violaze, they would have used him for target practice.

"Get up!" The Rashouwe ordered, kicking him in the chest.

Deltrin managed to pick himself up, holding his ribs with pain.

"Two choices: Translation or mutilation."

"I'm afraid I cannot pick the sane choice for your ultimatum." Deltrin whispered. "I don't know what the manuscript says, but I do know someone who does."

The extermination unit smashed Deltrin's face

232

with the butt of his gun, making him crash to the floor. The impact made him spit out the blood that filled his mouth, but he was out before he made contact with the floor. The Rashouwe turned to look at the other soldier.

"Send his ship up to the orbiter along with the manuscript. We'll meet you up there as soon as we've had our fun with him."

"Don't mess him up too much. We need him to talk." He responded back.

A malicious grin spread on the Rashouwe's face.

"Oh, he'll talk. But that's all he'll be able to do." He spoke wryly.

He picked up the comatose Deltrin by the arms and dragged him to his transport, while the other Rashouwe rocketed the ship up to the orbiter.

Deltrin awoke silently, during the trip to the Rashouwe base. As he opened his eyes, the coagulated blood on the side of his face cracked and fell in pieces. He made sure the lone driver didn't hear him wake up.

He panned his eyes around to examine his surroundings. Only an empty artillery shell rolling up and down the seat next to him was his only asset.

He felt a metal ring around his right wrist, along with another ring around his left. The cuffs were rather primitive, and Deltrin knew exactly how to free himself. He twisted his fingers and found the latch that held the trap together. Swiftly, he freed himself.

The Rashouwe must have felt he gave a stronger blow to Deltrin. Otherwise, he wouldn't have made such a poor choice in securing the prisoner. Deltrin looked to see if he had aroused the attention of his captor. Fortunately, the Rashouwe heard nothing.

He slowly and quietly crept his left arm from underneath his body to take a hold of the empty shell.

The noise he made was heard by the Rashouwe, who turned around to see if everything was all right. Deltrin's arm was set a little ways away from his body, but the Rashouwe thought that the bumpy ride was to blame. Luckily, he also didn't notice the cuffs were no longer around Deltrin's wrists. He must have been in a hurry. He turned back to the path and ignored the apparently comatose prisoner. Deltrin sighed as quietly as he could and continued to find the shell.

Eventually, he was able to clutch the tube in his hand. He put all his force into his swing and slammed the empty shell into the side of the Rashouwe's head. In reflex, the Rashouwe slammed on the brakes and recklessly swerved the vehicle left and right. Deltrin hopped into the front seat, and took another swing at his prey. He connected the shell to the right temple of the Rashouwe, knocking the villain out cold. Deltrin pushed him out of the vehicle and stopped the moving transport completely. He hopped out of the transport, with his weapon still clenched in his left hand. He hovered over the torpid pile of flesh, still quivering from nerve damage.

Deltrin proceeded to undress the Rashouwe, down to his undergarments. Deltrin then took his clothes and swapped uniforms. Soon enough, Deltrin was a Rashouwe officer, and his prisoner was nothing more than a drifter. He carried the Rashouwe back into the vehicle and threw him into the back. He didn't have to worry about his hostage making any trouble. He was killed instantly by Deltrin's second and final blow.

Deltrin drove the vehicle to the Rashouwe base. The war was over by the time he got to the battlefield. The green field that once was had been coated with blood and littered with an endless count of bodies. The stench would have knocked out Deltrin, but he lost his sense of smell when the Rashouwe broke his nose.

He drove into the compound and parked the vehicle next to the main tent. He looked around, getting a feel of what it was like to be in a Rashouwe camp.

There were thousands of soldiers wounded, hobbling from the battlefield to get to the medic. Unfortunately for them, Deltrin couldn't locate any medical tent. The Rashouwe didn't want wounded. They left them behind if they couldn't keep up.

The machinery was awesome and frightening. Blood was splattered on most of the walkers, but the heavy artillery looked brand new. They must have not used them. Correction, they didn't *need* to use them.

The organization of the camp was astounding. All the vehicles were positioned as if they were ready to go back into battle. The buildings were hidden in the forest area, like weeds in a garden. Deltrin tried to locate a vacant ship, but couldn't find any around. Suddenly, he heard a grunt from behind. He turned around to see who the annoyance was. It was a soldier of lesser rank.

"Is that the prisoner, sir?" He asked pointing at the beaten corpse in the vehicle.

Deltrin nodded and ordered him not to touch him. He complied and walked off into the dark mist of the Rashouwe camp. Deltrin still could not locate any ship, so his plan was raised to another level. He swallowed a huge breath, and walked into the main tent.

"I need a ship." He blurted out into the stale air in the tent. A general slowly lifted his head to see who it was that dared ordered him.

"Since you have something we need, I'll let you live. But next time you come in here ordering me around, I'll plunge my fist so far into your chest, I'll rip your skeleton out and hang it on my wall, along with the rest of my trophies."

Deltrin stayed silent, feeling his heart pound so fast, he could barely hear anything. The general got up and walked toward him.

"There's a ship in back of this tent. It's mine. If it's so much as scratched when you get back, I'll beat you so hard that you'll be begging me to carry out my earlier threat."

Deltrin held his breath and walked out of the tent. The general told him to stop, and he feared the worst. Deltrin whipped his head around to see what the filth was about to tell him.

"Did you crush him?" He asked without emotion.

Deltrin managed to stretch a smile across his thankful face. "Like a pulp, sir."

The general smeared a diabolical grin and waved him off.

Luckily for Deltrin, the officer he was impersonating was obviously not a well known officer. He thanked the stars for his good fortune and raced to the ship. He carried the corpse out of the vehicles and climbed into the metallic beast and accustomed himself to the controls. There were many more controls in this ship, than in his own, but all he needed was a steering wheel and an on/off switch. He succeeded in lifting off and set a course for the orbital.

His ship had not docked with the main ship that was orbiting the planet, yet. This was good for Deltrin. He made contact with the other Rashouwe, who was piloting his own ship.

"Is anyone there?" he called into the COM.

The Rashouwe picked up. "This is Lextous. Is that you lieutenant?"

"Obviously, you half-wit, who else would it be?"

"Sorry, sir. But you sound different."

Deltrin forgot about one tiny detail. He thought of an explanation as quick as he could.

"Our friend gave me a little trouble, but I convinced him to quit. He managed to hit me in the throat."

"Sorry to hear, sir. Do you want me to dock with you and ditch this ship?"

It sounded like a good idea.

"Yes. Bring the manuscript with you. I'll get closer to you. Out."

Deltrin hovered right next to his ship and docked. He then walked to the door with a plasma rifle in his hand. The door opened and the Rashouwe was on the other side. He wasn't looking up.

"I have the manus..." He looked up with a confounded countenance, as Deltrin pointed the weapon at his head.

"What?" Deltrin asked. "Aren't you happy to see me?"

He waved his free hand, asking for the manuscript.

"Give that to me." He ordered. The Rashouwe's trembling arm extended, revealing the manuscript. He placed it in Deltrin's hand.

"Now get into this ship." The Rashouwe didn't hesitate, and quickly moved into the other ship, while Deltrin moved into his own. Deltrin raised the gun back up to the eye level of the Rashouwe and callously pulled the trigger.

The bolt of plasma ran through the Rashouwe's eyes and exploded within his skull. The lights in his eyes faded as the stream of plasma scorched every cell in his skull. The Rashouwe's graceless body collapsed backward onto the metal floor and crashed onto the grid. A stream of blood trickled from out of his nose and ears, but no exit wound was made. Deltrin looked at his mystery weapon with glee, and thought to himself how much he liked his new toy. He then stared down at the body and the pool of blood that was accumulating.

"I didn't want to dirty up my ship, anyway." Deltrin said. "Violaze?" He called. "Where are you?"

A little ruffle could be heard and a terrified dragon emerged from underneath the bed. He was beyond ecstatic to see that his partner was alive, and that they were out of danger. He flew onto Deltrin's shoulder and hugged Deltrin's face with his tiny arms.

"You're going to want to see this."

Deltrin got back on the general's ship and sat into the pilot seat. The weapon's terminal was relatively simple to operate. All you had to do was point and shoot. He armed the ship with the heaviest artillery and opened fire on the main ship, tearing the unsuspecting orbiter to shreds. Billions of pieces of metal sprayed in all directions. The largest piece of metal that could be found in the wreckage was about a meter in length. Everything was destroyed. Deltrin laughed maliciously at his triumph. Violaze displayed the same response.

"All right." He began, "Let's clean this place out."

It took only a few minutes for Deltrin to take all the valuable equipment out of the general's ship and put it in his own ship. When he finished he thought to himself about what to do next. Just then, a faint transmission could be heard over the communicator. Deltrin picked up the instrument and slyly responded.

"Yes?'

"What is going on up there?" The furious general asked.

"Oh, the prisoner got out of hand and I had no choice but to blow the ship up. You don't mind do you?"

"Don't mind? You mindless waste of flesh. I'm going to

tear you apart when you get back down here!"

While Deltrin was listening to the furious babble the General was spurting, he wondered what he could do to really make him angry.

The coup de grace was finally worked out in Deltrin's unforgiving mind. He noticed the strange monitor on the dashboard that flashed several different numbers. The numbers accompanied hundreds of thousands of moving dots. Deltrin remembered the monitor that Rinar explained to Tyran in the manuscript. The dots were spread over a huge map that resembled the planet's landscape. Deltrin found the area where the base was located, and instantly knew what to do.

The explosion that the ship would make on impact with the surface would not only be enough to wipe out their communications, but it would also take out most of the army and the fleet. Deltrin set a course directly for the main camp.

"Are you still there, you idiot?" the general snapped over the intercom.

"I'm sorry." Deltrin answered. "But I'm going to have to scratch your ship."

He pulled the communicator out of the wall to save his ears from the annoying whining. He then timed the ship to blast towards the surface within a minute. He told Violaze to race for the other ship, as he raced as well. He shut the door and detached the general's ship. He pulled away and watched the doomed vessel turn towards the planet. Within seconds, it rocketed towards the base.

The explosion could actually be seen from where Deltrin and Violaze were watching. There was no way that anything could have survived. With the size of the ship along with the amount of weaponry in and on it, the explosion must have been the size of large city. Deltrin turned his head to talk to his partner who was perched on his shoulder.

"I hope you don't need to stretch your wings again."

He squeaked, giving a response to the pedantic statement.

Deltrin walked to his room to see if the book had been moved. Luckily, it had not been seen. Only the manuscript had been in danger, but it was not anymore. He didn't worry about them tainting the manuscript either. They would have killed him immediately if that was their mission.

"I don't know about you." He began talking to Violaze, who was sitting in his favorite chair. "But I'm beat. I need to tend my wounds first, but afterwards, I'm going to crash for a while. He walked down to the cockpit and set the course for the scientists once again and walked back to his washroom.

Everything seemed all right except for his nose. A field dressing would be all that he could do, because he didn't have the right instruments to do the job correctly. He walked into the kitchen and gathered a bottle of alcohol. He walked back into the washroom, took a generous drink from the bottle, placed his hands over his nose and broke it back into place. Luckily, he could barely feel it, because his face was numb. He cleaned the blood off of his face and cleaned his mouth out. He bandaged his reset nose with gauze and walked back into his bedroom. Violaze had already fallen asleep in the chair. Deltrin smiled at the picture and then walked to his bed and crashed upon the mattress. He slept for several hours and dreamed of success. Nothing particular, just the pure feeling of succeeding.

The headache that arrived when he awoke was nothing to envy. He could still feel the butt of the gun crushing his nose. The gauze had stayed on through his nap, but it was bloody and needed to be changed.

He walked to the washroom and bent over the sink. He took a look into the mirror and shuddered at the image he saw. He turned on the faucet and took a cloth that was draped over the side and washed off the coagulated blood from his upper lip and took a new bandage from the cabinet. He pulled the old one from his nose ever so gently, feeling every particle of the tape try to stick to his skin. The agony of the pulling sensation added on to the broken cartilage unsettled Deltrin's stomach, causing him to sit down after every inch of the bandage he drew.

Eventually, the bandage was completely off and the new bandage was in its place. Deltrin stumbled out of the washroom and sat down in his chair. His vision was slowly returning to its normal accuracy, but objects in the distance were still a little blurry.

Deltrin got up from his chair after sitting for about fifteen minutes and walked to the cockpit. He squinted at the terminal, which showed that there were still ten hours before the ship would reach the planet.

"Well." He thought, *"There's no way we're going to stop anywhere. I'd say I have plenty of time to finish the manuscript."* He sat down in the pilot chair and relaxed. *"But not right now."* He could feel his conscious slipping away, along with the memories of his past emerging from the deep vaults of his sub-conscious. The stars sang a lullaby as they flew past the window. Within seconds, Deltrin found his present turn suddenly into his past...

...After waiting almost a year to get to the fourth planet, Deltrin was becoming very claustrophobic. He and Violaze had made several pit stops for the past year, but it had been five weeks since last he stepped out of his ship. His partner was also becoming restless. He knew the riddle like the back of his hand and was very impatient to finally see the arm stretching out of the ice-land.

Finally, after seven weeks of waiting in the ship, Deltrin came across the frozen world. Its bleak surface hardly reflecting anything, making it night everywhere. It was a good thing that Deltrin knew exactly where to land, because he would not have survived for very long, traveling across the black ice.

He took hold of the ship's controls and penetrated through the thin layer of the atmosphere. His only sense of sight was on his computer, which gave him the coordinates on where to land. He could see faint outlines of the planet's surface, but nothing he could steer from. The tall protuberance finally appeared on the computer. Deltrin looked out through the window and saw a grand shadow directly in front of him, coming out of the darkness suddenly and without warning.

The landing pad was about a hundred meters in diameter, about twice the size of the ship, but Deltrin needed all the space he could get to land safely. He slowly descended onto the peak, using both the terminal and the peak itself as guides. The touchdown was rough, but nothing was hurt.

Deltrin got out of his seat and walked down the hall to the door. Before he got there, he took a warm coat and cloaked himself with it.

"If you want to come out and stretch," He told Violaze. "Only stay out for a couple minutes. I don't want you to freeze. I want you to stay inside for as long as you can."

He opened the door and could feel the freezing air push against his body with all its force. He shivered and shook, feeling his nerves sink into his body, trying to keep warm. Violaze felt the wind and didn't hesitate to fly to the bedroom, burying himself under the covers. Deltrin sighed and proceeded to walk into the dark, lifeless world in front of him.

He took several flares and began to light them, setting them all over the mountaintop. Just out of curiosity, he dropped two flares off the side and watched them plummet to the surface. He didn't see them hit; they were lost in the haze that twisted around the trunk of the ice-tree he was on. That display of terror was enough to make him move as fast as he could.

The frigid air was seeping through his suit, biting at his vulnerable skin with its jagged teeth. He located the 'ring of the hand' and set two flares next to where he kneeled. He pulled at the casket's door, but it didn't budge. It was frozen stiff. Deltrin didn't have the time to fool around, and without thinking, he ran back into the ship, found a huge metal bar, ran back out into the cold and proceeded to break the seal of ice. He beat the tube with repeated blows to its side. Finally, the casket burst open. Almost instinctively, Deltrin threw his hand into the wind and barely caught the piece before it was lost. He smugly grinned at his quick reflects, yet only for a second, for the ground beneath him suddenly cracked and split open, swallowing him inside.

As if the map meant more to him than his own life, Deltrin still held onto the parchment with all his might, as he slid down the slightly angled tunnel with gaining acceleration to whatever waited at the bottom of the pit.

The tunnel was too organized and structured to have been naturally formed. The surface was smooth and almost perfectly circular. Also, there was no source of heat or water to burrow through and mold a tunnel in such a frozen world. Something had already created this transit. The question that beat Deltrin's mind, while the freezing ice beat upon his backside was were these creatures still roaming around beneath the surface? What was even more confusing was the fact that the cave was becoming more lit the further he fell.

As he plummeted, he quickly stuffed the map inside his jacket, freeing his hands to create more friction. He dug them into the walls of the tunnel, trying to slow himself down, yet it was only a few seconds before the ice bore into his skin, leaving thin streaks of blood behind him.

He wailed in pain and clenched his fists, bringing them into the pockets of his coat. Finally, the tunnel began to level out, yet Deltrin was still falling at tremendous speed, and to add to his troubles, he was about to collide with a bed of stalagmites. He looked around for anything to grab a hold of before he was impaled.

In the distance, he could see a new opening in the ceiling of the tunnel. He positioned the heels of his boots to dig slightly into the ice and slowly lifted himself upon his feet.

Swiftly, his chance for salvation approached, and with great effort, Deltrin leapt off the ground. He quickly extended his arms and caught the edge of the opening with his injured fingers. Ignoring the pain it brought, Deltrin climbed up into the next tunnel, which was much more stable, and level.

He stood up and checked his pockets for the map.

Still there. He sighed with relief and looked up through the vertical tunnel from which he just fell. There was no way for him to escape that way.

With slight dismay, he turned around only to find the new tunnel was without conclusion in the near distance. Yet, there was a tiny hint of warmth felt in the air, mysteriously out of place for such an arctic world.

His choices were but few, so he began to jog down the icy corridor, hoping the exertion would raise his body temperature.

Only the echo of his breathing breached the silence, giving him less hope than before. As he ran, he studied the walls, trying to find another opening that led up to the surface, but failure was all he found, until a new sound was heard.

He stopped in his tracks, sliding a few feet from the sudden interruption, and listened.

There is a strange sensation that underwater divers experience when they are below the surface. Every creature that moves can be heard within a certain distance, especially crustaceans tapping rocks as they move or build a home. In a liquid medium, sound becomes omni-directional, which is exactly what Deltrin was experiencing in this ice world. There was a soft tapping that emanated somewhere from one of the walls.

Deltrin tried to calm his breathing down to acquire a better sense. After a few deep breaths, he was relaxed and quiet.

The noise sounded like pointed objects chipping away at the ice, as if something were trying to escape or dig through the walls. The more Deltrin listened, the closer the object sounded, allowing him to zero in on the location of the source.

Based on his judgment, Deltrin lowered his head

and placed his ear against the wall where the sound was strongest. Patiently, he heard the tapping come closer, beating against the ice with the rhythm of a heart.

Suddenly, he felt tiny pieces of ice fall into the cavern of his ear, followed by eight tiny legs. Before he could react, the tiny creature lodged itself into Deltrin's ear and continued to rap upon the inner walls, confusing it with the ice. Deltrin jerked his head away from the wall and screamed in torment, as the creature's miniature, yet sharp, appendages chiseled away.

He recklessly threw his head from side to side, hoping to dislodge the creature, yet the small insect had an evolved grip, allowing it to work upside down with at least six of its legs.

The pounding burrowed deeper into his senses, driving him to madness. With rash intentions, Deltrin grabbed for the knife attached to his belt, unsheathed the tiny pick within it and jammed it into his ear. Almost professionally, he stabbed the insect without running the spike into his skull.

A deafening shriek rang in his ears and the beating upon his drums ceased. Slowly, Deltrin pulled the pick out of his ear, revealing a small arachnid skewered at the end.

It was black in color, save the under-belly, which had small blooms of green and red. Each leg was a centimeter in length, armed with a tiny spike at the end. They were still slightly moving. Deltrin flicked the tiny creature on the floor and stepped on it, refusing to study it any longer.

But all was not quiet for long, and this time, there were multiple sources. Before he could move, another insect broke through the ceiling and landed on Deltrin's head. He shook wildly about, and brushed his hair with both hands, being careful not to stab his own head with the knife he still held on to. The little creature fell to the ground and skittered across the floor. A storm of insects fell to the ground, as the frozen sky above Deltrin turned ominously black. His foreign presence was now a threat, most likely alerted from the tiny insect's cry from his ear. The floor swelled with the keepers of this realm, all racing towards the intruder. Some were quick enough to already have crawled up his leg. Deltrin bounced up and down, trying to shake them off his body, and as he did this, he stepped on numerous insects, infuriating them more. A symphony of high-pitched squeals peeled the ice off the walls, as the army cried to their comrades all around the planet.

It was time now for Deltrin to run.

He stopped bouncing around and simply sprinted away from the dark wave pursuing him. His pace increased as more crawled from out of the woodwork. As the freezing temperature continued to eat away at his muscles, he knew he was done for; a meal for millions, until a light source could be seen at the end of the tunnel. Just as things started to look good, the floor below became too thin for support, causing him to fall through again.

This tunnel was not as vertical as the first, yet it still sent him rolling into a new room. At least for him, there were no insects who decided to fall with him.

As he came to a halt, Deltrin hesitantly picked himself up off the ground, fearing any sudden movements would send him plummeting to another cavern. He didn't notice where he was until he stood fully erect with both feet firmly planted to the floor. He lifted his gaze off the floor as his concentration crept up the walls only to see thousands of tunnels, varied in diameter.

Breathless, he stood on the outer diameter of the main heating room. In the center, there was a large hole dug in the ground, which was not ice, but solid rock. Deltrin walked up to the edge of the monstrous aperture and looked down.

Only a dim source of light could be seen, yet Deltrin could easily feel the vapors of heat rising up from the planet's core. He looked around and saw thousands of little insects crawling along the floors and walls, making new smaller tunnels within the larger ones, obviously ignoring the alien's presence.

Deltrin began to forget the tiny trickles of blood that escaped from his injured ear, as well as the shattered capillaries in his fingers. He remembered the riddle speaking of some sort of race of creatures that roamed beneath the planet's surface, and could only assume the new lot was creating the next civilization using the old tunnels and heat source as a foundation.

It is strange the fascination brought forth by such primitive methods executed by smaller life-forms, yet Deltrin ignored the irony and simply watched with wonder as the tiny workers burrowed deeper into the walls. The millions of tiny claws striking at the ice echoed throughout the transit system, but could not be heard above the surface, muffled by the strong currents of wind.

Deltrin finally broke free from his trance and began to plan his way back to his ship. He knew it would be literally impossible to find the arm on the surface, so he had to backtrack his way to where he fell in the first place.

He took off his coat and began ripping off portions of the material. One by one, he tested the accessible tunnels, using the pieces of material as markers to indicate the directions he ventured.

Hours passed until he gave up his search, vindicating his fear that there were no ways out but straight up, and all he had to use was his knife. It was hopeless. He collapsed on the ground and continued to devise a plan, unaware of the squeaking behind him over all the insects.

Finally, he heard the foreign noise and turned around to be introduced to a new sense of joy and relief he had never thought imaginable. There was Violaze, chirping madly, struggling to carry the same pneumatic gun and clip Deltrin used to save his own life on Violaze's home planet.

"Oh buddy, am I glad to see you!" he yelled.

Violaze dropped the gun into his hands and started to flip in the air, ecstatic to see his partner still alive.

"Let's get the hell out of here!"

Apparently, Violaze had become worried of Deltrin's prolonged absence and decided to venture out. When he saw the hole in the ground, he immediately flew into the ship and found the tool he was familiar with and brought it down, hoping to help out his friend, if he were still living.

Deltrin followed his friend back to the original tunnel's opening.

"Come to think of it," he began, "there's only about two hundred meters of rope on this thing." He looked up the tunnel. "I'm pretty sure there's more than two hundred meters going up."

He thought for a moment.

"Violaze, I'm going to need you to tie a rope to the hull of the ship and lower it down about fifty meters. I'll fire this up as far as I can and climb the rest of the way up with the other rope. Can you do that?"

He chirped compliantly and flew straight up the tunnel. Deltrin waited a few minutes for his friend to clear the line of fire and then launched the hook as far as it could go. As soon as it found its hold, Deltrin took two large pieces of torn material and substituted them for gloves.

He held tightly and swung out above the bed of spikes and slowly climbed. After a long and painful assent, Deltrin finally made his way to the end of the rope, where Violaze was waiting.

Without any hint of warning, the hook began to slip out of its holding place, and Deltrin saw he still had a few feet to climb. With unimagined strength, he planted his feet into the wall and leapt up into the air just as the hook released its grip. With divine assistance, Deltrin did not fall. It was a sight to behold, his bloody hand gripping with all his might on the rope above. He swung his other arm up and grabbed hold with both hands and fervidly climbed up.

The knot Violaze made on the hull of the ship was more than Deltrin could have ever expected, giving him an appreciated and unconditional faith in his partner. Never would he doubt his dragon's loyalty and devotion to keep the team alive.

They were too cold and tired to hurry into the ship. He and Violaze strolled through the hatch and closed it calmly. Deltrin walked to the thermostat and raised the heat inside the ship.

He then sat in the pilot seat, waited a few seconds to catch his breath, and then left the superficially dead world as fast as he could.

As soon as he was past its gravitational pull,

Deltrin let the ship float in space, while he would regain his strength. The adrenaline that poured out of his body and the freezing temperature suddenly ceased his functioning and Deltrin passed out. Luckily, the temperature rose quickly, and the ship was back to its normal state.

Deltrin awoke, with an incredible headache. He crouched in his chair and waited a few seconds for the blood to get to his brain. He slowly got up and walked to the map room. The ice on his face and in his hair was melting and dripping down into his eyes. He wiped the cold water off and pulled the fourth parchment from out of his coat. It was not smudged, thankfully, so there was no problem matching with the other pieces. The bottom half of the map was complete finally and another stanza was given...

No siblings have I that I see in the sky.
Just a friend who sits on the throne.

Violaze was still under the covers when Deltrin walked into the bedroom. His little head poked out from the sheets and tested the air of the ship. It was finally warm, so he emerged from the blankets and flew to the shoulder of Deltrin. As soon as he dropped his talons on Deltrin's shoulders, he felt the freezing skin and bounced off even quicker.

"Sorry." Deltrin said. "Let me warm up for a second. Then you can perch."

Violaze didn't bother. He flew to the bedpost and sat there for the duration. Deltrin grabbed a blanket from the bed and draped it over his shoulders. He walked back to the map room, picked up the map, and proceeded to the cockpit and sat down in front of the computer.

The fifth riddle spoke of a planet that had no stars, no planets, nor any moons near it. Deltrin began the search with the basics.

He told the computer to search for a planet with the aforementioned description. Nineteen choices came up on the screen. By process of elimination, Deltrin read every description, trying to determine which one fit most comfortably with the riddle. Only one planet fit the criteria, considering that most all of the other planets were just dead rocks, floating in space. The estimated time of arrival was two weeks. It would be a long time, but it sure beat one year of travel. Deltrin set a course for the planet and walked back to the kitchen. He grabbed something to eat, along with a drink and walked back to his pilot seat.

He sat down and wallowed in the pacific realm of the stars. He was soon accompanied by Violaze, who cautiously tested the temperature of his partner's shoulder. As soon as he found it was safe to land, he settled down and enjoyed the serenity of the atmosphere...

Deltrin's memory began to fade and he found himself back in the present. The sea of stars was much the same as it was many years ago, but things were different. The universe no longer gave Deltrin a safe haven within its dark cloak. He shook his head and regained full consciousness. He got up from his seat and went back to his room to continue reading the manuscript...

The Death of a Comrade

"The Rashouwe have begun to move into the target area."
The General spoke over the intercom.
"As we expected." I responded, "They are getting ready to
meet their reinforcements."
"How long before the bomb is launched, Retnar?" I asked.
"Anytime you're ready." He responded. "Commander
Rinar has contacted the ground forces ahead and they're
awaiting orders."
"Good." I replied. "Let me know when they have
confirmed that all the Rashouwe soldiers are in the
designated area. Out."

A sensation swept over me that I had not felt in
many years. I had been anxious many times, but I never
felt this type of anxiety except when I was fighting. I could
feel the sweat roll down my brow in estuaries, but I was not
scared. I was excited. About five minutes passed of silent
radio until Retnar broke in with the news I wanted to hear.
"Targets are in position." He spoke.
"Deploy the bomb."
"Yes sir." Retnar returned. He radioed his friends up above
and ordered them to fire.

Terinsa lied back in the seat and looked up to the
sky. I did the same. I can remember the sky was blue and
serene, with only a few clouds, but that tranquility was
soon to disappear. The clouds parted with a huge blast in
the sky, which was followed by a violet halo that deprived

the sky of its blue shade. The explosion swept the heavens, leaving the Rashouwe fleet in ruins. Pieces of the crafts rained upon the Rashouwe below.

"Order the troops to swarm the Rashouwe soldiers!" The General yelled into the COM.

We carried out the orders and moved closer as well. We approached the valley and could see our soldiers mowing down the Rashouwe with a never-ending wave of terror. A few of our men were taken down, but considering the ratio, we had achieved an incredible victory.

"Let's move in!" Rinar yelled to us. We hopped out of the vehicle and armed ourselves. Our objective was to follow any of the Rashouwe who managed to escape the slaughter. The six of us ventured beyond the valley and watched for any survivors. We picked off any stray soldier we could locate, but were unable to get all of them.

"We can't let one escape, Admiral." The General declared.

The Admiral nodded and ordered all of us to follow the Rashouwe who escaped. The firing in the distance began to quiet down, which meant that the day was ours, but our mission was not yet done. We ran after the surviving enemies like lions running after wounded prey.

"Red squadron, this is Telkord." The General spoke into his communicator. "We need back-up. Meet us at these coordinates."

The leader responded and informed the General that they would be there in a few minutes. They were still cleaning up.

"Understood." The General said. "See you in a few. Out."

"Why do we need back-up?" The Admiral asked.

"I don't trust the Rashouwe to send all their forces. There is the possibility they may have a veritable force dug in the land somewhere. I don't want to run into an ambush. I want the squadron to close in on the runners, so we can trap them and dodge the possibility of falling into a trap of their own."

The Admiral nodded, but was disheartened by the possibility of another army. We proceeded at a slower pace, but were still able to keep the runners in our sights. We passed through a small brush of trees and came upon another valley. The runners had slowed down for some reason.

The squadron had not reached our rendezvous yet, but we could not pass up the opportunity that was presented to us. We all pulled our weapons to our chest level and began to fire. The plasma blasts ripped through the air with tremendous velocity, and tore open the runners with every shot that hit them. There were two dozen Rashouwe soldiers that we followed, and within a couple seconds, the two dozen bodies were cut to pieces and were spread over the landscape. Even though it seemed we had finished them off, something was still bothering me. I turned over to face Terinsa, who was right next to me.

"Why did they stop?" I asked, breathing heavily.

She shrugged her shoulders and gave me a discouraged look.

"We better go check it out." She finally said. "Just in case."

"Shouldn't we wait for the squadron to get here?" Retnar asked.

"That's probably wise." I responded. "Shouldn't the squad be here by now?" I asked the General.

"Yeah, they should." He replied with uncertainty. He placed his gun down and pulled out his communicator. "Red squadron, this is Telkord. Why aren't you here yet?"

A faint hum could be heard over the COM, and then the leader's voice came through.

"Sorry sir. We got hung up. We'll be there in one minute."

"You'd better be." The General hissed over the instrument.

He turned it off and shoved it back into his jacket pocket.

"Admiral?" He said. "You and I will move out into the

255

open for the squad to see us."

The Admiral looked at the General in disbelief to the incredibly foolish order.

"Are you sure it's wise to expose ourselves?" He asked.

"I believe that the Rashouwe would have made their move by now."

"But General," He continued. "I don't think that everything is clear. Didn't you see how they stopped up there?"

"I did." He answered. "They stopped because they new they were lost and made their last stand. Don't be afraid, just come with me to direct the fleet."

"We'll cover you two." Rinar spoke up. He didn't seem to agree with the General's decision, either. The thrill of defeat must have taken hold of the General's spirits and clouded his thoughts. The Admiral walked out from the brush slower and with more trepidation than the General, who strode out with pontifical confidence.

We stayed behind and watched for any surprise attack. Nothing came, and within seconds, the fleet came into view. Foolishly, we all took our attention away from the valley, and looked up to the hovering fleet. From out of the distance, bolts of plasma whizzed by our heads, originating from an apparent hole in the ground. They were hiding in the well!

The General was hit immediately from the ambush, while the Admiral fled for cover. The General could not move quickly enough, and was soon crippled by a bolt that blew apart his left arm and another that took out his lower right leg. He fell to the ground, screaming in agony, but he did not scream for long. His penitent form was soon destroyed with the next wave of bolts. His head and chest were instantly blown apart with an array of blasts, and nothing was left but tiny pieces of his body. I couldn't believe what I had just seen. I could see the Admiral making flight for the cover. "Move it, Admiral!" I yelled, but I was too late. I watched in horror as a bolt of plasma connected and blew out a portion of his lower hip. He crashed to the ground, but was still alive, barely.

Terinsa and I jumped from the cover and fired all we could at the enemy, trying to get to the Admiral, who was barely crawling and bleeding profusely. Our shots were hitting the enemy with accuracy, and we could see blood sprouting from the ground. The squadron was firing on them as well. The plasma emanating from the sunken bunker began to cease. We dodged the sporadic blasts as best we could, and reached the Admiral, who was breathing heavily. Before I could bend down to help him, a stray bolt grazed my right arm. I could feel my skin burst open, but the heat of the plasma cauterized the wound immediately. I fell to my knees and turned around to continue to fire on the enemy.

"Get him out of here!" I yelled to Terinsa.

"I'm not leaving you out in the open!" She yelled back.

"I insist!"

There was no time to argue. She left me angrily and pulled the Admiral to safety. I fell to my chest and drew my other gun and began firing both weapons. I reaped the ground of any Rashouwe heads poking out of the well with my firepower, along with the help of the fleet. The attack finally ceased, and I hurried back to the brush.

"Don't you ever tell me to leave you in danger again, damn you!" Terinsa yelled. I didn't even listen. I was too busy gazing at the dying Admiral.

It seemed he was seeing right through me. He glared at me for an eternity, and then extended his arm. I grasped his hand with extreme pride, knowing it would be for the last time.

"Set me free with my father." He said. A moment of the past flashed in my mind and instantly I knew exactly what he meant.

"I promise, I will." I swore to him. A single tear trickled

257

down my cheek. I felt sorry that I had cried in front of the Admiral, disrespecting him, but I could not hold back.

"Do not grieve." He told me. He struggled to place his other hand on my shoulder. "Finish this. I don't want to see you again until the mission is done."

The blood sloshed in his eyes, as he panned to Terinsa, who was crying as well. "You two are the greatest beings I have ever met." His breathing began to slow down rapidly. He swung his arm from my shoulder and landed it on the ground in front of her. She quickly placed it in her trembling hand. "Stay together." He whispered. "In life and in death." Terinsa lowered her head to hide her tears. The Admiral smiled and loosened his grip. A final breath poured out from within his soul and he closed his eyes.

I couldn't let go of his hand. I wanted to stay there and keep hold. Terinsa released her grip and took hold of my hand. My eyes were glued to his lifeless expression. I could hear her saying my name and telling me to let go, but I couldn't respond.

"Tyran!" She yelled into my ear. I jerked suddenly and whipped my head to face her. I stared at her, still caught in a daze.

"Let him go."

I looked back down and hesitated. I knew that he would have ordered me to if he were still alive, so I reluctantly let go. I could feel the anger fill within me, cutting off my supply of air. I stood up and walked out to the open area, towards the General's scattered carcass.

"Tyran?! Where are you going." Terinsa yelled, as Rinar and Retnar looked on bewildered. I turned around and told them to cover me. I then walked through the pool of blood and found the General's communicator. I took the instrument and walked back to the brush. I then contacted the squadron.

"This is Captain Tyran. I am assuming command of the mission in consequence of the deaths of the General and the Admiral. I am ordering you to stuff that hole with every bomb you can muster. Is that clear?"

"Crystal, sir." The fleet leader spoke without hesitation.

Ten of the ships began to fire several missiles into the ground, as well as dropping bombs down the hole. The well started to resemble a chimney, the way the smoke poured out from the top. After a minute of bombardment, I ordered the fleet to cease fire and to land. They complied and soon anchored their ships. I greeted the leader and asked him if he could fly the four of us into the well. He agreed to do it and took Rinar, Terinsa, Retnar, and myself down to the cavern in the ground.

It was a good thing that we had piled the explosives into the subterranean world, considering there were hundreds of Rashouwe scattered everywhere. There was a whole new army underground.

"Are there any other wells we need to worry about, Captain?" The pilot asked me.

"No." I replied. "We've eliminated this planet of all Rashouwe presence, present company excepted."

"Good to hear sir."

I remembered the cavern was where we wanted to set the map, so it was imperative we cleared the place of all the bodies. I turned towards the pilot and presented him with a question. "Is there any way that you can burn all the bodies down here?" He looked at me, unsure of what I was doing.

"Without problem, sir" He said, confused.

"Excellent." I said. "In that case, let's torch the place."

"As you wish, Captain." He took us to an elevated area, right below the hole in the ceiling. He then dropped several incendiary bombs to the floor, setting the ground ablaze. He then piloted the ship out of the cavern and brought us to the surface.

We waited about a half-hour for the fire to simmer. We went back down with the intention of placing the piece of the riddle in its designated resting area. Terinsa and I walked out of the ship as soon as it landed on the warm ground with the tube tucked under my arm. Retnar stayed and watched, as we searched for an appropriate place to put the casket. We had to look for something in haste, for the humid air was difficult to breathe.

We finally located a hole in the wall and wedged the casket into it. The metallic surface of the tube hissed as it came in contact with the scorching rock. She and I pushed it in as far as we could and then rushed to the ship. As soon as we were secure, we began our ascent to the surface. The third portion was finally at peace and we were ready to finally leave this planet.

The pilot elevated the ship out of the radiated cavern and took us back to the surface. I climbed out of the vehicle and walked to where the Admiral was laying. I carried his body into the open and set him down on the ground.

You see, when he mentioned to me that he wanted to be set free with his father, he was asking me to cremate him. His father received the same burial. I remember because I was there.

I remember when the ritual was complete, they handed the urn with the ashes inside to the Admiral. For several minutes he stood still, just looking at the lifeless vessel that was in his hands. After some time, he ceased to look at the urn and glanced up at me.

"Father would not want to stay put in this jar." He told me. "And I wouldn't allow him to be imprisoned in this tiny cell for eternity." He then took the lid off and waved the urn around, letting the wind pick up the ashes and carry them off.

"My final gift to him was to set him free, Tyran. I want you to do the same to me when I am gone." He looked at me with all seriousness and I swore to him I would fulfill his desire. Secretly, I had hoped the day would never come, but here I was, and I had a promise to keep.

I set his body on fire and watched the wind embrace his ashes, carrying his soul to another world, a world I'll only see in my dreams. Finally, all was done, and I was ready to leave this world of death. All four of us gathered back into the ship and the pilot transported us all the way to where we left Retnar's ship.

We climbed out of the warm vehicle and took all our equipment with us. We were allowed to keep the weapons, just in case we ran into some more trouble. The plasma rifles we were given were innovations of an earlier model. The improvement was the actual ammunition that was fired and not the way it was fired. When the beam of plasma hits the target, it leaves a minute entry wound but no exit wound. Instead, the bolt stays inside the target and spreads around, singeing everything. Eventually, the plasma disintegrates, but everything inside is burnt to a crisp. One shot anywhere is fatal. This was a weapon that we all could use. It would have been nice to think that we wouldn't need them, but we were through with looking towards the future through rose-tinted glasses.

The probability of us falling into another battle was very high, and the threat of such an event loomed over all our heads. We accepted the risk and were ready to conquer all odds against us. The death of the Admiral filled our spirits with hatred, which inspired us all the more to destroy the Rashouwe. Rinar felt the same way about the death of his General. I could see the passion ignite within his soul, almost making his eyes glow red. He walked us back to the ship and gave us each an individual farewell.

"Tell your Troctie friends hello for me." Rinar said to Retnar, extending his hand. Retnar smiled and formed an extremity to return the good gesture.

"You can count on it, Commander." He said in return. "It has been a pleasure."

The Commander then walked to Terinsa and

261

extended his arm. "The truest warrior I have ever seen." He stated. She blushed at the compliment and shook his hand. "Close second." She replied.

He smiled and then walked over to me. He paused for a second, looking deep into my eyes. "It is an honor to fight for this cause by your side." He told me. "I only wish that we had been fighting on the same side so many years ago."

"The honor is all mine, Commander. You have shown me that you are of excellent character. I wish we could fight side by side again, and If it were within my power, I would have you join us, but we have different missions. But our cause is one in the same, with the same determination. That is all I need to know."

"Understood and agreed, Captain." He said, extending his arm. "I am sorry that you have lost a valuable friend."

My emotions pierced my heart with their unforgiving talons as soon as he mentioned the Admiral. I lost my speech for a brief second, and then was able to thank him for giving his condolences.

"Likewise, my friend." I said in return. He smiled, and shook my hand.

"I'll see you on the other side." Was the last thing he said to me. I laughed quietly and patted him on the shoulder, and then proceeded into the ship. The others said a final good-bye to Rinar, and followed me into the spacecraft.

Terinsa and I found a seat to relax in, as Retnar took hold of the controls and began to lift off from the battle-scarred planet. We could see Rinar waving to us on our departure, as we ascended into the blue sky. He eventually stopped waving and walked back to the vehicle to join the pilot. They flew off towards the mountain, as we said our good-byes to what we left behind. Soaring out of the planet's grasp, we made way for the fourth planet.

The Creae

Deltrin's hands were glued to the manuscript, overwhelmed from what he just read. He took a deep breath and placed the book in his lap. He took a long drink from the glass next to him, and sank in his chair.

One good thing about what he just read was that he learned how Violaze came into being. Tyran mentioned that the well was radiated, which would explain the advanced evolution of Violaze's species. That was why the nest was inside the cavern. The Radiation must have hung around inside for quite some time, genetically changing the little lizards that crawled around the planet's surface. Some must have found a way inside.

Deltrin took a moment to cool down and then dove right back into the read, excited to hear about planet four. But before he could even read one more word, he heard a noise coming from the cockpit. He placed the book down, marking his place, and headed down the corridor.

The new system that Deltrin had purchased was more critical than he had thought. The noise he heard was the computer informing him that he had seven hours left before he reached his final destination.

"You called me all the way here just to tell me that?" He asked confused and frustrated. The adrenaline he was feeling before changed suddenly into fatigue, and he instantly felt the affects. He still had twelve hours before he had to finish the read, so he decided to sit down and relax.

Blast it. He thought, wishing he were still in the mood to continue on with his reading. *Oh well. I still have plenty of time.* In seconds, he was asleep again, dreaming of the fifth portion of his journey...

...Deltrin knew that the trek through the fifth planet would be an arduous one, considering the riddle spoke of needing another 'lung'.

As soon as the planet was in sight, Deltrin left the cockpit and went into the supplies room to find a respirator of some sort. Since the atmosphere he was about to trek through was not aqueous, he couldn't rely on his oxygen helmet this time.

The biography of the planet Deltrin received from the computer told of volcanic activity on the surface. It also spoke of an incredibly dense atmosphere around the red planet. Deltrin remembered the riddle clearly stated that the planet had a star 'within' it.

Since the atmosphere was very thick and dense, no gas could escape into space. The sulfuric gases from the explosions and the hydrogen sulfide and carbon dioxide from the geysers spread throughout the planet's limits. Deltrin was a being who could not process these gases with his lungs, so the 'third' one was a necessity.

Deltrin found all the equipment he needed in the supply room and dragged everything out into the map room. Violaze watched with curiosity, trying to understand what his partner was doing. He peeped out a question to his friend in haste, who stopped to answer him.

"I'm trying to get everything ready for the next planet,

Violaze."

Violaze peeped again.

"No. I'm sorry, little guy, but this is a journey I have to make alone. The atmosphere is poisonous and I have only one respirator. Don't worry. I will be just fine."

Violaze trusted his partner, knowing he had been in more precarious situations than this. Violaze simply stayed where he was and watched Deltrin prepare himself.

Deltrin set everything on the map room table and went back to sit down in his pilot seat. He took control of the ship and maneuvered it as best he could, trying to penetrate the atmosphere. Considering it was almost as thick as solid rock, Deltrin decided to slow his ship down greatly, as not to damage the hull. His plan was to slowly break his way through, instead of simply bursting through it.

The ship began to penetrate the planet's aura, gradually eating its way through to the inside of the sphere. After nearly an hour of intense heat and work, the ship made it through and splashed into the thick air of the fifth planet.

The heat emanating from the volcanoes below seeped through the fissures of the ship, causing the internal temperature to rise at almost fatal degrees. Deltrin quickly activated his coolant system to bring the cabin's temperature to a healthy level. He set the controls to automatic landing and ran back to the map room to gear up.

One of the great options of Deltrin's ship was the extendable chamber on the port side of the ship, which was an attachment to one of his outer doors. Normally, the air was breathable on most of the planets he would travel, but there were always exceptions. In order for him to safely pass through the different atmospheres, he needed a room to keep the foreign gases out of his ship.

As strange as it may sound, air does have a weight and mass. On any given planet, there will be a certain amount of pressure applied to the inhabitants of the planets, because the air is pushing down on them. Evolution, as well as adaptation proves to be the best cure for this apparent pain, but beings who are visiting the planet do not have this luxury.

Normally, the only things to worry about when passing through atmospheres are the air canals in the body, which are the exposed areas where the pressure attacks. The air pockets in the body are very delicate, and when an outside force or pressure acts upon them, the air inside is pressed further down, causing extreme pain. The opposite effect happens when the being crosses into an atmosphere with a lesser force than what the air pockets have adapted to. Instead of pressing down, the pressure works in the opposite direction. By simply applying force through the tubes, releasing the imprisoned air and clearing them out, the imbalance of pressure when passing through atmospheres has barely any affect. However, the problem with the weight of the gas on the entire body remains unsolved. Unfortunately, there is no way for Deltrin to protect his body from the difference in pressure, however, he is able to protect his lungs, which are the most important organs in this case.

He relies on a special computer attached to his tank that tells him the amount of pressure forcing down on his body, as well as the time he has before his air supply runs outs. The pressure of the atmosphere also effects the air supply. The more extreme the pressure gets, the more effort is needed to expand the lungs, which means that more air will be used for each breath.

Before Deltrin made his final preparation for the departure into the foreign atmosphere, he made sure the air in his tank was properly compressed to the right measurement. His cockpit computer informed him that the planet's atmospheric pressure is four times as strong as the internal pressure of Deltrin's ship. In order for his lungs to avoid the risk of collapsing, Deltrin had to compress the air.

The mouthpiece attached to the tank acts as a regulator to increase the amount of air Deltrin breathes in. As aforementioned, the more pressure, the more effort needed to expand the lungs. Since the fire planet has a pressure four times as strong as what Deltrin was used to, Deltrin had to make sure that with each breathe he took, four times as much air would need to be compressed into each inhalation. This would allow his lungs to expand to the normal size, which incidentally, makes the compressed air seem like the air Deltrin is used to. The air in the tank is compressed to incredible measurements, and the regulator makes sure that the amount of air Deltrin takes in is the right amount. Simple as that.

Deltrin swung the heavy tank over his shoulders onto his back and activated the flow of his air-stream. He placed the respirator and mask over his face and began to breathe in the strange tasting air. He turned to Violaze and gave him a reassuring wink. He then activated the decompression chamber to extend out of the ship's hull. He waited a moment for it to fully stretch out before he opened the outer door. He stepped into the chamber and closed the door behind him, as not to let the air of the planet get inside his ship. Once the door was closed he made sure everything was in working order. After his safety check, he took a deep breath and opened the door to the planet.

The extreme heat of the world tangled its talons around Deltrin's body, making him feel the unforgiving temperature already. It was extremely hot, and Deltrin was completely exposed except for what the mask was covering. He could feel the gas invading his skin, and he knew he could only spend a few hours before the gas would infiltrate his blood stream and poison him.

He attached the computer to his wrist, untangling its wire from around his neck. The terminal read that Deltrin had seven hours and thirty minutes before he would run out of breathable air, but he did not have to worry too much. The planet was small and would not take much time to travel. Besides, he knew what to look for: A single geyser of some sort with an everlasting flame guarding the cave where the fifth piece was hiding.

The ground Deltrin walked on was pushing its heat through his boots. Walking for only half an hour, Deltrin was beginning to wonder if he could ever make the full seven-hour trek.

He didn't worry too much about any Rashouwe force based on this planet. Considering it was not placed in any strategic position, nor placed in a huge solar system, there was no reason for the Rashouwe to come to this planet. Besides, there was no trace of intelligent life. It's a good thing they were unaware of the map's presence here.

The air was so thick, Deltrin was basically trudging to his destination. The heat literally dripped from the burgundy clouds above and splashed onto the ground in a series of vapor waves. The ground itself was blood red, almost appropriately colored for the planet's individuality.

Curious, Deltrin kneeled down to feel the strange

powder that littered the planet. It was soft regolith, possibly the remains of ancient explosions, for no asteroid or comet could have made it through the atmosphere to create such material from impacts. There were mountains all around, but none in close range. The powder Deltrin was walking on was actually sediment that was carried by the wind or some other force from an actual blast zone into this region. He pondered this, and then let the thought leave silently from his mind. He had other things to worry about. He waved his hand through the thick mist and let the fine grains glide to the surface, where they rested. He lifted himself off the ground and proceeded on his quest to find the everlasting geyser.

Deltrin walked through the sulfur fog, trying hard to concentrate on his search, but he found it difficult not to stare and wonder at the strange environment. The trees were orange, with a little hint of yellow. They all had blossoming that could be seen, but the colors of the flowers were no different than the leaves' color.

On the ground, Deltrin noticed small animals that crawled in and out of their little holes in the ground. They had their differences from other lizards Deltrin had seen before, but relatively speaking, they could have been indigenous to a planet that accommodated air breathable to what Deltrin was used to. Just the fact that there were so many of them zooming around like sand-crabs was what captured his attention. He had to watch every step he took to avoid hurting any of them.

"So where are your big brothers?" he asked, crouching down to have a conversation with one of the locals, forgetting this planet should be void of life.

Deltrin eventually found the geyser within two hours of his journey. Considering it would take him the same amount of time to get back to the ship, he had three hours to do what he pleased.

He approached the area, surprised at what he saw. There was a pond-like body of water the size of a small tide-pool with a cylindrical tube extending out of the water. The flame was floating at the opening of the small tunnel, only about a meter in height. The water around the tube was bubbling, either from a gas being released, or from the extreme heat coming from the tube. Deltrin dipped his hand in the water near the tube and solved the mystery very quickly. Luckily, the burn was not severe enough to leave a scar, but it did teach him a lesson.

The cave in front of him was just big enough for Deltrin to crawl through. There was no light from within, nor was there any type of commotion inside that could be heard. However, Deltrin could sense the presence of some sort of being inside, waiting for him to come. It whispered out to Deltrin, singing the song of the sirens, luring him to come closer. His eyes spastically moved from side to side, trying to adapt to the dark interior, but nothing could be seen. One thing was for sure; there was no turning back. Deltrin had no choice but to get inside the cave and recover the artifact, regardless of the possibility of a phantom guardian.

Deltrin probed around in his vest pocket, searching for a flare he could use. There was the possibility of a geyser inside the cave that could set off an explosion, if a flame were to come in contact with it. He found an illumination rod, which did not have any exposed flame, however, he only had one. He couldn't just throw the rod into the cave, considering it could break, so he had to crawl through the Cimmerian tunnel without a beacon.

The further he plunged into the tunnel, the less he could hear, until finally, the only thing that made any sound was Deltrin. His low, wheezing breaths echoed irregular patterns in his ears. The only thought that crossed his mind, as he twisted his unwilling body through the burrow, was if his breathing would be the last sweet sound he would ever hear.

Inch by slow inch, Deltrin crawled in a spiral formation, feeling his uncomfortable body rub against the warm rocks. The sweat soaked his body. The heat produced from the energy he spent, as well as that from the planet tore at his skin. His tank was being scratched, but not damaged too severely. He made sure he did not get caught in a snag that could tear his tank open. Speaking of which, he also cradled the computer's wiring in his chest, so as not to it get scratched, or even worse, ripped to shreds.

The sarcophagus he was crawling through finally opened up into the cave, where Deltrin literally poured himself into. He splashed down to the floor and noticed the floor was covered with tiny holes. He groped around to find an area that was uneaten, but could not find any such place. He was not in a cave; he was in a nest.

With the hint of light from the outside, Deltrin hurriedly probed around in his pocket, trying to find the glow rod. He took hold of it, pulled it out, and ignited it immediately. Before his eyes, the room lit up and exposed a vast transit system of openings.
"Find tube and get out." He told himself, making the directions as simple as possible.

The tube rested in a patch of fine powder. Deltrin rushed for the tube, picked it up, and started for the tunnel. In his haste, he stumbled on one of the holes, and sank his right leg into it.

He tried to pull his leg out, but couldn't. He was stuck. He clutched the tube with one hand, and pulled at his leg with another. As he was doing this, another strange noise, apart from his sporadic breathing, began to echo in the dungeon. The glow rod Deltrin lit was lying on the ground, shattered from being dropped. To add to the gloomy atmosphere, the little light from outside was receding.

It was black. Deltrin let go of his leg and looked at his computer terminal on his wrist. He activated the internal light and read the computer. 04:23 was the time left before his air would run out. He began to panic heavily, screaming through his mask for anyone, or anything to hear. It was hopeless. He turned off the green light on his computer, and noticed something was still glowing in the cave. Whatever was making that strange noise before was now in the room with Deltrin.

All around him, new lights assorted in colors appeared and flared intensely in the dark. He could feel tiny claws poke into the skin of his sunken leg, as well as hear the tiny creatures scattering across the floor. The noise began to solidify to a more organized march, as if the unknown hosts were preparing for something. He could feel tiny feet crawling up his back and around his neck, until all the lights in the cave were in front of him, revealing tiny iris' floating within each of them.

A laser scanner emanated from one of the blue eyes, and scrutinized the mystery guest. The azure beam glided up and down Deltrin's face for a few seconds and then turned off. Instantly, all the tiny creatures crawled towards him, dug around the hole that held onto his leg, and freed him. Completely confused at the unexpected help, Deltrin stayed where he was, instead of fleeing for his life. Even so, it would take him half an hour to get through the tunnel. Instead, he stared at the armada of glowing eyes, which stared straight back at him.

The little creatures quickly averted their attention from the traveler and crawled towards one of the corners of the room. Deltrin pulled his leg out of the hole and walked towards them. The room began to shake and suddenly, the corner of the cave broke free and exposed a walkway. He could feel their tiny heads at his heels, nudging him to go in. Since the little helpers had saved him once, he felt they would not trick him now.

He dauntlessly walked through the doorway and followed the glowing eyes in front of him, leaving the cave behind. The tube holding the map was still cradled close to his heart. No matter where he went, he wouldn't let go.

The dark hallway began to light up and soon enough, Deltrin could see where he was going. To his surprise, the guides were the same types of tiny lizards he saw on the surface of the planet. They had looked so real before. Whatever created these tiny machines was certainly a magnificent artist.

A metallic door stood in the path of the hallway. As soon as Deltrin reached it, the myriad of lizards turned around and flocked back to the cave. Deltrin was alone again, and this time, he was really lost. He looked at his terminal. 03:46. He had less than an hour and a half before he had to get back to the cave.

The tiny creatures had led him to this door for a reason, but now that he was here, he was lacking a key. They had left him without any way of getting inside. He turned around, hoping to find a slow robot from the pack to follow back to the cave. He began to walk back, when the door behind him slowly opened with a hiss, welcoming Deltrin to come inside.

He stayed in his tracks, contemplating the choice. He had the chance to go back to the cave and get back to the ship. He also had the chance to meet who it was, or what it was that created the little creatures. He knew he would regret his decision if he left without knowing, so he turned around and went beyond the metallic threshold.

What he saw next would be troublesome even for a poet to describe. Deltrin found himself on a balcony overlooking a cavern that stretched as far as the eye could see. The walls were glittering silver, with not a hint of the red planet exposed. There were thousands of pipes and cylindrical tubes running up and down from the floor to the ceiling. Machines were pumping gases in and out of the transit system. There were wheels and gears moving in all different directions. Billions of creatures, ranging from tiny insects to giant golems roamed around on the ground or in flying vehicles, making sure the grand machine was working. What was this machine controlling?

The balcony on which Deltrin was standing began to change form, turning into a tube of some type. Stupefied at the incredible scene in front of him, Deltrin barely noticed that the tube was closing in around him. Within seconds the transport shut tight and rocketed through an intricately built tunnel system, flying past a myriad of structures that Deltrin could not recognize, considering the speed the pod was traveling at.

It finally rested on another platform, opened up, and revealed another area of the city. It could have traveled only a mile, or it could have traveled to the other side of the planet. There was no way for Deltrin to find out.

He slowly lifted his arm and checked the terminal. 03:41. Five minutes had passed since he was in the hallway. Five minutes was all it took to leave one world and find another.

The city was completely different from the surface of the planet. Where were all the volcanoes now? Instead of the constant blasting and sounds of explosions, this city was filled with sounds of machines, flying overhead or dancing on the ground. The only familiar noise of a city that could not be heard was conversation. Nothing talked. One thing was for sure; of all the cities Deltrin had seen, this one was the most active and vivid. Strange how these machines were capable of showing more life than a living being.

A heavily built creature with three eyes walked towards Deltrin. It extended an extremity with three joints, instead of just one. All three eyes looked at Deltrin, whose sanity was far from recovered.

"Don't be alarmed." It said, sounding monotonic and systematic.

Deltrin was well beyond any state of alarm, already traveling through the state of utter disbelief.

"You can speak?"

The triclops smiled as best it could, and nodded, jerking its huge head up and down.

"If you want an explanation," It continued, "Follow me. The Creae is waiting for you."

Like a zombie, Deltrin followed his new friend. For several minutes, they walked down a pathway, leading to one of the largest buildings in the city. It was a wonder to behold.

Apart from the thousand of other houses and buildings built within this metropolis, this one seemed out of place. Every structure was positioned and built to fulfill a purpose for the grand machine. There were buildings that had several pipes run inside it, most likely a factory that provides air to breathe for the plants and

275

animals. But this didn't make sense to Deltrin, for all the life on this planet was robotic. What need did they have for breathable air? There were other buildings of gigantic size, where several flying crafts docked, most likely an airport of some sort. Everything was moving to a unified beat, all performing set tasks to keep the machine running, except for this one building.

Towering over everything around it, this creation was fit to house a god. There were several spires jetting straight up to incredible heights, most likely the work of a master craftsman. The whole building was made of a metallic substance, different from every other building. It was smooth, yet it gave the illusion of a rough stone, like a medieval castle. There were no guard towers, or spikes adorned on the sides of this structure. Everything about it was welcoming. What made this palace especially welcoming was the fact that it was the only building with lights on in the windows.

When he first laid eyes upon this metropolis, Deltrin could not see any buildings. They must have been hidden behind the pipes. There was also the possibility that the transport had taken him to another part of the planet. Whatever the case may be, he was about to get the answers he wanted. Unfortunately, the answers could be as confusing as the world he was in. Revelation is not always the best possible outcome.

The guide finally reached the door of the heavily decorated building, most likely the home of this 'Creae' being. He stretched out his triple-jointed arm and placed his four-digit hand a few inches away from a black orb resting on a pedestal in front of the doorway. Three tiny connectors emerged from his hand and attached themselves to the orb. The orb jumped up from its cradle and floated in mid-air. The guide released his tiny connectors and reeled them back into his appendage.

The orb slowly twisted around, revealing a tiny slit running horizontally around the circumference of the ball. The slit began to widen, until it revealed a hemisphere. Inside the orb, there rested a green eye, with blue feathered into the iris. It stared at the creature that awoke it, and then turned to Deltrin, whose mind was completely blown at this point.

After scrutinizing Deltrin for a moment's time, the eye turned its attention to the door behind it. Triggered by some invisible force, the door slowly opened. The black orb began to shut as the door opened wider, until it was nothing more than a black ball. It descended back onto the pedestal and gently came to a rest.

"In there, my friend." The creature said, pointing.

The triclops smiled and walked away, most likely on his way to find some other job to do. Deltrin watched the creature walk off, and then turned around. He shook his head in disbelief and started walking into the unknown temple.

The entrance hall looked like a converted church without the pews. The upper half of the room had several stained-glass windows allowing colored light to fill the room. Unfortunately they were too high for Deltrin to see what they depicted.

The floor was white marble with erratic black streaks splashed within the design. Each step Deltrin took echoed loudly throughout the large room. He proceeded further, but eventually stopped. In the center of the room, there was bridge built over a stream of electricity. Deltrin walked to the bank of the virtual river and peered down to see what was inside. Within the millions of streaks and currents, Deltrin could see his own reflection. *Incredible*, he thought. This stream had the illusion of reality and was able to produce the same attributes as a real river. It was an internal moat, there simply to entertain whoever gazed upon it. Deltrin could even see robotic fish swimming about within it.

Deltrin got up from his knees and walked over the bridge to the other side of the room, only to find other spectacles pleasing to the eye.

There were three paintings, gargantuan in size, hanging on the wall in front of him. One depicted a large being, standing in a black atmosphere, holding a large sphere on his back. Deltrin walked closer to see more.

The being was in obvious pain, straining to balance his burden. The sphere he held looked like a collection of stars and comets and other heavenly bodies all culminating together on this poor creature's back. The painting to its left was even more intriguing.

Deltrin had never seen this painting before. In the middle of the canvas was a star, with five beings surrounding it. To him, it was merely a primitive depiction of some kind of ritual. Oblivious to the hidden significance, Deltrin simply smiled at the aesthetic quality and passed it after only admiring the work for a few seconds.

Deltrin still had another painting to see. He walked closer to the third one to get a better look, for the lighting was not that good. With each step he made, he slowly saw the details of his own face emerge from the canvas. He stopped in his tracks, beholding himself frozen in art.

There he was, standing gaunt and noble on an unknown planet, holding a manuscript under his arm. The sky was blue above him, with not a cloud in the vicinity. Behind him was his beloved transport, shining brilliantly in the sun. *Pity*, he thought, *it never looked so nice before*.

Deltrin walked closer to see more detail. A smile appeared on his face, when he was able to see Violaze perched on his shoulder.

Suddenly, the painting split down the middle and slowly parted, presenting the doorway to a new room. The light emanating from the other side illuminated the entrance hall. Deltrin had no choice but to follow the light's invitation.

The walls inside were completely adorned with paintings and windows depicting scenes of all sorts of different events. The room was large enough to be filled with thousands of them, which it was.

The art was so vivid and alive; Deltrin could hear voices talking to him and to each other. There were tables and shelves scattered all around, with artifacts and decorations literally covering all the surface area possible. There were fully detailed dioramas on every table, each of them portraying a different world. On one, there were thousands of tiny soldiers and vehicles of war scattered about a mountainous land. On each side of the table there stood two mighty castles, each standing proud and sturdy in the face of the battle taking place on their land.

There were several conflicts all around the highlands, the favor of each battle swaying back and forth from one side to the other. There were soldiers left behind, wounded and helpless on the rough terrain. There were brothers helping each other, fighting to stay alive. Crude catapults and other projectile weaponry launched countless stones and arrows into the air, landing indiscriminately into whatever they could find. How would this battle conclude?

Deltrin walked over to another realm, where the scene was much more jubilant than the last. It was a depiction of a small gathering in the center of a small town, where a wedding was taking place. The bride was beautifully gowned in white, looking as elegant as a goddess. Her bridesmaids were obviously jealous of her appearance, yet were still pleased to see their friend was soon to be wed. The groom looked a little nervous, but was still incredibly pleased to be loved by such an enchanting creature.

Together, they stood at the Altar, where the priest conducted the ceremony, holding each other's hand in a tender, yet firm grip. Before their family and friends, they confessed their undying love, promising eternity to each other.

Everywhere Deltrin walked, a different world was laid in front of him in a marvelously detailed work of art. The decor was brilliant.

"I find it peaceful here." A voice emerged from somewhere in the room. "Perhaps this is the only place I can experience true emotion."

Deltrin spun around to locate the speaker.

Sitting in a throne surrounded by several display tables, a being was found staring at Deltrin.

"Are you the Creae?" Deltrin asked.

"You don't see any other creatures around, do you?" the being asked, playfully sarcastic.

The Creae stepped down from the chair and walked towards Deltrin. She was wearing a purple and silver gown, flowing gracefully down her beautiful shape. Her eyes glowed vehemently, a black pearl surrounded by a field of gold. Her hair was just as radiant, like waves of energy laid upon her perfect curves.

She gazed into Deltrin's silver eyes.

"Do not be afraid." She said with a soothing accent.

She placed her gentle hands over his mask and slowly pulled it off. At first, Deltrin was terrified and jerked back. She understood his reaction and assured him he would be safe. Trusting this celestial being was no problem for Deltrin, so he allowed her to remove his apparatus. Her movements were almost undetected. She took his mask and dropped it on the floor beside her.

With tenderness, she placed her hand on his cheek and caressed it softly.

"You're much more beautiful than I thought, especially without your mask."

"I'm surprised I can breathe. I thought the air was sulfur based." He said, closing his eyes in response to her touch.

"The air is what I choose it to be. My team of walkers, whom you encountered in the cave, studied your respiratory system for me so I could make the air breathable for you."

"When did they do that?" he asked.

"Don't you remember the laser beam?"

He chuckled and looked around the spacious room.

"Where am I?"

The Creae smiled at the irony and removed her hand from his cheek, much to his disappointment. "Isn't that the question you all ask yourselves in life?"

Deltrin turned suddenly confused from her statement.

"What do you mean 'you all'? Don't you classify as a living creature?"

"No." She said. "I am metallic, just like the other creatures you saw on your way here. The only difference between us is that I was chosen to lead them and I have a layer of skin."

"Impossible." He said. "You're too passionate to be a

281

machine."

"Even machines have feelings." She quietly said.

Deltrin lowered his gaze in humiliation at the incredibly rude comment he made. "I'm sorry." He said humbly.

She accepted his apology with a smile and a nod. Deltrin tried to change the subject immediately.

"You were saying you were chosen to lead this city?"

"That's right." She said.

"Who gave you that power?" Deltrin asked.

"I'm so glad you asked." She said, taking his hand in hers.

She led Deltrin to the throne she was sitting in before. There was another chair next to it, so Deltrin made himself comfortable.

"You are the traveler I have been told to wait for."

Deltrin could not believe she knew who he was. He nodded his head.

"How do you know about me?"

"The ones who created me were the same beings who orchestrated your quest. It is obvious you have not found the treasure yet, so that means you don't know anything about the mechanics behind this journey."

"No, I don't. At least not yet."

"I should have figured that. I should warn you I have been programmed to give you information concerning this planet and its history, however, I cannot give away too much."

"Why not?" He asked.

She sank her eyes into his questioning stare and smiled at him, as if she were about to reveal something.

"I know things about your future, Deltrin." She said. "Things you will soon accomplish." She sank back into her throne.

"I'm sorry, but I find it hard to believe what you are saying. How could you possibly know who I am, or about this mission? I can understand that the people who created you knew about the quest, but they had no idea who would take the mission."

Her smile turned to a neutral position.

"Open the tube, but do not show me what is inside. To prove I know about the mission, I will tell you what you will find."

"You could have opened it yourself and looked." He responded.

"If I opened it, Deltrin, the parchment would be dust, considering what the air would have done to it once it got inside." She concluded. "Now, written on the paper will be the following phrase: *his wings stretch out and keeps my kin safe from the horrors that we cannot see. Cloaked by space, his shaded face leaves two eyes where once were three.*"

Satisfied, she leaned back and relaxed, waiting for Deltrin to confirm what she had said. He read the riddle and slowly looked up to her.

"Paranoia is a terrible emotion to have, my friend." She said. "I forgive you now, but do not let it plague your soul again."

"I am sorry." Deltrin said with humble sincerity. That was the second time he insulted her. No more, he thought. From now on, I will listen without objection.

"But tell me, how did you know my name?"

"My creators told me to watch for your arrival." She began. "When I say arrival, I do not mean your arrival on this planet. I mean your arrival into the mission. The tube that informed you about this mission, which you found orbiting the moon was being monitored." She smiled again. "We have been watching you ever since you

283

opened that casket."

"What about my future?" he continued to ask. "You said you knew about my future."

"I know about the mission and its entirety. What happens to you during this mission is up to you, and is unknown to me right now. However, if your past experiences are previews of what is to come, I am looking forward to watching you."

That was the first time Deltrin ever saw a machine blush. He smiled at the flattering statement and enjoyed the moment of silence after it was made.

"Tell me about this planet." He said, breaking the silence.

She got up from her throne and began to walk around the tables.

"I enjoy telling stories while walking. I feel constricted in a chair."

Her glowing eyes smiled at Deltrin. "Please walk with me." Without any hesitation, Deltrin bounced out of his chair and went to her side. She enjoyed his haste and began to tell the story.

"After the creators left this place, they gave me instructions to take care of the planet and make sure it would be protected. That was two billion years ago. I hope my age isn't showing."

"I'm afraid you look younger than I do, Creae. And you look more beautiful than anything I have ever seen" He said in response.

She stopped in her tracks and smiled brightly, placing her hand on his cheek again.

"How gracious of you to say so. Be that as it may, I still feel old."

She turned around and continued her stroll.

"I stayed put for several millennia, sitting in a single

area, watching the sky repeat itself and watching the planet slowly die. Besides the orders, the creators gave me one other thing; an emotion."

She stopped in her tracks, caught in a daze from remembering a time when one emotion was all she had to worry about.

"What was the emotion?" Deltrin asked.

A single tear emerged from her eye and rolled down her pale cheek.

"Hope."

She turned her attention to Deltrin, who noticed the streak.

"I bet you thought machines were incapable of tears. That's the trouble with emotions. They can't stand to be alone."

Deltrin lifted his hand to wipe the tear from her cheek. She gazed into his eyes and cupped her hand around his wrist. She smiled and continued her story.

"Despair came soon after and as I watched the planet die, I felt sorrow. I did not want to see it become a dead rock. With the metals blasted out of the volcanoes, I started to make myself some friends, who would help me save this planet. Love was the next emotion. I felt a deep connection to the friends I made and with their help, we built a city in the core of the planet. The creators did not foresee the planet's destruction, not realizing they left me on a dying planet. That was the next emotion; forgiveness. In time, my band and I have rejuvenated this planet. The city you are in is actually the main computer that runs the planet."

"The city runs the planet." He repeated. "That's incredible. But why does the planet still look like it's dying?"

"My orders were to watch for the traveler to come and to

make sure no threatening force, like the Rashouwe, would have the chance to infiltrate the planet. Considering the planet is very violent, there is no reason for anything to tread upon its surface. In order to keep that protection alive, I had to make sure the volcanoes stayed active and that the atmosphere remained toxic to foreigners. The vast tunnel system you saw when you entered the city is actually running the gas into the atmosphere. I have the power to change that, and since you are breathing right now, I have proven my worth."

"So this planet is actually dead, but has the illusion of life?"

She nodded.

"Strange you should mention life and illusion in the same sentence. I am a robot, but am capable of exercising the same emotions as any living creature. We are alike, you and me. If you want to use the argument that a machine does not have a spirit or a soul, then let me retort before you begin. Emotions are the bread of life. We feed our spirits with the sensation of passion. I have a soul, Deltrin, just like you."

She paused for a moment and walked up to Deltrin.

"You have much to do. I hate to see you go, but you must return to your ship and finish your quest. Violaze is waiting."

"You know about my friend?" he asked.

"Of course. I must admit, it is nice to have a companion."

She closed her eyes and leaned forward to kiss him. The warmth from her lips could have fooled anyone. She was not a machine. She was alive. Passion for life was what made this possible. Something that can be forgotten or taken for granted by those who are born with it.

"I would like a companion, myself." She whispered. "Come back to me when you are finished."

He stared into her golden countenance and promised he would return. She smiled at him, knowing his sincerity. She walked him out, but before he left, he asked a final question.

"Explain to me you choice of decor."

She looked around her magnificent room and looked back at him.

"The soul needs to be fed, Deltrin. Beauty is one of my soul's favorite dishes. On the surface, the planet is hot and void of life. My workers and friends are incapable of experiencing emotion. In my home, there is life everywhere. The paintings, the windows, the scenes you see on the tables, they are all alive, speaking their thoughts to me, keeping me company. Like I said, I find peace here. There are things I know you will soon find out, which I try to forget by surrounding myself with color and life."

She spoke her last words like a plea.

"When you finish your quest, leave your world of death and live with me in this world. Feed your soul with the right sustenance"

He did not know how to take her last comment. She gave him a reassuring smile, handed him the piece of the map he almost forgot, and sent him on his way.

When he reached the surface of the planet, he noticed he was no longer using his regulator. Instead, he was able to breathe in the fresh air.

The planet also changed from when last he saw it. The trees were green with vivid blossoming all around. The mountains were calm, the breeze was cool. Everything was peaceful.

287

He walked back into the ship, without making a stop in his chamber. He opened the hatch and stepped into his ship. He was quickly greeted by his little friend, who was very glad to see him.

"Have I got a story for you."

The Dream

Deltrin began to awake from his flashback, and noticed he had been asleep for two hours. He stretched his tired body and wiped the solidified water from his eyes. He scratched his head and got up from his seat to walk back to his bedroom.

Violaze was sleeping on the pillow. Deltrin made sure he was quiet, trying not to awake his slumbering friend. He sat in his chair and made himself comfortable. He picked up the manuscript, opened to the last page he read, and continued on with the story...

Everyone will lose their father sooner or later, but not twice. I was silent most of the way to the fourth planet. I sat in a chair for hours, looking at the passing stars, trying to find some sort of meaning. Unfortunately this time, they were just stars.

I needed something to crash into my life, like a message or an impacting statement. I looked to the brilliant specks of light waiting for a spark of clarity, but the stars kept their silence and just looked at me as they brushed passed my horizon.

I had created those stars. Where was that awesome power now, when I needed it most?

Terinsa and Retnar were also in the room, but I barely noticed their presence. Nevertheless, I spoke.

"I keep trying to tell myself that he's not gone as long as we keep him in our hearts, but I don't want to drown myself in sanctimony." I said.

I didn't take my eyes away from my lonely window. "What do you want to tell yourself?" She asked, disconsolate.

"I don't know yet." I responded.

I took a final look out into the silence before I turned to face her. The soundless space was frightening. I could feel inner peace by just looking into it, but the further I looked, the more the peace dissipated and turned into confusion and uneasiness. Something was out there, bigger than my comprehension and it was frustrating.

"I have never really believed in an afterlife. I've never believed in death, either."

A sigh of weariness emerged from my lungs.

"I've dedicated my entire existence to creating life, and yet I stand helpless to the force that dictates what happens after our life has expired."

I turned to the window and stared back into the void.

"Right now, Octan and the Admiral are asking questions that we don't even have the knowledge to consider. But what scares me the most is the possibility that there is no one out there to listen. Perhaps that is why I didn't want to think of an afterlife in the first place. I did not want to come to the realization that we become something different than what we are now. Even worse, I didn't want to find out that we don't change, at all. There I would be, dead. Cognizant of my past life, but not being able to enjoy it ever again.

Terinsa and Retnar said not a word to my statement. I was glad they didn't. I was not in the mood for someone to stop my train of thought.

"I feel content with the knowledge I have for the mechanics of life, but I don't have any knowledge about the

290

mechanics of death. I feel that is appropriate because death is another realm of which we are not a part. What I'm most afraid of, though, is that I would find myself in the universe of death, with the same knowledge of life, and the same lack of knowledge about death."

I paused for a moment and stared out into space. The stars outside the window began to whisper as quiet as a soft breeze. I could tell they were leaving me.

"I look out into the stars and I feel lonely. What if there are no stars where death looms?"

"Tyran." Terinsa interrupted. "I know the loss of the Admiral weighs heavy on you right now. It's doing the same to me."

She walked over and placed her hand on my shoulder.

"Stop looking for answers. They'll only bring you grief."

She was right. Knowledge does bring grief. It would be so easy to just rely on something else to provide the answers I was looking for, but I did not handle things in that fashion. I was my own provider and what killed me inside was this impotence to reward myself with the revelations I desired. Maybe I didn't want answers at all.

I had two choices; to either continue on with my never-ending interrogation and receive no remuneration, or stop now and concede to the power whose land I was trespassing on. I chose the latter.

"Perhaps you're right. I need to stay within the boundaries of my own field of expertise."

"There is something we Trocties like to think." Retnar included, with a relatively easier mood than Terinsa's and mine. "You remember how I told you that all life is electricity?"

We nodded our heads.

"Well, death acts in the same manner, only with a slight twist. You see, electricity has no death. Instead, it changes form. If it were possible to steal electrical currents in open space like we do with other beings, we would be able to hear the stories of millions of different creatures."

I must admit, it did sound somewhat inconceivable, but it was a nice thought in comparison to my pessimism. "The Admiral and Octan's memories can be found, but their presence would be indistinguishable. Whatever forms of electricity they have become has a completely different language than ours."

I listened to what Retnar's words, but nothing helped. I was in a pensive state, where even the reasonable answers were ignored. I didn't want plausibility in my theories; I just wanted to find a way to subdue all my stray thoughts.

I went to bed, with the trailing thought that Retnar's outlook on death was not that eccentric. However, I did not need to learn any ancient art of stealing thoughts to find anything. The memories were there to begin with. All I had to do was clear my mind with any unnecessary garbage and simply concentrate.

There was a window next to my head, inviting me to gaze into its mystery. Memories began to flicker before my eyes, and I found myself drifting into the warm nostalgic hands of the memories that danced with the stars. Before long, I fell asleep. For the first time in many months, I dreamed.

Usually, I am aware of when I am dreaming and when I am walking along the plains of reality, but considering the clarity of the dream I was having, I couldn't tell where I was.

From my many years of experience, I have found there are actually three states of being instead of just two. The two known states are the conscious and the subconscious. The third state is a threshold between the two worlds, where they collide and mesh together.

We would like to think that we spend the majority

of our lives in the 'real' conscious world, but in actuality, we spend just as much time in the fantastical world of our sub-conscious. We understand our conscious world because it involves a tangible existence, whereas the sub-conscious world is purely cerebral.

Early philosophers of ancient Universes would preach the idea that the lives we live are actually dreams themselves, and when the time came when our lives would end, we would simply wake up in another 'realm'. They would explain that the eccentricities of our dreams were not understandable on the premise that they were essences of a different form of existence. Only when we reach the next realm would they become intelligible. When we reached that future world, the dreams we would have in that life would be of the next world in the time-line, and so on. Dreams are nothing more than a preview of what's to come.

The third state of being of which I aforementioned is a bridge that connects the conscious and the sub-conscious. Think of it as an interpreter.

The sub-conscious realm is like a mist, or a fog, where nothing seems to make sense. In order for it to gain some clarity, a guide is needed. That is where the bridge comes in. Without this exegetic essence, the two worlds would not connect and the transition from one to the other would be very rough, like traveling over violent waves of unforgiving waters.

I mentioned our lives are constantly plagued with confusion, where we are gradually trying to understand which world has the greatest impact. In actuality, the bridge between them is the most influential.

It's common sense that nothing can be understood without a medium or a tool of translation. Both the conscious world and the sub-conscious world could not be rationalized without the help of the interpretive third world. That is the reason why the interpreter is the most influential. I am telling you all this because the dream I had was literally representative of these three worlds.

I felt myself drifting away from inside the spaceship to a world I was unfamiliar with. The transition between worlds was as gentle as the strings on a violin and as soft as its melody.

My landing into the dark domain was as light as a feather, but it was not the landing I noticed. I concentrated more on the bleak atmosphere of my dreamscape. I didn't move from where I stood for several minutes, trying to absorb all I could about my new surroundings. The air was cool, almost haunting, as if the wind I felt was the caress from a forgotten spirit. I couldn't smell anything, which probably meant my sense of smell was inoperable in my subconscious state. I could, however, hear perfectly well and could sense I was not alone.

There were trees all around me, swaying back and forth, amused at my present situation. They were all colored the same radiant green, with the occasional blossoming of flowers on their branches. Pedals from above repeatedly fell on my face, tickling the hairs on my skin. They gently settled upon the ground, creating a rather splendid garden at my feet.

I was surprised to see such a display of extreme radiance of color in this dark atmosphere. It was as if the trees and the land they rested on produced their own light. But then again, I was dreaming, and from what I have experienced in my dreams, anything is possible.

I finally decided to leave my fallen garden and journey off into this strange land, unafraid of the mysteries that lurked in the shadows. The ground was soft, and with each proceeding step, it grew softer, like the ground was liquefying while I walked upon it. The trees began to sway with more meaning and I could hear the leaves and the wind laughing at me as I fell deeper into the earth. I began to panic, desperately trying to find something to hang on to, but no matter what I grabbed a hold on, it would break or shatter and I would continue to sink. I was running as fast as I could, feeling the blood pump through every vein in my body as hard as it could. In my dream, I could feel the sweat pour down my brow, and feel the shortness of my breath.

The snickering wind and the cackling trees grew more emphatic in their enjoyment, as I fell further into the shifting land. I was up to my knees in no time, and the effort it took to press on increased exponentially. It was getting harder to move my legs.

I could no longer move. I was prisoner to the earth below me. The trees bent down to gaze upon their captive, finding pleasure and amusement to their latest catch. I was helpless, a feeling I had forgotten due to my ignoring of such a weakness. Where was my universal power now? How dare these simple creatures entangle me and stick me into their muddy grave. Is this how they displayed their respect to the one who created them? With this thought of my own divine providence, I sank deeper into their grasp.

"What do you want with me?" I demanded of them, the guardians of nature who hovered above me. "How can you hold me captive, when I am one of your creators?"

"Realize this." A faceless voice emerged from the trees. "You are not forever, rather just a link in the circle of time, destined to be eventually replaced. Your glory in creating life was indeed exceptional, yet you forget that you yourself are a product of your own creation; a single, yet gifted life that grew within another universe. You are no different from me."

"But you are nothing more than trees and dirt, whereas I am a mobile, intelligent being, with the experience of over two-billion years of life."

"Yet, you forget I am holding you captive." The voice responded. "You are at my mercy. How tragic that your

life can end by your own arrogance and short-sightedness."
"To what?" I asked. "What am I not seeing?"
"Your mortality is catching up to you. Tell me, how did you feel when the Admiral died?"

I remained silent, waiting for the voice to inform me of my emotions.

"You have forgotten you will eventually die. This delusion of grandeur that has kept with you for so long has left you with the presumption that you are a god and will not die. But there are forces greater than you, Tyran. The forces you tried to comprehend not too long ago, but failed because you refuse to accept their existence. I am holding you captive because I want to show you you're not as great and powerful as you would like to believe."

The wind around me transformed into a tangible essence, manifesting into what I could only describe as a spirit. The white shade twisted around me like a cyclone, seeping in and out of my body, until it finally culminated in front of me and solidified into a cloaked figure. I watched in a stupor, as the specter glided towards me, reached out for my hand and said, "Follow me, Tyran".

Normally, I am not one to argue with an unknown specter who incidentally, knows who I am and was on a mission to reveal my faults. Without hesitation, I took hold of his hand.

He pulled me out of the liquid earth and I was once again free to roam. However, I was not free to go where I wanted, considering the mysterious host had other plans for me.

I was no longer touching the ground with the steps I took. Being with the mysterious host must have enchanted my travels, so I didn't have to worry about falling into the bottomless land any more.

We finally came to one of the destinations. Extended from the green land of this shifting world was a sturdy bridge made of a material that looked like wood of some sort.

We stopped at the base of the trestle and waited. The seas it towered over were incredibly violent, but the waves did not splash upon the shores. Instead, the water calmed down to a sit-still at the foot of the shore.

There were no ships to be seen, nor was there anything floating in the water. Just the white waves that covered the blue, rocking back and forth. I wondered to myself if it were possible for anything living to survive beneath the course waves. Thank the Heavens I never did get the chance to answer that question.

The entity shifted and stared at me with its phantom eyes.
"Do not fear anything, Tyran." It said, with a dark accent. "This bridge will take us to a world of your dreams, literally." It chuckled at its last statement.

It stepped onto the bridge, suddenly realizing I was no longer holding its hand. The specter turned around and stared at me with a puzzled look. I looked at it, displaying my true emotions, showing with my eyes how scared I was. "I'm afraid." I told my guide, with as much sincerity as I could command.

It looked at me, pleased to see my humility.
"Take my hand. My intentions are not to harm you, but to teach you."
"Think of this bridge as a transport. It is simply a doorway between existences. You must trust me. Take my hand and follow me."

His arm swiftly extended towards me. I could not resist anymore. With an unexpected sense of confidence, I took hold and pulled myself onto the bridge.

I began to walk again, this time on solid ground. However, the solidity of the bridge began to change with every step I took. I held tightly to my companion's hand.

The scenery began to change. Not the sky, no, the sky stayed dark and peaceful. It was the atmosphere below the bridge that began to change. The water that was once violent had calmed down, finally reaching a state of serenity, making it look like a satin cloak.

I then began to hear voices. They were faint at first, but grew louder as time passed. The voices were very familiar. The wind they traveled on brushed against my face, rushed through my ears and pervaded my mind. Before my eyes, I saw the air in front of me shift into pictures and scenes of random memories of my past. The whispers morphed into the voices of my family and friends as the atmosphere transformed into the memories corresponding with what was being said.

"What's happening?" I yelled up to my friend. I could not see where he was, but I could hear his response.

"You are leaving the world of your existence. What you are seeing now is a reaction to your virtual death. You are reminiscing on what is familiar to you. Call it a cushion for an unusual journey."

The bridge began to evaporate as soon as the specter explained the phenomena. Suddenly, I was walking on thin air with only the water below me.

Memories passed through the mist at irregular intervals for brief moments of time, hoping I would remember them. I experienced every feeling possible of the emotional spectrum as the reunion of my past played through its entirety. It was like I had traveled back in time and was watching myself grow up and older.

I wanted to reach out my hand and touch the head of my younger self, promising a long and eventful life for him to come. I saw my parents, young and unafraid of the future. How I longed to grab them in my arms and thank them. I tried, but failed at every attempt. I waved my hands through the clouds in front of me, but as soon as I attempted, they faded away just as quickly as a breath on a mirror.

The memories dissipated all too quickly. Soon

enough, I was once again walking on the bridge. I looked down at the water, which was now violent. We walked few more steps and suddenly, we stopped.

The ghost turned around and smiled. It let go of my hand and walked forward a couple steps.

"We have reached our destination."

With the wave of his shroud, the specter revealed a gateway to the world on the other side of the bridge. How can words describe such a sight? I am not blessed with such descriptive talents. All I can say is that all my fears were lifted from my soul; all the pain I experienced throughout my entire life was forgotten. I was in the presence of greatness, in a realm where happiness was something I could embrace. I could feel its purity surround me and animate my countenance. It was life in a physical presence. It was the soul of existence and I could see it, feel it, and become one with it.

The specter asked me if I were willing to take its hand once again and penetrate the brilliant gates that guarded the esoteric world. Without a second thought, I nodded, still entranced by the beauty before me.

He took my hand and led me closer to the gleaming threshold. With a gentle embrace, the gate absorbed us into its aura and became one with us. I cannot remember a time where I felt so alive in a dream. I became pure energy, pure in everything as I passed from the bridge to the majestic world in front of it. I opened my eyes and could not breathe, completely dazed at the view.

We had passed through the golden threshold and were now standing on a mountain, overlooking a landscape I thought impossible to create, even in a dream.

I was still holding on to the hand of the specter and tried to let go to explore the world on my own. It did not let me.

"I assure you," it said, "You'll want to hang on."

Hang on? I thought. This, as you can imagine, was quite

frightening.

Before I could blink, the specter jumped off the mountain, with me holding on for dear life.

It chuckled at how hard my grip was.

"Relax. This is the best part."

Hours passed, or so it seemed, for us to fall down the mountainside. I should have been afraid, but I could not produce the emotion. I also should have felt at peace, but I could not feel that as well. I was impotent to produce any emotion.

The ground suddenly came closer at an accelerated rate. Without me realizing it, we plunged into the earth below. I didn't feel a thing. Considering the distance we fell, we should have been flattened paper thin. Instead, we dove into the land as if it were liquid.

"Things are different here apart from your existence." It spoke. "However, I can remember what it was like living in that realm."

The specter looked at me with its glowing eyes and playful grin.

"I want to show you something."

I was pulled out of the liquid ground and led to a different realm.

The only solid ground was a tiny patch of land, floating in a sea of stars. We were in space, but we were still able to breathe.

"Are you creating these worlds?" I asked.

"We both are." The ghost responded, perhaps deliberately to confuse me.

"How could I be making this world if I have no clue where I am? I don't even know how to control my emotions."

"Feeling humble yet?"

I turned around, almost sickened by the revelation of its intentions.

"Is that why you brought me here? To scare me?"

"Were you not paying any attention to your experience on

the bridge? Look around you, Tyran. You're dead! Doesn't that mean anything to you?"

"But this is a dream, isn't it?" I asked, feeling my hands fidgeting at my side.

"How can you be so sure?"

Suddenly, I couldn't breathe anymore. Strange that I hadn't noticed I was breathing before. I couldn't tell if I was breathing during my adventure on the bridge, but now I felt the lack. I was suffocating in this realm of space.

I could tell the spirit was watching, waiting for something.

"You are indeed passionate, my friend." He spoke with a new accent, like that of a parent trying to teach their child. "But what are you passionate about?"

I could breathe again. I took a moment to respect my new breath of air.

"Have I not shown enough passion for life?" I began "I have dedicated my life to building a realm of existence."

"No you haven't." The spirit quickly interrupted. "Existence has always been here. What you did was build a new realm for it to expand."

"But my work paved the way to new life."

"And now you want to destroy it."

"Yes." I said, taking a few seconds to realize what I had said. "I regret that destroying this existence is the only way to pave way for new life."

"What gives you the right to decide the fate of countless beings?"

For an instant, I felt ready to answer, but I could not. At that moment, I realized I had no authority over any being. I produced a realm for life to grow and flourish, but that did not give me the right to take it away. I remained silent, contemplating questions I thought had been answered in the past.

"Why do you want to kill everything? I thought you had passion for life?"

Tears began to fall upon my cheek.

"I do." I said. "But I can't think of any other way to save life from the Rashouwe."

"It seems to me that your destructive weapon holds much more fear than the entire Rashouwe faction. Why should anything fear them when it is you who threatens their existence? Could it be that you have become what you hate the most?"

"No. Unlike the Rashouwe, I fight for the perseverance of life." I responded rather hastily.

"But so do they. Remember, they helped create the universe so that life could expand."

"Yes, but only to kill it."

"Not unlike yourself."

This was a response I did not like.

"How dare you compare me to such a vile race! I don't create just to destroy."

"But what do you think you are doing now? You created this universe and now you're going to eliminate it. Don't you find that ironic?"

"But if I don't," I continued, "Everything will die."

"You forget, Tyran, all things eventually die. Why are you hurrying things up?"

I was feeling agitated from all the interrogation and did not give him the satisfaction of an answer. Instead, I asked him a question.

"Do propose something better?"

He seemed intrigued from my participation.

"Tell me, my friend, do you feel there is no hope if the Rashouwe are not destroyed?"

"You know I do."

"That's where you're wrong."

The spirit paused for a moment and began to remove the cloak from his head. His countenance was still hazy, fogged by the mist around us, but soon I was able to recognize who my guide really was. He was me.

302

There I was, starring into the eyes of myself, this doppelganger I would soon become, or have already been. "I am your proof there is hope in the future. I am your future."

"My future? I asked, terrified at the sudden revelation. "So, you're a product of our final universe?"

"No." He said smiling. "I am a being of the next realm of existence, a realm separate from this collection of universes that you're so familiar with. I am your next life. You see, each realm of life is caught in a circle of time. You are never in the same realm twice, yet your one life in your realm is repeated over and over again, hence the circle of time. When you are gone from your present life, you will become me in this realm."

"But when does my realm complete the circle?"

"Very soon, which brings me to my next point. You must change the manuscript of equations before it is discovered."

"And do what?"

"Put back the gravity barrier."

"And let the Rashouwe continue their reign of terror."

"Let me finish." The spirit quickly said. "Make sure the explosion takes everything out, like you wanted in the first place. In time, gravity will take over and the universe will decrease in size, giving room for more universes."

Finally it hit me.

"This future explosion is the end of the circle, isn't it?"

The spirit smiled.

"Very good. So you see you are subject to an even greater force? Something called fate?"

I had. I realized I was not as powerful and authoritative as I believed. This dream's purpose was to show me I was just a mortal being, like any other I have encountered in my travels. One thing still confused me.

"But I will still be destroying all life as I know it. I thought you told me that was bad?"

"It's fate. I had to realize, as you soon will, that the

decisions I made were already planned out. But, this is not a bad thing. As long as we believe what we do is deliberate, we feel content with our actions."

"But now I know my life is predestined. How can I ever feel content with my actions?"

"You needed to be reminded that you are not a god. The only way to do this was to show you your death, and that life would continue without your intervention. You are an important figure in your realm, but you do not have the authority to guide the path of existence."

"But how can I be even remotely important if I am nothing more than a empty transport for some higher power to control?" I asked, feeling destroyed inside.

"Do you remember the passion you felt for life before you met me?"

I nodded faintly.

"Regain that feeling again. You are no longer above the beings you feel you are fighting for. Now, with this revelation, you are fighting with them. You now feel the fear of death approaching you, which inadvertently makes you respect life."

"How?" I asked "How can I possibly enjoy life knowing that everything I will do is already planned out?"

"Do you know how and when you're going to die?"

I shook my head.

"Do you know what is going to happen when you wake up?"

Again, I shook my head.

"You never will until it happens, and it will hold the same surprise it would if you had never met me in the first place. All I had to do was remind you of your place in life. You have obviously shown your humility to the power and sublimity of your universe. For that, I am inspired. However, your actions to dictate how life should continue were not yours to decide upon. Do you see now why I brought you here?"

I nodded, feeling once again the humility I felt when I first saw the universe born out of the black void. I felt new to life, realizing once again I am nothing in comparison to the grand scheme of things. My spirit was right. I had no idea how my life would eventually turn out. All I knew was that my life was not forever. I had lived for so long that I had forgotten. That is what had bothered me so much about the Admiral's death. It was the vision of my delicate existence that frightened me, but I did not want to admit it. Not to anyone. Not to myself.

"You are a good man, Tyran. Remember that. You wish to protect life and will to the day you leave your realm. But remember you are doing this not because you are their protector and god, but that you are their brother in life. Keep your humility and passion for life and remember that nothing is forever, except the circle of time. Evil will sometimes triumph, as will good, but they will never fully win. But that's what makes life so extraordinary; the challenge. Continue your fight for your cause, Tyran, but remember you are fulfilling a mission given to you not by yourself. Awake, and live again."

With that, he was gone and I found myself alive in my quarters, with a strange new sense of being. I felt my mortality catching up to me, but I was no longer afraid. I stayed in my bed for quite sometime, wondering if I was happy, or just feeling a new challenge.

The City-Ship

"I didn't expect to see you so cheery this morning." Terinsa said, as I walked into the dining room. She was showing a bit of jubilance to see I was feeling better.

"I had a wonderful dream." I told her. I stopped where she was sitting and gave her a kiss.

"Are you going to tell me about it?"

"No." I replied. "I think I'll keep it for myself. Rest assured that I'm not afraid anymore."

"I should hope not." She said. "Because we are at planet four. Guess who gets to place the tube on the surface?"

I didn't give her the satisfaction of answering her. I instead dipped my finger in the glass of water on the table and flicked a little in her face. She laughed and walked out of the room to the cockpit. I followed her.

Retnar was sitting in the seat, manually flying the spacecraft to the icy surface below.

"Did Terinsa tell you the good news?"

"Yes, Retnar, she did. It's so nice to know you two are conspiring against me. In all seriousness, though, is there anything that should concern me about the planet?"

"Apart from the freezing temperatures," he answered, "It should be completely void of any action. I would, however, put on heavy clothing if I were you."

"Well," I said, playing the part. "I was going to run out there naked and spend some time enjoying the sun-light. But now that you have pointed out the tiny flaw in my plan, I guess I should get dressed."

The operation did not take long. I stepped out into the cold atmosphere and finished the job in about ten minutes, added time due to the fact that a broke through the ice in one area of the hand, but that is unimportant. Luckily, Retnar landed perfectly on top of the pedestal, right next to the 'finger' that we wrapped the tube around.

I was, however, freezing when I got back into the ship. Retnar and Terinsa were waiting for me when I entered through the outer hatch. As Terinsa kept watch over me for any side effects, Retnar pulled anchor and set off for planet five.

I wish to spare you the details of our adventure on planet four, considering you've been there yourself and know there really isn't much to talk about.
Deltrin laughed to himself.

For that reason, I want to spend more time discussing the events that took place on planet five. They are much worthier of being told.

The fire planet had been on my mind ever since we left the temple. I had never been there before, but from what Terinsa had told me, it seemed to be an extraordinary place.

I was pleased the fourth part of our mission was brief. I did not look forward to spending time on the dead planet. I knew the next mission would be much more arduous, and would require all the energy we had.

The night before we landed on the red planet, the three of us gathered around the dining table and had a nice drink and a pleasant conversation.
"What do you plan on doing after we're done, Retnar?" I asked him.
"I haven't really given it much thought. I suppose I will

return to my home planet and live out my days there. All this traveling is enough to last me a life-time." He said, chuckling. "Do you two have any plans set out?"

"We haven't decided yet." Terinsa said. "We just know we'll be together. That suits me just fine."

He smiled and saluted her with his glass.

"I must admit." He continued after he drank. "I will be very sad to see you two leave. You have been the closest friends I've ever had.

"Likewise." I said. "But I think you would eventually grow tired of us, especially Terinsa."

She elbowed me in the chest and looked me sharply.

"Watch it." She said. "I could leave you marooned on a planet, and stay with Retnar."

She winked and kissed me on the cheek.

"Remember what you have."

I chuckled at her last comment. As if I needed to be reminded. Retnar eventually spoke up.

"I just want you guys to know what you mean to me, while I still have the chance. If I die tomorrow, I will die happy, knowing I've helped pave the way for peace and new life. You have given me that gift and I am forever grateful to you. I will never forget you."

He raised his glass for the final time that night and said his toast.

"A being of great wisdom once told me that the greatest love is the one fought hardest for. The blood that we have shed on this mission has baptized our bond of friendship, and has made it the most cherished love of all. Here is to the mission. The impetus of our bond."

We all drank to his eloquent toast and placed our glasses on the table. With that, we all went to bed to rest for the adventurous day ahead of us.

The fire planet glowed in the dark space, like the eye of a prowling hunter. It waited for us, instilling false hope and security into our spirits. We accepted its superficial hospitality and placed ourselves into its fiery claws. It blazed with laughter as it snatched us up. Another trophy for its case. The heat of its belly swelled up into our ship and drained our energy until we collapsed and allowed ourselves to be the unsuspecting prey of the demon within.

Hours passed until we finally awoke in a dark cell, underneath the smoldering surface. Strangely enough, it was cool in the damp oubliette, however, that did not please me one bit. We were all prisoners in an unforgiving world.

Footsteps could be heard, approaching us from the dark hallway behind the cell's door. A key rattled and the door opened. Three figures stepped forward, but could not be distinguished due to the lack of light.
"The Constructor General." One of them said. "What a surprise. I thought you bought it on the Phantom Hunter, Captain Tyran."

I knew that voice. Pity. I thought I was going to live the rest of my life without ever hearing it again.
"Where's the rest of your friends, Frolton? Did you stab them in the back as well?"
"Spare me your sarcasm." He spit back at me. "They are no concern of yours. You should be more concerned about your present condition."

He slithered towards me and glared at my tired face. "Where is the manuscript?"

I could not help but to laugh at the pathetic question.
"All you villains are the same. Always asking stupid questions when you know none of us will give you the answer you're looking for."

I don't think he liked my response that much. I think it was the sudden blow he smashed my jaw with that clinched my suspicion. I was still conscious, though.
"I'm not your typical villain, my stupid friend." He hissed.

309

"Many will often overlook certain characteristics of their enemy, being blinded by their vanity. I, on the other hand, know it is important to study your opponent before attacking. You are a very intelligent being, as hard as it is for me to admit. The combined forces that rally behind you are without a doubt, very strong. However, I know we will eventually beat you, but that is not what we want. We want a new arena for our festivities. We do not have the necessary information needed to know in order to create a universe. That is why you three are valuable assets to have."

"A stalemate would still be a victory for our side." Terinsa blurted. "We'll all three die before we tell you where the manuscript is. Fortunately, we are the only ones who know its hiding place. Our forces know we will die eventually. Perhaps denying you of your macabre desire to kill is what we really want."

He turned his head.

"Still thick-headed, are you, my dear?" He taunted. "You never were a player. I'll have you know we are so spread out, we'll eventually find it, even if we have to tear all of space apart. But I think you'll talk before it comes to that."

"What makes you think that?" She retorted.

"Simple. Pain." He walked over to me and pulled out a jagged blade. "I'll give you a preview of what you have in store."

I can barely remember what happened next. One second, I could see him aiming the blade at me, and the next, he plunged the fang-like knife into my left shoulder. He didn't stop there. He kept the knife inside me for a few seconds, twisting it left and right, until everything was serrated inside. As hard as it was to hold in the pain, I never wailed, denying him the satisfaction of breaking me down.

He finally pulled the weapon out and wiped the blood on me. He chuckled to himself and walked out of the room, his escorts following close behind.

The moment he left, I passed out from the pain and did not wake for almost an hour. When I did, I noticed I could not move my left arm at all. I couldn't even move my fingers.

"What happened?" I whispered through my daze.

"How much do you remember?" Terinsa asked, with Retnar by her side.

"I remember being stabbed, but that's about it. Come to think of it, the stabbing's pretty hazy, too."

Retnar got up and looked at my arm.

"What can you move, my friend?"

"Nothing. I can't even tell if my arm's there. The bastard must have cut everything inside."

"They'll heal in time, Tyran." Terinsa said, trying to console me as best she could. "But it won't be for a long time."

She took a moment's breath before she said her next line.

"I'm so terribly sorry I provoked him. It should have been me he wounded, not you."

"Don't take the blame for his cruelty. Nothing could have prevented it from happening. What's done is done. Besides, I think we should try to come up with a plan on getting out of here. Do either of you know how we got here in the first place?"

"We were asleep for as long as you were, Tyran." Retnar said. "We're just as lost as you."

The days that passed were routine. They fed us once a day, and left us alone. I found that rather strange, considering Frolton seemed very interested in knowing the location of the manuscript. We never saw him again after the initial meeting. Not that it was a bad thing. What was bad was the fact that we were left in suspense. I would have rather had them torture us, instead of leaving us in

311

anticipation of the worst. It was our impatience that ate away at us.

"Is this part of our torture?" Retnar asked with little energy. He barely wheezed the question from his beaten lungs. I shrugged my shoulders, just as confused.

"You know what bothers me?" Terinsa asked. We turned our heads to face her in anticipation of her answer.

"We shouldn't be able to breathe the air. Even though my thoughts are scattered and vague, I still distinctly remember the atmosphere being sulfur based. We should be dead."

"Maybe were in a controlled cell." I suggested.

"Come on Tyran." She said. "You know as well as I do the Rashouwe don't keep prisoners, let alone control a cell for their captured to survive. Something's wrong with this scenario. The only reason we are being kept alive is to tell them where the manuscript is, but we haven't seen hide nor hair of Frolton for the past five days. Why are we being kept alive?"

My brain did not want to work, so it was very difficult to come up with an answer. We all three tried to come up with a plausible explanation, but failed at our attempts. We simply did not have the energy to think.

Another day passed and we were still left in the dark, literally. I could barely move, glued to the hard floor. Terinsa was leaned up against one of the walls, and Retnar was on his back in the middle of the room, staring straight up.

We didn't get food that day. Instead, we were greeted by Frolton, who did not seem as happy as his usual mad self. That was because of the unwelcome visitors who led him into our cell.

Three hooded figures walked close behind him. One had a weapon poking Frolton in the back. The armed figure took his hood off. Even though I lacked the energy, I could tell my features lit up when I saw who it was.

"Rinar!"

He threw Frolton down to the floor and bent down, hovering over me.

"Good to see you again, Captain."

"I thought I'd never see you again."

He chuckled. "Yeah, well. Here I am." He looked over at Terinsa and Retnar and greeted them with the same demeanor.

"Are any of you hurt?"

"Tyran was stabbed in the left arm." Terinsa exclaimed. "He can't move it at all."

Rinar bent down to have a look at my arm. He could see the bones exposed, as well as my severed muscles. He sighed deeply and looked me in the eye.

"That's a pretty deep wound. I'll have my surgeons look at, but they won't be able to heal it completely. Did he do that to you?"

I nodded. Rinar pulled a ragged knife from his vest pocket and proceeded over to Frolton.

"If you were a true Rashouwe," Rinar told him, "you would have done the job right."

With a single motion, Rinar swiftly drew a sharp weapon, cutting the air around his knife, and took off Frolton's left arm.

The cut was incredibly clean, almost undetected. At first, Frolton had no idea what had just happened to him, but as soon as his arm fell to the ground, the realization hit him hard. The shock took his power of speech.

"Don't think I'm through with you." Rinar said, putting his knife back into his pouch. "Tie him up."

His two companions leapt to the order instantly. Rinar moved to Terinsa and helped her up. As soon as she got to her feet, she was able to move around. He told her to get out of the cell and wait for the rest of them to follow. She did as he asked and left the cell. He then lifted Retnar to his feet and told him the same.

"We need to get out of here quickly." He told me as he

313

lifted me up. He made sure my arm was secured, so not to disturb the wound.

Frolton was soon bound, and bleeding profusely. Rinar took notice of the loss of blood and told me to wait outside, but I could still hear what he did inside the cell.

"I wouldn't want to kill you that easy." He hissed at Frolton. He took a flare from his pant's pocket and lit it. He then put the flame up to his open wound and cauterized it. The blood stopped, as did Frolton's silence. He bellowed with pain as the fire cut deeper into his skin.

"If you were just another enemy, I would have killed you long ago. But since you harmed my friends, I have to make you pay. Getting rid of you is probably doing the Rashouwe a favor. However, that's a regret I'm going to have to live with. Taking the good with the bad is something I can deal with."

Rinar turned around and left the room, stepping on the severed arm as he exited. He slammed the door behind him and led us through the dark tunnel.

"Can we breathe the air on the surface?" Terinsa asked him.

"We're not even on the planet." He answered.

We were all too tired to completely absorb what he had just told us, but we were still taken off guard.

"We're on a ship. A Rashouwe City-Ship to be exact. You were being held in a D.C. Unit."

"A what?" I asked.

"A Download Chamber." He continued to take us through the maze, while explaining. "Before I became part of the resistance, the Rashouwe Construction Agents were able to build a type of facility that took the place of truth serums. I assume the habitat was very cool, but damp, right?"

"That's right."

"The dampness you were feeling was a type of gas. It turns liquid at fifteen degrees Celsius, which explains the cold temperature. However, even at something below that marker, it still leaves a type of mist."

"What does the gas do?" Terinsa asked, a little concerned.

"It invades the bloodstream by either inhalation or epidermal exposure. Once the gas mixes with your blood, it travels up your nerve column until it reaches your brain. That is where it begins its work. We have concluded that messages in the brain are conveyed by means of electrical current."

I wanted to tell him that was old news, but I was too tired.

"The gas acts as an articulation device, which makes the brain waves leave the body and travel freely in space. The room you were in was equipped with mechanical devices that absorb the waves and download them into a terminal. The terminal then relays the messages onto a monitor, which is what Frolton and his drones were reading."

"So that would explain why he never bothered to check up on us and beat the information out of us. One thing though, Rinar." I continued. "He told us that he would use pain to get what he wanted."

"Actually, he was." He said. "The gas slowly eats away at your skin. The extreme fatigue that you were feeling was a result of your body spending all its energy trying to keep you alive. In a couple of days, you all would have been dead."

"Did he find out where the manuscript is hidden?" Retnar asked, deeply concerned.

"No. Fortunately, the three of you all have an incredibly strong and multi-layered sub-conscious. With your collection of memories, and their incredibly long life, they had a lot to wade through to get what they wanted."

"That's good to hear." I said.

"For everyone." Rinar concluded.

Soon enough, we reached the end of the hall and found ourselves in an engine room.

"Where are we?" Retnar asked.

"All these gadgets you see control the amount of gas inoculated into the cell's atmosphere."

Rinar walked over to one of the levers and pushed it further on the wheel.

"God help me, I wish I could see him rot."

From what I could read, Rinar increased the gas emanation by three hundred percent. I never got to see how long Frolton lasted, but considering how much gas pervaded the room he was in, his skin probably melted within two hours.

"We have twenty minutes before this ship is completely poisoned." Rinar exclaimed, already leading us to his ship.

We reached the outer hatch within five minutes and climbed aboard Rinar's transport. He closed the hatch and detached himself from the ship.

I got a great look at the City Ship from one of the windows. It was enormous, completely covered with different terminals and cargo holds. This must have been the type of ship they used as a base when they were bombarding solar systems. Taking one of them out was advantageous to our side of the battle.

"Back to the surface, I take it." Rinar asked.

"To a safe place." Terinsa concluded.

"Tyran, I want you to lie down while I fetch my surgeon."

Rinar left the three of us and came back within minutes, accompanied by another Rashouwe.

"He'll take care of your arm Tyran. We won't reach the surface for another three hours. We'll rest for a couple and then I'll tell you our situation."

He and Retnar proceeded down to the cockpit, while the surgeon and Terinsa stayed with me. He worked on my arm for about an hour, stitching here, cutting there. By the time he was done, I was able to move my arm, but very slowly and gently. He told me I would be able to move it with more reaction in a day and would be able to use very soon in case of battle.

Great, I thought. *Just the reason why I wanted it healed.*

We were all gathered around a table, discussing our next move. I was more alert now that I had some rest, as was Terinsa and Retnar.

"The deprival of your energy on your descent to the planet's surface was not caused by any gas that dwells within the planet's boundaries. It was the Rashouwe who penetrated your ship's hull with a vapor that essentially drained you of your energy."

"Are you implying they knew we were coming?" Terinsa asked.

"The Rashouwe have been based on this planet for many years. Though it gives them no tactical advantage, considering it is basically lost in space, it does produce a valuable resource."

Rinar got up from the table and left the room for a brief moment. He returned with three flasks. He set them on the table in front of us. He pointed to the flask that seemed to be filled with a mist colored orange and red.

"The gas inside this jar is the same gas the atmosphere is comprised of. In the jar to its left, you will notice it is filled with a liquid. What you cannot see is that it is comprised of the same elements. However, it is missing one, which brings me to the next jar."

In the third jar, it seemed like there was nothing inside.

"In the cooling process of turning the gas to liquid, an element is released, the gas you cannot see in the jar." He picked up the jar carefully and held it up for us to see. "There is enough gas in this jar to poison an entire planet."

"My God." Retnar exclaimed. "How does it work?"

"When a creature takes the gas within its lungs, it is instantly poisoned, though it does not realize it. The gas is very thin and is inhaled almost without detection. It is the tingling sensation traveling up the nerve column that

317

signals the primary stage of the creature's death. You see, the gas is able to seep out of the lungs and throughout the entire body, tainting the blood stream. What makes it so lethal, however, is its power to change the body cells into its own molecular structure. The element clings to every cell in the body until the blood stream is saturated. Then, it manipulates the cell's original composition and turns it into its own composition. One minute goes by and the entire body is filled with the tainted cells. With every exhalation, the creature expels an enormous amount of gas into the atmosphere, which other creatures will eventually inhale. The time it takes from inoculation to death is three minutes, approximately. It that time, the creature has exhaled enough gas to infest a small community. One by one, the creatures of the planet inhale the gas and end up spreading it profusely."

The power of the Rashouwe has always astounded me, but this new discovery of theirs was the most devastating weapon they have ever placed their squalid hands on.

"Have they used it on anything yet?" I asked, deeply disturbed.

"The only place they could have is this planet, which incidentally would be a foolish move. We have been able to jam their transmissions and intercept their messages, so they couldn't tell any of their ships about it. That is how we found you. To tell you the truth, I knew you would get into more trouble, so I made sure I watched you from a safe distance. It looks as though my suspicions were correct."

"Why would it be foolish to use it on this planet?" I asked.

"Because there are no creatures to test it on."

I forgot about that bit of information.

"To get back to our problems," Terinsa said. "We need to figure out a plan." She turned to Rinar. "How powerful is the Rashouwe force on the planet below?"

"I have not been on the surface to see for myself, but from

318

what I gathered from the many transmissions we intercepted, they have quite a veritable force down there."

"Okay." She said, hoping he would accompany the bad news with good news. "What do we have fighting on our side."

"We are outnumbered three to five."

"Well then." She said. "Let's get started."

There were no allied forces on the surface, fighting with the Rashouwe. To be sure, there never had been. The Rashouwe force residing on the planet was there just for the resource. They seemed to have no clue about the resistance's presence. This gave us a tactical advantage. The element of surprise.

We all deliberated in a dark room, sitting around a table with several maps lit up on an illumination board. Rinar led the discussion.

"Since they no longer have the City-Ship to communicate with, they will have to consolidate their efforts and have their stations come closer together so they can communicate with each other. The City-Ship was their link, so naturally they cannot relay any message around the planet. Without a satellite, they are left in the dark."

He pointed to one of the larger maps.

"Our radar gave us this photograph three days ago, before we rescued you. As you can see, there are many camps scattered all around the planet. On this photograph taken a day ago, which you will remember being slightly after the rescue, you can see the camps have moved closer to each other."

He grabbed another map and placed it in front of us. "This picture was taken twenty minutes ago. The camps have culminated around this area, which is protected by mountains. There are no other traces of Rashouwe life anywhere."

The picture was detailed, showing a very

mountainous area in the northern region of the planet's axis. All the rest of the planet was level ground. If the Rashouwe had placed themselves anywhere else, they would have been open to attack. Something didn't seem right, though.

"So what's our first move?" I asked.

"We wait." He replied. "Our reconnaissance team will scout the area first, to see what part of the camp is the easiest to penetrate."

Two small drop ships detached from the main ship we were on and fell to the surface. Soon enough, they established themselves on the surface and made contact with us.

"Raven Base, this is Raven's eye. The unkindness has arrived."

"Affirmative, Raven's eye." Rinar responded. "Proceed as planned. Out."

We were in video contact with the team in minutes and could see the terrain for ourselves. That's when I realized what had bothered me. There were mountains everywhere, not just in that one vicinity. I turned to Terinsa.

"You told us there were several mountains everywhere before, right?"

"That's right." She said, not realizing her mistake. "I told you that..." She stopped. The horror on her face appeared instantly. She looked down on the maps and studied them.

"Oh, no." she said to herself. She quickly turned to Rinar. "How did you get these photos?"

"We have a camera that takes pictures of the surface, which sends the photo back electronically. The camera downloads the photo onto a terminal, which is where we make a hard copy."

"These photographs are fake." She exclaimed. "I have been on that planet myself, and I distinctly remember the terrain being incredibly mountainous and volcanic. Someone has been giving you false information."

"That's impossible." He said. "No one onboard would do such a thing. I handpicked my army myself, and they are all loyal."

"But what about an outside force?" She retorted.

A faint voice could be heard over the COM.

"Captain, are you there?"

The Captain looked confusedly at Terinsa and picked up the receiver.

"Go ahead."

"We've reached the coordinates and have gone into the mountain."

"And?"

"It seems to be deserted."

"What?!" Rinar burst out. "There were over ten thousand Rashouwe on that surface. Are you telling me they are hiding somewhere else on the planet?"

"Not exactly, sir." He replied. I could detect a little hesitation on the other line, as if he were afraid to tell the Captain what the team found. "The camp is still here. We have done a life-scan for a two hundred mile radius, and there is nothing. They have evacuated the planet."

"To where, Lieutenant? There is no ship they can get to. We poisoned the hull, remember?"

"Yes sir, I do, however, that does not exclude the possibility they knew about the tainted ship and simply put on gas masks."

"How could they have known."

"They must have been watching over us as we were of them. Another thing, Captain." He continued. "The maps we acquired from our camera are wrong. There are thousands of mountains here."

Rinar looked up at Terinsa, whose satisfaction was easily seen through her facial expression.

"I'm sorry I doubted you, Terinsa."

She nodded, accepting the apology.

"Lieutenant, I want you to get out of there at once and get back here."

"Understood, Captain. We're already on our way out."

We watched them evacuate the area on the screen. There was absolutely no movement in the area, besides our team. Before they left, the Lieutenant noticed a terminal on the ground that was turned on.

"Captain?" he asked with shortness of breath. "I think you should see this."

Rinar glanced at the screen and looked at the object the Lieutenant was kneeled in front of.

"What does it say?" He asked.

The lieutenant wiped the dust away from the screen and read what was on the screen.

"Everyone get out!!" He screamed. He jumped up and yelled to his troops to move as fast as they could. But it was too late.

We had seen what was on the screen. A timer that had five seconds left on it, accompanied with a message that read, "Death to Traitors."

The Lieutenant made five steps away from the terminal, which was nowhere near enough for him to get away. It was a trap. The Rashouwe knew about us and had set explosives for us to run into. The explosion wiped out the entire team and killed every soul within a five-mile radius. The Rashouwe had played their cards well, and were on their way to alert their allies to track us down.

Rinar placed his receiver down on the table and stared at the maps for a moment. If the fire burning within him could have flown to his fingers, he could have burnt our ship down with a simple touch.

"So let me get this straight." He said as he ran his fingers through his sweat-drenched hair. "They found the planet and tried to alert their allies. Instead, we jammed their transmissions and stole their messages. We then infiltrated

322

their main ship, killed the passengers and rescued you. We then took photos of the planet's surface, which were actually false because the Rashouwe stole our messages and replaced them with others. We cheated the cheaters who in turned cheated us right back."

We didn't say anything.

"Our only redemption is to go back on the City-Ship and make sure they don't get anywhere."

"Don't we have enough fire-power to blow it completely up?" Retnar asked, rather reluctantly.

"No." He replied. "Besides, their firepower is much greater. They could have blown us up, but that would have wasted their time. They want to tell their forces about this planet, but since we destroyed their communications, they need to find a ship in the vicinity that can communicate and alert the main forces."

"So what do we do to stop them?" I asked.

Rinar thought to himself, trying to figure out what the best plan would be.

"They need all of us to go down to the planet, before they can leave. They need to make that our forces have been completely eliminated. In order to portray that illusion, we need to send all the ships down to the surface, save one. They don't know their little ruse has worked yet. If we send everyone down on the surface and keep them there for a long enough time, they'll think we've fallen into their trap and are dead, and they can leave safely. Once they have started to leave, we can then follow them and infiltrate their ship before they can make contact with anyone else. The problem is not getting down to the surface. We can do that without any complications. The problem is getting on board the City-Ship. We need to be undetected."

I looked at Retnar, who had already thought of the solution.

"My ship has a invisibility drive that has proven effective against the Rashouwe before." He claimed. Rinar was pleased to hear this stroke of luck. "The problem is, I can only fit about thirty inside."

"That is a problem" He replied. "However, I think there is a way we can defeat them with only thirty."

He left the room and brought back a familiar jar.

"We have ten jars of this size filled with the toxin. Three to a team should work. We will find which areas are the most populated and release the gas in the vicinity."

"Isn't the ship already permeated with the other gas?" Terinsa asked.

"Not any more. As soon as they realized the ship was contaminated, they would have cut off the gas current and allowed the gas to dissipate. The air is most likely breathable by now." He took a deep breath and continued with the plan.

"If we can get enough Rashouwe beings to breathe in the toxin, the whole ship should be contaminated within half an hour."

He smiled and turned my way. "So let's have it Tyran. Are you ready for another operation with incredibly bad odds?"

"I know Terinsa is."

She looked at me with eager eyes and smiled wickedly.

"How about you Retnar?"

"What else am I going to do?" He asked sarcastically.

"Well." I said. "Looks like we're all ready. Have your elite force ready in ten minutes and we'll board the ship."

I find it incredible the many things that could take my mind off the original manuscript mission. Never did I think I would have such an eventful odyssey. But then again, the mission would have become incredibly boring without a little excitement.

There were thirty-one of us onboard Retnar's ship, all crunched together. Thankfully, we weren't in uncomfortable positions for too long.

Rinar, Terinsa, Retnar, and I were all in the cockpit, planning our strategy. Fortunately, Rinar had blueprints to one of the City-Ships, which he kept for a purpose such as this.

"How well do you know the infrastructure of this ship?" I asked.

"The City-Ships are all the same. I should know, I've been on a few of them, and their blueprints are all identical, so we don't have to worry."

He began to point out areas of the ship's hull. There were twelve main rooms and about thirty smaller areas. The main rooms were sleeping quarters, whereas the rest of the ship was used for engines and computers.

"We'll dock the ship right next to one of the engine rooms and penetrate through the hull. Our presence will be unknown, because no one hangs around the engines. They take care of themselves. Once everyone is through the opening, we'll spread out and attack the sleeping quarters. Two of them will be untouched, but considering how many will be hit with the first stage of the gas, they'll all be dead before they know what hit them. The operation should take us thirty minutes. What do you think?"

We all agreed. Terinsa, Rinar, and I left the cockpit to tell the others about the plan. Retnar stayed and piloted us to the ship. Operation Vengeance had begun.

All ten teams were equipped with a flask of the gas. Each of the team members had a mask and respirator, as well as a single weapon in case of emergency. We did not want our presence to be known and gunfire would surely give us away.

We penetrated the ship's hull and made our way through the engine room, unnoticed.

"You all know where you're going." Rinar addressed to his team. "Stay silent and do the job effectively. We have thirty minutes. We wait for no one, so make sure you're back here in time. Good luck to you all."

325

They all saluted him and went on their way. He turned to the three of us and turned on his regulator. He told us to do the same.

"Good to go?" He asked us. We replied with enthusiasm and were on our way.

Rinar was the navigator, I held the flask, and Terinsa and Retnar were the gunmen. Rinar led us through dark tunnels until we reached our target area.

The sleeping area was rather quiet, but filled with Rashouwe soldiers. There was minimal movement.

The room's dimensions were enormous, probably a thousand meters in area.

"Where do we drop the flask?" I whispered through the mask.

"I don't know yet." He murmured back. "Our best possible place would be in the center of the room, but the gas may take a while to get to them. Besides, the breaking of the glass would alert them."

He turned to Retnar and Terinsa.

"You two cover us. Tyran and I are going to release the gas on the outside perimeters of this room."

They assented and watched us leave. I removed the lid off of the flask and released the gas. The dye had been cast. Quietly, Rinar and I crept behind the headrests of the beds. Most everyone was sleeping, and never knew they were being poisoned. The few who woke up were dead before they could say a word. One by one, the soldiers died where they lay. We circled the entire room in about fifteen minutes and met up with our two teammates.

"Done, now let's get out of here."

Rinar led the group, with Retnar close behind him. Terinsa was behind me, guarding the rear. In five minutes, we were back in the engine room. There were six other groups there, with similar success. In another five minutes, the other three groups came. No one was killed. It was an incredible victory.

"How do we know if we did the job, and everyone is dead." I asked.

"I forgot to tell you about the incendiary properties of the gas. With one flame, I can set this whole ship on fire, which is precisely what I'm going to do."

He ordered all of us into Retnar's ship. We scurried inside and waited for him. From out of his pocket, he took a small explosive and placed it on the ground as soon as we were all secure. He ran into our ship and ordered Retnar to close the hatch and get the ship out of the blast zone.

"I gave it thirty seconds." He told me with a smile.

I watched with my three teammates in the cockpit. The City-ship was serene, floating silently in space for a brief moment, and then, it was turned violently into a ball of fire. The airless space of which it blazed around stole the fire's breath, turning the flame into nothingness.

Countless small pieces of the ship, black and charred, blew away from the main hull. Nothing could have survived. Not even my talent for manifesting the apparent impossible could give resilience to our fallen enemy.

Our mission was not yet complete. We still had to place the fifth piece of the manuscript in its appropriate place. We told this to Rinar, who escorted us to the planet's surface.

We never took off the respirators, considering we would need them for our walk through the thick atmosphere. Rinar joined us, after he dropped off his troops on his ship so they could rest.

Terinsa led us through the terrain, searching for the tiny geyser she visited so many years ago. Through the valleys and mountains, we trekked, until finally, we found the geyser. It was a strange phenomenon. A cylindrical tube with a single flame atop, surrounded by a boiling pond.

"The cave is right behind the pond." She said, pointing straight ahead.

We all four followed her into the dark cavern, eventually fitting ourselves through the tiny opening. She walked over to one of the corners of the cave and gently rested the tube against the wall. Five down, two to go.

We were almost done. At least, it seemed that way for the moment. When we got back out of the cavern we were met by a huge regiment of Rinar's forces. It seemed as though our troubles were not yet over.

"Sorry to give you the news, Captain, but there's a huge force of the Rashouwe orbiting the planet. They should be entering the atmosphere within ten minutes."

The Fire Within

The City-Ship must have asked for reinforcements before we destroyed their communications. Fortunately, we were not outnumbered this time. Their numbers were similar to ours. I thought we would be all right, and the battle would be over soon. Perhaps it was this confidence that elongated the war.

For months, we fought with their forces. Luckily, they had no back-up. I think the main Rashouwe force had found a different toy apart from the deadly gas on this planet to pay attention to. The force we were fighting was forgotten by their race, but that didn't stop them from fighting. They continued to fight with the same persistence and fury every day, never giving up or surrendering.

There were fights in the mountains, fights in the valleys, fights everywhere. There was never daylight, but with the constant bursts of lights in the sky, I never noticed its absence.

You are probably wondering how we lasted for so long with the toxic air. Before we started fighting, we built tents and buildings that circulated breathable air. We made chambers that kept the poisonous air out of our camps. We also had compressors that filled our tanks with breathable air. It was very difficult fighting at first, but after awhile, we got used to the extra burden. The Rashouwe did the same, which took away our advantage.

After weeks of fighting many skirmishes, we were

able to beat the Rashouwe down to a minimum. We had also suffered many casualties, but the ratio was in our favor.

Rinar, Terinsa, Retnar and I all survived to the last battle. However, in that final push, which concluded in the total annihilation of the other side, one of us did not return.

The first few hours of the final battle were indecisive; however, we eventually pushed the Rashouwe into the mouth of a large crater. They were trapped inside, with no means of escape. That didn't stop them from fighting. They wanted to go until the last soldier fell. Because of this, we could not rush them. We did have good cover on the ridge, though. It was just a matter of time before we took them all out.

When the firing stopped from down below, we thought the war was won, but if there is one thing I have learned from the Rashouwe, it's never trust a dead man.

We got up from our cover and proceeded down to the center of the crater to confirm our victory. Halfway down, we fell into their trap, and they began firing on us. This time, neither of us had any cover. Our reactions weren't quick enough, and many of our men fell within seconds. We began to fire back, tearing our enemy to shreds with the plasma bolts, as well.

The final battle was bloody, even compared to the many months of fighting. Soldiers left and right were being cut down to pieces and after awhile, no one knew who they were shooting at.

After an intense couple of minutes of heavy firing and quick deaths, the fighting began to cease. However, the smoke did not dissipate as fast. It was like fighting an invisible force. From out of that invisible force, a single bolt flew past my ear, grazing the top of my shoulder, leaving a tiny cut. Retnar, who was standing right behind me, was not as lucky.

The blast slashed right through his right arm and

through his tank. The plasma tore open a gigantic hole, releasing all of his breathable air. I saw him fall to the hot ground, crashing violently in his own pool of scorching blood. I quickly dropped my gun and went to his aid. I could no longer hear the fighting, but that didn't mean it stopped. I was in a whole different world; cradling my dying friend in my arms and watching him breathe his final breath.

His blood shot eye rolled around until it locked in a dead stare with me. I was panicking, telling him he was going to be all right, but the blood from his open wound poured richly onto the ground. His torso could not close up the wound and stop the bleeding. Instead, he just listened to me, and did not say a word. I could tell that my talking was doing nothing for him. I knew he would not last for another minute, but that didn't matter. My brother was dying, and I wanted him to live. I refused to accept the fact he would soon die, until he cupped his hand around one of mine and smiled. He managed to open his mouth and with his final breath, he spoke his last word. "Hope."

His eye turned placid and hid behind the closing lid. I felt his soul leave his body and lose itself in the smoke around us, setting itself free at last.

I didn't notice that Terinsa and Rinar were behind me. The fighting had stopped long ago, and they had been watching ever since. Rinar bent down and looked at me, but didn't touch me. He could tell I was lost.

There was no response I could give to justify what I was feeling. He had given his life for a cause he barely understood. His pure love for life drove him to fight with valor and to overcome all obstacles, and that he did. While I sat there, I realized I did not want his memory to die, even though in writing these lines it never will.

I picked myself up, and carried Retnar up to the crest of the canyon. I placed his body down on the ridge and simply gazed into the dark mist that cloaked the night sky. The planet was dying, and that was because of our extremely harsh treatment. I wanted to make sure it stayed alive and eventually rejuvenated itself to its original health.

I was a constructor of life, and with this talent, I wanted to leave this planet a gift. I got to work immediately, with the help of Terinsa and Rinar, and created a single life form, mechanical, of course.

It was our intention to have the creature stay on the surface and to alert us of any future threat. We did not stop there. We had to give it a gift, as well. A machine is capable of experiencing emotions if it is programmed to do so. Luckily, I knew how to do it.

"There is a final gift I would like to give this being." I told them. "Something that Retnar reminded me of in his last words."

I proceeded to program into the machine a single emotion. In time, the emotion would influence the life form and allow it to act upon the strange sensation. When all was done, we had created a beautiful creature, with hope implanted in its steel heart.

I shook the hand of my friend, saying good-bye again.

"When we meet again." He said. "I promise we won't have to go into battle."

I wish he could have kept that promise. I have not seen him since, and fear I never will.

Rinar lent Terinsa and me a ship, since there was no way either of us could pilot Retnar's ship. We left it where it was and hoped that our creation would make use of it.

We piled ourselves into the foreign ship, acquainted ourselves with the controls, and took off for planet six. The fire planet left our sights in minutes, leaving us with a bleak realm to travel through. I said good-by to Retnar, and promised him immortality.

The Paradise Rediscovered

I was not lonely. On the contrary, I enjoyed the company of Terinsa, and she enjoyed mine. We reminded each other of that as many times as we could. I just missed my friend. All the things he taught me, all the things he could have taught me. It was pleasing and painful at the same time, like most memories are.

It did not take long for us to get to planet six. I wished the Admiral and Retnar could have seen it. It was magnificent, to say the least. It was incredibly mountainous, but it was more burgundy than blood red as on the fire planet. It had more life to it, as well as on it. Trees had managed to find nice areas to grow, giving a more verdant glow to the surface. Small animals scurried around, jetting in and out of their little homes in the trees, in the ground, and in the mountains.

"I never thought this planet would turn out so vivid." Terinsa said, staring in awe at the beautiful landscape. She smiled contently.

We walked together for miles, taking the trip slow. It seemed there was no need to rush the expedition. Even if we had to, we still would have taken our time. We had been fighting and trying to complete the mission in haste, and never stopped to behold the planets we visited.

I missed the simple purity of adventuring; perhaps I even ignored it. How wonderful it was to walk on a planet for the first time and feel its youth. The smell of the air, the coolness of the breeze, nothing could ruin it. I felt that same sensation as I walked with Terinsa on the picturesque planet.

There was only one star the planet circled around. It had a purple haze around it, with a little hint of blue. The clouds in the sky lined themselves with that brilliant color, making the horizon look like a delicately woven web.

The humming of the tiny insects and the whistling of the birds were much more pleasant than the echoing sounds of weapons firing in the corners of my mind.

We walked until nightfall and decided to rest, knowing it would be a long time before we would get another chance to lie down on such soft ground.

I had forgotten how soothing the music of the night was. The creatures that managed to stay awake as long as we did sang lullabies for Terinsa and me. Their blanket of notes covered our world, as Terinsa relaxed in my arms and slowly fell asleep. I stayed awake a little longer, taking time to realize what I had, and where I was. The distant stars, with their watchful eyes, watched over the two of us, keeping us safe from any trouble. For the first time in a long time, I felt safe. We felt safe. With this thought, I closed my eyes, and joined my love in slumber.

We awoke the next morning to the sun shining in our eyes. Terinsa kissed me on the cheek and slowly got up. She stretched and took in a deep breath. I watched her silhouette dance in the sunlight, her cloak spreading outward, making her look like an angel.

She bent down, playfully grabbed my hands and pulled me up to my feet. She kissed me again, only this time much more passionately.

"Good morning." She whispered in my ear as she embraced me.

"Indeed it is." I agreed. "Any morning is good when I'm with you."

"Took the words right out of my mouth." She giggled, and began to strap her equipment pack on her back.

"So how far do we have?" I asked as she began the trip.

"A full day's hike." She answered back.

"Oh great." I quietly said to myself. Even though the planet was filled with incentive to traverse upon it, I still didn't look forward to the long walk.

Along the way, several little animals decided to follow us on our trip. They walked cautiously at our heels, making sure not to get stepped on. They chirped and peeped and made all the little noises they could, each of them happy to see someone new on the planet. When we sat down to rest on occasion, some would crawl up our legs or over our chests and pile onto our bellies. They rested there for the duration, until we would have to leave. But as soon as we would continue on, they would be right behind us.

The night began to fall again, thankfully, and we were at the foothills of the mountain. Our little friends decided they would come no further and took off, saying good-bye to us in their own particular fashions.

The mountain was by no means steep, and was surprisingly easy to climb. We made it to the area with the three caves and made camp. I looked into the distance and saw the gigantic mountain, which was the key to our riddle.

"On second thought." I began. "Lets just carve three faces over the threshold of each of the caves, instead of having to make three full statues."

"I think I'm in agreement." She said, breathing heavily from the climb.

We pulled out a couple chisels and began working.

The sky was completely black by the time we finished our work. The faces were somewhat crude, but they would do the trick.

"When morning comes, we'll watch to make sure our

experiment works." I said. "If all goes well, the peak of that mountain will cast its shadow onto this area, pointing to the right cave. Inside the two other caves, we'll dig a hole in each, which will act as a trap. I don't think we need a fire-pit. The holes we'll make will be deep enough for the traveler to not be able to get out of. The fall alone will kill him or her."

She agreed and threw down her working tools. I did the same. We had a full day's work and it was time to rest, or so I thought.

"How tired are you?" She asked, with an intended sensual accent.

I looked at her and smiled. She waited for an answer, but got none. Instead, I walked over to her, grabbed her in my arms and kissed her as passionately as I could.

"Well, that answers that." She said, and pulled me down to the ground.

The sun appeared in good time, and proved to us that our experiment worked. The peak of the mountain crawled slowly up the mountain we were on and pointed the way to the right cave. We predicted that at the speed it was moving, it would point to the next cave in two hours, but we did not spend that much time. We needed to get back to the ship and journey to the final planet.

The trek back took another two days and sure enough, we had a parade of small animals follow us all the way. It was rather tough to say good-bye to them. They were so friendly and trusting. We petted as many as we could and climbed into our ship. As soon as we did, they peeped and chirped their good-byes and left for their homes.

I piloted us out of the planet's orbit and plotted a course for the final planet. Our journey was coming to an end.

The Illuminated Key

Deltrin placed the book down on his lap and took a sip from the glass by his side. His quest was coming to an end, as well, and he did not know how to cope with it. Even so, he would never be able to find a mission that could match the significance of this one. He was not only saying good-bye to this mission; he was saying good-bye to everything that made him who he was. He had no choice but to give up his occupation as a Questor.

His eyes were tired, and he figured he needed to rest them. He placed the book down on the table, picked up his drink, and headed off for the map room.

The maps had not been used for quite some time now and the pieces were beginning to fade due to its extreme old age. Deltrin swung an overhead light to try and read the writing, which he barely could. The sixth and seventh pieces were all he could read. He smiled and read the final stanza to himself...

Alone I sit, in a temple of shards, coming out when my fathers embrace.
The skeleton bands, with the jewels in their hands, will uncover my illustrious face.

As soon as he finished the last sentence, the stanza faded. The map was gone. Deltrin turned off the light and sat down next to the table, thinking back to when he placed his hands on the two final pieces for the first time...

"Two more to go!" Deltrin enthusiastically cheered to Violaze. The violet-eyed dragon smiled and chirped back a similar response.

After the unusual meeting with the Creae, Deltrin acquired a glow about him, as if something had filled his spirit with confidence. He was always smiling, always cheery. Nothing could take away his animated disposition. His vigor was becoming epidemic and soon enough, Violaze was chirping all the time, flying around wildly and glowing himself. They were both alive with color.

"The sixth planet is in view, buddy." Deltrin said. "Do you want to join me?"

Violaze flew to his shoulder and plopped himself down, resting next to Deltrin's right ear. His glowing eyes looked into Deltrin's, which incidentally gave Deltrin his answer.

"Good." He said. "I'd like your company."

He landed the ship with ease and equipped himself with the necessary climbing tools. He knew, from what the riddle told him that he would need to do some heavy hiking, so he wanted to go prepared.

He opened the hatch and walked out, with Violaze clinging to his shoulder.

"All right. We're looking for a mountain with three caves on it. The riddle said the key to choosing the right cave lies in the hands of 'the father'. That means the single star in the sky is the key. We'll figure out how to use it when we get there. For now, let's find us a mountain."

Luckily, Deltrin remembered to take a pair of binoculars with him, so he wouldn't have to climb every mountain to find the three caves. All he had to do was look with the binoculars at the base of each mountain.

There were little animals everywhere, with the occasional larger ones nearby. Deltrin and Violaze paid little attention to the larger ones, as not to pose themselves as threats.

They eventually came to a grand mountain that stood in the light of a smaller one. It looked conspicuous, so Deltrin decided to take a look.

"There seems to be nothing on the big mountain." He said, after scrutinizing the entire rock. He shifted his attention to the smaller mountain, and found what he wanted.

"Got it! There are three caves lined up side by side. It's halfway up the mountain, so that shouldn't be too hard of a climb. However, we're about half a day's walk away, so we have our work cut out for us."

The night came quickly, but there was no problem in finding a soft spot on the ground. There were many meadows along the path the two adventurers were taking, so they just had to pick one and sleep under the hood of the trees.

Violaze got up and walked over to where Deltrin was lying and perched on his chest. He then cuddled up and fell asleep. Deltrin took the hint, and did the same.

They slept for a few hours, until the sun came up. The meadow's many trees cut the star's rays and let the tendrils of light sneak up on the two unsuspecting creatures. The light pierced their eyes and woke them up. They picked themselves up from the ground with surprising energy. Deltrin strapped his equipment on and they were off.

The journey to the base of the mountain was only three hours, and the climb up was another two. By midday, the two adventurers were facing the three caves, trying to see how the sun was connected to solving the riddle.

"The riddle said something about the morning." He said, while scratching the hairs on his chin. "And that if we wait too long, we're toast."

He looked up to the three statues, hoping to find another clue. All the faces were the same, so there were no clues there. Each of the openings were black inside, so he couldn't see the right path. But when he turned around to see the other mountain, the solution presented itself.

"I think I got it." He said with delight. "Only in the morning, it said, so when the morning sun is out, it is in a particular position. As the day progresses, it moves in a clock-wise rotation, which means it changes position. The sun is pointing the way. But how can I tell where it is pointing?"

He looked down on the ground and saw the shadow of the greater mountain's peak cast on the ground, slowly moving.

"You see!" he yelled with jubilance. "The peak of the mountain is the arrow! Ha ha! We've got it! Now all we have to do is wait for morning."

He turned around to Violaze, who was sharing the enjoyment. He was flying in circles, dancing around.

"Let's stay here and just relax. I'm pretty tired myself, so I think I'm going to sleep."

He lied down and closed his eyes. He was asleep in seconds. Violaze thought the idea was a good one. He stopped flapping his wings wildly and fell upon Deltrin's chest. Deltrin didn't wake up. The excitement turned to fatigue instantly, and he was dead asleep. Violaze made himself comfortable and followed his friend to the land of dreams.

The sun was peeking out of the horizon when Deltrin awoke. It poured its light onto the planet's surface, a sea of red drowning all the life on the surface.

He stretched his rejuvenated body and noticed the morning had come and his timing was perfect.

"It's time." He told the barely animated Violaze. "Let's watch."

Slowly, the sun moved behind the greater mountain and cast its shadow on the ground. The black arrow crept closer to its three choices, ever so slowly. The anticipation was painful. The detail of the mountain's peak grew in clarity as it crawled to its destination. Finally, the arrow found its target and pointed directly to the cave on the left.

"Let's see what's behind door number one, shall we?"

He crept into the dark tunnel, with Violaze perched on his shoulder. He lit a flare, and illuminated a cavern, with the beautiful casket resting peacefully in the center of the room.

"God I love this job!"

He picked up the tube and made his way back to the ship. The journey was a little under two days, considering he did not stop to rest. His beloved transport was waiting patiently for the two of them and welcomed them as they walked through the outer hatch.

Deltrin and Violaze walked into the map room and placed the tube on the table. He opened the hatch and read what was inside. It took him a minute to understand, but as he studied it, he realized something.

"I don't believe this!" He said, with changed attitude.

"It's incomplete! The stanza's there, but it's cut in half!"

The map fit just right, but the stanza was cut right down the middle. The final piece had the other half, which gave Deltrin all the more reason to go and find it.

He jumped into the pilot seat and searched out the final planet through his galactic road map. He found it rather quickly and set a direct course for it.

"I could use some rest." He said. His frustrated attitude mixed with his lack of sleep knocked him out cold. Violaze didn't even make it to the cockpit. He was fast asleep on the map room table...

...Deltrin awoke from his nostalgic sleep and focused in on the aged parchment in front of him. He wiped his brow, and chuckled to himself.

Violaze was awake, as well, and had made his way into the map room. He landed next to the map on the table and looked at it. He cocked his head to the side and made a melancholy face. He was sad to see such a magnificent piece of art vanish into memory.

"I was just thinking about how much fun we had on the last two planets."

Violaze glared up at Deltrin, not sharing the same outlook on the last planet. He chirped in disagreement, remembering what a tough time he had on planet seven.

Deltrin chuckled to himself, since Violaze would not join him in the joke.

"Now let's see." He began. "Everything was going great, until we got to the island, right?"

Violaze didn't answer.

"Then you got incredibly hungry all of a sudden and went searching for food. By the time I found the casket on the shores of the island, you had already eaten enough of those strange berries to feed an army."

Violaze chirped in anger at the teasing he was receiving.

"Well, it wasn't my fault! I didn't know that the berries were sedatives!" He laughed hysterically at the silly situation.

"Anyway, you didn't miss much. You still got to see the beautiful night sky, and the mysterious glow of the surface. You basically saw what I saw. I just wish you could have seen that temple where the manuscript was."

He picked up the dragon in his hands and talked to him eye to eye.

"I tell you what. When we get the chance, I'll take you there. Does that suit you?"

The little winged creature washed his anger away and smiled at the suggestion. He chirped gleefully and hugged Deltrin's hands.

"All right then. I have to finish the book. We have about three hours before we get to the scientist's planet. That should give me plenty of time."

Violaze chirped again.

"Don't worry. I'll tell you all about the book when I'm done."

Violaze was content. Deltrin walked down the hall into his bedroom with the happy dragon perched on his shoulder. Violaze took flight and flew on the bed. He relaxed and fell asleep for the time being. Deltrin would wake him when they docked on the planet.

Deltrin took a sip of his drink and sat down in his chair. The book was almost finished, as was the mission. He made himself comfortable, and began the ending...

The Tail of the Serpent

I couldn't wait to get to the seventh planet. It was simply gorgeous. Its placement in space was perfect, the way it floated in a black sea, surrounded by a ring of stars. Terinsa had never been there, so I looked forward to giving her a grand tour of the area.

"Is the last casket ready?" I asked her, as we began our descent to the glowing surface.

"You bet!" she answered, excited to see the planet's surface.

"Great. We should land in about thirty minutes, so get suited up."

We opened the outer hatch after we suited ourselves and allowed the ship to land. The illuminant ground was breathtaking. It was like we set foot on a panel of light, instead of rock.

"Wow." Was all she could say. She stared at the night sky and saw the halo of stars circling around the planet. No other stars could be seen in the vicinity. It was such a peculiar phenomenon; the way the stars circled around in such a meticulous pattern.

"Is there any explanation for all of this? The glowing surface, the ring of stars?"

"Not that I know of, but I'm sure there is one." I replied. "Personally, I don't want to know. When I got here for the first time, I was too awestruck by the mystery of the planet and the neighboring stars to take the time to find out.

Truthfully, I thought it would ruin it. Me. A scientist; thinking that a scientific explanation would ruin something."

"Don't worry." She said. "You're not the only one who feels that way."

She held out her hand, offering me to hold it. I took the invitation.

Hand in hand, we searched for the secret island.

The planet was like a fairyland. The trees were beautiful, the breeze was soft. Every step we took was in soft sand and rock. There was nothing to bother us. No explosions or heat waves to drain our energy. It was glorious.

We journeyed for several hours, and to my displeasure, I noticed that Terinsa was lacking the energy to keep up with me. I asked her if there was any problem. She told me there was none. I didn't believe her. Something was wrong, but I did not let her know it was troubling me.

The island was in sight soon enough. The water was the most brilliant blue I had ever seen. It was a shining crystal sheet that was only three feet in depth. We walked into the sea and made our way for the island.

Those final steps to the end of our journey were difficult to make. I knew that as soon as I placed the casket on the shores, we were done.

We walked to the other side of the island, where there was a growth of trees that shaded a patch of land. Together, we dropped to our knees, and placed the casket down. We smiled at each other, not realizing what we had just accomplished.

I looked into her face, realizing suddenly that her countenance had turned from jocular to terror and distress. She stayed put for a brief second, hoping her pain would leave. Her colorful face turned pale and she fainted backwards. I jumped to her side and caught her before she fell. Completely terrified at this sudden turn of events, I quickly asked what was wrong.

With her remaining energy, she kept her consciousness and tried to figure out the problem.

"The immortality potion must have worn off."

"This quickly?"

"It can't be anything else."

She smiled weakly. Her pale eyes looked into mine.

"Thank God I finished the quest with you before this happened."

"Well, let's not just sit here, I have to get you to the ship and fix you up."

"No." She peacefully whispered. "I want to stay here."

The tears began to fall from my eyes.

"I won't leave you here, you're coming with me."

She kept her calm and watched me panic, pleading with her to reconsider. I could not change her mind.

"Don't leave me alone, Terinsa."

She placed her hand behind my neck and pulled me towards her. She kissed me with little energy and pulled me away.

"I won't." she said. "You are everything to me, Tyran. I have always loved you. Leave me here upon this paradise. Come back when you are ready to join me."

"I have always loved you, and always will. I promise to return."

She tightened her grip around me and smiled.

"Terinsa." I uttered. "I need to go back to the temple to consummate our project. No questions. Just trust me."

"I always have." She said through her faint smile. "Whatever it is you have to do, finish the job."

She pulled me closer and said her final words.

"For us."

With her remaining energy, she pulled me in and kissed me. She exhaled her final breath into my lungs as I felt her soul pass from her lips into my body. Our spirits entwined in that final embrace, and never let go. Her warm lips turned cold and I released our physical embrace, still holding on to her soul. Her motionless body sank in my arms and I knew my love had left me. I caressed her cheek with my trembling hands. The rest of me couldn't move.

I carried her body to the meadow in the center of the island and placed her on a bed of leaves. I looked at her expressionless face and remembered how beautiful it was when it had life. I would never be able to gaze into her captivating eyes, nor would I feel her warm embrace again. Once in the arms of an angel, never again.

On her grave, I vowed I would come back to die by her side, but I needed to complete the mission entirely. I left the grave she laid on and made my way back to the ship.

I set the course for the temple planet and reached it within a week. Those nights were impossible. I could still hear her voice in the silence, whispering my name. Occasionally, I would even awake to her gentle, yet phantom touch.

I see your face, radiant as the stars and just as distant. Will I ever see you again, or will you haunt my soul and sing to me like sirens who flee like a dream from daylight? If I do not see you in the next life, I will feel the lack. I only pray that my memories will die with me and I will be left with a clean slate. But I never want to lose you, my love, my life, my breath, my lost soul. Wait for me in the next life. Give me, once again, this pain and pleasure I can't live with, or without.

The ice-planet was still beautiful, as was the temple, when I saw it. However, I lacked the sensation I once felt. I did not have my three comrades by my side as I walked down the hill, yet I still felt their presence as their empty footsteps followed mine.

The labyrinth was still intact, looking as though it

had not been touched, which I hoped it hadn't. I reached the door to the temple and opened up the pathway to paradise.

It welcomed me with its warmth, though I could not welcome it with mine. I walked up to the second level and waited for the star to cease its eclipse and reveal to me the manuscript behind the wall.

In that time I have waited, I have been writing this manuscript, and though it hurts me to say it, I have come to the end. However, I must tell you what I am going to do, as soon as the manuscript is revealed.

Since I was told the universe we will soon give birth to is actually the first universe in this existence, I have to make sure the primary explosion does not go on forever. I will make the necessary changes to have the universe contract after a huge expansion. Of course the other universes will be destroyed, so there is no possibility that the mission will be a failure. By the time the universe begins the second phase of its pulse, it will have wiped out everything in its path.

Throughout these long years I have been writing this, I have always wondered what you look like. I don't even know who you are and yet, you are my savior and my friend. I wanted to make sure you knew how much you have meant to us and with the telling of this tale, you have been informed of your importance to this mission and to the continuation of our existence.

Our lives are etched upon the pages of this manuscript. What we have learned, what we have taught, everything. I used to believe what we did would solve all our problems. I am glad to say they didn't. This existence is locked in a circle, as is every realm of existence. Who am I to change that? Our sacrifice was already fated, but I did not want to think of it that way. I wanted to think that every move we made was our choice. We fought for life and it's eternity, because we felt it was the right thing to do.

I hope you feel the same way. In all truth, I know you do. I just want to make sure you know how much I respect you.

I sometimes catch myself thinking back on the many memories I have stored in my mind and did not write down. Those memories, along with the ones I didn't mention, will keep me happy for the short period of time I have left to live. Before I leave this temple and reunite with Terinsa, I would like to tell you to take advantage of the wonderful opportunity you have to live your life to the fullest. The memories that will cradle you in your frail old life will comfort you until it is time to pass on to your next one.

When you have completed this mission, find your paradise and lose yourself in it. When the time comes, all of us will be waiting for you on the other side. Until then, farewell.

For a brief moment, Deltrin stared at the final sentence. He was finished with the book and was nearly finished with his mission. His emotions were stagnant, for he knew not how to react. Five years of emotional torment all coming to a conclusion with the final words he read. He had one final step and could then officially celebrate the end of a long era.

The sweat on his brow sparkled in the light over his head. He closed the book and walked down to the map room. He placed the manuscript on top of the map and stared at it for a few minutes. He had lost a family of friends he never met, and yet he knew exactly what they were like. He knew he would never forget any of them for as long as he lived. He brushed his hand on the cover of the book, making a final connection with the book of magic that created his family.

He called out to Violaze to warn him they were in

orbit of the scientist's planet.

What could he tell them? He tried desperately to come up with an excuse to coax the scientists to perform the experiment. Simply shoving the manuscript in their faces would probably turn them away, or even worse, threaten them.

As Deltrin lowered his ship down into the city area, he thought to himself. Once the scientists see the intensity of the equations within the book, there is no way they would turn it down. Just as long as he doesn't confuse them with the story behind the manuscript, everything should be just fine. He dismissed his fears of rejection and continued to lower his ship to the surface.

He docked in a heavily used bay and picked up the book of equations. Violaze perched on his shoulder. They both exited the ship and started the first steps to the end of their journey.

It had been a long time since Deltrin had been in a city. For the past decade, he had been traveling to desolate planets with barely any trace of life. Things had changed since last he walked down a metropolitan area. Beings rushed from building to building. Vehicles in the air and on the ground were flying all over the place. Everyone was in a rush. Violaze watched in amazement as he witnessed a city work in super-speed.

Deltrin was able to stop one of the pedestrians to ask him a few questions.

"Excuse me, but are you familiar with the project known as 'Hyperlight'?"

The pedestrian gave Deltrin a condescending look and answered him.

"Everyone does." He said.

"Oh great!" Deltrin said, ignoring the patronizing

response. "Do you know where the labs are?"

The pedestrian peered into Deltrin's eyes with suspicion; however, he did not pursue anything.
"In the building you see down there, with the five spires."

Deltrin looked where he pointed and saw the building. He thanked the pedestrian and began to walk to the laboratories.

Many beings stopped to stare at the two Questors, but it was not Deltrin they were staring at. Obviously, they had never seen a dragon before. Strange. And this was supposed to be an advanced civilization.

The entrance to the building was adorned with several statues. There were some in the courtyard, some right at the doorway. There were several trees in the courtyard, as well as a fountain. It almost seemed that the building didn't belong in this chaotic mess.
"Do you think we should knock first?"

Violaze chirped in answer to the question.
"Okay, but If you're wrong, you're to blame."

Deltrin opened the doors and walked right in, suspecting that some type of guard would soon meet him. He was right.
"Can I help you?" The guard asked.
"Uh, yeah." Deltrin stuttered. "I'm looking for the scientists of the project known as Hyperlight. I don't have an appointment, but I do think they will be interested in what I'm presenting."

The guard looked down and looked back up at him.
"I'll let you pass, as long as you make sure your strange pet doesn't cause any trouble."

Deltrin held back his chuckle, and looked up at Violaze, who did not find the remark as funny. The violet eyes glared at the guard. It was a good thing Deltrin thanked the guard quickly and left, for Violaze would have done something rather rash if he were allowed the time.

"Don't worry about him. He knows nothing. You are far better than he."

Violaze chirped impassively, but let the comment go. He didn't care about what the guard thought.

Deltrin took a transport up to the appropriate floor, and walked into the laboratory, where he was met by one of the scientists.

"Good day." The scientist said cheerfully. Deltrin was pleased to see the scientist was polite.

"Good day." Deltrin responded. "I am here to give you this manuscript I found during one of my travels. It contains equations I can't understand. That is why I have brought it to you. I have heard about Hyperlight, and feel your group of scientists would be the perfect ones to contact."

He handed the book over to the scientist. He began to flip through the pages, astounded by the dense amount of information.

"Do you know what it's dealing with?" He asked.

"In truth, yes I do, sir." Deltrin responded. "But I must warn you the information I am about to tell you does not leave this laboratory. Your group of scientists must not tell a soul."

"Agreed." He said, intrigued by the mystery.

"It is the formula for building a universe."

"A what?" He said, not believing his ears.

"A universe. I know it sounds absurd, but you must believe me. Do you know who the Rashouwe are?"

"Of course I do." He said. "They have been attacking our area for many years now."

"This is what they're looking for. Don't let them have it. Find a sanctuary and complete the formula."

The scientist looked into Deltrin's eyes.

"You're serious?"

"I'm afraid so. In time, you will complete what has been done by generations of constructors before you. Whatever you do, don't change anything. Do exactly what the manuscript tells you to do, no matter what. It is imperative that you do so."

The scientist did not breathe for a second, but caught his breath eventually.

"I promise we won't change a thing."

"Thank you, my friend."

Deltrin began to walk out of the room, feeling good about what he had accomplished.

"Just one thing." The scientist remarked before Deltrin left. Deltrin turned around to see what he wanted.

"Who are we doing this for?"

Deltrin thought for a brief moment at the strange question. Wasn't it obvious? Just before he was about to say 'everyone', he held himself back. With a tender, yet faltering voice, he uttered his response.

"For us."

He smiled with a sense of contentment and walked out of the room with Violaze on his shoulder.

Tyran had told Deltrin to live his life when the mission was complete and to find his paradise. With this in mind, Deltrin and Violaze made their next and final journey to a familiar planet, where a beautiful creature was waiting to feed their souls with the bread they desired.

The scientist watched as this magnanimous creature strolled with dignity out of the lab.

Concealing a smile, this constructor placed his

hand upon the aged cover and took a moment to reacquaint himself with the manuscript he hadn't seen for over two-billion years. Now that Deltrin had acclimated himself to the universe mission, and had proven his loyalty to the preservation of existence, he was a valuable ally, and would be called upon in the near future. But first, serious planning by two strategic geniuses was required. The final act of war was approaching.

"Was that him?" a soft voice asked from behind.

"It was indeed, my love," he whispered, "It was indeed."